The Regional Development of the American Bildungsroman, 1900–1960

Modern American Literature and the New Twentieth Century
Series Editors: Martin Halliwell and Mark Whalan

Published Titles

Writing Nature in Cold War American Literature
Sarah Daw

F. Scott Fitzgerald's Short Fiction: From Ragtime to Swing Time
Jade Broughton Adams

The Labour of Laziness in Twentieth-Century American Literature
Zuzanna Ladyga

The Literature of Suburban Change: Narrating Spatial Complexity in Metropolitan America
Martin Dines

The Literary Afterlife of Raymond Carver: Influence and Craftsmanship in the Neoliberal Era
Jonathan Pountney

Living Jim Crow: The Segregated Town in Mid-Century Southern Fiction
Gavan Lennon

The Little Art Colony and US Modernism: Carmel, Provincetown, Taos
Geneva M. Gano

Sensing Willa Cather: The Writer and the Body in Transition
Guy J. Reynolds

Gertrude Stein and the Politics of Participation: Democracy, Rights and Modernist Authorship 1909–1933
Isabelle Parkinson

The Regional Development of the American Bildungsroman, 1900–1960
Tamlyn Avery

Forthcoming Titles

The Big Red Little Magazine: New Masses, 1926–1948
Susan Currell

The Reproductive Politics of American Literature and Film, 1959–1973
Sophie Jones

Ordinary Pursuits in American Writing after Modernism
Rachel Malkin

The Plastic Theatre of Tennessee Williams: Expressionist Drama and the Visual Arts
Henry I. Schvey

Exoteric Modernisms: Progressive Era Literature and the Aesthetics of Everyday Life
Michael J. Collins

Black Childhood in Modern African American Fiction
Nicole King

The Artifice of Affect: American Realist Literature and the Critique of Emotional Truth
Nicholas Manning

Visit our website at www.edinburghuniversitypress.com/series/MALTNTC

The Regional Development of the American Bildungsroman, 1900–1960

TAMLYN AVERY

EDINBURGH
University Press

Edinburgh University Press is one of the leading university presses in the UK. We publish academic books and journals in our selected subject areas across the humanities and social sciences, combining cutting-edge scholarship with high editorial and production values to produce academic works of lasting importance. For more information visit our website: edinburghuniversitypress.com

© Tamlyn Avery, 2023, 2024

Edinburgh University Press Ltd
13 Infirmary Street
Edinburgh EH1 1LT

First published in hardback by Edinburgh University Press 2023

Typeset in 10/13 ITC Giovanni Std Book by
Cheshire Typesetting Ltd, Cuddington, Cheshire

A CIP record for this book is available from the British Library

ISBN 978 1 4744 8996 6 (hardback)
ISBN 978 1 4744 8997 3 (paperback)
ISBN 978 1 4744 8998 0 (webready PDF)
ISBN 978 1 4744 8999 7 (epub)

The right of Tamlyn Avery to be identified as the author of this work has been asserted in accordance with the Copyright, Designs and Patents Act 1988, and the Copyright and Related Rights Regulations 2003 (SI No. 2498).

CONTENTS

Acknowledgments vii

Introduction: The U.S. Bildungsroman's Regional Complex 1

Part I: Midwestern Naturalism
1. Industrial Folklore and the Regional Ingénue in Dreiser and Sinclair 25
2. Developing the Countryside: Cather, Hughes, and the Poetics of Rurality 45
3. South Side's Overdevelopment: Farrell and Wright's Extreme Youths 69

Part II: The Northeast's Young Aesthetes
4. Emplacing Modernism: The Fitzgeralds and the Artist's Regional Complex 99
5. Thurman and Fauset's Portraits of Harlem's Regional Artist 140

Part III: Southern Underdevelopment
6. Imagining the Region of Underdevelopment 179
7. The Way of the World: Hurston's Folkloric Bildungsroman 186
8. Caught and Loose: McCullers, O'Connor, and the Gothic Bildungsroman 201

Part IV: Southwest Frontiers
9. Mathews at the Limits of the Bildungsroman's National Framework   231

Afterword: Situating the Bildungsroman's Transnational Afterlives   244

Works Cited   247
Index   258

ACKNOWLEDGMENTS

This book is indebted to many brilliant people—above all, I thank Sarah Gleeson-White, who provided consistent guidance and support at every stage of this project; for her mentorship, I am beyond grateful. Joy McEntee was a jovial writing companion who kept me on task. Elizabeth King was a supportive friend and magnificent research assistant; her commentary improved the pages and made drafting enjoyable. Many colleagues and students encouraged me along the way. I'd especially like to thank my University of Queensland colleagues, whose collegiality grounded me throughout the process. I greatly appreciated the School of Communication and Arts generously awarding me two grants to finalize this manuscript.

At this project's inception, two of the scholars I most admire, Barbara Foley and Leigh Anne Duck, gave invaluable feedback that inspired me to write this monograph. For their encouragement, I am sincerely thankful.

Good fortune brought me the most caring, patient editor at Edinburgh University Press in Michelle Houston, who was delightful to work with. I am truly grateful for her assistance. I'd also like to thank the rest of the EUP publishing team for their kindness and efforts, as they worked with me in bringing this work to publication: Susannah Butler who took over from Michelle, Caitlin Murphy, Fiona Conn, and Fiona Screen.

Thanks goes, too, to Genevieve Ellerbee on behalf of the Sheldon Museum of Art, for her assistance in facilitating the cover image.

I also thank the series editors, Mark Whalan and Martin Halliwell, for supporting this project, as well as two anonymous readers who provided reassuring, incisive feedback.

My parents, Jennifer and Alan; my grandparents, Neville and Margaret; and my sister, Jess gave unconditional encouragement and love, for which I am eternally grateful.

I dedicate this book to Julian Murphet, for always supporting me and anchoring this project's uneven development with boundless love. He, Ezra, and Rufus are my "we of me," and for their companionship I remain thankful every day.

INTRODUCTION

The U.S. Bildungsroman's Regional Complex

The Unfixed Figure of Youth as the Expression of Uneven Development

In the twilight of the American Literary Renaissance, an era later labeled *America's Coming of Age* (1915) by Van Wyck Brooks, Nathanial Hawthorne's *The Dolliver Romance* (c. 1868) ironically intimated that youth "is the proper, permanent, and genuine condition of man" (21), a phrase Herman Melville also quoted in his unpublished novella *Billy Budd, Sailor* (1891). It was an ironic refrain of *Nature* (1836), in which Ralph Waldo Emerson had peered into New England's woods and envisioned in these "plantations of God" a region of "perpetual youth," where "the currents of the Universal Being circulate through me," offering "something more dear and connate than in streets or villages" of preindustrial society (10). Those social spaces that form the substance of nations—streets, villages—were to be rethought in the pursuit of an imagined place untainted by the condition of industrialism and political fragmentation. The Young American in Literature was to steer the nation's future toward that chimeric region of youthful innocence (Emerson 211), a place where self-reliance could be facilitated, a philosophical concept that echoed the German concept of *Bildung*, denoting youth's development into the civic ideal through education and culture (Jeffers 4). The Civil War arrested that development. Instead of uniting into a nation delimited by a centralized culture of nationalism, a collection of loosely interconnected localities, states, and regions were cast adrift in the disorienting transnational flows of industrial capitalist modernity. Without a national culture to anchor the nation's rapid development from the 1880s, that symbolic figure of youth, unable to return to that region of stability, had prematurely arrived upon the precipice of adulthood: an unknown future of national destiny and capitalist modernity.

These anecdotes form a prelude to the history this book will rehearse, which is the story of uneven development in the United States, as it related to the literary genre that narrates the end of the season of youth: the Bildungsroman, often interpreted of late as the *novel of development*. The Young American was experiencing what I will call American literature's *regional complex*: not simply a textual strategy of regionalism so much as a preoccupation with the geography of local difference and a loss of faith in the universal subject that region as a term insisted upon, resulting not only from the cultural shock of modernization, but the arrival of an era defined by the U.S.'s augmented concentration of power in an increasingly globalized world-system. This book explores how the Bildungsroman and its protagonist, Youth, became the symbolic form of the cultural preoccupation with America's uneven development and decentralization, politically, economically, and socially circa 1900–1960, as it configured the profound reorganization occurring across the cultural landscapes of the many regions where the genre took root. In the absence of a coherent national character and culture into which the nation's ideal young citizen can "[grow] in national-historical time" during periods of instability and change, which Mikhail Bakhtin influentially proposed was the ideological logic of the European Bildungsroman (*Speech Genres*, 25), the genre's formal and teleological apparatuses underwent substantial reorganization, offering multiple visions of a youth caught between regional and national temporalities. This regional complex became one of the defining features of the Bildungsroman there, even after 1919 when "local color" fiction was pronounced dead by one editor of *The Nation* ("Local Color and After," 426).

By the 1920s, regional fragmentation—both politically and culturally—had translated into a preoccupation with local difference that was pervasive in American writing; one reason why I will argue that unconventional approaches to the Bildungsroman's generic themes, forms, and characters proliferated then. This unevenness resulted in clusters of regional variations, as authors repurposed the genre's universal features to contend with the asymmetrical effects of national development—culturally, politically, and economically. Guided by capitalism's geography of uneven development, the Bildungsroman not only reflected the profound changes occurring in American culture and politics circa 1900–1960 but also evolved with them, diffusing into generic variations across different regions: the Midwest, where urban and rural naturalism apprehended the region's ethnic heterogeneity and industrial overdevelopment; the Northeast, where development of the regional artist narratives flourished; the South, which blended the realist Bildungsroman with rural folklore and gothic tendencies that stylistically simulated the jagged effects of the region's underdevelopment; and the Southwest, which contemplated the arrested development of the nation's frontiers. The Bildungsroman's responsiveness to regional difference formed the core impulse of a genre I will call the *novel of uneven development*, the protagonist of which is the *unfixed figure of youth*, whose development within the national-historical time of Americanization is unsettled by their preoccupation with regional difference: that immobilizing entanglement I call American literature's *regional complex*. This awareness of regional difference ultimately left the unfixed youth, and the Bildungsroman genre with it, irreconcilably caught and loose within the homogenizing processes of Americanization.

This process of generic transformation resulted from one of the defining issues of early twentieth-century U.S. culture: the realization that although regional affiliation came first now, industrial modernity would centralize national life in a way that would irreversibly alter the organic differences of local cultures in the future. This was imagined as a generational shift, in which Old America—untidily conceived as an imagined community, at best—was developing into a yet unclear new character. Although mass production, transit lines, and the new mechanical media were the most conspicuous agents of national unification at the U.S.'s disposal from the 1880s, communities were suddenly exposed to differences in how people lived in other counties, states, and regions; this exposure inspired the genre of "local color" fiction, which depicted touristic versions of regional life often in ways that were seen to serve the "bourgeois fascination with the other" (Foote 19). Region may have been politically imagined as the nation's Other, but on a practical level, it also created a container for imagining the everyday lives of communities caught between two primary modes of being: local, everyday life, and national-historical time. As a literary signifier, region denied the stabilizing function nationhood played in the development of modern European symbolic forms, including the Bildungsroman; yet, it could not guarantee an alternative place for the uprooted subject to potentially finalize their development within an ever-expanding set of possible identifications brought on by globalization. The stability region offered was almost always associated with childhood in American literature, a realm into which the unfixed youth cannot fully reintegrate after their season of wandering.

Localism was thus construed as offering alternative narratives and subject positions to those presented by the official account of national destiny and development; nevertheless, the protagonist's struggle to finalize their development common in such novels reflected the wider struggle to accept cultural centralization as a suitable alternative to many decentralized literatures. This sense of uncertainty informed the geographical logic of uneven development within the twentieth-century American Bildungsroman. Many influential commentators arguably conscripted the local and the regional into the service of a broader, idealistic patriotic allegiance to the United States, in the search not only for a "usable past" but also a "usable place" upon which to center an American literary tradition; a perspective emulated in the influential editor and novelist William Dean Howells's advocation of "our decentralized literature"; and the prominent philosopher John Dewey's lament that the "Great Society" of the nation in the 1920s was not yet a "Great Community," as he put it in *The Public and Its Problems* (1927, 142). Despite his growing concerns over America's fractured national culture toward the end of the decade, Dewey had observed in 1920 that although people think "largely in terms of national integers," the U.S.

is a loose collection of houses, streets, neighbourhoods, villages, farms, towns. Each of these has an intense consciousness of what is going within itself . . . and a languid drooping interest in the rest of the spacious land. Very provincial? No . . . Just local, just human, just at home, just where they live. (685)

In defense of localism and suspicion regarding the lingering effects of the wartime centralization of federal powers, Dewey influentially claimed that the "local" is the "only universal." He imagined the local to be a cultural portal into what civilization "used to be," prior to a postwar mode of existence characterized by increasing global interconnectedness but decreasing local connectedness. These localities were where an otherwise abstract U.S. culture registered most palpably, even if only as a set of similarities within difference; but they were also where capitalist development had not yet fully reorganized encrusted community customs and social structures. The Bildungsroman—as a genre closely related to the centralizing imperatives and augmentation of nationalism—ambivalently registered the failure of a national literature to "merge into a unit" even after Reconstruction ended, but remained a heterogenous "spread of localities," "a loose collection of houses, of streets, of neighborhoods, villages, farms, towns," while "the nation" remained "something that exists in Washington and other seats of government" (Dewey 684–5).

As indicated above, the Bildungsroman has historically informed the Western project of cultural nationalism; as a genre, it was thus implicitly and directly implicated in these debates. Though certain American novels disrupted the traditional definitions of the genre's European iterations, the reasons behind this have never been fully elaborated apropos this formative period in the Bildungsroman's evolution.[1] From the late nineteenth century, the U.S. was

[1] Sarah Graham's chapter "The American Bildungsroman" in *A History of the Bildungsroman* (Cambridge University Press, 2019) abridges the genre's national transformations. Karen R. Tolchin's *Part Blood, Part Ketchup: Coming of Age in American Literature and Film* (Lexington Books, 2007) traces historical tendencies across nineteenth- and twentieth-century narratives. Other works that discuss aspects of American identity and ideology are Barbara Foley's *Radical Fictions* (Duke University Press, 1993); Geta LeSeur's *Ten Is the Age of Darkness: The Black*

experiencing an unprecedented growth spurt: economically, geographically, and ideologically, the fractured nation was reconsolidating while expanding in many directions. Yet, a discourse of nationalism was being established in the absence of any culture of nationalism. As the poet James Oppenheim wrote in *The Dial* in 1920, any "society of states, in which each state is a society of races, is not a nation in the Old World sense; it is not an organic fusion, but a collection, in which the differences are more marked than the likenesses" (238). That dilemma was popularly likened to the awkward development of an adolescent, as we saw in Emerson's reversal of the axiom laid out in Franco Moretti's account of the Bildungsroman in European literature, *The Way of the World*: a "*Bildung* is only truly such . . . if, at a certain point, it can be seen as *concluded*: only if youth passes into maturity, and comes to a stop there" (26). Such was the originary logic of the Bildungsroman genre as it emerged out of the aftershock of the French Revolution of 1789, when the potential crisis of "permanent revolution" found its ideal symbol in the figure of youth who, by the end of the classical Bildungsroman, forgoes youth's boundless mobility and conforms to their society's civic ideal. In Mikhail Bakhtin's chronotopical account of the Bildungsroman, upon which Moretti draws, the genre registers how "man's individual emergence is inseparably linked to historical emergence," whereby the "visible movement of *historical time*" becomes spatially "inseparable from the natural setting and the entire totality of objects created by man, which are essentially connected to this natural setting" (*Speech Genres*, 23). In that context, literary realism's emphasis on the present signaled "an aesthetic need to avoid recognition of the deep structural social change . . . and contradictory tendencies within the social order;"

Bildungsroman (University of Missouri Press, 1995); Alicia Otano's *Speaking the Past: Child Perspective in the Asian American Bildungsroman* (The University of Michigan Press, 2004); Martin Japtok's *Growing Up Ethnic: Nationalism and the Bildungsroman in African American and Jewish American Fiction* (University of Iowa Press, 2005); Yolanda A. Doub's *Journey of Formation: The Spanish American Bildungsroman* (Peter Lang, 2010); Stella Bolaki's *Unsettling the Bildungsroman: Reading Contemporary Ethnic American Women's Fiction* (Rodopi, 2011); and Jesse Raber's *Progressivism's Aesthetic Education: The Bildungsroman and the American School, 1890–1920* (Palgrave, 2018).

the young protagonist adduced "an instrument for the exploration of the new possibilities of bourgeois society," in Fredric Jameson's terms (145). The symbolic figure of youth thus formed a key to understanding modernity's new temporalities of social development; but it was also suggestive of the mutually informing relationship between historical and literary geography in the development of Western culture.

The late nineteenth-century Bildungsroman became the cultural expression of that state Georg Lukács famously labeled the Novel's "transcendental homelessness—the homelessness of an action in the human order of social relations, the homelessness of a soul in the ideal order of a supra-personal system of values" (61). Transcendental homelessness refers to the aesthetics of a moment when "periodicity [is] lost" and "genres cut across one another, with a complexity that cannot be disentangled" (41). The Bildungsroman grasped for the illusion of permanency in the "modern" figure of youth whose development—which Moretti deems the metaphor of capitalist modernity—masked the permanent revolutions and boundless expansion enveloping the nation-state, by giving shape and form to its civic ideals. Though the *fin de siècle* connotes the West's cultural preoccupation with time and temporality, and the decline of the European nationalist epoch, "a space of common sense," "knowledge," "social practice," and "political power, a space thitherto enshrined in everyday discourse, just as in abstract thought, as the environment of and channel for communications" had also "shattered," as Henri Lefebvre notes (25). Not only the temporalities of *Bildung*, but the borders of its narrative geographies, and the closure of development that could be achieved within the national-historical framework, shattered with it.

While I will not dwell on whether this genre possesses any "consensus of meaning" as countless others have (see Hardin x), one currently influential interpretation of the Bildungsroman is that the genre bound "national experience to the life of [its] hero," and was thus "connected more than any other to the rise of modern nationalism," as Tobias Boes contends (3). The genre's teleological logic of development was thus contingent upon the historical reorganization of the nation-state by the end of the nineteenth century, when the genre underwent distortion. Subsequently, scholars have contemplated whether to apply terms like antidevelopment, "failed initiation," or "problematic formation" to describe what resulted (Moretti 15). It makes sense, then, that the American Bildungsroman tradition is full of such problematic narratives in the period between 1900 and 1960. When concepts like *local*, or *nation*, or *region*, and other "parameters that we use to evaluate space fall apart," which is precisely what occurred from the late nineteenth century, then "the complexity of reproducing the local seems especially precarious: an obsession with space and its objects becomes paramount" (Yaeger "Narrating Space," 13). This is precisely what occurred, as countless American novels deviated from the classical soul-nation allegory, plucking themes, character types, and paradigmatic plots about youth's development from the classical model, appropriating them to represent not only the increasingly complex social networks of modernity but the regionally fragmented nation's decentered subject.

My own interpretation of why and how the Bildungsroman evolved unevenly in the U.S. context is in dialogue with Jed Esty's persuasive hypothesis that "the developmental logic of the late bildungsroman underwent substantial revision as the relatively stable temporal frames of national destiny gave way to a more conspicuously global, and therefore more uncertain, frame of social reference," leading to a proliferation of modernist antidevelopment novels that contend with this dialectic through the figure of the unseasonable youth who does not grow up (6). Modernity's erosion of the preconditions of Bildung meant that the novel which managed the risk of national disintegration required new narrative schemes, themes, and characters to consolidate the "open-ended temporality of capitalism and the bounded, countertemporality of the nation" (5). Given the "crucial symbolic function of nationhood, which gives finished form to the modern subject" (4), the genre encountered a hurdle when the symbolic status of *nation* proved itself too unstable a point of reference. Accordingly, narratives of arrested development proliferated in European literature, demonstrating "a shift in scale, where the thematics of uneven development attached increasingly to metropole-colony relations within the global frame rather than to urban-rural relations within the national frame"

(6–7). Although Esty's argument gainfully reframes the horizons of Bildungsroman studies around the geographies of uneven development, it also narrows the formulation of unevenness in literary space into more traditional dichotomies: modernism's globally enframed metropole–colony relation arguably replaces realism's nationally enframed urban–rural relations in this model, creating an optical illusion in which region is always already divorced from the metropolitan, but also the national or global. This reflects a broader tendency in transnationalist models of modernism, which have often neglected the "polytopic quality of modernist writing" including its "innumerable 'places'" that register at hypercomplex scales, one of the untidier scales being that of region (Thacker 20–1). As the case studies in this book cumulatively demonstrate, region played a much more significant, complex role in reorganizing the dynamics between the local, national, and the global in the twentieth-century Bildungsroman, and is thus far more critical to the genre's development than has previously been recognized.

The meaning of an aesthetics of *uneven development* that I refer to throughout is informed by the geographer Neil Smith's theory of uneven development, which stipulates how capital "produces distinct spatial scales—absolute spaces—within which the drive toward equalization is concentrated," but that it can only achieve this "by an acute differentiation and continued redifferentiation of relative space, both between and within scales" that "themselves are not fixed but develop (growing pangs and all) within the development of capital itself." Nor are these scales "impervious" to global fluctuations; qualifiers that define the borders between the local or the cosmopolitan, urban or rural, or regional and national are themselves "products of world capital and continue to be shaped by it" (196). The Bildungsroman represents how the individual comes to know themselves in relation to their social totality through their mobility, gradually assuming a stabilized civic identity consecrated in education, labor, and courtship, as pertains to the customs of their local context. In the American iteration, establishing the limits of region formed one crucial means by which the young protagonist understands their role within that totality. The genre thus implicitly registered the conditions Smith describes as the "changes and developments in relative space" that accompanied capitalism's uneven development, which "are neither accidental nor arbitrary but integral to the production of the national scale and its differentiation into rising and declining regions" (194). Given how the genre centralizes the initiation of the young subject into the adult world of labor, sexuality and the reproduction of the family, and social hierarchies against the background of their local social and environmental context, it tends to either implicitly or explicitly formulate what David Harvey describes as the "spatial fix," narrativizing how the global class struggle "dissolves into a variety of territorially based conflicts which support, sustain and in some cases even reconstitute all manner of local prejudices and encrusted traditions" (*Limits to Capital*, 420). The novel of uneven development was responsive to these transformations and interruptions capitalist development posed to local life.

While European modernism's bifocal preoccupation with uneven development has been described in terms of "far-flung colonies" held in opposition to "the proximate metropole," many "U.S. modernist novels" were responding to "the challenges of the universal" while "worrying about the implications of the local," writes Harilaos Stecopoulos (21). This unevenness was responding to a period when the nation's only unifying logic for managing its internal differences was through the homogenizing economic rhythms of capitalist progress (Duck 5). Places, by which I mean those social spaces that form conceptual containers for the lived experiences of people, seemed to offer representational and imaginative alternatives to the more abstract, uncertain borders of national, capitalist space. As public commentators, intellectuals, politicians, and writers grappled with how to integrate or assimilate regional distinctiveness into national-historical time, these debates provided distinctive geographic contexts for a range of generic experimentations, in which the figure of youth grappled with those same uncertainties and instabilities. If the dissolution of the universal subject had unsettled the only universal truth, which is that all youth must come to an end, the novel of uneven development questioned whether "the local [was] the only thing that is universal" after all, as Dewey had proposed (685). Regional affiliation appeared particularly salutary in the context of the destabilizing, variable effects of capitalist development. If regional affiliation at times operated as a constrictive container for both authors and their youthful protagonists, it nevertheless simultaneously offered a possible anchor point for their development.

These aesthetic concerns over the shifting epistemologies of the "local" and the "universal," which related to how authors and commentators processed the incongruities between regional and national time, were contingent on the ongoing colonization of the continent, and a shift from state to federal administrative power that was augmented by America's restrictive immigration policies and political interference abroad. Between circa 1880 and 1950, American literature tended "not only to be saturated in locality but also to understand that locality as a guarantee of its own authenticity and its patriotic allegiance" (Giles 19). Yet many Bildungsromane of that period suggested how the multidimensional aesthetics of regionalism not only facilitated but in various ways obstructed American exceptionalism, challenging the mythologization of place and identity that informs that ideology while presenting the possibility of seemingly alternative temporalities to that of a national-historical time synchronized with the rhythms of capitalist development. An increased awareness of the differences, rather than the unity, of the American civic body had significant repercussions for the genre's logic of development: rather than resolving these differences, modernist American Bildungsromane tended to probe and accentuate them by narrating the protagonist's struggle to integrate in national-historical time. The United States' involvement in World War I amplified earlier preoccupations with "how local affinities articulated in specifically aesthetic terms might relate to the nationalizing imperatives of war and its concomitant centralization of political power," according to Mark Whalan (*World War One*, 106). Evidently, such observations apply to the twentieth-century American Bildungsroman, in which the genre's representational resistance toward the "normative regime" of nation (Boes 3) related to an abstract nationalism that always already diffused into multiple particularities and pluralities.

As a construct, region did on one level serve nationalist ends, as the concrete realm of American exceptionalism, 100% Americanism, and white supremacy that embraced unique local cultures and diverse landscapes to insist upon the nation's political might. It also consolidated oppressive political structures designed to curtail the mobility of the Indigenous population and minority groups and sectionalize the proletariat; Jim Crow is a clear example of that function. Yet region encompasses multiple contradictory meanings and perspectives. For many, especially those most marginalized within the nation-state, region also signaled those subversive peripheries, localisms, folk cultures, and modes of living connected to the fact of land, and other complex heterotopias that offered some distance from the homogenizing effects of nationalism. From multiple ideological focal points, then—liberal and conservative, reactionary and radical—region recodified the political boundaries of nationalism within the Bildungsroman genre. In the novel of uneven development, the protagonist's broadening sense of modernity's rapidly changing world-system is managed through regional difference. This became the symbolic conceit for delimiting and navigating alternatives to an abstract American culture that was in this period conditioning of a modern civic identity centered upon the processes of economic standardization and cultural homogenization that accompany capitalism's uneven development.

Critical Regionalism: A Literary-Geographical Methodology

In U.S. literary studies, the term region brings with it significant historical and ideological baggage. Although region is not in essence synonymic or antonymic of nation, I recognize that many influential early commentators on literary geography presumed as much. As Neal Alexander and James Moran note, "the term 'regional' has often been resented by those who are regarded as residing in a dependent and satellite position to a notional center" (11). Such views led the Southern novelist Eudora Welty to determine that although the "location of a novel" held political significance in contemplating aspects such as theme and character, the term "'regional' writing" in criticism neglected "to differentiate between the localized raw material of life and its outcome as art," as it was construed typically through pejorative value systems that privileged the false universal over the local (Welty 781). Others, like Flannery O'Connor, protested that "regionalism" had become an accusation used to dismiss works that did not try to universalize American literature by refusing local specificity ("The Fiction Writer," 806). Modernist studies once insisted that "the key cultural factor of the modernist shift is the metropolis," because unlike the heterotopic inadequacies of provincial life, "a large city seems to nurture ideals of cosmopolitanism and worldliness" (Herring 1), as argued in Raymond Williams's *The Country and The City* (1973). In this history, the modernist text believes "it has uprooted itself from provincialism as a way of life and the provincial as a geographic entity," a position early critics like Malcolm Cowley and Carl Van Doren supported, the latter of whom in 1922 derided America's "moribund local color" fiction, with its "'quaint interiors scrupulously described; rounds of minute activity familiarly portrayed; skimpy moods analyzed with a delicate competence of touch'" (qtd in Herring 1). Heightened regional scrutiny informed Van Doren's "revolt from the village," to manifold political ends, as authors attempted to rewrite the mythologization of "place" that sentimentalist local color fiction emphasized, without ever actually erasing regional specificity. That said, when critics Lewis Mumford and Frank Lloyd Wright coined the term "regional modernism" in the 1930s pertaining to urban design and architecture, it activated a reactionary response to what they perceived as internationalist modernism's homogenizing "metronormativity" and the dilution of local aesthetics (Herring 1), a view that coalesced with influential but problematic regionalist theories, like that pioneered by the Fugitive Agrarians in the South. As the following discussions of the Bildungsroman's regional development will substantiate, region evidently played a more dialectical role within literary geography than early critics of regionalism, along with some of its most passionate proponents, imagined.

Although key debates over the proliferation and waning of "local color" fiction remain relevant touchpoints throughout this book, I use the terms "region" and "regionalism" neither in defense nor repudiation of this historical mode. "Local" and "localism" are terms I also apply to designate "a narrower geographic base for group or individual identity" than region, given terms including "local color" and "local history" are often considered "part of the regionalist's project to describe the local as part of or imbedded within a larger set of natural or cultural relationships" (Katz and Mahoney xi). One key finding of this book is that the preoccupation with region that reorganized the Bildungsroman's literary geography after 1900 often stemmed from an urgent geopolitical desire to reconceptualize how the novel as a symbolic form mediates local, regional, national, and transnational networks of affiliation, by contemplating how individual development is impacted by these overlapping forces. Building on Lefebvre's theory of social space,[2] Neil Smith explains how scale condenses "the oppressive and emancipatory possibilities of space" into

> a distilled expression of spatial ideologies: nationalism, localism, regionalism, and, in some forms, racism and xenophobia. The production and representation of scale therefore lie at the centre of a spatialized politics even if in much political discourse this spatial struggle is often implicit in arguments over nomenclature, naming places, and much as explicit in boundary struggles. (230)

As I demonstrate through examining how different regional literatures emphasized different kinds of textual strategies for registering the preoccupation with regional difference, redeveloping the genre's classical formal attributes in unexpected ways became a way of comprehending the multiple affiliative entanglements of the nation's uneven development, as a loosely interconnected society caught in the face of economic inequality and red-baiting; xenophobic immigration policies; state-sanctioned racial segregation; settler colonialism and imperialism; and patriarchy. Reflecting the many inconsistent layers of affective loyalty an individual might possess, the American Bildungsroman discursively engaged in those boundary struggles, as the narrative of development evolved alongside emerging sociological understandings of how human growth and capitalist-industrial development operated across different environments.

---

[2] According to Lefebvre, modernity poses not "one social space" but an "uncountable set of social spaces . . . No space disappears in the course of growth and development: the *worldwide does not abolish the local*. This is not a consequence of the law of uneven development, but a law in its own right . . . Considered in isolation, such spaces are mere abstractions. As concrete abstractions, however, they attain 'real' existence by virtue of networks and pathways, by virtue of bunches or clusters of relationships" (86).

Though my readers may be more familiar with a view of region that is static, reactionary, and homogenous, and definitions of regionalism and localism that are patriotic and 100% Americanist, that is an impartial picture of what region signaled, especially as authors blended literary and geographical discourses in their novels of uneven development, striving to provide more authentic depictions of "real" Americans where they "really" lived than they felt local color fiction had delivered. In literary studies, the term *region* often implies the embodiedness and subjectiveness of *place*; whereas in the field of geography, the term is empirically applied to delineate "spatially distinctive collective phenomena including ways of life that have evolved through human social action over time," including "classifying, on a territorial basis, data about the different modes of life encountered around the globe" (Harvey *Cosmopolitanism*, 171). Indeed, Harvey notes that the "objective and subjective meanings" by which we approach geographical scales such as "region" falter when faced with "understanding political organization," given that "regions, states, or nations may appear at one level as mere imagined abstractions," and yet "the sense of a territorial bond and of an affective loyalty to it has enormous political significance" (*Cosmopolitanism*, 8). Novelists often contributed to public debates over localism and nationalism, drawing upon geographical discourses as well as contemporary sociological, anthropological, political, and philosophical discourses of space, place, and culture to inform a decentralized aesthetics of individual development, which accounted for the lived effects of capitalism's reorganization of local life. The novel of uneven development regulated both objective and subjective connotations of region, to represent the multifaceted dimensions of political and social affiliation and loyalty that enframe the young protagonist, who contemplates the end to the season of mobility that the adult world of labor, politics, economics, and civic obligation poses to them.

These findings intersect with the interdisciplinary field of critical regionalism, which investigates how the untidy spatial concept, region, dynamically structures social, cultural, and economic activity, rather than serves as passive container of human activity. Critical regionalism, first theorized by Kenneth Frampton in architecture, originally invoked "vernacular traditions and icons of place" in order to facilitate "a politics of resistance to the homogenizing force of commodity flows and monetization" (Harvey *Cosmopolitanism*, 179). Gayatri Chakravorty Spivak and Judith Butler were among the earliest to import the concept of critical regionalism into the discursive networks of theory, to conceptualize a "trans-frontier jurisdiction" beyond the abstractions of the state-structure, including those repressive apparatuses that Louis Althusser argued connect the "'imaginary relationship of the individuals to their real conditions of existence'" (Spivak 75). As an heurmeneutic, critical regionalism unsettles the nationalist reductionism of literary interpretative practices by configuring the hypercomplex role that geographical scale played in modernist literature, retiring the more reductive categories upon which modernist studies previously relied, such as the metropole–colony and center–periphery binaries.

Though various historical arguments apropos American localism and regionalism form important referents in what follows, my approach revisits those accounts in light of recent critical regionalist scholarship.[3] As various scholars have noted, there is much to learn about the transnational circulation of literature by tracing regionalist concerns, given how regionalism—even in its most patriotic evocations—only "gains in aesthetic interest . . . to the extent that it is (and was) seen to circulate in a transnational network of distribution" (Evans 777). To that end, the many American Bildungsromane discussed in this volume engage in what might be described as regional cosmopolitanism, a concept conceived by Tom Lutz to disambiguate the paradox of literary valuations that have historically denied the centrality of inclusive cosmopolitanism within literary regionalism, which becomes visible through the recognition of difference in many regionalist works (see Lutz 9–49). More recently, Jason Arthur suggests that "articulating commonalities across cultures" rather than "articulating differences" became one of the defining impulses of twentieth-century American culture; it was regional cosmopolitanism as a "literary register" that mediated

---

[3] Examples include Andrew Thacker's *Moving Through Modernity: Space and Geography in Modernism* (2003); Leigh Anne Duck's *The Nation's Region: Southern Modernism, Segregation, and U.S. Nationalism* (2006); Scott Herring's special issue for *Modern Fiction Studies*, "Regional Modernism: A Reintroduction" (2009); and Neal Alexander and James Moran's *Regional Modernisms* (2013).

"the concentricity of the local, the national, and the global," while negotiating "such polarities as 'nativism' and 'pluralism'" (xii). In rethinking the paradox of how modernism's literary perspective can be simultaneously "'rooted'" in "both the local landscape and the cosmopolitan world," Jessica Berman also theorizes how the situatedness and embodiedness of everyday life are not separated from the global; rather, they intersect in regional cosmopolitanisms that traverse the "multidirectional flow of global literature and culture" (150). In the American Bildungsroman circa 1900–1960, the unfixed figure of youth broadly represented this state of simultaneous situatedness and potentially boundless mobility, a dialectic which brought the many interfaces of the regional, national, and transnational in modern, everyday life into view. Judith Fetterley and Marjorie Pryse have observed that regionalisms vacillate

> between urban and rural/"regional" places; while cosmopolitan attitudes might assume clear barriers between the modernizing life of the cities and the presumptively premodern world of the regions, for the writers themselves and in their regionalist texts, these barriers become permeable and transitive. (4–5)

Building upon this consensus on region as a dynamic, permeable, and transitive literary scale, it seems that the ever-shifting dynamic between regional and national affiliations in an increasingly uncertain global framework created a paradox within the Bildungsroman's logic of development, provoking many authors to probe that aesthetic uncertainty and produce innovative responses that formalized the logic of uneven development. Region not only anchored development in the American Bildungsroman after 1900, simultaneously posing both a stabilizing and constraining force to the individual's growth, but also pointed to the inadequacy of a unified national culture within the ever-expanding forces of globalization. Region, as a spatial construct, thus portended to the difficulty the individual experiences in managing competing and contradictory affiliations and social difference, within the nation-state's official discourses of pluralistic liberalism.

Though the unfixed figure of youth may futilely look to region to anchor that future, I will not argue that region implicitly stood in for an integrative nationalist center. To formalize those growing pains of a period of abstract, fragmentary, and placeless Americanism, the open-ended, future-oriented Bildungsroman offered an ideal scaffold for locating, conveying, and experimenting with that political uncertainty. National history becomes visible as it is compressed into literary space; in the twentieth century American context, its present tense is governed by the overlapping perception of a stable past anchored in locality, embodiedness, and emplacement, and the prospect of an uncertain, unlocatable future tense. The itinerant protagonists of those aesthetics—who wander through their towns and cities, cross physical and social borders, worry about the impacts of national politics and culture, and try to comprehend an incomprehensibly widening world—were as much the unfixed youth as the authors themselves. Each of the novelists featured in this book contemplated how the evolving dynamic between "the local" and "the universal" impacted their society's cultural life through this symbolic form. Their regional complex was indicative of an urgent critical response to life under an ascendent global hegemon. For a genre all about the formation of the nation-state, this preoccupation assured the Bildungsroman's transformation into a less clearly enframed political apparatus.

A Roadmap of Uneven Development

In what specific ways did this regional complex underwrite the genre's formal incoherence between circa 1900 and 1960, including the many variegations in themes, plots, and characterization that became visible in that period? To address such a question, we require an heuristic—in this case, a roadmap—to configure and interpret the dynamic role that region played within the novel of development. If the twentieth-century's "complex geography of modernism" appears "quite different depending on where one locates oneself and when," in David Harvey's words, it follows that the "the particularities of place" will necessarily tabulate "the diversity" of modernist experiments in a range of generic situations (*Cosmopolitanism*, 170), including in the Bildungsroman. This book not only asserts that the Bildungsroman was responsive to regional cultural transformations rehearsed above during America's rising nationalist period, circa 1900-1960; it creates a map of key regional transformations that reorganized the genre's heterotopias, thereby producing an aesthetics of uneven development that tested the limits of representing local difference within a globalizing capitalist framework. My method for navigating these particularities involves remapping the American novel of development from a critical regionalist perspective, drawing a literary atlas of the genre's most significant transformations. The case studies in this book account for how this regional complex translated into formal innovations that unsettled the co-optation of the local under the capitalist-industrial banner of Americanization.

The map of the American Bildungsroman's uneven development this book assembles is not intended to give full coverage of all possible authors and novels. The discussions shall culminate, from section to section, to create an overall sense of similarity in difference between regional literatures. I acknowledge that there will be exceptions to the tendencies described in what follows. All literary geographies risk self-legitimization, inevitably delimiting the interpretive possibilities of such discourses rather than providing open-ended hermeneutics. This is certainly true of regionalist discourse, which "imposes its own definitions and boundaries" to legitimize them, as Wendy J. Katz and Timothy R. Mahoney advise (xi). To discuss "renaissances and localized literatures" may simultaneously open "conventional entry points for previously disregarded groups of authors and texts"; even as it presents critical problems inherent in "the notion of the 'regional' novel,'" given the term "implies that some novels are about specific geographic space, while others are about life," or "a specific society," "human experience," "the working class," or "people in general" (Cappetti 8-10), creating a hierarchy of literary value that risks marginalizing those who do not fit within those categorical boundaries. For Giles, "to adumbrate a regional map of American literature is" always "merely to consider how these different forms of misrecognition have become institutionalized: which geographies have become normalized and why" (223). By constellating texts in a way that emphasizes how an aesthetics of unevenness transfigured the Bildungsroman into a genre that scrutinized and unsettled how regional difference was culturally regulated and accepted, this map looks to denaturalize some of those institutionalized misrecognitions. Finally, although this book engages in historicism, it does not trace the emergence of the American Bildungsroman or attend to its current state; that is a far larger intellectual project, ambitiously initiated in Sarah Graham's chapter on the matter in *A History of the Bildungsroman* (2020). I maintain that in historicizing symbolic forms, like the Bildungsroman, geographical thinking remains a crucial imperative within the critical climate we inhabit for approaching "the culture of a political entity that goes from colonial outpost to global power in a little over a century," as Jennifer Rae Greeson suggests in a related context (2). Drawing momentum from several related fields, including Bildungsroman theory, modernist studies, literary geography, and scholarship pertaining to the regional literatures under discussion, this book contributes to broader critical efforts to reframe the diachronic as well as the synchronic parameters of modernism, the Bildungsroman, and American literature.

Below, I have outlined this critical regionalist map of the American Bildungsroman c. 1900–1960. Section One locates us in the Middle West at the *fin de siècle*, a chronotope that laid much of the groundwork for reconfiguring the relationship between mobility in the Bildungsroman genre and the role that region played within modernity's untidy geographies. Chapter 1 discusses how naturalist novelists Theodore Dreiser and Upton Sinclair adapted the bourgeois Bildungsroman to allegorize that region's rapid industrialization. In doing so, they radically re-engineered the sentimental teleology of development in "local color" realism. Their new poetics of labor showcased the antidevelopment of immature regional types whose dreams of fulfilling labor are churned through the charnel house of Midwestern industrialism. Building upon those findings, Chapter 2 examines naturalist regionalisms after 1919. I consider how the new social politics of rurality engulfing the postwar Midwest informed the denial of rurality as ethnically homogenous spaces in Willa Cather's *My Ántonia*, and contoured the proletarian regionalism of Langston Hughes's *Not Without Laughter*. Chapter 3 then observes the socialist and sociological theories of adolescence, urbanity, and regional development which underwrote Richard Wright's *Native Son* and James Farrell's *Studs Lonigan* trilogy, two portraits of "extreme youth."

Section Two then shifts to the Northeast region's modernist Künstlerroman of the 1920s, which saw the emergence of the development of the regional artist subgenre. Chapter 4 discusses how in F. Scott Fitzgerald's *This Side of Paradise* and Zelda Sayre Fitzgerald's *Save Me the Waltz* the young modernist artist's development is contoured by their regional complex: their sense of regional difference, within the centralizing imperatives of New York's culture industry. Chapter 5 contemplates how this same tendency was applied to those Künstlerromane, including Jessie Redmon Fauset's *Plum Bun* and Wallace Thurman's *Infants of the Spring*, which challenged the nationalizing imperatives of the New Negro Renaissance by insisting that Harlem was built up of many seemingly contradictory regionalisms. These texts simultaneously contended with the difficulties of being relegated to a segregated "region" within American literature's white-dominant marketplace of ideas.

Section Three transports us across the Mason–Dixon line, one of the most scrutinized regional borderlines in modern history. Chapter 6 contextualizes the early twentieth-century trope of Southern underdevelopment. Reacting against the amplified social mobility of Northern modernism and the New Negro Renaissance, the Fugitive Agrarians designed a regionalist manifesto to counteract that trope. Their reactionary definition of regionalism loomed over the Southern Literary Renaissance from the late 1920s, when many authors utilized the Bildungsroman to explore more nuanced methods of representing the uneven temporalities of nation and region than touristic local colorism afforded. Unsettling the Agrarians' narrowing regionalism, while correcting the pervasive cynicism toward rural folk culture in the New Negro Renaissance, Zora Neale Hurston's ethnographically informed *Their Eyes Were Watching God* blended the realist Bildungsroman with what Mikhail Bakhtin called the "realistic fantastic" of folkloric narratives, as Chapter 7 observes. Leaning into such generic incongruity, Hurston illustrated the hazards of integrating folk cultures into the soul-nation allegory. Chapter 8 discusses how the gothic mode, a term which in the mid-twentieth century typically referred to Southern texts that juxtaposed the region's banal, everyday features with images of violence, deprivation, and estrangement, merged with the realist Bildungsroman to similarly represent the jagged effects of modernization upon underdeveloped rural communities, as reflected in Carson McCullers's *The Member of the Wedding* and Flannery O'Connor's *The Violent Bear It Away*.

That discussion carries us into this literary tour's final destination, Section Four, located in the Indigenous borderlands of the Southwest. The concluding discussion of John Joseph Mathews' *Sundown* reflects the curious role that region played in the Indigenous critique of the ideologies of nation-formation in the early twentieth century, in the context of the federal Allotment policy. At the limits of the nation and the Bildungsroman, *Sundown* exemplified the logic of the novel of uneven development, as it contested the viability of the ideologies of civilization, progress, and modernization that the genre's national-historical time insinuated.

Part I
Midwestern Naturalism

CHAPTER 1

Industrial Folklore and the Regional Ingénue in Dreiser and Sinclair

This expedition begins with the symbolic Midwest that emerged in the Bildungsroman at the *fin de siècle*, a literary region in which the young individual's development allegorically demarcated the nation's potential for unrestrained growth. That region was imagined as an open thoroughfare for industrial modernity's ideology of westward territorial expansion, both domestically and abroad. The precipitously developing plains "exposed the fault lines in previous American institutions without clearly replacing them with new ones," as its seemingly boundless "prairie, grids, transportation corridors, and cash crops" informed "the genteel standardization or rationalization of social and business life" of middle-class America (Katz and Mahoney xxii). Chicago formed the strategic junction in the ebb and flow of intraregional rail traffic, contributing to the city's reputation as offering limitless mobility, which denied the rationalization of local life under industrial development. Train lines created the "geographic terms" by which the city-region's "cultural and literary identity" communicated the story of self-making through migration, as "told from the provincial point of view," Timothy Spears observes (8). Chicago posed a curious paradox, as various scholars note; despite its metropolitan ascendency, it still performed the role of a "provincial city" within the nation's regional imaginary (Cappetti 8–10; Spears xviii).

Midwestern naturalism was forged within that paradox. From the Progressive Era, many writers presented the uneven landscape of the Midwest as being concentrated in its new metropolises, especially

Chicago, the local writerly "atmosphere" of which "challenged the traditional approaches to [news] feature writing" (Hricko 4), by descriptively accentuating "strikes, slaughterhouses, railroads and poverty" as being elements of the region's modern character (Woolley 9). Novels such as *Sister Carrie* (1900) by Theodore Dreiser and *The Jungle* (1906) by Upton Sinclair evinced how the effects of industrialization upon the character of the Midwest also shifted the ontologies of individual autonomy, labor, and leisure that were central to bourgeois realism. Such novels often recalibrated the Bildungsroman's poetics of the local—specifically, local color fiction, which had become the sentimental stigma on the face of an emergent class within American literary realism that privileged unforgiving representations of the effects of industrialism on everyday life: urban naturalism. This mode provided an alternative to the classical Bildungsroman's model of development, based upon sociological models of social development. In the rupture of the social order precipitated by industrial modernity, man's intervention in the region's natural order expedited the "density of urban life and factory work" that shattered the classical Bildungsroman's bourgeois dreamscape of individual *"little worlds"* by forcing "people into increased contact with one another" (Corkin 38–9). The "little plots, little scenes, little characters" of the Midwestern hinterlands that comprised the genre of local color fiction, as it was later skeptically described in one anonymous editorial for *The Nation* in 1919 ("Local Color and After," 426), needed to be customized to complement the transformations of labor and the environment in ways that did not repress the effects of the nation's mass-industrial revolution, but rather, explained them sociologically from the standpoint of the masses.

In that sense, naturalist novelists were no less preoccupied with the local than other authors, often writing about the increasingly multifaceted tensions between regional identity and national character, especially in relation to industrial development and its impact upon human development. Writing during the first wave of Spencerian and Darwinian sociology, Dreiser and Sinclair perceived how the natural world and its "natural processes were necessary to the proper functioning of the city," a harmony that was lost the further society removed itself "from the biological rhythms of nature, of the land," argues Richard Lehan (128-9). Their naturalist novels reversed the classical Bildungsroman's teleology, in depicting the story of a young protagonist's removal from nature as they become caught up in the region's destiny, which is to operate as a factory for the mass production of the necessary fuel for national progress: non-perishable food. Narrativizing the possibilities of the unregulated world of industrial labor that Chicago encapsulated, drawn in contrast to the prairies, these novels narrated the young, regional protagonist's apprenticeship in a modern, yet volatile labor environment. In contrast to the harmonious regionalism informed by the idle pulses of provincial life in local color fiction, the mental life of the new Midwestern subject who resides in Chicago's rapidly developing urban sprawl was now consistently framed in extremes and an accelerated temporality.

Within the region's literature, the "Chicago novel" subset imagined the city's densely populated built environment in stark contrast to the Midwestern hinterland's slowness and starkness, according to Sidney H. Bremer; its skyscrapers and "street-car monopolies [that] deepen social divisions by oppressing labor and segregating residential districts" gesticulated toward "a future of 'indefinite continuation,' of constant expansion 'in anticipation of rapid growth'" (75-6). That description adumbrates the boundless potential for development that must be strategically managed in the originary Bildungsroman by drawing a close to the season of youth. The Chicagoan Bildungsroman instead depicted spatialized psychological tropes of volatile overdevelopment, foregrounding the voices, perceptions, and responses of ordinary young workers whose individual destinies are fodder for the symbolic structures of the new industrial order. Such is the metaphoric environment that the naturalists reflected, by squaring the hostile conditions of labor initiated in Chicago's factories and stockyards into the circle that is the Bildungsroman form. If, as Moretti argues, "the 'harmony' that characterizes work" in the classical Bildungsroman only succeeds in that it eschews a "strictly economic logic," for Dreiser and Sinclair, the individual whose primary enterprise is to seek out meaningful vocation dissolves into dissonance in a society in which capitalistic work and the "god of profit" effectively "betrays the very essence of work, what it is 'in and for itself.' Beautiful. Ennobling" (Moretti

30). Rather than abandon the Bildungsroman altogether, naturalists repurposed its formal attributes, even as they promoted deterministic, materialist visions of capitalist development's impact on human maturation.

New plots, tropes, themes, and characters needed to be developed for the Bildungsroman to aptly register the region's extremes as they are experienced by the young laborer who is dialectically shaped by the modes of rural and urban life they simultaneously inhabit, in ways that realism was seen to have not previously captured. That shift was guided by Frank Norris, who in one influential essay on American naturalism, argued that realism can only reach the mere "surface of things," while fiction ought to plumb the "depths of the human heart, and the mystery of sex, and the problems of life, and the black, unsearched penetralia of the soul of man" (76). For many apprentices of Émile Zola's naturalist "experimental novel," including Dreiser and Sinclair (Pizer 190), the role of literary fate in the Bildungsroman was to be substituted for socioeconomic forces to answer Norris's plea for "romantic" (read: naturalist) fiction. Such forces appeared to govern the lives of the principal characters of the Bildungsroman in ways that reassembled sociological theories of human development, especially those being developed by the prominent Chicago School of Sociology. Naturalism could not provide the "definitive stabilization of the individual, and of his relationship to the world," because the "'maturity'" reached at "the story's final stage" was "fully possible *only in the precapitalist world*," in the bourgeois Bildungsroman's original teleology; for, only "far from the metropolis" can the "restless impermanence of youth be appeased," Moretti explains (27).

In this chapter, I examine how the regional migration plot undertaken by Dreiser and Sinclair, whose respective novels *Sister Carrie* and *The Jungle* forged a new sociologically derived poetics of labor and development for the Bildungsroman, enabled them to map the geographical logic which was aesthetically and politically rooted in the industrial and cultural transformations of the Midwest. Among the early literary responses to the region's developments, these two novels placed young, provincial migrants into that city's transformational labor force, transfiguring the "quintessentially ideological" discourse of bourgeois realism upon which the Bildungsroman genre formerly relied (Foley *Radical Representations*, 321). As the young protagonist becomes unfixed from their regional mode of existence by relocating from the organic temporalities associated with the provinces, the disorientation, discomfort, and uncertainty they contend with is suggestive of the effects of capitalism's uneven development internal to the national-historical time of America's industrial modernity, an unevenness metaphorized by the paradoxical "provincial city" of Chicago.

Theodore Dreiser's *Sister Carrie* (1900)

Though Fredric Jameson suggests that the protagonist of the realist Bildungsroman was not a "new social type," so much as "a kind of registering device" that recorded the new possibilities of bourgeois society (145), it was precisely the industrial Midwest's new social types that the urban naturalist novel appropriated in *fin de siècle* American fiction. Novelists such as Theodore Dreiser scanned sites such as Chicago for modern labor types, around which they could create "experimental" plots that revealed the deterministic effects of the new frontiers of urban modernity upon human development. Although Dreiser arguably preserved elements of Howellsian realism and the Jamesian novel of manners, which observed the educative experiences of the bourgeoisie,[1] *Sister Carrie* was in his words "close[r] to life" because it was never intended as "a piece of literary craftsmanship," so much "as a picture of conditions done as simply and effectively as the English language will permit" (Dreiser *Interviews*, 6). Contiguous with Lukács's claim that the Bildungsroman's "hero is picked out of an unlimited number of men," and is only placed at the "centre of the narrative because his seeking and finding reveal the world's totality most clearly" (134), Dreiser's protagonist Carolyn Meeber's development formed the conceit by which he could scrutinize the wider totality

---

[1] Dreiser's use of sociological types deviated from the more complex characterology Henry James was engineering in psychological novels such as *What Maisie Knew* (1893), written at a point in James's late career when he abandoned his earlier preoccupation with American scenes. Nevertheless, *Maisie* shared a similar premise—i.e. the vicissitudes of bourgeois American women's maturation—with earlier novels such as *Washington Square* (1880).

of the capitalist nation-state. The stark economic unevenness that resulted from national growth driven by free market capitalism captured Dreiser's interest, as he noted at the moment he turned his attention from journalism to fiction in the late 1890s, when he resolved to novelize how the rapid industrialization of the United States meant that "one eighth of the families in the United States in 1895 controlled seven-eighths of its property" (Dreiser qtd in Hakutani 23). Rather than take the bourgeoisie as his focal point, Dreiser scrutinized the new sociological types that arose within the unremarkable, unsalaried masses, finding his ideal medium in the young, single, American born, and white protagonist, Carrie, who steps aboard a regional train in the Midwestern hinterland headed toward Chicago. Carrie perpetuated the stereotype of the regional young woman adrift, whose provincial innocence is betrayed by the inharmonious world of labor into which she is inculcated. Such is the basis of the naturalist allegory of development at the heart of *Sister Carrie*, as it is first articulated by its sociologizing narrator: "Among the forces which sweep and play throughout the universe, untutored man is but a wisp in the wind. Our civilization is still in a middle age" (Dreiser *Sister Carrie*, 83). The symbolic "middle age" of the Midwest region's industrial development is synonymous with the protagonist Carrie's youth, her "middle age" between childhood and adulthood.

Between 1880 and 1930, when Dreiser produced most of his novels, Chicago's female labor force expanded, from 35,600 to 407,600, at roughly three times "the rate of increase of the female labor force for the nation as a whole," given the U. S. female workforce had only increased by 171% (Meyerowitz 5). This produced a sociological generality ripe for literary investment in telling the story of the region's development: the New Woman. As one of many *fin de siècle* novels that centered on that type, *Sister Carrie* reimagined Chicago's heterogenous demographics by representing its working class as young, female, white (Meyerowitz 6), but no less crucially, regional. As one of Chicago's many new apprentices of factory labor, Carrie metaphorized the region's changing mode of production, and the new narrative possibilities it offered the "experimental novel" (in Zola's sense). Because Carrie is first characterized as a regional type—innocent, naively ambitious, and unfamiliar with modern labor settings—she ironically exemplifies the type of character that can only flourish in the preindustrial capitalist, non-metropolitan world she renounces in the novel's opening.

Bourgeois individualism, the presiding ideological tenet of the Bildungsroman genre, is observed when Carrie distinguishes herself as exceptional from the workers; her provincial sensibilities mean she does not fit the type.

> The machine girls . . . were in a sense "common." Carrie had more imagination than they. She was not used to slang. Her instinct in matters of dress was naturally better. . . . They were free with the fellows . . . and exchanged banter in rude phrases, which . . . shocked her. (Dreiser *Sister Carrie*, 37)

The reader's sympathy is directed toward the protagonist who cannot parse these crude conditions of collective labor, an environment without "the slightest provision" for the "comfort of the employees" (37). After less than an hour on the job, an exhausted Carrie wonders how her colleagues endure such mindless labor. When a workmate retorts that "It isn't hard . . . You just take this so . . . and start the machine" (34), the attendant's nonchalance is an ironic companion to the violence the machine's language communicates: "punching, with sharp, snapping clicks, cutting circular bits." Carrie submits to the machine's orders; her body is quantitatively articulated into "an average speed," lest "the work would pile up on her and all those below would be delayed" (35). Her "imaginings," too, seep into the "humdrum, mechanical movement of the machine" (35) until the foreman descends upon her, spluttering distressing imperatives: "Don't keep the line waiting!" (35) That this stressful, alienating factory environment is an unsuitable backdrop for the bourgeois subject only recently arrived from the provinces is not only signaled by Carrie's incompetency here, but also her general disorientation when riding the factory elevator up multiple floors, and her refusal to socialize with her colleagues.

Intruding on these proceedings, the narrator pauses to sociologically interpret Carrie's instinctive dissatisfaction, interpreting her outlook as a premonition of the trade unions' fight to advance workers' rights. The narrator excuses Carrie's derision toward her fellow workers because her attitude reflects those social relations before the idea of "the new socialism which involves pleasant working conditions for employees" had taken "hold upon manufacturing companies" (37). These narratorial intrusions—distinct from the free indirect discourse that is focalized upon Carrie—enunciate many of the historic agendas that might otherwise be concealed by the individual development narrative, reflecting Dreiser's own struggles as an author regarding how to represent the individual's development within a totality into which they cannot truly be integrated. Although in the novel's terms the coarseness of the machine girls morally binds them to a fate of hard labor, Carrie's sexual intrigues do not result in her downfall, as they would have in the provincial working-class girl rubric of Rebecca Harding Davis's *Life in the Iron Mills* (see Hapke 78). Dreiser exposes the cultural myths surrounding the "self-protective" nature of "feminine economic activity" in the proletariat by substituting feminine desire for capitalist consumption (Hapke 156). As Laura Hapke observes, the narrator later clarifies that Carrie is not a prostitute, despite living "in sin" with her gentleman friend, the drummer Charles Drouet; the transaction between them is, somehow, not the same as that in Stephen Crane's *Maggie: A Girl of the Streets*, often considered the progenitor of American literary urban naturalism (156). Though Carrie is shocked by the crude bawdy of her proletarian peers, any expression of her erotic agency as a fallen woman, by her society's moral standards, is sublimated into the intensities of consumerism: she feels orgasmic "relief" when "[holding] the money in her hand" (Dreiser *Sister Carrie*, 60). Absolving her of potential immoralism, capital catapults her out of a simple, puritanical local framework and into the vertiginous warp and weft of transnational exchange.

To engineer this conceit, Dreiser reproduces regionalized mythologies of Midwestern innocence: the subject who is yet unspoiled by the consumerism resulting from Chicago's capitalist overdevelopment but is soon to be corrupted by it. Carrie's lack of identification with her co-workers foreshadows her estrangement from her lover George Hurstwood—a prosperous Chicagoan businessman, who abandons his wife and children and attempts to rob his employer in an impulsive whim to win Carrie's affection, and thereby absorb what personal possibilities her youthfulness affords an aging, married man. That plan is foiled after they flee to New York, when his inability to secure work forces him to scab at the Brooklyn strikes, his economic decline inverting the heroine's ultimate removal from the working class when against all probability she becomes a celebrity actress on Broadway. Inversely, Hurstwood's accidental participation in Brooklyn's Great Trolley Strike of 1895 reflects the radical response to the uneven development of national modernity. Hurstwood's perspective becomes the more powerful lens through which to view the region's radical transformations, giving the former journalist Dreiser the opportunity to import his own investigations into the trolley strikes that unfolded across the Midwest in the ten years prior in Twin Cities, Minnesota (1890), Detroit (1891), Milwaukee (1896), Cleveland (1899), and St. Louis (1900), where the struggle became so intense that labor activists dynamited the lines. Thus, when Carrie shuns Hurstwood outside the theater toward the novel's end, she symbolically recoils away from those labor struggles he witnesses, and her career progression from laborer, to kept mistress, to celebrity comic actress on Broadway is revealed to be ironic.

By juxtaposing the class antagonism represented by Hurstwood's demise against the representation of bourgeois character development central to the Bildungsroman genre, Dreiser reconceived of Horatio Alger's appropriation of Bildung in his bestseller *Ragged Dick* series (1868) on the one hand, which popularized the rags-to-riches paradigm in urban popular fiction about young manhood. On the other, Carrie's seemingly boundless socioeconomic growth also cut against the grain of the more obviously deterministic, character-focused "growing down" rubric in women's fiction of that period.[2] Annis Pratt and Barbara White's influential definition of the female Entwicklungsroman holds that it is "the novel of mere growth ... from one age to the other without psychological development," in which the author's undertaking to "accommodate their

---

[2] Examples include Edith Wharton's *The House of Mirth* (1905), which portrays the rise and tragic decline of a Northeastern socialite, Lily Bart, in the face of that region's conservative class system; and Kate Chopin's *The Awakening* (1899), set among Louisiana's Creole gentry.

hero's *Bildung*, or development" fails to project "a self-determined progression *towards* maturity" (36). Yet the transformative process of "observation, contrast, emulation, and consecutive change" in *Sister Carrie* cannot culminate in "the transcendent wisdom or stable marriage of its heroine," Clare Virginia Eby observes ("Psychology of Desire," 195). Unsettling the genre's harmonious teleology in which individuation is developed through meaningful vocation and acculturation, Dreiser's labor plot squared the regional ingénue into the circle of a sociological model that determined how the American masses enter the workforce through networks of geography, race, class, and gender. Dreiser's satire of the childish regional ingénue who is unfit for factory work masked the novelist's deeper anxiety, which was that labor and comfort were no longer mutually inclusive, as they once appeared to be in the classical Bildungsroman. He thus anticipated concerns that would preoccupy the region's naturalist Bildungsromane for decades to come.

Upton Sinclair's *The Jungle* (1906)

In *The Jungle* (1906)—another Midwestern Bildungsroman about human growth under the new industrial order—Upton Sinclair also adhered to the same basic aesthetic principles of naturalism and Zola's experimental novel hypothesis. Sinclair, however, came to that form as an unapologetic propagandist. From a socialist perspective, Sinclair's novel of uneven development explored the many faultlines caused by the practice of unregulated regional development with limited federal oversight in Progressive Era politics, including food security, immigration and public housing, and workers' rights. In revealing the consequences of the largely unregulated development of regional and private interests in the Midwest, *The Jungle* ultimately provoked the extension of federal powers over interstate commerce, as its shocking revelations over biosecurity in agricultural production and the meat-packing industry gave President Roosevelt license to investigate and intervene in the Midwest's agriculture and food production.[3]

---

[3] Sinclair's exposé forced the Department of Agriculture to legislate a federal statute in 1906 to protect consumers from misbranded consumables, marking "'a radical

Sinclair's experimental Bildungsroman, in Zola's sense, places a young, regional worker into the framework of Illinois's burgeoning industrial sections; however, unlike Carrie, that figure is proletarian and an immigrant. Jurgis Rudkus emigrates with his extended family from their bucolic Lithuanian home so that Jurgis can afford to wed his fiancée, Ona, by obtaining work in the stockyards of Chicago, which advertisements depict as a modern locale of great prosperity and happiness. The extreme struggles they face there formed the basis of Sinclair's multilevel allegory of the material transformations of the region. As industry in the region attempted to outcompete the Northeast's industrial hegemony by exploiting labor, it contributed to a nationwide tendency to accrue capitalist gains through overproduction. Companies ruthlessly exploited the limited workers' rights in place at the regional level. Without federal oversight into industry practices, corporations routinely bribed local politicians to disregard dangerous loopholes in health and safety regulation. As a naturalist Bildungsroman, *The Jungle* depicted a determinist view of individual development, in order to expose the local and national political corruption that was fostering Chicago's rapid development: the region's industrial model depended on exploiting the rapid influx of cheap foreign labor to stimulate its astronomical economic growth.

To accomplish this task, Sinclair needed to develop a "proletarian novel" alternative to the bourgeois Bildungsroman tradition, managing the ideological implications of shifting a bourgeois form onto an entirely different class. As Sinclair reflected, his novels—of which he wrote more than ninety—all promoted "one favorite theme, the contrast between social classes; there are characters from both worlds, the rich and the poor, and the plots are contrived to carry you from one to the other" (*Autobiography* 9). Was such a theme commensurate with the Bildungsroman, which Barbara Foley describes as the "classic form" of the bourgeois novel (*Radical Representations*, 321)? In that genre, while the environment may

departure from previous governmental methods,'" as proof of "'the centralization of power in the United States and a corresponding decrease in the old time sovereignty of the states, or of the individual,'" as one newspaper reporter indicated (Braeman 464).

descriptively factor into the narrative, it merely forms the "stage" upon which heroes display traits of character, forcing writers of proletarian novels in this period to adopt and adapt formal strategies such as paradigmatic plots, political mentor characters, and narratological ironies that locate meaning somewhere between what the reader reads explicitly and understands implicitly (321). As Foley concludes, socialist authors like Sinclair not only contemplated *how* an individualist, bourgeois genre form could be re-engineered to effectively inspire class consciousness; they also needed to consider the question of whether "the new wine of literary proletarianism" can be poured "into the old bottles of bourgeois convention" as a rule (323). *The Jungle* begins by presenting many recognizable motifs and themes of the genre, such as courtship, initiation into the labor sphere, and the formation of identity in relation to the social and environmental totality. As the novel unfolds, it shifts into more radical presentations of uneven development, including the power struggles between regional, national, and global forces that are visible in telling the story of Jurgis, whose provincial worldview, outsider status, language barrier, and limited understanding of the American capitalist mode of production results in the systemic betrayal of his innocence. As we shall see, rather than form an unconquerable impediment to his development, Jurgis's exploitation activates a more authentic self-cultivation than in the classical Bildungsroman; namely, his awakening as a socialist radical. This distinction constituted Sinclair's radical revision of the form's poetics of labor.

This modification formed part of Sinclair's larger political project to instrumentalize bourgeois forms to socialist ends, including reformulating the bourgeois depiction of regional and local life within the imaginative commons. The institution of slavery had formed the Southern-born Sinclair's labor theme in his first novel, *Manassas* (1904), a historical romance set in Civil War Baltimore, written a year before Thomas Dixon's infamous revisionist saga, *The Clansman* (1905). *Manassas* opened with a preemptive rebuttal: "That the men of this land may know the heritage that is come down to them" (*Manassas*, 2). By the time he finished writing *The Jungle*, the self-declared "idealist" Sinclair was already running for Congress on the socialist ticket, the culmination of a period of increasing engagement with the radical left (Sinclair *Autobiography*, 105). Between writing *Manassas* and *The Jungle*, Sinclair discovered his ideal platform, *Appeal to Reason*: a left-wing regional publication based in Girard, Kansas, with a circulation of 500,000. For this magazine, he produced radical analyses on the Chicago stockyard strikes, and socialist regionalist pieces, including one article entitled "Farmers of America, Unite!" He furthermore organized the distribution of 30,000 copies for residents in rural New Jersey (105).

In a series of high-profile pieces for *Collier's*[4] national audience, Sinclair—who in his own words, had become "a red-hot 'radical'" of the rural Midwest—outlined socialist literature's response to what Californian novelist Gertrude Atherton described as the conundrum of "why American literature, with so many opportunities to be so robust, should be so bourgeois" (Sinclair *Autobiography*, 105, 107). Atherton's article for *The North American Review* entitled "Why Is American Literature Bourgeois?" advocated an aesthetic break with the Howellsian realism—"or would it not be better to call it Littleism?"—which she felt had herded a "new drove of literary sheep" devoid of "style" or "distinction," searching "for copy, for local color," but with their "eyes ... closed to great things" (Atherton 781). Howells, among the most influential literary editors of the period, had recently promoted the search for new American scenes in the "decentralized literature" of local color America (Howells 221). Sinclair noted the irony that Atherton was "the most bourgeois" author of the day, and really ought to be redressing "the literature of Capitalism" by challenging bourgeois forms—such as the Bildungsroman—that furnished the "organized system of repression" through the transmission of ideas (Sinclair "Our Bourgeois Literature," 24). Sinclair, who staked his career on the position that "*All art is propaganda*" (*Mammonart*, 9), saw that the Bildungsroman urgently required an anticapitalist uplift, given its idealistic depiction of labor and development. In the 1925 literary critical volume *Mammonart*, Sinclair then redressed what

---

[4] *Collier's* was an Ohio-based general interest magazine, which ran between 1888 and 1957. It notably featured short fiction by prominent writers including Henry James, F. Scott Fitzgerald, and Willa Cather, but also published investigative journalism by left-wing writers such as Sinclair and Jack London who espoused social reform.

he felt was actually deficient in Howellsian realism, which was that it recoiled from "sordid tragedy" to concentrate on "'the more smiling aspects of life'" (*Mammonart*, 334–5). Sinclair sought to destabilize that school through naturalistic realism in novels such as *The Jungle*. He criticized Howells's bourgeois disciples, who had retreated from the politics of uneven development into the terrain of "local color" realism that was formulated by rejecting "extremes, whether base and cruel, or heroic and sublime" (334–5). People raised "in different parts of the country wrote stories describing in detail the peculiarities of speech and costume and manners there prevailing," along with "the everyday and obvious events of humdrum life," contented "to observe and not to think" to gratify the major publishing houses, he claimed (335). Sinclair instead wrote for the "new generation of clear-eyed young workers," whom his protagonist of *The Jungle* represented: youth shaped not by some abstract sense of national identity but through class struggle and solidarity, who were unable "to imagine themselves" in the parochial regions of Howellsian fiction, and would read the "mild and gentle" scenes of local color realism "as one studies relics in a museum" (336–7).

Judging by the terrain of his novels, written for and about diverse ordinary working folk across the U.S., Sinclair became a champion of "our decentralized literature" in a way Howells had not anticipated, by creating platforms for marginalized voices of the nation's regions. Sinclair's regionalism proposed a necessary alternative to the standardizing imperative of bourgeois literary nationalism, given what interested him most about the decentralized United States was its heterogenous proletariat. The editors of *Appeal to Reason*, great admirers of *Manassas*, asked Sinclair to do the "same thing" for "wage-slavery" as he had done in portraying "the struggle over chattel slavery in America," leading him toward Chicago in October 1905, to write what would become the first "proletarian" novel in American letters (Sinclair *Autobiography*, 108). Importantly, it assumed the generic scaffold of a Bildungsroman, because Sinclair understood that this genre had historically served ruling class interests by depicting the emergence of the bourgeois subject into national-historical time in ways that suppressed the potential of revolutionary tendencies. *The Jungle*'s explicit social exposé inverted that anti-revolutionary teleology, by critically reimagining the poetics of labor and development that furnished the bourgeois Bildungsroman, as in this early narratorial observation:

> Here was a population, low-class and mostly foreign . . . dependent for its opportunities of life upon the whim of men every bit as brutal and unscrupulous as the old-time slave drivers; under such circumstances immorality was exactly as inevitable, and as prevalent, as it was under the system of chattel slavery. (Sinclair *The Jungle*, 104)

As this passage illustrates, Sinclair frequently "preaches by telling things and showing things," which is precisely what Norris—at that point, Sinclair's strongest local influence—famously cautioned literary naturalists against (Norris 27). The "elemental forces" that inform any novel must "find expression" in the "concrete;" any "social tendencies must be expressed by means of analysis of the characters of the men and women who compose that society, and the two must be combined and manipulated to evolve the purpose—to find the value of x," Norris advised (27). Accepting naturalism's formulaic principles without subscribing to Norris's advice to disengage from explicit politicization, Sinclair developed his subject with impatience, often focusing on ethical observations that are extraneous to the protagonist Jurgis's individual development.

Instead of the harmonious integration of a young worker into his society, what transpires in *The Jungle* is the story of wage-slavery set in Chicago's disharmonious labor environment. Sinclair's plot about the "unsuspicious workers" who confront the industrial "river of death" that was the Chicago Stockyards foregrounded the effects upon psychological and social development that resulted from the city's rapid transformations after the Great Fire of October 1871, as the industrialization and growth that followed the rebuilding of the city led to a population density and labor crisis (Hricko 1). Chicago had grown from a modest town of 200 in 1833 into a metropolis of 1,099,850 by 1890, comprised of "young farm and small town people," "freed American blacks," and "Germans, Irish, Scandinavians . . . Poles, Czechs, Italians, and other Europeans and Asians," who sought the economic opportunity that typically accompanies density (David D. Anderson 4–5).

Chicago's growth inspired Midwestern naturalism's village-to-city migration plot, which narrativized not only the new social divisions of space, but the new division of labor that accompanied metropolitan growth. That growth had precipitated new dimensions to the nation's labor struggles, which were often depicted in those plots. Of Chicago's diverse workforce, over 300,000 men and women belonged to trades unions in 1872, although membership fell to 50,000 by 1878 "due to unemployment, wage cuts, union busting, and hard times" following the 1877 mass workers' strikes (Ashbaugh 18). Changes to the daily temporal division between labor and leisure steadily came into effect, underscored by violent struggle: the residual vibrations of the labor rally of May 4, 1886, resulted in deadly confrontations between workers and policemen that culminated in the Haymarket Square bombing. The retaliatory hangings of eight men accused of the bombing strengthened the backbone of America's labor movement, with subsequent international May Day rallies marking the onset of years of city strikes in support of the eight-hour working day (see Roediger and Foner 124–77).

The Jungle's plot addresses these political developments in its reformulation of the Bildungsroman genre's poetics of labor, tracing the onerous working life of Jurgis, his bride Ona, Jurgis's father Dede, Ona's stepmother Elzbieta and her six children, and Ona's cousin Marija. The cost of Jurgis and Ona's traditional Lithuanian marriage ceremony in the novel's opening chapter leaves them with steep debts, forcing them to seek work of any kind. The family's decision to purchase property leads Jurgis to Chicago's legendary meatpacking district. As Mark Seltzer explains, Sinclair foregrounded Chicago's "bourgeoning commodity distribution centre and relay point between the industrial East and the agricultural West," a locale "dominated and defined by its stockyards and slaughterhouses," that expanded from butchering 3,000 cattle per year in 1839 to 700,000 by 1871 through seamlessly "mechanized organic *dis*assembly lines" (203–4). Sinclair's graphic vision of Chicago vis-à-vis the development of the subject accentuates a "traumatic component in the project of self-making or self-construction," where the modern subject resides in a perennial "state of shock" (205). Discussing Jurgis's first introduction to The Yards, where he is brought by an acquaintance early in the novel, the narrator remarks of the cattle:

> It was uncanny to watch them press on to their fate, all unsuspicious—a very river of death ... Our friends were not poetical, and the sight suggested to them no metaphors of human destiny; they thought only of the wonderful efficiency of it all. (Sinclair *The Jungle*, 34)

If his characters are unaware of the poignancy of their plight, as is suggested in the cynically regionalist imagery of bovines, rivers, and death, Sinclair himself is nevertheless an overdetermined poet of the "metaphors of human destiny" (34), as the symbolism of that imagery makes clear.

The young worker's body and character, too, become denaturalized regionalist metaphors of the exploitation necessitated by national destiny. Sinclair's didacticism accentuates the explicit political awakening of Jurgis, a young, former agriculturalist who, despite his "mighty shoulders" and "giant hands" (6), "was like a boy, a boy from the country," the kind of exploitable employee "the bosses like to" complain endlessly about being unable to "get a hold of" (23). Sinclair deliberately trades in sociological types to achieve that political didactic: Jurgis's body and much of his idealistic dialogue capture Sinclair's archetypal worker—physically robust but not vainglorious; principled, if naive. Jurgis, a regional innocent in an inhospitable industrial environment, exemplifies a poetics of proletarianism common in the U.S. proletarian Bildungsroman to come, as Barbara Foley defines that subgenre, which accentuated "physical details" crudely "invested with the rhetorical power to generalize about class-defined essences—which, while 'material,' are hardly signalled by bodily features" (*Radical Representations*, 345). The development of Jurgis, through whom the sociological positionings of the novel are focalized, breaks with the provincial idealism of the classical Bildungsroman—signaled in his idyllic memories of his Lithuanian homeland and childhood—as it is dissembled by the machinery of capitalism.

The bourgeois logic that labor is an edifying component of individual cultivation formulated the harmonious development plot in early nineteenth-century Bildungsromane. *The Jungle*, however, approached the prospect of development from the perspective of the proletariat; thus, it documented the new industrial order's grotesque labor environment, its plot following a series of trials and hardship faced by the residents of Packingtown. The arbitrary cutback of shifts and laying-off of factory workers increases the Rudkuses' vulnerability and desperation; they are tricked into a mortgage with astronomical interest rates they cannot afford on their menial, irregular wages. On several occasions, Jurgis succumbs to gruesome injuries that leave him unable to work, forcing the family's youngest children to work in abominable conditions. To keep up with the cost of living, a pregnant Ona secretly turns to prostitution, and Jurgis is arrested for attacking her abusive *souteneur*. After Ona dies in childbirth, Jurgis attempts to raise baby Antanas; however, the infant drowns in flood water surrounding their house. Everywhere faced with unrelenting horror and tragedy which robs him of his home, family, and faith in humanity, Jurgis abandons his remaining family to roam the Midwestern countryside as a vagabond, before returning to Chicago to work as a union buster in a criminal organization.

Although Sinclair's prematurely wizened protagonist ventures through modernity's most concentrated precincts of shock, alienation, and political fragmentation, the novel does not cynically conclude with his arrested development. Although Jurgis initially succumbs to corruption, he converts into a socialist organizer brimming with radical potentiality toward the novel's end, signaling Sinclair's belief in the younger generation's potential to fulfill the revolutionary promise of the democratic republic. The novel's overdetermined message is voiced through a socialist organizer's impassioned speech, which Jurgis overhears at a union meeting:

> [The politicians] will not give the people of our city municipal ownership . . .; all that they will do is give our party in Chicago the greatest opportunity that has ever come to Socialism in America! . . . Chicago will be ours! *Chicago will be ours!* CHICAGO WILL BE OURS! (328)

Avowed stylistically through the emphasis on the collective pronoun and exaggerated lettering, Sinclair's point is that the reorganization of local life must be seized through radical agitation for political reform, not unregulated capitalist development. There can be no return to the "smiling" escapism of local color. While Jurgis and his community's punishing struggles transform him into a budding revolutionary hero, in contrast the predicaments of small-town Midwestern Carrie in Chicago's industrial order are quickly relieved, leading to her exiting the region altogether to seek fame and fortune in the Northeastern culture industry. Carrie's remarkable social ascendance nevertheless comes at the expense of her lover Hurstwood—who epitomizes the values of Chicago's cultureless middle-class, and thus in the novel's logic, must die in a Brooklyn flophouse to ensure that Carrie's otherwise inexcusable socioeconomic ascent reads as an ironic and uneven rather than aspirational story of capitalist development. Without an ironic foil like Hurstwood, Jurgis's reflection upon his social position must lead to action; rather than serve as a cautionary character, he models the awakening of revolutionary consciousness that Sinclair sought to inspire in the minds of the young workers, who might recognize in the image of its protagonist's development a viable future. The wider message of *The Jungle*, then, was that to seize the means of production, the proletariat must first seize the means of the imaginative production of labor, nature, and social space, which for Sinclair included their literary representation in forms such as the Bildungsroman.

Like a building to be demolished and reconstructed into a more ideal form, the literary naturalists thus recalibrated the bourgeois Bildungsroman's scaffold to depict representations of the vicissitudes of localism and everyday life facing the proletariat, as the nation's mode of production shifted from an agrarian economy into an industrial one. Dreiser and Sinclair reconceptualized the genre's development plot through naturalist theories of socioeconomic determinism, in ways that clearly revolted from the American village at the height of local color's vogue. Jurgis Rudkis and Carrie Meeber, unfixed figures of youth based on sociological types, were installed into migration plots that foregrounded the challenges of deserting the romantic, rural-agrarian mode of their childhood including the folklore of labor that belonged in that world, to navigate the uneven political landscape of the urban-industrial reality of adulthood. As these novelists contemplated the effects of regional development, they created a new poetics of labor that presented maturation itself as contingent upon the class struggle inherent within national progress; this struggle was registered ironically, in Dreiser's Bildungsroman, and didactically, in Sinclair's. In both novels, the regional complex—expressed through the protagonist's struggle to reconcile their regional idealism (rurality/childhood) with the reality of national destiny (industrialism/adulthood)—metaphorically exposed the broader challenges of capitalism's uneven development. Their Midwests represented a marked deviation from the harmonious visions of everyday life in the nation's regions that local color characters and settings arguably reinforced.

CHAPTER 2

Developing the Countryside: Cather, Hughes, and the Poetics of Rurality

For the literary naturalists who narrated the uneven development of the urban-industrial Midwest, the pathway into adulthood they conceived through deterministic plots metaphorized modernity's effects upon regional distinctiveness and the everyday life of the region's workers, while anticipating the implications that unrestrained national expansion and industrial development would have upon the future of democracy and the consolidation of a national culture. In their novels, national progress took the narrative direction those authors imagined modernity itself to have taken, whereby "the countryside is abandoned for the city, and the world of work changes at an incredible and incessant pace," as outlined in Moretti's account of the European Bildungsroman (4). The harmonious little worlds and scenes that sustained the classical Bildungsroman of Goethe and Austen, locales that managed the restless mobility of youth and provided an end destination to their travels, found anachronistic equivalents in the local color depiction of the rural Midwest, a region conceptualized as the land of the pioneers, and the plains of prosperity where the nation's Manifest Destiny was headed. Yet, region also came to signify sites of isolated, homogenous, backward communities devoid of action or curious characters, where nothing ever happens but the banal drama of place itself.

Dreiser and Sinclair both implicitly utilized such geographical mythologies, if only to starkly contrast the harsh labor environment of the region's industrial centers. Their Bildungsromane implicitly subscribed to a connotation of regionalism often understood through "nostalgic portraits of preindustrial rural communities and people," as Stephanie Foote has observed apropos responses to regionalist fiction in general (3). They ultimately sidelined that mode of living to focus on the malaise of modern industry. To return to that place of rural innocence, for Carrie or Jurgis, would be as impossible as aging in reverse. The seemingly unstoppable forward march of modernization, which such unfixed figures represented, meant that the "colourless and uneventful" society in which the "old youth" existed was no longer tenable for narrativizing modernity, now that capitalism had imposed "a hitherto unknown *mobility*" and catalyzed the turn toward interiority, giving rise to the Bildungsroman as modern society's symbolic form (Moretti 4). If to be young is to be mobile, something must elicit the subject's removal from the stabilizing properties of local life. This process of becoming unfixed, caught in the flux of geographic unevenness of capitalist modernity, we have already seen, formed the central tension of the Bildungsroman genre in the Midwest during the period.

Rurality—a geographical category referring to low population density and some degree of physical separation from urban areas—often connotes images of communities that are insular, autonomous, homogenous, and culturally resistant to change or external interference. Although the depiction of rural folk that regionalism was often concerned with "constructs a common national past for readers concerned with national matters" (Foote 6), Midwestern rurality served a curious role in the Bildungsroman and its relationship to American nationalism's search for a usable past. The rural Midwest simultaneously became one key imagined social space for disrupting, delaying, and denying modernity's unfolding development by situating the scene of youth's emergence in rural communities symbolically wedged between the agrarian past and industrial present. Raymond Williams, writing of the "political dividends" afforded by English literature's "lulling illusion of old country life," and the shifting imaginative associations between the "country" and the "city," describes how in the realist novel, a

> natural country ease is contrasted with an unnatural urban unrest. The "modern world" . . . is mediated by reference to a lost condition which is

better than both and which can place both: a condition imagined out of a landscape and a selective observation and memory. (180)

Though Midwestern-based writers including Dreiser, Sinclair, and Norris projected some nostalgia for the older, passing order of "country" life, even if their young subjects abandon it to expand their professional opportunities, their novels facilitated a critical break with the local color fiction of Bret Harte, Sarah Orne Jewett, Hamlin Garland, Pauline Hopkins, and Charles Chesnutt, which typically catered to bourgeois Northeastern readers' views of provincial America. The region's rural hinterlands facilitated a nostalgic intervention into the forward march of progress, by creating an idealized landscape onto which to rehearse the malaise of modernity. As Garland put it:

> Then there is the mixture of races . . . the deepening of social contrasts . . . a great heterogeneous, shifting, brave population, a land teeming with unrecorded and infinite drama. It is only to the superficial observer that this country seems colorless and dull; to the veritist it is full of burning interest, greatest possibilities. (15–16)

His statements on rurality, which challenged the "'narrow interests'" attributed to regionalism, not only attempted to theorize and legitimate local color realism, but furthermore, claimed that the local was synonymous with the national (Fetterley and Pryse 35; Foote 57). Like Howells, for whom region served as a patriotic synecdoche of an ideal but "decentred" national whole (Howells 221), Garland's patriotic belief in the diversity of local cultures meant to fortify a deep connectedness between the disparate dimensions of the Midwest through literary representation. The parochial rural landscape attributed to local color, by that same logic, became the ideal symbolic setting onto which to rehearse American exceptionalism and the ideology of white nativism, both in the Midwest and in the South, with some key differences in how that dynamic translated into fictional representation. In that paradigm, rurality played a key symbolic function in the development of American cultural exceptionalism in the early twentieth century, as the ideal locality for rehearsing a 100% Americanism rooted in the unique ecology of the "indigenous" countryside, which was imagined to be populated with uncreolized communities of white Americans. This was especially the case after the onset of the Great War in 1914, which brought heightened scrutiny to the nation's external borders, meaning that the nation's internal borders—its regional ones—were perceived to offer potential barriers to external influences.

Concurrently, as locomotives and automobiles sublated disparate rural and urban districts into an interconnected region, these imaginative associations increased in complexity. The "empowered wartime state had wielded homogenizing cultural power ... through the mass mobility ... that capped off the demographic sea change of the large-scale urban migrations of the recent past," Mark Whalan explains (*World War One*, 107). Within that context, the idea "that American regional distinctiveness was in decline" was loudly propagated even as "regional, ethnic, racial, and linguistic differences were often being downplayed ... in the name of ensuring national, martial cohesion" (107). Thus, from the Progressive Era onward, many literary regionalists entered public discourses on localism and the aesthetics and politics of region in ways that disputed the "100% American" fantasy of "region as ethnically 'pure space'" (115). As urban Midwestern fiction revolted from the village as part of the debates over regionalism and realism from the late nineteenth century, the unfixed figure of youth that had facilitated that revolt also became a strategic trope for imagining what would become of the Midwest's rural communities after they were culturally integrated into the framework of national-historical time, which was synced to the clock of capitalist modernity and globalization.

The notion that rural areas were ethnically pure spaces had informed the European Bildungsroman's metropole–periphery relation, given how "long-established links between ideas of rurality, ethnicity and ethnic purity" within nineteenth-century European society formed "a method of interpreting the new and emerging social relations produced by the exigencies of colonialism, and were inscribed within the urban–rural dichotomy" (Agyeman and Spooner 197). The rural Midwestern Bildungsroman—which still filtered the region's development through the deterministic lens of naturalism—became an important symbolic form for disentangling those associations, while addressing the widespread belief that local distinctiveness was waning. As a mediating agent between the local and the national, regionalism both gave and imposed upon rural communities, and those who wished to read about them, a culture that would form the basis of an affiliative identity that was both separate from and connected to the urban dimensions of the nation. In the context of these new regionalisms, told from the perspective of the rural Midwest that appeared in literature after 1919, aesthetic naturalism continued to play an important part in how the development of that region was depicted, especially in terms of conveying how rural communities were responding to the transformation of local heterogeneity into a homogenous nation-state unified by its commitment to capitalist modernity. Although these texts subscribed to similar deterministic worldviews, they attempted to delay and deny those processes within the uneven temporalities of region and nation that underwrote those novels. The two texts that I consider in this chapter, Willa Cather's *My Ántonia* and Langston Hughes's *Not Without Laughter*, situate the effects of capitalist development within a generational rift instigated by the region's youth, who struggle to conform to a national destiny guided by capitalist modernity due to their entrenched childhood affiliations with the land and place. Despite these two authors' clear differences regarding the politics of form, each novel tells the same basic plot: the young protagonist must find a way to reconcile their cosmopolitan ambitions for growth with their enduring bond to the rural communities that are being profoundly reorganized due to industrial development and the consolidation of national powers after the draft was imposed in 1917. These novels of uneven development exposed the shifting epistemologies of region, creating a poetics of rurality that unsettled the cultural imperialism of national destiny.

Willa Cather's *My Ántonia* (1918)

> There was nothing but land; not a country at all, but the material out of which countries are made.
> —*My Ántonia* (5)

Jim Burden, the first-person narrator of Willa Cather's *My Ántonia* (1918), here recalls his first consciousness as a child of Black Hawk,

Nebraska, evoking the natural wilderness as a geographical anchor for his unfixed social identity as an orphaned, intraregional migrant from Virginia. Even through his child's eyes, Jim remembers how his sense of self took root in the sublime Midwest landscape, the affiliative qualities of which offer him greater cultural stability than those more abstract concepts of "country" or "nation." Narrated in the style of the protagonist Jim's autobiographical account of his youth, Cather's Bildungsroman depicts Jim's upbringing in a rural landscape undergoing the first signs of capitalist development; it also portrays the social transformations of the prairie communities, as the wilderness that has sustained the peoples of the region is subdivided into private and state property, thus becoming interconnected with the abstract national whole through transportation infrastructure. In this fictional version of the author's hometown Red Cloud in Webster County, Nebraska, Cather weaves an allegory of a region awkwardly emerging in national-historical time, where the act of narration itself and its attentiveness to narrating rural customs is an attempt to put the brakes on the forward march of national progress. *My Ántonia* retroactively tracks Jim's childhood alongside that of his Bohemian playmate and friend, the novel's other protagonist Ántonia Shimerda: an immigrant whose lack of autonomy contrasts with Jim's upward mobility. The unresolvable paradox of Jim's personal development is that although he directly benefits from the opportunities facilitated by the rural Midwest's industrialization, including new trainlines, cities, and educational institutions, he also questions the frontier mentality of illimitable expansion and laments the passing of the preindustrial epoch immortalized in the epigraph above.

Describing the assimilation of regionalist fiction into the Americanist nationalist movement from the late nineteenth century, Susan Gilman attributes the selective memory of nation-building to the construction of "a more harmonious, 'imaginary' past" that turns its gaze "away from and toward the disturbing present," not unlike how categorical regionalism itself "constructs region as both separate from and engaged with nation" (115). Arguably shifting away from that quest for an American usable past, Cather's historical reconstruction of the prairies onto which Jim's childhood memories are layered—as he recalls a time prior to the privatization of the land for individual and corporate development—produces a literary framework for reinterpreting the Midwest's modernization as a generational conflict occurring between regional youth and their ancestors. The novel opens with an introduction, told in the first person by a friend of the protagonist, who resides in New York City. A chance encounter between two former acquaintances on a train passing through Iowa prompts them to reflect on an insular regionalism that exclusively belongs to those whose mode of existence is shaped by a shared past:

> While the train flashed through never-ending miles of ripe wheat, by country towns and bright-flowered pastures and oak groves wilting in the sun, we . . . were talking about what it is like to spend one's childhood in little towns like these . . . [and] agreed that no one who had not grown up in a little prairie town could know anything about it. (Cather *My Ántonia*, vii)

Though he is a "legal counsel for one of the great Western railways" by the present tense of the frame narrative, Jim recounts his youthful experiences centered around his childhood friendship with a Bohemian girl named Ántonia Shimerda, with whom he still ostensibly shares a deep affinity despite how they have grown apart in distance and experience. The conceit of the two-page "Introduction" is to situate the narrative to follow as a reflection that Jim has written to share with the frame narrative's unidentified narrator, inspired by their railroad journey, so linking Jim's development to that of the expanding railroad frontier (viii). The ideology of national destiny that underwrites the region's material development implicitly determines Jim's growth; despite his self-perception as a young man with a "romantic disposition" (regionality) in the initial narrator's words, his "personal passion" toward "the great country through which his railway runs and branches," and "faith in it and his knowledge of it have played an important part in its development" as an employee of one rail corporation (viii). Over the course of Jim's retroactive narrative, we observe the rural landscape transforming from uncultivated wilderness dotted with open-grazing farmlands, into fenced-off pastures that follow "surveyed section lines" (76), which he leaves behind for the college town of Lincoln, and again for New York City. From the latter setting, the narrator's mind's eye returns to the West of the past, to his childhood, in the novel's closing images.

Like Dreiser and Sinclair, Cather contemplated the meaning these changes posed to different generations of prairie folk, by appealing to the "'youthful' attributes of mobility and inner restlessness" of modernity's symbolic form, the Bildungsroman (Moretti 5). Modernization encouraged the abandonment of the countryside for the city, where "the world of work changes at an incredible and incessant pace" in comparison to the "colourless and uneventful socialization of 'old' youth," and the representation of youth's development instead becomes "an uncertain exploration of social space . . . through travel and adventure, wandering and getting lost," writes Moretti (4). For such reasons, Cather was very drawn to this form, with a view to harness these uncertainties of social space unfolding in the region; earlier novels such as *The Song of the Lark* (1915), and later ones including *A Lost Lady* (1923) and *Shadows on the Rock* (1931), can all be classed as Bildungsromane. A century after *Wilhelm Meister*'s epoch, Cather's Bildungsroman narrativizes the co-existence of the older and younger generation within regional spaces, in ways that challenge the view that those rural communities are premodern, backward, "colourless," and "uneventful." This is suggested by the first-person, past-tense narration of the adult Jim, who has left for the East Coast to further his education and job prospects but returns to the Nebraska of his childhood physically and in the act of his narration. This act of returning heightens the significance of a narrative space that was "not a country at all," but simply Jim and Ántonia, existing in the raw materials of a yet undefined, inconclusive national space (Cather *My Ántonia*, 5).

Seeking to unsettle that national space and its symbolic relationship to its internal regional parts, Cather rejected the "belief that snug access and easy money are the real aims of human life," a mindset that had "settled down over our prairies," but not "yet hardened into molds and crusts," as the author suggested in her 1923 piece for *The Nation*'s series on the regions of the United States (Cather "Nebraska," 236–8). Cather suggested how modernization incited "machine-made materialism" and a surfeit of "prosperity," "moving-picture shows," and "gaudy fiction" that had "colored the tastes and manners of . . . these Nebraskans of the future" (236-8). Many of her contemporaries, including the Marxist critic Granville Hicks, subsequently interpreted her regionalist politics as the source of a major aesthetic defect; namely that her inability to adapt her material to the political economies of national development left her out of sync with the innovativeness of novelists like Dreiser, who deftly narrativized the region's modernization and labor struggles (Hicks 703-10). Cather's recurring theme of "heroic idealism, the joyous struggle against nature sustained by a confidence in the ultimate beneficence of that nature against which it fought," could no longer be sustained after writing *My Ántonia*:

> The story of this new West could scarcely take the form of a simple, poetic idyll. Heroism and romance, if they existed, had changed their appearance. Characters could no longer be isolated from the social movements that were shaping the destiny of the nation and of the world. (Hicks 706)

Compared with the "robustness" of Dreiser and Sherwood Anderson's prose, Cather's poetics of rurality dwelled on the stabilizing temporalities of "survival" rather than accelerating temporalities of "growth" (710), an assessment that raises interesting ideological implications regarding the Bildungsroman's logic of development, as a genre Cather often utilized. Hicks's Cather was a modern novelist who returned to an anachronistic world out of sync with the rhythms of industrial modernity, by reprising the primary task of the classical Bildungsroman: "to show how pleasing life can be in what Goethe called 'the small world'" as the individual is integrated into the organic whole of their society, in Moretti's words (36). For Van Doren, Cather overcame her local colorisms by gradually liberating "herself from the bondage of 'plot'" and thus "from an inheritance of the softer sentiments," that she might discover how "the ultimate interest of fiction inheres in character" and the epic presentation of their moods; Cather's regionalism thus distinguished itself from that of women writers of local color, such as the New England fictions of Sarah Orne Jewett—to whom Cather's 1913 novel *O Pioneers!* was dedicated (Van Doren 121).

What substitutes the "bondage of 'plot'" in Jim's development is not merely an appeal to *place*—a term that inflects the people's relationships to certain locations—but the more dynamic, obstruse concept of *space*. Cather's Old Nebraska invoked what Neil Smith describes as the nineteenth-century "moral geography" of the American landscape, which comprised the "poetic fusion of physical geography with cultural myth" (18). This moral geography of the natural environment—a key settler-colonialist symbol of the New World—infuses "the scientific experience of nature" with the "poetic experience of nature" (18). While this scientific-poetic dichotomization of nature was often considered uniquely American in influential mid-twentieth century literary studies by Henry Nash Smith, Leo Marx, and others, Smith notes that such moral geography exceeds national borders, as "a result of emergent industrial capitalism" and its processes of deterritorialization (19). Cather assumed responsibility for this moral geography, but then ultimately discarded that vision in decentering the human from that ecology at key points in Jim's development. The demotion of human action to description of space is a more accurate description of *My Ántonia*'s narrative work; Cather's most significant gesture was turning literary space itself—both the natural ecology, and the humans who attempt to cultivate those environments into a *place*—into a series of events that could sustain narrative momentum. As Tom Lutz notes of Cather's *sui generis*, the author's representations of the prairies establish her novels' broader "proto-ecological" undulation between "the human and nonhuman," distinguishing in the geologic world "a set of values distinct from the values of civilization and related to the prehistoric, animal existence of human beings rather than to their contemporary social existence" (107–8). In *My Ántonia*, the narrator acts as an anthropological and poetic interpreter of the region's geography, imagining an ecology before the invention of regional or national space and time. The effect of such narration is to disclose "the ways in which regional culture both is an aesthetic object to be discovered by the perceptive anthropologist/artist and is composed by the anthropologist or artist representing that culture through the shaping process of selection," as Eric Aronoff observes (102). The natural world, in Cather's aesthetics of development, forms the ideal space upon which to project and rehearse the social complexities of rurality and regional difference, and to capture the disorienting effects as those distinctive heterogeneous cultures are swept into the homogenizing flows of national destiny, scientifically and poetically.

The novel does not insist upon the corrupted innocence of the protagonist who ultimately aligns himself with the rhythms of that destiny; nevertheless, Jim's complicity in the economic and cultural expropriation of the natural and ethnic spaces of the tablelands clearly renders his development problematic, as the following quotation insinuates:

> ... I felt that the grass was the country, as the water is the sea. The red of the grass made all the great prairie the colour of winestains, or of certain seaweeds when they are first washed up. And there was so much motion in it; the whole country seemed, somehow, to be running. (Cather *My Ántonia*, 10-11)

These images that arrest Jim, as he remembers himself as a young child first becoming conscious of the new "country" to which he has been transported over the Mason–Dixon line, clearly invoke the nineteenth-century transcendental logic that bound democracy to nature, exemplified in Walt Whitman's *Leaves of Grass*.[1] Because in the novel's backward-facing narratology, Jim exists to the reader as both a youth and an adult, he is partially detached from what Cather saw as the ambulatory generation of Young Nebraskans "now in the driver's seat," who were "scudding past those acres where the old men used to follow the long corn-rows up and down" (Cather "Nebraska," 236-8). Coupled with his regional indeterminacy, having been born in Virginia but raised in Nebraska, and educated and professionalized in Massachusetts and New York, this unfixity informs Jim's naturalist detachment as a first-person narrator. Through Jim's forward-looking reflections, Cather interleaves the determinism of urban naturalists with the fatalism that underwrote the ideology of the unstoppable progress

---

[1] Cather ambivalently admired Whitman, finding elements of his encyclopedic ambitions "ridiculous," and yet praising his "passion for the warmth and dignity of all that is natural" (Cather "Walt Whitman," 902).

of civilization that was Manifest Destiny, producing a sense of irony that looms over Jim's and Ántonia's individual fates. The rhythms of this anthropomorphic landscape resemble what Jennifer Fleissner has described as a gendered perception of naturalism as "either fatalistic or nostalgic in the face of modern life," engendering a naturalism that will revert "masculine power and adventure to a vitiated modernity" (7).

Examining the novelist's oeuvre and what he saw as her revolt from the (local color) village, Van Doren observed that Cather's recurrent universalist theme was "the struggle of some elect individual to outgrow the restrictions laid upon him—or more frequently her—by numbing circumstances" (115). Such is the case regarding the two young protagonists at the center of *My Ántonia*, whose uneven pathways into adulthood signify the inharmonious aspects of rurality in ways that challenge the classical Bildungsroman's ideological apparatus. Their unevenness manifests in the unequal constraints they experience due to their different ethnicities and genders. Whalan notes that regionalist novelists writing in the wartime period "often strained to consider the question of how local affinities articulated in specifically aesthetic terms might relate to the nationalizing imperatives of war and its concomitant centralization of political power" (*World War One*, 106). *My Ántonia*'s "multiple vision of citizenship, refused to turn the region into a mere metonymy for a national identity of '100% Americanism,'" refuting the notion "that regionalist identities and cultures might provide the grounded specifics that would flesh out the ghostly abstractions of national community" (115). Such ambivalent effects are captured through the lens of Jim, who is captivated by the diverse immigrant satellite farming communities around the township of Black Hawk who inhabit the natural world that is slowly but visibly being colonized by capital over the course of Jim's childhood, in ways that provide a symbolic stage for reckoning with the bigger implications of industrialism, ethnic pluralism, and the consensus of a "100% Americanism" that national-historical time then implied.

Jim's youthful restlessness is distinctive from the frontier spirit; his adventurousness is offset by a literary naturalism that emphasizes his empathy toward nature, but also the migrant communities who live by its rhythms—such as the Bohemians, Norwegians, and

Poles of Black Hawk. Jim's mobility as an unfixed subject, caught and loose in this place, forms a vehicle through which Cather examines the unevenness in the region's sociological order, including its ethnic, gender, and class hierarchies. At one point, Jim's recollection of having navigated the bewildering spatial logic of unfenced land by following the "sunflower-bordered roads" reflects discrepancies between empirical and nationalist epistemologies of place. The character Otto Fuchs led him through these fields as a child, and he recalled Fuchs's folk history of the land, using it as a compass. The legend went that the Mormons' first exploring party introduced the species "when they left Missouri and struck out into the wilderness to find a place where they could worship God in their own way" by creating a trail of sunflowers to lead the women and children across the plains to Utah in the summer (Cather *My Ántonia*, 19). The botanists' theory of how the Nebraskan ecology evolved, however, contradicts Fuchs's folk history of these roads; the sunflower is found to be "native" to those plains, and not introduced. Yet the story of the sunflower cannot be entirely replaced by this empirical explanation; it has accrued the power and gravitas of a "legend" that has "stuck" in Jim's mind, so that "sunflower-bordered roads always seem to [him] the roads to freedom" (19). Jim's metaphoric nostalgia is shaped by these two competing understandings of place and history. The signification of those summer sunflowers operates as a roadmap to the traveler; though the "new country [lies] open before" him without any "fences" (19), Jim recalls how to follow the sunflower-bordered roads to find his way, remembering the Mormons' map. This lesson proves important for the youth who will later in life become a lawyer for the railroad's surveyor expeditions, and whose career will be devoted to literally smoothing the connections between regional centers and outposts—yet who retains strong, visceral childhood memories of this "poetic experience of nature" the Bohemians have facilitated for him. Jim's powerful nostalgic desire to return to a purer state of childhood, so that he might recover something of the Nebraskan wilderness before the effects of modernization and industrial development, render this place unrecognizable.

These differences between his destiny and that of Ántonia become more pronounced as Jim moves with his grandparents from remote farmlands into the township of Black Hawk, which requires him to assimilate into the more upbeat daily rhythms of that more modern setting. Over the course of a month, the family suddenly find themselves becoming "town people" rather than "country" people (96); he begins to unlearn the old country ways, to integrate into a more connected, yet somehow alienated, mode of living, as suggested in the paradoxical description of the Burden family's "new world" house on the far-edge of Black Hawk's municipality, which to Jim resembles an unfixed "country hotel," where their former "country neighbors" can visit (96–7). The difference is that town life incurs a "lost freedom" that "farming country" life offered, restructuring the social relations of the country folk and town folk (96). As an interregional and now intraregional figure, moving from the more undomesticated land to the realm of the landed country society, Jim starts to detect the social complexity underwriting the small-town mode. As he grows into an intelligent, white, "native-born" young man, opportunities for mobility and thus self-cultivation open to him in ways they do not for the country youths; he cannot remain in a state of childhood innocence, where such social demarcations of class, race, and gender that govern the adult world seem strange and inconsequential. He displays racial essentialism toward the Black inhabitants of the rural Midwest, such as the piano player Johnnie Gardner, who strikes Jim as possessing a "soft amiable negro voice, like those I remembered from early childhood [in the South], with the note of docile subservience in it" (121). Through his close affinity with Ántonia, Jim nevertheless appears better equipped to critically observe the gendered constraints conditioned by regional spaces. He narrates his concerns for those "country girls" who move to the towns for work opportunities that will lift their families out of poverty, who are then sexualized and subjected to scandalization by judgmental townsfolk (129). These foreign girls, as Jim ironically detects,

> were considered a menace to the social order. Their beauty shone out too boldly against a conventional background. But anxious mothers need have felt no alarm. They mistook the mettle of their sons. The respect for respectability was stronger than any desire in Black Hawk youth. (131)

As a young man seeking his place in that parochial social order, Jim nevertheless finds that he is outgrowing the regional identity that constrains the Norwegian, Bohemian, and Polish farmers who befriended him as a young child, including Ántonia's family. Blessed with opportunities they can but dream of, he eventually leaves Nebraska altogether to attend law school at Harvard University. After graduating, he becomes a New York-based lawyer, retained in the services of the surveyors for the railroad industry; despite his early trust in the sufficiency of the path to freedom set out by the sunflowers, Jim's career ultimately overwrites those folkloric borders. In returning physically and symbolically to Black Hawk as an adult, he discovers that his own childhood home "had been ploughed under when the highways were surveyed" (Cather *My Ántonia*, 239). The lost paradise of place still haunts Jim, who "had only had to close [his] eyes to hear the rumbling of the wagons in the dark, and to be again overcome by that obliterating strangeness" (240). The land's swift development has advanced the town's veneer so profoundly that he cannot recognize it, until he ventures "into the pastures where the land was so rough that it had never been ploughed up, and the long red grass of early times still grew shaggy over the draws and hillocks," where he "felt at home again" (239). Momentarily fixed in this proto-nationalist space, which seems to exist outside of historical time, Jim recalls his early youth, standing with Ántonia on the verge of "the road of Destiny," where "fortune" has "predetermined" for them "all that we can ever be" (240). Cather's naturalist perspective here leans into the rhetoric of Manifest Destiny, where Jim's futurity as a character stretches temporally backward, as much as forward. This is both a geographic materialist and a romantic image, superimposed into the one visual layer: this road forces him and Ántonia apart, yet also reunites them in Jim's imagination, as he attempts to recover whatever they "possessed together," namely "the precious, the incommunicable past" (240), the usable past of a "country" beyond the borders of national citizenship or ethnicity.

The ambient nostalgia of the rural communities that informs Cather's depiction of rural cultures nevertheless effaces the naturalist objectivity of her forward-marching representation of national-historical time, slowing that rhythm down to a standstill.

The dialectical effect is the image of the unfixed individual who now stands immobilized between the Old and the New, between regional and national time, opposing temporalities that undercut the sense of finalization achieved by the protagonist reaching adulthood. The final paragraphs of the novel impart the sense that the old regionalisms, defined by "authentic" cultural attachments to land, place, and community, are passing over into a new generation of regionalisms that are defined by the "inauthentic" cultural production associated with urbanization, consumption, and individualism. So long as Jim stands still in this uncanny space, his arrested development forecloses that erasure of rural localisms, if only in the act of literary memorialization.

Langston Hughes's *Not Without Laughter* (1930)

Having recently relocated from Chicago's North Side to Cleveland, an aspiring young Midwestern poet, Langston Hughes, composed a poem "To Youth" (1918). Its final stanza reads:

> For today you have the strength of youth
> And youth is tomorrow's man.
> So work! Map out your life
> And with wisdom make your plan. (Qtd in Rampersad 27)

The poet was not insisting upon "youth" as a symbol of the permanent revolutions of capitalist modernity. Rather, the cartographic metaphor in the penultimate line tellingly suggests how Hughes linked personal development with labor (work) and geographic mobility: Youth, an explorer approaching the frontier of adulthood, begins his journey in a fixed place; but that map will widen, as he intrepidly strides toward manhood. It was a lesson derived from his own youth; as a child, Hughes lived in several Midwestern states—including Kansas, Missouri, Ohio, and Illinois—locales which left their marks on his poetics. His renowned poetry collection *The Weary Blues*, for instance, took its title from blues song lyrics he first encountered as an adolescent in Kansas City's Independence Avenue (Rampersad 16); while poems like "The Negro Speaks of Rivers" would reflect the Midwest's natural and social landscapes. His senior school years in Cleveland, Ohio introduced Hughes to one of the cities that flourished in the early years of the Great Migration there circa 1910–1920. Cleveland's growth and decline was subject to capitalism's uneven development; it was a center of concentrated wealth, due to the Lake Erie area's mineral resources, including oil and coal; but it was also an area of racialized economic disparity that disproportionately impacted its Black proletariat, a working class also comprising many Hungarian, Polish, Italian, and Russian immigrants. The unevenness of the Midwest of Hughes's youth remained a key concern for him as he turned to radical politics by the end of the 1920s, which prompted him to travel to Haiti and the Soviet Union, and to join the John Reed Club in California, where he drafted his influential short story collection, *The Ways of White Folk*.[2]

The poem "To Youth" is a fitting primer to Hughes's first novel, *Not Without Laughter* (1930), a key text of the New Negro Renaissance of the 1920s, not set in the region's vibrant cultural epicenters, such as Bronzeville or Cleveland, but in the rural hinterland. Set in fictional Stanton, Kansas, circa 1915—resembling Lawrence, KS, the rural small-town where Hughes lived with his grandmother—the young Black protagonist Sandy's upbringing echoes the author's own development. Sandy's restlessness and desire to explore the world beyond his narrow regional framework is on one level attributable to Hughes's own cosmopolitan childhood ambitions. Although youth formed a symbol of the liberative ambulatory dynamics that cosmopolitan signified for Hughes, that journey was complicated by the dilemma that although maturation seemed a universal rite of passage, its destination was racially and regionally predetermined due to white supremacism and segregation. Accordingly, the novel's plot follows Sandy's attempts to "map out" his "life" under an oppressive nationwide regime, even as it highlighted the pressures of modernization that pushed Black youth to migrate from the rural provinces into the cities to seek employment.

Situating *Not Without Laughter* generically, vis-à-vis the author's wider political outlook, has proven challenging, given the author's

---

[2] This collection impacted the aesthetics of James Farrell and Richard Wright, which they discussed at the 1933 American Writers' Congress (Denning 218).

politics were often conflated with a view of modernist cosmopolitanism that cynically repressed regionalism, while this novel clearly engages in regionalist themes and settings. The author's "revolutionary political ideas," including his views on how art might effect social change, "were conspicuously missing from the book" (Shields 612). One reason for that excision was Hughes's white patroness Charlotte Osgood Mason demanded Hughes write a novel that documented the exoticness of Black ruralism for white, metropolitan, paternalist liberals (Shields 602). As a result, *Not Without Laughter* arguably constituted a "proletarian fictional autobiography" rather than a "proletarian bildungsroman," because its "episodic and linear" narrative structure is necessarily more rigid than the "locus of causality" in a Bildungsroman, and "the narratorial voice addressing the reader is intuited to be roughly equivalent with both the protagonist and the author" (Foley *Radical Representations*, 329, 335). A proletarian reading of the novel is complicated by early reviewers describing it as the "First Novel of Negro Working-Class Life," even though it does "not assume a left-wing perspective" compared to the "revolutionary energies" of his poetry, according to Barbara Foley (204n). Michael Denning has alternatively suggested that Hughes refused to present Stanton's Black community in ways that would corroborate Mason's fantasy of regional African American communities as sites of ethnically pure folk aesthetics to be mined for Northeastern cultural reproduction (218), a perspective that tessellated with prominent left-wing radical regionalisms during this period. Despite the dominant assumption of the time that proletarian fiction needed to make an explicit case for the author's radical politics, Hughes's novel arguably engaged in the aesthetics labeled "proletarian regionalism" by influential leftists including Benjamin Botkin and Constance Rourke.

Building upon those aesthetic tendencies Denning suggests were crucial to Hughes's influence on proletarian short fiction in the 1930s Cultural Front, *Not Without Laughter* modeled a proletarian regionalist Bildungsroman that depicted and thus legitimized the experience of the heterogeneous, regional communities of common working folk in the rural Midwest that local color fiction often inaccurately portrayed in ways that damaged the radical cause. As Denning notes, in the context of the Depression and New Deal cultural mechanisms that were heavily investing in localist projects, "proletarian regionalism" also became an important mode "of 'national' thinking on the cultural left" (132). The New York Left often demoted the "multi-accented slogan" of regionalism, at a time when such affiliations were being conscripted by white-supremacist reactionaries, like the Southern Fugitive Agrarians (Denning 133). Members of The League of American Writers, including Botkin—who popularized the term "proletarian regionalism"—subsequently reinvested in synthesizing studies of "popular arts, industrial folklore and aesthetic ideologies" to refute those right-wing views (134). Likewise, Hughes's novel adopted a textual strategy that would place Midwestern rurality at the center of the political struggle against racial capitalism that conquered and divided ethnically and geographically disparate workers at regional, national, and foreign levels.

Whereas Sinclair, Dreiser, and Norris tended only to register the politics of rurality and labor in the peripheries of their Midwestern migration plots, *Not Without Laughter* opened a vivid portal into Black working-class life in the rural Midwest. That setting forms the backdrop to the limited but incrementally broadening worldview of Sandy, the unfixed figure of youth whose regional constraints gradually loosen as he becomes aware of a nation and world outside of that framework. Contrasting the fixedness of the town's social constructivism against the sublime forces of the natural world encircling it, Hughes's rural vistas formed a naturalist metaphor of the volatilities of the nation's wider social forces, particularly the volatilities of national politics, a storm from which the stability of local community life offered limited refuge. The proletarian regionalism Hughes constructs in *Not Without Laughter* is not necessarily idealist; that said, it arranges a set of conflicting generational ideas within Black political discourses—the Old Negro of sentimental local color fiction versus the more urbane New Negro. The novel questions how race, space, and affiliative loyalty are transmitted from generation to generation, as Hughes interweaves his memories into the rubric of a Bildungsroman. Sandy lives through the effects of the Great Migration—during which hundreds of thousands of Black Southerners voyaged northward into America's industrial centers via the nation's new rail networks. He discovers the unevenness of the nation and world through the stories that passing intraregional characters relay to him. His upbringing in this sense conforms to a proletarian regionalism that coalesces the many beneficial folkways of the rural Black Belt, including blues and jazz culture migrating from the South, religious practices, and facilities for youth. These forces counteract the alienation of segregation and exploitative labor conditions facing the region's Black proletariat: those elevator runners, porters, railroad laborers, maids, farmhands, and cooks whose menial labor made possible the profit margins of capitalist development and growth in the region.

Disrupting that organic, idyllic agrarian culture envisioned in right-wing Southern regionalisms, Hughes's novel opens with sublime, naturalist imagery of a "brown boy" and his grandmother, Aunt Hagar, standing in the "sooty grey-green light" at the center of a cyclone in America's tornado alley (Hughes *Not Without Laughter*, 2). That event disrupts the implied status quo of customary interracial interactions across ethnic and class groups in a racially segregated small-town. White and Black residents alike are thrown into chaos, searching for the dead and calculating the damage to private property. As with Cather's *My Ántonia*, this opening sets Hughes's intention for a novel that will explore the hardships of remote life for Black working-class people in the Great Plains, without ever denigrating those communities by presenting them as parochial, backward, and premodern villagers. Hughes's novel of development highlights the fact that the ideologies of race and place inherent in Jim Crow are not essentially rooted in any specific region. Moreover, Hughes's use of local color—a word which inflected racial overtones, in the context of the 1930s—formed a crucial part of his "Afro-planetary" wanderings and wonderings, as David Chioni Moore has argued, building upon Paul Gilroy's influential Black Atlantic thesis (51).

Although by the novel's ending, Sandy relocates to Chicago with his mother Anjee, Hughes does not romanticize the migration of young Midwesterners out of their rural hometowns; nor does he convey interminable loyalty to regional affiliation. Sandy's father Jimboy refuses to be bound by any roots; his cosmopolitanism seems only curtailed by the limits of the rail infrastructure, and the temporal patterns of seasonal labor that lure him from one place to another in search of a temporary wage. When he takes Sandy fishing, the idyllic stillness of "the flat brown-gold river," without "a ripple" or "a sound," is furiously interrupted by each passing train. Jimboy counts five trains that go "flyin'" past, each train disappearing "between rows of empty box-cars far down the track, sending back a hollow clatter as it shot past the flour-mills, whose stacks could be dimly seen through the heat haze," as Sandy's vision shifts from the box-cars to the river, descrying "the gold of wheat-fields and the green of trees on the hills. He wondered if it would be nice to live over there in the country" (Hughes *Not Without Laughter*, 46). Through such vistas, Sandy learns the way of the world, as it is symbolically regulated by the fixed railroad timetables that suture Stanton into a regional and interregional framework. But Sandy must also learn the racial and economic ideology of nature as cultivated private property, realizing first-hand the effects of the racial logic driving capitalism's uneven development that will contour his destiny. Without private landownership or political enfranchisement, Anjee is forced to leave her child Sandy to seek temporary employment in the Midwest's large urban centers, including long spells in Detroit and Chicago. Jimboy takes an alternative path: he becomes a traveling blues guitarist, one of the many "adventurers and vagabonds" who transit through Stanton, circumventing the restrictive laws of property ownership by relocating frequently, thus refusing to allow labor to define or constrict him. Or such is the case, until Jimboy is conscripted by the U.S. army to fight overseas: Hughes's telling reminder of the greatly increased powers of the nation-state after the draft was adopted in 1917, but also of the hypocrisy of the war effort's homogenizing nationalism, which was selectively blind to Jim Crow.

There are more limited opportunities for youth culture to operate here than there are in the urban Midwest, Sandy discovers, since Stanton's Y.M.C.A. is a designated whites-only venue; but there is still Windsor's pool hall, which provides an alternative outlet for lively socialization "for the Negro youths of the town," like Sandy. Though his time is mostly devoted "to bookishness" and his middle-class aunt "Tempy's prim plans for his improvement," Sandy finds the community venues such as the pool hall more amusing "than the movies, where people on the screen were only shadows" (189). Cudge's lunchroom—the semi-integrated establishment where locals often dine—is frequented by the "[a]dventurers and vagabonds" who pass through Stanton, ushering in regional cosmopolitanisms that operate through the intraregional tourism facilitated by the "side-door Pullmans" that connect remote Stanton to "far-off cites where things were easy and women generous," at least in Sandy's naive imagination (190). Sandy's imaginative mobility is one of the ways in which Hughes presents him as an unfixed character, whose inability to convert the potentiality of youth he possesses into meaningful action highlights the author's naturalist (i.e., determinist) understanding of individual agency, as it is subject to geographically determined social and economic constraints. Regional tourism, the bedrock of Stanton's social and commercial culture, crucially informs Hughes's representation of the mobility driving the transformations of the labor force of the small-town Midwest, as the region's townships are slowly assimilated into the rhythms of capitalist modernity.

The Drummer's Hotel is a major employer of Stanton's youth, and thus mediates their perspectives of adult behaviors, customs, and mores regarding race, class, and sexuality. Within Stanton's social system, the hotel forms a symbol of the region's culturally fluid and mobile properties; the Drummer's Hotel plays an important role in Sandy's growing critical awareness of the adult world and the social production of space. Although it provides necessary, albeit exploitative, employment for the town's proletarian youth, including to Sandy and his aunt Harriet, its implicit social function is to provide a coherent structure for Sandy to interpret the wider social antagonism between those in the community who enforce sexual prohibition and racial segregation, and those who subvert those laws. For, the hotel is a hotbed of sin in the opinion of Sandy's grandmother Aunt Hagar; indeed, it is the place where white prostitutes meet their clients, Sandy learns. Hughes's rural proletarian youth also forms a lens through which to examine the asynchronous constraints of small-town social networks upon young women relative to their young male counterparts. This is apparent in the disjunction between the ideal New Negro woman, Sandy's young, progressive aunt Harriet Williams; his proletarian, conservative grandmother Aunt Hagar, a former slave from the South modeled upon the "Old Negro" local color stereotype; and her bourgeois but equally conservative daughter, Sandy's aunt Tempy Siley. With Harriet's migration toward St. Louis, where she eventually becomes a successful cabaret singer, Hughes does not indicate that city life is liberative. Rather, he suggests that the confined character networks of rural life create more visible platforms for scrutinizing gender norms; because behaviors that unsettle the encrusted customs of a small community are more conspicuous than in large metropolises, any deviation from the norm tends to appear potentially more destabilizing.

While Stanton's youth grow up experiencing many of the cultural benefits of the region's new industrial interconnectedness, the rail networks also generate heavier currents of undesirable traffic. The chapter "White Folks" more overtly formulates region as a vitiated container for the "social equality" movement, and is particularly critical of the rural aspects of region, which at times act as a vessel for *de facto* white supremacy and *de jure* Jim Crow. As the Rogers's family friend Sister Williams—a former slave—and Jimboy discuss their experiences of violent dispossession following Reconstruction, these injustices are revealed to be not unrelated to the social exclusions and deprivations the younger Harriet faces in the North, she insists (57). Sandy, while working in the hotel as a bell-boy, later confirms this when he is accosted by a white Mississippian guest who demands that he "'hit a step for the boys!'" (162). Although Sandy refuses to cooperate, the comment forces him to reflect on the porousness of the border dividing rural Mississippi from rural Missouri, which the adults had first outlined to him, but which he had yet to experience himself. In Stanton, the heterogeneous Black community's mutual hatred of "White Folks," a term representing the ideology of 100% "Nordic" Americanism, unites two politically disparate generations: the ex-Southerners (the Old Negro) and Northerners (the New Negro).

When, late in the novel, Sandy relocates to Chicago, Hughes ultimately unties the center–periphery geographies that were invoked to discuss regionalism and Black cultural nationalism in the 1920s. This distinction becomes clear upon Sandy's arrival in Chicago, a faster-paced city, surely, but one that offers no chimeric reprieve from the systemic inequities of its hinterlands. Bridging the divide between the Midwest's rural and urban dimensions, Hughes represents regional differences through the eyes of a child, whose development is constrained only partially by small-town parochialism; in a much more direct, forceful way, his poverty results from federal inaction on the nationwide "race problem," systemic racism which could not be isolated to any one region, or to the nation's non-metropolitan areas. Segregation, coupled with a private property system that prevents workers from owning the means of their production, inhibit Sandy from becoming a fully autonomous subject of national-historical time: two issues that preoccupy the proletarian regionalist tract of the novel. As with *My Ántonia*, the literary regionalism that informed *Not Without Laughter*'s portrait of unfixed youth examines the small-scale, intricate operations of the proletarian small-town Midwest, highlighting its relationship both to the wider region and national whole in terms of its race relations, political forms, and division of labor. Sandy's widening understanding of the points of difference and connection between his local scene and the wider world are gleaned through his experiences in nature and the built environment, storytelling, literature, and the social relations of leisure and labor. These wanderings formed part of the author's proletarian regionalist revision of the Bildungsroman's logic of labor, as he reconceived of the ideological view of rural backwardness that dominated accounts of the Great Migration, by examining the political hopes, fears, and desires of the young, Black working class.

CHAPTER 3

South Side's Overdevelopment: Farrell and Wright's Extreme Youths

James Farrell and Richard Wright, two inheritors of Dreiser and Sinclair's oeuvre, produced novels of uneven development centered on the ethnic proletariat who were enslaved by the increasing standardization of national life that mass culture and urbanism demanded. Their novels heavily invested in the critical aesthetics of the "new" local color, or what I have been calling the critical regionalism that was essential to Midwestern naturalism's cultural logic. The 1930s nevertheless saw the Midwestern Bildungsroman transition from the "Dreiser school" to the "Wright school" of Illinois literary naturalism, a key aesthetic development that resulted from Chicago's Bronzeville Renaissance (Tracy 1–3). Wright's and Farrell's novels typified an emergent tradition of Midwestern realism in which the representation of social space reacted against the earlier reliance on rural migration tropes in novels by Dreiser, Sinclair, Norris, and others. For naturalist authors of the New Deal era, sociology—interpreted through the materialist rubric of Marxist theory—formed an empirical basis for a literary tradition that would not only reflect the conditions of the masses but transform their world for the better. As we shall find, the *Studs Lonigan* trilogy and *Native Son* drew upon sociological research into the effects of industrial built environments on human development, including Robert E. Park and Ernest W. Burgess's influential 1925 edited collection, *The City*, featuring essays by members of the University of Chicago's School of Sociology, who observed Chicago's multiethnic neighborhoods as primary fieldwork sites. Direct connections link Wright and

Farrell with that school: Farrell studied as an undergraduate with Burgess and Park at the University of Chicago, while Wright became acquainted with Park and Louis Wirth through the Federal Writers' Project in Chicago. One empirical model that *The City* offered their Bildungsromane was a discursive framework for articulating the city's maladjusted youth: they found that Chicago's tendency to fragment community support fostered what Park termed the "juvenile delinquent" type in his essay featured in that collection. Similar concepts were reconceived by Chicago School-trained, African American sociologists St. Clair Drake and Horace R. Cayton, friends of Wright who interpreted developmental patterns within Chicago's Black Belt with greater nuance in their volume *Black Metropolis* (1945). The literary innovations produced within the Chicago Renaissance's second wave were informed by the region's "sociological imaginary," as Carla Cappetti observes (1). In the simplest terms, the regional imaginary that conditioned the Bildungsromane there saw Chicago as a laboratory for studying how social development is determined by socioeconomic forces and the environment.

This transition accompanied the transformative effects of the Roosevelt administration's New Deal, which channeled investments into regional projects, including employing artists through the Works Progress Administration, which oversaw the Federal Writers' Project (Bone and Courage 7). To stimulate white-collar employment, the Federal Writers' Project (FWP) engaged historians, teachers, librarians, and writers in the production of an American Guides series that documented the environmental, cultural, economic, folkloric, and historic dimensions of the nation's states. The upshot was that disenfranchised artists from diverse ethnicities, races, and geographical backgrounds, whose "parents were sharecroppers, stockyard workers, domestics, and laborers" (Bone and Courage 7), now not only assumed ownership over the nation's literary future but also played a key role in redefining the parameters of cultural regionalism. Given how these paid positions gave authors time to work on their writing, the FWP indirectly invested in literary innovations that reorganized the role of the regional imaginary within the Bildungsroman.

Farrell's calls for cultural criticism to scrutinize "the quality of life, the aims, the wants, the actions, the things men do, and the values they want to realize among the different social classes that go to compose the population of these linked States" (Bone and Courage 7) were answered in Bildungsromane such as Wright's *Native Son* and his own *The Young Manhood of Studs Lonigan* (1934), which expanded into a trilogy. Such works of "serious American realism," in Farrell's words, often featured distracted, young protagonists unconverted to the politics of the author, who appeared as mere "social manifestations" of their disintegrated urban communities. Distinguishing themselves from the earlier naturalists, rural or urban, Farrell and Wright portrayed a Midwest utterly voided of the region's organic environmental features. They instead mapped the inorganic contours of the urban spaces that enclose the young protagonist's development, to accentuate the conscious and unconscious psychological effects of that mode of living upon developing subjects. The experimental method they enacted was this: a "delinquent" adolescent—whose emulation of racist stereotypes stalls their maturation—is situated within the confines of Chicago's South Side neighborhoods, a microcosm of the ethnic and class antagonisms that accompanied mass migration, including systemic issues relating to cultural integration, pluralism, and 100% Americanism. The Johnson–Reed Immigration Act of 1924, and the conflicting regional and state interests that simmered following its legislation, bore heavily upon these Midwestern Bildungsroman. Given Chicago's South Side comprised diverse ethnic diasporas of Italian, Polish, Jewish, Greek, Czech, West Indian, and Irish Americans, as well as African Americans from the South and rural Midwest, all vying for limited employment, resources, and space in ethnically zoned covenants, these neighborhoods formed strategic battlegrounds upon which these effects of national policies and regional development were rehearsed. The story of the region's uneven development as told by Farrell and Wright thus redefined the Bildungsroman's teleology of development that was configured by the soul-nation allegory.

James T. Farrell's *Studs Lonigan* Trilogy (1935)

Although James T. Farrell published prolifically over several decades across a range of forms and genres,[1] his most renowned works remain his large-scale cycles about young manhood in Chicago's South Side. Like Sinclair, Farrell approached novel writing with the political motivation to transform the bourgeois Bildungsroman into a more radical, populist form informed by sociological and ethnographic models of development and the Midwestern urban landscape, such as those provided by the University of Chicago's School of Sociology. In an essay entitled "Social Themes in American Realism" (1946), he marked 1929 as a watershed in "realist American fiction," which now foregrounded the nation's unequal distribution of wealth and resources, and the disproportionate effects of that uneven development on ethnic communities who were detrimentally impacted by immigration laws, public housing policies, and zoning. According to Farrell, American realism prior to the Great Depression failed to properly represent the "plebeian classes, the lower class, and group sections of the American population" ("Social Themes," 321). Adapting a term from Edward Dahlberg's Bildungsroman *Bottom Dogs* (1929), Farrell designated this new fictional mode "bottom-dog literature" (312). This term had "advantages over 'proletarian' literature," he argued, given "in the strictly Marxist sense" the latter term misleadingly implied works exclusively centered on the working class (312–13). Bottom-dog fiction precipitated a break with the Dreiser school of social realism, because it further revealed the basis of "social snobbery" to be "ugly racial prejudice" (313). Literary representations of "conditions of dirt, physical misery, and inner frustration" that appeared in Depression-era "bottom-dog literature" thus appealed to and engaged with the plebeian class on a "more human level than has been the case" (314). Richard Wright's *Black Boy*, Farrell proposed, was proven "equally important in the bottom layers of American society as it is in the world of Henry James" because it gave human figuration to how "one third" of the

---

[1] Farrell published 40 novels, 10 monographs, over 250 short stories, and numerous poems and essays.

nation's population actually lived (314). The regional complex in *Studs Lonigan*—its preoccupation with finding a form that would be intrinsic to its political representation of the proletariat in their urban provinces and localities—reflected a Marxist renovation of the bourgeois Bildungsroman. The misadventures of its restless young hero, Studs, who is locked in his regional framework, reflected the contradictory dynamics of the insular nation-state and capitalism's expanding, globalized networks as they are felt by the ordinary and *bottom-dog* classes of the Midwest's urban neighborhoods.

To summarize, Farrell's aesthetic concern, principally, was to represent how capitalism creates economic and social unevenness. His fictional oeuvre was set among these Irish communities living in South Side Chicago from 1900–30, which underwent class-based reorganization during the Great Depression. Influenced by Hughes, Wright, and other socialist writers, his conception of bottom-dog literature spoke to the Midwest region's aesthetic responses to the contradictory spatial character of its urban development, during what has been described as the second wave of the Chicago Renaissance (Hricko 5–6). In his literary critical works, notably *The League of Frightened Philistines: And Other Papers* (1945), Farrell historicized the generic evolution of the Bildungsroman, from Stendhal and Balzac, Dostoevsky and Tolstoy, to his interlocutor Joyce's modernist Künstlerroman, *A Portrait of the Artist as a Young Man*. Stephen Dedalus, the "rebel artist" and the champion of alienated youths, challenged "the whole moral sensibility of his age" by seeking "freedom in the realm of feeling and culture" (Farrell *The League*, 57). As a "rebel artist" who wrote for and about protagonists who were alienated from high art and culture, Farrell took his cue from Joyce: he theoretically revalued the political possibilities of the genre, by configuring a populist Bildungsroman the geographical imaginary of which depicted the metaphysical unfixity imposed upon immigrant diasporas in postwar America. Drawing upon Marxist theory of the novel as socialist praxis (Wald "Farrell and Trotskyism," 92–3), Farrell's novels of young manhood set in Washington Park and South Side retired the view that regional literature must either attend to 100% Americanism or serve a reactionary regionalism whose opposition to national development derived out of comparable xenophobia and racism.

Describing his outline for *Bernard Clare* to a friend (1946), Farrell proposed to "reduce the 'sociological' aspects of the book and try to, deeply, internalize it" (qtd in Flynn 119), emulating his idol, Joyce. In this way, he would narrativize "the soul of a young man, that being a battleground of ideas and the moral consequences of ideas" (119). A second letter in 1943 spoke of probing "the moral and intellectual consequences of the ideas of money, private property," how "capitalism poisons our lives from cradle to grave," and the developmental "effects of a whole system based on private profit, private ownership as a means of production," in which the "idea of property is poured into the depths of our consciousness from the earliest age" (119). As Farrell wrote in the authorial introduction to the Modern Library edition of the *Studs Lonigan* trilogy, the creation of Studs anticipated those tendencies, as a young imaginative character as well as a "social manifestation" of his context and capitalist interpellation (Farrell *Studs Lonigan*, xi). The "moral consequences of ideas" are faced by the second-generation Irish American Studs, the "young soul" whose development is obstructed by the spatial transformations of Chicago's ethnic neighborhoods after the Great Depression, including the corrosion of racial difference and class barriers between the proletariat and the petit-bourgeoisie, two kinds of social stratification that ultimately informed the classical Bildungsroman's ideology. As a youth whose mobility is constrained by these competing forces, Studs represented how nationalist ideologies and policies regarding race and immigration, as well as the superstructures of capitalist reproduction and the Prohibition Era moral fabric, unevenly structured and organized local life.

Studs's mobility as a young protagonist is gradually stagnated by the insularity of the neighborhood community he ultimately does not escape, as it contends with an impending economic depression and the xenophobic immigration policies that characterized 1920s America. That atmosphere provides Studs with a limited range of developmental possibilities. Rather than deliver cultural stability, Studs's insular neighborhood alienates him from any genuine ethnic identity or sense of community he might gain beyond those horizons. Despite Farrell's interest in the notion of the bottom-dog Bildungsroman of the proletariat, the South Side that he reimagines in *Studs* is not the "slum of his biological origin" but rather the "community of Irish American immigrants who had escaped the slum" only to have their economic security and sense of local autonomy undermined by the devastation of the Depression, with its accompanying reorganization of the ethnic demarcations of South Side (Cappetti 109). Farrell drew knowingly upon new Irish American stereotypes related to the 1925 Johnson–Reed Immigration Act. The opening of *Young Lonigan* opens a window into the social morality of an urban adolescent during a transformative period in Chicago's South Side, as he attempts to configure himself through media archetypes of ethnic identity: "Studs Lonigan, on the verge of fifteen . . . stood in the bathroom with a Sweet Caporal pasted in his mug," as "he sneered" (Farrell *Studs Lonigan*, 3). Poised to leave the "jailhouse" of his Catholic grammar school (3), Studs stands on the threshold between youth and young manhood. The derisive image presages the sociological discourses underwriting the novel's antidevelopment plot and the characterization of young Studs, a juvenile who sees an imaged version of manhood in various media, including popular film and radio broadcasting, and tries to emulate it. The "social manifestation" Studs reflects here foreshadows more rebellious images of young manhood later in the series, given how Farrell was not necessarily seeking "an extraordinary ethnic identity, only a practical one" (Dowd 156). Indeed, Studs's self-perceptions range from his idealized self, "The Great Studs Lonigan," to the alienated "Lonewolf Lonigan," and the pitiable "Pig Lonigan," an impotent drunk and hooligan (Farrell *Studs Lonigan*, 57). As a character, Studs Lonigan tested how abstract ethnic stereotypes were circulated within a xenophobic national popular culture, and the constraints such heavily mediated essentialisms posed to the social production of local life.

As with Joyce's *Portrait of the Artist*, *Studs Lonigan* creates a stylistic ontology of "development" where reflection and interiority often preside over the external narrative events. Yet Farrell obfuscates much of Studs's authentic inner life: i.e., the capacity for contemplation as well as action, two principal requirements of Bildung. Studs only knows himself through cultural referents, which include movie stars, baseball players, songs on the wireless at the pool hall—references which Farrell juxtaposes against Studs's religious and ethnic education. Throughout the trilogy, the influences of popular media on Studs's psychological development are encoded in Farrell's many stylistic intrusions, including traditional Irish ballads, such as "My Irish Molly," and "Little Annie Rooney" (15), as well as scrubbed-out handwriting (4) in *Young Lonigan*; hymns in Latin in *The Young Manhood of Studs Lonigan* (189); and images of advertisement posters (60), pop song lyrics (81), and newspaper headlines (197) in *Judgment Day*. Studs knows nothing about his Irish heritage, or life beyond 58th Street. Entire episodes occur which narrate Studs listening to the radio, inspecting a poster or advertisement, or viewing a movie, creating a sense that Studs's interiority is colonized by film and radio, substitutions for the capacity for reflection he requires to develop as a subject. This stylistic linking of the unconscious and media is exemplified in the third act of the trilogy, when Studs attends a film called *Doomed Victory* (in the novel, a movie poster is included), about a hardboiled Irish gangster.[2] Studs, yawning, "slump[s] into his seat ready to let the picture afford him an interesting good time" (61), and the reader is left to observe the film about the exploits of Studs's idol Joey Gallagher, a womanizing hoodlum who gives "cold lead as his answer to every rat who gets in his way" (64). Farrell is not suggesting that Studs is passively conditioned to adulate Chicago's glamorized criminal underbelly; rather, the film creates an ideal screen onto which Studs can project the uneven experience of his changing social environment, reading it through the basic filmic language of archetypical characters and contrived plots that resonate with his aspirational manhood. Studs's "thought patterns could be said to constitute an external stream-of-consciousness," Ann Douglas has suggested, meaning that "Studs, as a participant in and victim of mass culture, inevitably sees the world in terms not of institutions or even people, but of audiences" (494). Thus, when the feature's antihero dies in a blaze of glory, Studs feels like "a part of himself [was] dying" (*Judgment Day*, 70). Meditating on why the

---

[2] Farrell drew upon archetypal gangster films including Mervyn LeRoys's *Little Caesar* (1930), Howard Hawks's *Scarface* (1932), and William Wellman's *Public Enemy* (1931) featuring the "immigrant-gunboy" Tommy Powers on whom Studs's hero "seems modelled" (Douglas "*Studs Lonigan*," 496).

movie couldn't "have ended differently," he questions the sublimatory function of cinema as a means of managing one's internal affects through externalization, as the following excerpt conveys:

> Joey, unsuspecting, pointing to the advertising sign. . .
> THE WORLD IS YOURS
> Joey Gallagher again fading, in the mind of Studs Lonigan, into Studs Lonigan. Studs Lonigan, the world is yours. (*Judgment Day*, 69)

Studs does not enact his Joey Gallagher-inspired fantasies, though his foil, Weary, does by raping a young woman and assaulting Studs, crimes for which he is subsequently apprehended (*Young Manhood*, 409–11). What Studs's excursions into genre cinema reflect, above all, is the character's limited capacity for epistemological awareness: the inability to "know" himself through his restricted cultural education, to translate reflection into action, as a Bildungsheld must learn to do to successfully integrate into his social world. This inability for productive self-development stems from Studs's narrow understanding of the world outside of his neighborhood; he only interprets his situation through popular media and political slogans. The boy who longs to conquer "THE WORLD" never leaves his South Side neighborhood, except in his fantasies.

This alienation—Studs's spiritual rootlessness and culturelessness, which he displaces onto feelings of racism and xenophobia—is accentuated in his engagement with radio, which offers insight into how the competing influences of mediated regional and national interests directly impede upon his development. Consider the episode in which Studs, at home with his parents, sinks "into a rocking chair opposite the radio":

> The parlor suddenly filled with howling jazz, and Lonigan again tinkered with the dials . . . the notes of a saxophone came like a clear stream of fluid that seemed to flow into Studs . . . He leaned back, a brooding expression settling on his face, and again the saxophone was lost in a rising cacophony that crashed into a wild conclusion. (*Judgment Day*, 79)

Tuning out from the white noise of radio, Studs is suddenly consumed with thoughts of change and aging—thoughts of his neighborhood changing, of his family and friends inevitably dying, and of his own mortality—until he lets the "cloying-voiced radio crooner" lull him into a trance of mediated suspension from reality. The presence of "wild," "howling jazz" is not coincidental; it embarrassingly reminds the Lonigans of the perceived threat of cultural displacement in the wider neighborhood due to the Great Migration. The increasing presence of African Americans there underscores their own second-class status, as an ethnic diaspora whose difference is rendered conspicuous in the context of the Immigration Act of 1924. Popular music, cinema, and print media form sensory distractions that mask and reroute the disorderliness of the deeper political intuitions that Studs is frightened to acknowledge. Instead of acknowledging these fears, he displaces them onto these popular song lyrics:

> *Youth will pass away,*
> *Then what will they say about me?*
> *When the end comes, I know they'll say,*
> *"Just a gigolo,"*
> *And life goes on without me.* (*Judgment Day*, 80)

The Illinois blues song "I ain't got nobody (and nobody cares for me)," popularized by icons such as Bessie Smith and Sophie Tucker, here seems to impose an irrepressible moment of self-realization. The song's lyrics are parceled and dispersed throughout the narrative; the emasculating line that disturbs Studs upon its first hearing, "*Just a gigolo . . . ,*" recurs on pages 243–4 and 245. In narrating the family's responses to the music, Farrell also includes the advertisements that are spliced into the commercial radio program: "'And friends of Radioland, the Peoples Stores, situated all over the city for the housewives' convenience, will be gratified, and amply repaid if you have enjoyed this concert which they have sponsored'" (*Judgment Day*, 81). The men are shushed by one such housewife, Mrs. Lonigan, whose obedience to capitalist propaganda epitomizes what theorist Theodor Adorno later described as the "Radio Generation" type: "whose being lies in the fact that he no longer experiences anything himself, but rather lets the all-powerful, opaque social apparatus dictate experiences to him, which is precisely what prevents the formation of an ego, even of a 'person' at all" (*Current of Music*, 465).

Farrell presents modernity's new media, including film and radio, as structuring Studs's experience of living between an abstract "national" space and a closed-off ethnic identity in ways that prevent the "formation" of a genuine "ego," in Adorno's terms. Rather than facilitating his maturation, the neighborhood's "white flight" fuels Studs's physical and psychic decline, exacerbated by his increasing ethnic agitation and gradual immobilization. In *The Young Manhood of Stud Lonigan*, set in 1924 in the wake of a suite of xenophobic national policies curtailing immigration, Farrell is furthermore retroactively accounting for the fallout brought about at the local level by years of postwar policies, incendiary debates, and xenophobic hysteria blasted across popular media. We observe this clearly in his interaction with the Greek intellectual, Christy, who gives the following speech to the young patrons at the local pool hall:

> "Silly boys. They have no education. . . . The boys . . . grow up in poolrooms, drink and become hooligans . . . Or else they are sent to the capitalist war and they get killed, for what? . . . to make more money for Morgan and the bankers." (*Young Manhood*, 336)

Studs, who enters the room halfway through the monologue, is blindsided by Christy's disillusionment in the abstract Americanism he has absorbed through newsreels, films, and radio broadcasts. Observing Christy translate Whitman—the poet-prophet of the American *demos*—into Greek, Studs is suddenly overcome by a musicalized memory:

> A song of several years back jingled in Studs's mind, *Don't Bite the Hand That's Feeding You* . . . The first line kept returning to him: *If you don't like your Uncle Sammy* . . . The song hit the nail square. Studs had an image of Uncle Sammy in his brain . . . his eyes sad with sorrow caused by the ingratitude of all the foreigners who had come over here and been ungrateful to him. (337–8)

Thomas Hoier and Jimmie Morgan's 1915 jingle, written to bolster loyalty during WWI, sinks below consciousness, lying dormant there, feeding into the ethnic anxiety of the second-generation immigrant. In the hearings of the Committee on Immigration and Naturalization, brought before the House of Representatives, which ran from February 21st to April 5th, 1928, addressing the "acute problem" of immigration "particularly" from Mexico (U.S. State Congress "Immigration from Countries of the Western Hemisphere," 1), Morgan G. Sanders, a Democrat congressman elected by the third district of the State of Texas, quoted the same jingle on the House Floor. He did so in support of the Box Bill, which proposed caps and deportation reform for Mexican, Canadian, and South American immigration, even while he acknowledged the essential cheap labor that those migrants provided on developmental projects including the Southwestern desert railroads. Having been interpellated by these views, Studs longs to tell that "Greek sonofabitch, get the hell out of a white man's country," but instead asks his friends the most damning question he can muster: "Say, is that Greek an American citizen" (Farrell *Studs Lonigan*, 338)? Simultaneously, the mythical patriotism symbolized by Uncle Sam evokes powerful nostalgia in Studs for childhood's simplicity, when he read "cartoons with Uncle Sam in them in the newspapers," wishing "that Uncle Sam was a real man, the same to America as God was to the world. It made him wish that again, and wishing that, he was wishing he was a kid again" (338). Not only Christy's jeremiad, but the revelation of the abstract, emptiness of 100% Americanism strikes at the prematurely aging Studs's own ontological uncertainty as a character, who despite what should be his youthful mobility to seize the world, is increasingly aware that he is undeniably caught. His sense of reactionary political conservatism stems from his desire to recover some abstract unspoiled youth before President Wilson notoriously classified his own ethnic group as the "hyphenated Americans." Part of that fallout relates to how a progressive aesthetics of regionalism emerged to counter such federal interference. As Foley suggests of the "proletarian Bildungsroman," we are meant to "hear" more in these episodes than we observe at the literal level (*Radical Representations*, 335). What we hear are snippets of public debates over place, locality, and regionalism. Farrell's sympathy is with those 'unrelenting tides' of migrants targeted by the unprecedented postwar push toward 100% Americanism.

Approaching his late twenties by the end of *Young Manhood*, Studs still has not reached actual *manhood*. He still resides with his chauvinistic parents, who resolve to vacate the neighborhood to escape the influx of African American migrants against whom Studs's gang launch targeted attacks. Stirred by anti-Black propaganda, Studs's mother becomes *"more religious every day,"* believing her son has been corrupted by "bad companions" (*Young Manhood*, 342). Meanwhile, the class struggles of South Side translate into violent territorial confrontations between the youth of ethnic diasporas competing for space. Because Studs cannot understand the abstract regional, national, and international political spheres that grind against one another in his daily life—a life that is structured by the invisible webs of hearings, policies, legislation, blueprints, and zoning restrictions, as well as the unplanned merging of different social groups and interests that spring out of such designs—his resulting failure to integrate harmoniously into his world instead manifests as a physical illness from which he never recovers. This "sickness" is contagious among his crowd, as friends like Hink begin to look "crazy," "queer," or act "far away," exhibiting the alienation of a rootless existence (339). In the parlor room as much as the pool hall, Farrell's narrative references national debates over migration and immigration policy, and their regional applications: what happens to individual development when the community support systems and resources that reinforce civil society are eroded by urban overdevelopment and ethnic redlining? Such a question preoccupied researchers at the University of Chicago regarding the physical environment of the metropolis.

The bigger political question Farrell was interested in, however, was how civil unrest could be mitigated if city planning and zoning was constructed around racist and xenophobic notions about whose access to democratic rights matter most, and which ethnic groups have the right to occupy certain spaces in America. In an ideal world, Farrell's solution to secular development, like Christy's, was socialist revolution: to rouse class consciousness in the masses, by emancipating them from the conditions that alienated them. Yet the novelist Farrell obeys Frank Norris's aesthetic directive for the naturalist author not to "preach" to the reader, even airing the conservative view through the mouthpiece of the Lonigans'

Catholic priest, Father Shannon. Shannon preaches against "'movements started by vicious men and women who philander with the souls of youth," including "jazz, atheism, free-love, companionate marriage, birth control," and all "miscalled tendencies" (the term *tendencies* suggesting his distrust toward the Chicago School) that "are murdering the soul of youth'" (*Young Manhood*, 349). Youth comprise either those who attend Mass, or those who fill "'those seats of the godless—the universities," attend "those iniquitous incubators of vice, cheapness, and trash—the movies," and read blasphemous "modern authors'" like Sinclair Lewis's 1927 bestseller *Elmer Gantry*, a regionalist satire that lampooned fundamental evangelicalism in the provincial Midwest. They also read that "'noisy, vociferous'" H. L. Mencken, who incites youths to "'Read Nietzsche!'", an irresponsible recommendation given the famous juvenile delinquents Leopold and Loeb read Nietzsche "'almost in this neighbourhood'" (352–3). The appearance of Danny O'Neill, the protagonist of Farrell's next eponymous pentalogy about young manhood, offers an alternative pathway of development altogether. Danny, having indeed read Nietzsche while at the University of Chicago, uncovers that Father Shannon speaks not out of *"ignorance and superstition"* but rather a *"downright hatred of truth and beauty"* (369). This realization liberates him from his inherited spiritual guilt, allowing him to imagine *"a better world . . . of ideals such as that the Russians were attempting to achieve"* and resolve to *"study to prepare himself to create that world"* (370). At present, he remains *"a disillusioned young man"* surrounded by bullies like Studs, whose own capacity for reflection and action is limited. Unlike Studs, Danny can liberate himself from the constraints of place, realizing that he can *"drive this neighbourhood . . . out of his consciousness with a book"* (372).

Studs, however, remains immobilized by the disconnection he feels between his local mode of living and the patriotic, Americanist ideal he has imbibed. His function as a naturalist character operates not simply as a "stereotype" or "product of forces," but what Farrell differentiated as a "social manifestation" (xi) of juvenile delinquency molded by the South Side environment. The bourgeois individualism of the traditional Bildungsroman is subverted, to that end, in Farrell's naturalistic detours into the effects of the

Depression. In the pervasive, typically two-page streams of consciousness of other characters—usually italicized to mark their separation from Studs—Farrell offers montages of other South Sider lives, creating a microcosm of the regional and national totality into which the Lonigans' lives unfold, and the pressures on postwar youth. In one instance, we observe a character called Mr. Le Gare's tears as he is laid off for protesting wages, having been replaced by "Yellow Scabs!", while his son Andy, whose brain is "not very good," seeks employment to help out (*Young Manhood*, 104–5); in another, we witness Mrs. Sheehan's "premonition" of her "son, the football star, lying dead at her feet" (114–15); a third focuses on Davy Cohen, "a poor sick Jew" who steals a library book, while coughing up blood (150–1).

Farrell's key political messages are the aspects of these conversations about ethnicity, mobility, and the constraints nation was imposing on regional life that are missed by Studs, this irony being one instrumental way in which Farrell's trilogy of young manhood widened the political horizons of the genre's bourgeois teleology. Farrell notoriously refused, on Marxist grounds, "to reduce the category of aesthetic value to a relativistic functional aspect," and Alan Wald observes how *Studs* reflects his "adamant rejection of the political coding of literary form" (*Writing From the Left*), such as the bourgeois Bildungsroman. Instead, *Studs* constituted a "bottom-dog" Bildungsroman in Farrell's definition, that assumed responsibility for but ultimately rejected the stereotypes of class and ethnic structures in the bourgeois regional imaginary of the Midwest. Farrell exposed his young protagonists "to multiple instances of exploitation and abuse that reveal . . . the devastating physical and psychological effects of capitalism on producers" (Foley *Radical Representations*, 329), as well as nationalism's psychological effects upon the heterogenous collectives that comprised its regions. Was the Bildungsroman, as a form, really commensurate with radical leftist politics? Farrell appears to have believed so—pending some re-engineering of the bourgeois individualism upon which the genre was predicated. By adapting that bourgeois model of development through a socialist lens, *Studs Lonigan* powerfully scrutinized the disconnection between the abstract nationalism of 100% Americanism engineered toward capitalist interests and the lived effects of regional development upon culturally diverse local communities.

Richard Wright's *Native Son* (1940)

In *White Man Listen!* (1957), written late in Richard Wright's career, the author referred to himself as a "rootless man" who did not believe in cultivating "many emotional attachments, sustaining roots, or idealistic allegiances" (xxviii), having finally left the United States after enduring years of political persecution and red-baiting (Gilroy 146–7). He was responding to criticisms against his character made by the Southwestern-born writer Ralph Ellison, a formerly close friend who notoriously cast Wright as an anti-regionalist with an incurable regional complex, which he felt drove a wedge between them "by geography and difference of experience" (Ellison 198–9). Ellison's Wright never moved past his brutal upbringing within a closed-off, Jim Crow community in the Deep South, a region which once he left it, he never desired to revisit except in literature (198). Since Paul Gilroy's influential interpretation of Wright foregrounded the author within a transnationalist theory of the Black Atlantic (Gilroy 145–86), the author's intellectual legacy has been recognized as expressing a more contradictory relationship to regional identity than those earlier assessments afforded. Wright's personal investment in Black Southern folk expressions and dialect fiction early in his career certainly broadened into visions of the "Negro" as "America's metaphor," a figure which he later placed at the center of his long-term political project tracing the history of civilization and the West, and the global history of imperialist struggles (Gilroy 149). Indeed, few American writers have ever grasped the untidy, vicissitudinous dynamics between the regional, national, and transnational in modernity's cultural project more perceptively than Wright.

The formative stages of this multistoried geographical imaginary commenced in Wright's early career in Chicago, a context in which he often deliberated the advantages of aesthetic regionalisms rooted in folk customs and vernacular, a localist aesthetics that might provide cultural stability out of which the more abstract affiliative capacities of nationalist and internationalist political movements might grow. Chicago's Black Belt was the setting of his most famous—and infamous—novel, *Native Son* (1940), a sociological Bildungsroman about a young Black proletarian living on Chicago's South Side. As an apprentice writer, Wright resided on Beale Street, Memphis, followed by Chicago; and was struck by the following impression of that city as the metaphor of unfinished youth: "Because Chicago is so young, it is possible to know it in a way that many other cities cannot be known. The stages of its complex growth are living memories" (Wright "Introduction" to *Black Metropolis*, lx). Young Chicago, struggling to culturally mature under the effects of its rapid but uneven development, formed the fraught regionalist muse of his Bildungsroman, *Native Son*. Like his comrade Farrell's South Side trilogy, *Native Son* delivered a determinist narrative of arrested development that was informed by the pressures of the environment its youthful protagonist inhabits, approaching that theme through what we might describe as Wright's sociological regionalism.

Whereas Farrell's novel disclosed the pressures of immigrants to conform to "100% Americanism" and the challenges these ideological borders posed in everyday life, Wright's novel created a provocative portrait of interregional Black communities with conflicting customs and cultural norms, picking up where the proletarian regionalism of Langston Hughes's *Not Without Laughter* (1930) geographically left off. While Hughes's Sandy Rogers arrives in Chicago from the rural hinterland, wanders past the oppressive tenements of Chicago's Black Belt, and contemplates his destiny there in contrast to his rural roots, Wright's Bigger Thomas was born in rural Mississippi, and is thus an official part of the Great Migration out of the South. The Northern cities' Black Belts, rural and urban, were densely populated with relocated Southerners only a generation removed from slavery, who were kept deliberately undereducated to preclude political agitation (Wright *Black Boy*, 148). Upon relocating to the industrial North, these Southerners often struggled to integrate into the customs expected of them by an established Black bourgeoisie, as Hughes famously argued in his essay "The Negro Artist and the Racial Mountain" (1926). This displacement led to systemic exploitation which, in turn, contributed to crippling generational poverty, as well as the popularity of extreme reactionary politics. As Wright explained in the novel's preface after-the-fact, "How 'Bigger' Was Born," *Native Son* consciously exposed the discrepancies between their lived reality and the empty, abstract nationalisms forced upon young people through representations of "daily American life" in "newspapers, magazines, radios, movies." Such cultural education left them unable to combat the "deep sense of exclusion" (858) that is structured into local contexts where urban industrialism has fragmented the common bonds of community, as they were traditionally organized around folk culture and religion, rather than mere survival.

Native Son thus disclosed the conflict that accompanies the protagonist's migration from one region—the South—into another—the urban Midwest. Wright represents the imagined temporal differences in these modes of living by superimposing "regionalist" imagery and rural tropes onto imagery that is inflected by mass media, as Leigh Anne Duck notes (190). The disparity between regional politics of racial segregation and class exploitation within a nation that presents itself as a liberal democracy also has significant bearings on the denial of Bildung for the protagonist of *Native Son*. As Bigger is tried for murder, the defense of his life becomes less about his criminal guilt and more about race in the nation's regional imaginary, including the deep psychological divisions of hatred that fester over generations along those imagined lines of racial, geographical, and ideological affiliation. Resulting from these unsettling divisions and "competing [regional] temporalities" (Duck 190), the literary geography of *Native Son*—set almost exclusively inside South Side's Black Belt—stakes a higher claim in the regional imaginary than is often attributed to it, given its title's reference to postwar American nativism. The intervention Wright makes in the Bildungsroman form hinges on reconceiving the novel of development and the unfixed figure of youth in ways that echo Midwestern naturalism's tendencies. Wright's novel of antidevelopment thus aligned with the similar geopolitics of Farrell, with the intention of revitalizing the bourgeois Bildungsroman of national destiny with a sturdier generic scaffold for containing the nation's ethnically but also regionally variegated proletariat.

The regional complex informed *Native Son* in the following way: Bigger Thomas, an unfixed figure of youth who migrates from the one region to the other, and becomes penned into that alien, adverse environment, forcefully comes to terms with the disjunction between the North's regional imaginary (how Black life there is imagined to be, relative to the underdeveloped Jim Crow South) and regional determinism (how life really is for the Black masses in urban Midwestern environments). It was not a dissimilar operation to that in Wright's autobiography about his own Southern upbringing, *Black Boy* (1945—later republished as *Black Boy/ American Hunger*), which describes how the "dream-maker" Black metropolis of Chicago became the mecca "to which Negroes were fleeing by the thousands" (Wright *Black Boy*, 115), an exodus of former agricultural and domestic laborers escaping both the Klan's tyranny and ruinous poverty. In *Native Son*, the Southern-born Bigger joins the city's racialized division of labor as the chauffeur of a white millionaire, Henry Dalton. The narrative soon veers into a disastrous collision course between Bigger's individual aspirations for rootlessness—symbolized in his whimsical fantasy about becoming a fighter pilot—and his predetermined fate as a young, Black, and criminally undereducated proletarian.

Like Farrell, Wright reformulated the Bildungsroman's narrative apparatus to deliver a sharper image of the urban, multiethnic proletariat than literature had previously provided. According to Martin Japtok, the Bildungsroman genre's "focus on the self" forcefully imposes the "subjective element into the genre of realism," ensuring that the reading act is inflected by seeing society and its apparatuses of power "through the eyes of the protagonist" (148). While the "form is individualist in nature," and thus conforms to a "European world view that is foundational to modern capitalism," the author who writes about ethnicity or the proletariat within a genre that centralizes an individual's "experience in the world" will encounter both limitations and new possibilities (148). The inner workings of form are deceptive, for as much as the Bildungsroman "invites views" of the state of things from "any angle," the genre in many ways conforms to that individualist capitalist worldview that so "often arises on the backs of ethnic groups and colonized people" (148). Yet, because the politics of members within ethnic groups may greatly differ, Barbara Foley suggests the alternative categorization, the "proletarian bildungsroman," to describe how the genre's belief structures were expropriated by left-wing writers (*Radical Representations*, 321–61). Given the Bildungsroman's principles stress a "typicality and narrative transparency" that render it unfit for "the proletarian novel," a proletarian Bildungsroman necessarily internally "eschews the normative political premises upon which such criteria are based" (Foley "The Politics of Poetics," 197). These poetics require closer attention to the geographies underwriting that proletariat's story. Wright's novels, according to Cedric Robinson, intended to "reconstruct and weigh the extraordinary complexities and subtleties of radical politics as he and others had experienced it" (292). These extraordinary complexities included the difficulties of revolutionizing a fragmented national Black community split across contrasting regional affiliations, who did not trust the sympathies of a predominantly white-led internationalist movement. One of Wright's target audiences in *Native Son* was his white comrades in the Communist Party U.S.A., who had limited contact with the Black proletariat they championed, even though they endorsed the Soviet Union's Black Belt thesis as a blueprint to revolutionize the peasant U.S. South (Robinson 296).

In *Black Metropolis*, Wright indicated that *Native Son*'s portrait of race relations in the North was underwritten by his sociological interests, which emerged in the wake of the intellectual attention brought to the region via the School of Sociology at the University of Chicago. Seeking a scientific model that could heighten the novel's appeal to political verisimilitude, he encountered the School's research. Wright explains, "I did not know what my story was ... until I stumbled upon science," which disclosed "the meanings of the environment that battered and taunted me" ("Introduction" to *Black Metropolis*, lix), and offered him a rubric for understanding the link between space and both racial and class-based oppression, something which the undereducated Bigger cannot articulate. Wright

> found that sincere art and honest science were not far apart, that each could enrich the other. The huge mountains of fact piled up by the Department of Sociology at the University of Chicago gave me my first concrete vision of the forces that molded the urban Negro's body and soul. (lix)

Such inorganic forces were not conducive to the philosophical ideal of Bildung. Though he "was never a student at the university," Wright attributed "the meanings" of *Native Son* to "the scientific findings of" sociologists "Robert E. Park, Robert Redfield, and Louis Wirth," whose "scientific facts" about the impacts of racism upon social development inspired the short stories comprising *Uncle Tom's Children* and his autobiography *Black Boy* (lx). Despite these overt influences on Wright's writing, he did not uncritically reinforce the influential findings of their sociological volumes. Davarian L. Baldwin notes how the Chicago School sociologists failed to critically disambiguate systemic racism from generalizations about racial "temperament" in prominent works such as *The City*, which skewed their findings; this reinforced the logic of "Black primitivism" in their writings about Bronzeville, and their dismissal of its vibrant business center, The Stroll (D. Baldwin 127). Such sociological terminology was easily mainstreamed as an apologia for political complacency regarding the "transitional" areas of the city, as Wright himself pointed out in *12 Million Black Voices*. The field's myopia formed the basis of Black sociologists Horace Cayton and St. Clair Drake's critical intervention in *Black Metropolis* (1945), for which Wright wrote the introduction; it revised the Chicago School's emphasis on "ghettoization," by reconceiving Black communities' creative expropriations of the spaces they were forced to inhabit: the Black Belts. *Native Son* grew out of "Drake's and Cayton's scientific statement" in *Black Metropolis* "about the urban Negro, [which] pictures the environment out of which the Bigger Thomases of our nation come" ("Introduction" to *Black Metropolis*, lx).

Bigger thus exemplifies what Zola would have called Wright's "experimental" literary subject: an unfinished and thus yet unfixed youth on the verge of manhood, whom the author places in a controlled or fixed environment to determine what plot would result. The irony of his status as an unfixed character is that despite his youth, the season of mobility and possibility, Bigger's path to development in Chicago is predetermined by ethnicity, like that of Studs and Jurgis; though he moves from one regional system of oppression to another, he cannot break out of his metaphysical confinement, even if he attempts to become a radical free agent unbounded to any political, racial, or geographical affiliation through violence. Wright thus found the trope of an unfixed youth, who has become stuck in an alien regional framework, was a medium for examining political, intellectual, and scientific understandings regarding the nation's uneven development, restyling those findings into a theory of the novel in his 1937 landmark essay, "Blueprint for Negro Writing," and subsequently the Bildungsroman that emulated its principles, *Native Son*.

Backed by Dorothy West, who recruited Illinois-based writers to transform the periodical *Challenge* into the more left-leaning *New Challenge*, Wright published the "Blueprint." While it does not mention the Bildungsroman specifically, it posited a socialist theory of fiction that led him to write one that would reorganize the genre's symbolic depiction of national destiny. Tellingly, to describe the responsibilities of the Black author, Wright shifts from images of an inorganic, stunted nationalism to a set of unmistakably regionalist metaphors, where the "origins" of a more organic, healthier nationalism must sprout: "By placing cultural health above narrow sectional prejudices, liberal writers of our braces can help to break the stony soil of aggrandizement out of which the stunted plants of Negro nationalism grow," and help "to weed out these choking growths of reactionary nationalism and replace them with sturdier types," Wright determines ("Blueprint," 1387–8). One obvious sectional prejudice is regional affiliation, especially those regionalisms rooted in "the stony soil" of the South, the cultural health of which clearly preoccupies *Native Son*'s regional imaginary, as we shall see. Following Wright's path of Black urban modernization, the "Negro writer must realize within the area of his own personal experience those impulses which, when prefigured in terms of broad social movements, constitute the stuff of nationalism" (1384). Wright configured this nationalism within a larger scale of political responsibility, too: that of a socialist globalism, which unites the Black nationalist movement with the global struggle of the oppressed. The word of resistance Wright cannot articulate, given its reactionary overtones at this historical juncture (especially for an avowedly troubled ex-Southerner), is clearly "region": the writer must tend the soil out of which national and international solidarity will grow by cultivating grassroots political modernization across the regions, the local element where "the interdependence of people" (1387) is most acutely felt.

The literary geography of *Native Son* transpires in a section of the city distinct from the artistic and intellectual haven of Bronzeville, out of which a regional Black literary renaissance was emerging. As such, Wright's regionalism in writing *Native Son* was furthermore informed by his involvement in the New Deal investment in localisms and regionalisms, the context in which he was professionalized as a young writer. The FWP—one of four large-scale arts projects conceived in 1935 by the Works Progress Administration, with a $5billion budget—promoted aesthetic localism as a means of seizing cultural continuity across the nation in social pluralism and regional diversity. The Chicago and Illinois Writers' Projects subsidized the formation of the South Side Writers' Group, which included Wright, Gwendolyn Brooks, Margaret Walker, Alden Bland, Willard Motley, William Attaway, and Arna Bontemps: a regional cluster of writers committed to cultivating social protest literature and fostering local African American culture (Barnes 52). Although criticism has neglected the connections between Wright's coverage for the FWP and his fiction, both his geographic essay "A Survey of the Amusement Facilities of District #35", reporting on Chicago's South Side culture, and *Native Son*'s fictionalization of that neighborhood, explore "the ambiguity of Chicago's racial boundaries in the 1930s," Rosemary Hathaway argues (92). Only by migrating into the whites-only sections of the city as an underpaid worker does Bigger fully understand the oppressive boundaries that will "ultimately trap him" as he attempts to hide from the police within the Black Belt in the novel's climax (93).

These ideological agendas converge in *Native Son*'s first searing sound-image: the *"Brrrrrrriiiiiiiiiiiiiiiiiiinng!"* of an alarm clock (*Native Son*, 447). Daylight unveils "a black boy standing in a narrow space between two iron beds" in a one-bedroom kitchenette (a one-room unit with a sink and gas stovetop) in a tenement building, beside his siblings, his mother, and a "huge black rat" (449). The alarm clock reinforces the psychology of the white real-estate capitalists' exploitation of space and resources described in *12 Million Black Voices*, which produces a "war . . . in our emotions" between feeling grateful to have escaped the Southern plantation, even as they are imprisoned by Chicago's exploitative "transition" phase, relegating non-whites to specific underdeveloped neighborhoods (Wright *12 Million*, 105). The alarm signals the collapsing of time and space into the reified mechanical chronotope of the "working day," suggesting how Chicago's racialized ghetto transforms time into an oppressive abstraction. Every aspect of the young worker's waking life, from his dwelling to his labor, contributes to his becoming one of the "warped personalities" of the ghetto (108). Given the caps on European migrant workers introduced by the Johnson–Reed Immigration Act of 1924, poor Black and white domestic migrants seeking jobs during the Depression now competed for housing in the cities' working-class zones; but there simply were "not enough houses for us to live in" (100). Farrell's *Studs Lonigan* attested to how competing claims to national legitimacy led to factional instability and even violence between ethnic youth co-habiting in cramped neighborhoods, including the Irish and Black communities of South Side. Black people were forced outside of the city's "business belt" into "transition" areas commonly referred to as ghettoes, filled with time-worn tenements in which apartments were subdivided into seven tiny, overpriced rental units by real-estate capitalists, "the Bosses of the Buildings" (103–4). Because there was limited white-collar work available for Black applicants due to segregated hiring practices, domestic workers such as maids, janitors, elevator runners, cooks, and other servants could barely make rent, which on average was $6 per week per kitchenette ($42 per week for the whole unit). Meanwhile, racist policies meant that white renters were charged only $50 per month for the undivided unit. Housing scarcity, Wright concludes, nevertheless meant that Black workers were "glad" to get these rooms (105). With five to six people living in each of these heavily subdivided units, upward of thirty had to share one toilet, making the kitchenette "the author of the glad tidings that new suckers are in town, ready to be cheated, plundered, and put in their places" (105–6). The kitchenette "is our prison," Wright muses, "our death sentence without a trial, the new form of mob violence that assaults not only the lone individual, but all of us" (106). *Native Son*'s establishing descriptions, symbolically prison-like, create a laboratory for Wright's experiment in creating a plot that was sociologically modeled on that environment's impacts upon psycho-social development.

Native Son takes the perspective of one of South Side's "warped personalities." That condition is tellingly described in regionalist imagery: Bigger is a "strange plant blooming in the day and wilting at night," without any "sun" or even "cold darkness" (*Native Son*, 471). The fact that he is the son of a murdered Mississippian sharecropper and spent his childhood segregated from whites because of Chicago's racist social production of space, coupled with his naivety regarding his place within that world, begets the plot's tragic determinism. Bigger is soon revealed to be racially "rootless." Having interviewed for a job with Mr. Dalton—one of those avaricious "Bosses of the Buildings"—he feels trapped in a "shadowy region, a No-Man's Land, the ground that separated the white world from the black" where "this white man, having helped to put him down ... held him up now to look at him and be amused" (508). As the personification of the maladjusted personalities ghettoization creates, Bigger's increasing racial alienation symbolically registers through the motif of "blindness;" namely, an incapacity for self-recognition, which worsens with Bigger's increased presence in the gentrified white neighborhoods of Kenwood and Hyde Park.

Just as regional determinism collides with Irish American nationalist identity politics throughout Farrell's trilogy, Wright's novel explores how the Black urban masses engage with abstract nationalisms. Such is the case in the following passage, in which Bigger contemplates his situation following Mary Dalton's murder:

> There were rare moments when a feeling and longing for solidarity with other black people would take hold of him. He would dream of making a stand against that white force, but that dream would fade when he looked at the other black people near him ... he hated them and wanted to wave his hand and blot them out. (Wright *Native Son*, 550)

As a personification of the South Side ghetto's negative potential, Bigger's reactionary masculinity stultifies what Hegel (593) referred to as the Bildungsroman's "philistine" trope of the young hero who successfully courts his lover, and thereby continues the bourgeoisie's cycle of reproduction. Hallmarks of Bigger's sexual "delinquency" (in the Chicago School's definition) persist throughout the novel, in the way he recoils from his overbearing mother; in his violence against his rival Gus early in the novel; when Bigger and his friend Jack masturbate in the movie theater; in Bigger's equal terror and arousal toward Mary Dalton; and in the rape and murder of Bessie Mears. Modernist Bildungsromane often undermined the trope of the sexually successful male protagonist, creating narratives of increasingly explicit sexual initiation that attempted to liberate masculinity from puritanical morality.[3] However, if *Native Son* poses a warning signal about the racism of overdevelopment, it also deftly reveals the double standard of race and masculinity in the national imaginary, which proliferated out of the South's definition of Black manhood, a concept which signaled "a power shift white men have historically resisted through terror, violence, and lynching," as Michael Bibler explains (9). Dissatisfied with the Bildungsroman's generic constraints upon Black masculinity, Wright presents Bigger's killing of Mary Dalton as part of his unconscious revenge against Mr. Dalton: the landlord who personifies the white capitalists who supported the principles of a separate-but-equal America, while dictating the terms by which millions of ethnic people lived in Chicago, the nation, and throughout the colonized world. Mr. Dalton's daughter Mary—who rebels against her father by joining the CPUSA's inadequately integrated Chicago chapter—triggers a death drive that implicates Bigger in these transregional racial and class struggles, transfiguring Mary's lifeless body into a symbol of white supremacists' worst fear: forced miscegenation. What begins in Bigger's mind as a noncommittal assessment of his individual actions is ultimately overturned through forceful introspection, as he accepts that his behavior has reified a racist trope:

> He was black and he had been alone in a room where a white girl had been killed; therefore he had killed her. The hidden meaning of his life—a meaning which others did not see ... —had spilled out.... There was in him a kind of terrified pride ... that some day he would be able to say publicly that he had done it. (542)

[3] Examples include Joyce's *Portrait*, Farrell's *Studs Lonigan*, and Fitzgerald's *This Side of Paradise*—which I discuss in Chapter 4.

The narrator does not insist upon Bigger's innocence, retaining the narratorial objectivity typical of naturalism. Wright does suggest that while Bigger is legally guilty, his actions are an unconscious politicized reaction against systemic white supremacy. As Wright suggests of his craft in the preface to *Native Son*, the "imaginative novel represents . . . an intensely intimate expression on the part of a consciousness couched in terms of the most objective and commonly known events" (Wright "How 'Bigger,'" 853). Wright's own Southern upbringing, filled with his private experiences of rage, terror, and deprivation, suggested to him why other "Negroes, in moments of anger and bitterness," might sympathize with Japan's colonial annexation of Chinese territory during the Sino-Japanese War, "not because they believed in oppression," but because they had no outlets for their own oppression (865). Wright could appreciate, too, why some Black Americans supported charismatic ideologues like Hitler, Mussolini, Stalin, or Marcus Garvey—the architect of the controversial Back to Africa movement (865). Wright also understood why others might recoil from their race amid a flood of misinformation, as Bigger does. On the verge of adulthood, Wright himself first observed how the South and the Midwest were distant and yet similar, when he realized that as a paperboy his job was to sell "racial propaganda" advocating "Ku Klux Klan doctrines" and lynching "as a solution for the problem of the Negro" in Chicago (*Black Boy* 115), a reality Bigger also uncovers during his trial. Wright insists that the Left must understand the historical dimensions to this mentality of regional *and* psychological dislocation Bigger experiences, and respond appropriately to the diverse, even at times uncomfortable, fears, motivations, and desires of individuals; whether they be fieldhands in Mississippi, elevator runners in small-town Kansas, or young men, robbed of their childhood, who become felons prowling Chicago's South Side tenements.

This messaging is articulated through the mouthpiece of Bigger's CPUSA-appointed lawyer, Boris Max. He declares that white society wants to convict Bigger in a kangaroo court for his symbolic crimes against white America, rather than for the legal crimes for which an adolescent should be held responsible following a lawful trial. Max notes the irony that the liberal nation-state lionizes the racial charity of Dalton, a millionaire whose fortune is predicated on Northern real-estate capitalism modeled on the South's Jim Crow. The twist in the trial comes as Max alters Bigger's plea from guilty to not guilty, a strategy which hinges upon two points: firstly, the "'mental and emotional attitude'" into which Bigger has been conditioned by his living situation; and secondly, but no less crucially, his "'extreme youth'" (792), exacerbated by the fact he has only finished eighth grade education (which was remarkably all the self-taught Wright completed). Max's updated defense provokes the racist views of Buckley, the State's Attorney, who deems Bigger "'just a scared Mississippi boy'"; "boy" being the epithet used to disempower and emasculate Black men of all ages in the South. Max emphasizes this double standard: if he is just a "'poor boy,'" Bigger cannot be tried as an adult, it logically follows (796). "'This boy is young, not only in years, but in his attitude toward life. He is not old enough to vote. Living in a Black Belt district, he is younger than most boys his age, for he . . . has had but two outlets for his emotions: work and sex—and he knew these in their most vicious and degrading forms,'" Max futilely clarifies, Wright's self-reflective meditation on the impossibility of genuine Bildung for the maligned "type" Bigger represents (798).

The court nevertheless condemns the "juvenile delinquent," leaving Bigger unable to ever psychologically or legally transcend the restrictive Southern identity that has been imposed upon him. Wright's plot of arrested development thus exposed the dichotomy between the nation's liberal democratic principles and the system of oppression uniting all regions, North and South, East and West. The novel's sociological and political articulation of the impediments of overdevelopment clearly "penetrate[d] the flow of social concealments and urbanities to the passions," as Wright's hero Mencken advocated in favor of an anti-puritanical, naturalist realism (Mencken qtd in Rowley 46). Living by "the brutal logic of jobs," mankind inhabits "a world of things," utterly alienated from "the soil, the sun, the rain, or the wind" (Wright *12 Million*, 100): that organic connection to the agrarian mode of life that sustained Bildung. Like Farrell, Wright means his reader to hear a revolution that exceeds the enraged individual social "type" represented on the page, which in this case, is the "juvenile delinquent" or "extreme youth." For James Baldwin, an apprentice of Wright who became one of his most perceptive critics, the "story of the Negro in America is the story of America, and it is not a pretty story;" its protagonist, Bigger Thomas, is "gloomily referred to as that shadow which lies athwart our national life" (*Notes*, 18–19). Although the abstract nationalism Bigger "killed for" may have come to nothing, that "sturdier" type of Black nationalism Wright *aesthetically* kills for in telling Bigger's "story" hit its mark, drawing not only national but international visibility to the underbelly of the Midwest's industrialism, disentangling that situation from the convoluted politics of region that governed the nation's racial imaginary.

If internalized racism's lies take root in "a region in" the "mind" (J. Baldwin *The Fire*, 296), an image Baldwin borrowed from *Native Son*, Wright's novel was clearly the tale of that region's arrested development, mapped onto the industrial growth of the Midwest. As case studies of the nation's regional complex, which was also a racial complex, Farrell's and Wright's novels articulated into a larger political allegory of social conflict on national and global fronts, one that was shared by those Midwestern Bildungsromane covered in previous chapters. Like a storm in a teacup, the Midwest's social extremes and contrasting environments contained rich material for novelists scanning for more precise methods of narrating the uneven development of man in national-historical time.

Part II

The Northeast's Young Aesthetes

CHAPTER 4

Emplacing Modernism: The Fitzgeralds and the Artist's Regional Complex

Given the close historic association between Anglo-American modernism and New York City, critical engagement with novels about the Northeast tend to focus on those representations of modernity and the metropolis that purportedly revolted against local color fiction there. Influential literary critic Carl Van Doren praised young writers like F. Scott Fitzgerald for rejecting the stultifying provincialism of "Old Style" local color fiction by writers such as Sarah Orne Jewett and Pauline Hopkins, a post-1919 shift demarcated as the American novel's "New Style," the unifying logic of which was its "revolt from the village" (173). This aesthetic of newness was predicated on a geographical shift from old New England to the Northeast's ascendant mecca of cosmopolitan modernism: New York. Usurping Boston as the functional central nervous system of the nation's cultural life, where the majority of writing, publishing, and circulation of high literature was said to occur, "New York publishes" America's decentralized literature, "criticizes it, and circulates it, but I doubt if New York society much reads it or cares for it," and is thus not "the literary center that Boston once was, though a large number of our literary men live in or about it," William Dean Howells lamented in 1902 (179). Literary culture thus became associated with the development of a cultural nationalism intended to replace local color's stultifying regionalisms by satirizing, ironizing, and ultimately rejecting small-town America. Its five boroughs accommodating a population of 7 million by 1930, eclipsing the birthplace of the skyscraper, Chicago, with a population of 3.4 million (Dennis 21), New York's unbridled growth exploded the nineteenth-century novel's character network. Its concentration of literary culture seemed to open the borders of regionalist fiction to more culturally porous transnationalist aesthetics. The city's "impressive structures" that were "planned specifically as symbolic expressions of modernity," in Marshall Berman's words, offered on the one hand "the reassuring authenticity of permanently assembled history usable by art," yet on the other were "still in that process of quick formation which is modern art's parallel and incentive" (289). As a "port to America" and "to the world," New York formed the emblematic theater of cosmopolitan modernism (Douglas *Terrible Honesty*, 58).

As a subgenre that narrates developments in how culture is produced and valued within a given society, the Künstlerroman registered more complex dynamics than afforded by the traditional narrative of metropolitan modernism. That genre recognized how the modernist mythologies of the cosmopolitan metropolis overwrote the local geocultural landscape and mode of cultural production and exchange connecting Manhattan to other parts of the nation, including the internal contradictory, competing regionalisms those metropolitan myths both repressed and perpetuated. Sara Blair has suggested of modernist Bloomsbury that as an "object of critical attention," it invites closer examination of its function "as a local world," including "the specific circuits of production and exchange in which its work and works participate," and "the geocultural landscape in which they unfold" (814). Künstlerromane about New York City's modernist cultural revolution often invited such closer examinations by presenting a young aspiring artist from farther afield who struggles to integrate into that vertiginous new cultural and political order, succumbing to the idleness of metropolitan life. As the Great War precipitated expanded federal powers from circa 1917, a renewed push to imagine the national center from the vantage of everyday, local life occurred, this time, with cynicism. This return to the scene of the local resulted from the administration's careening imperialism, including President Woodrow Wilson's divisive military interference in Haiti; the legal hardening of Jim Crow within and beyond the South, as well as the resurgence of the Ku Klux Klan, which incited white-supremacist terrorism in the nation's bloody summer of race riots in 1919; the anticommunism surrounding the Red Scare of 1919 and 1920, including the incarceration and deportation of left-wing organizers; rising antisemitism and xenophobia, flames of hate that were fanned by anti-immigration policies directed at Irish, German, Italian, Russian, and Jewish migrants, i.e., those ethnic diasporas Wilson notoriously labeled the "hyphenated Americans"; and the growth of organized crime in response to Prohibition. Wartime patriotism buoyed Americanism but also perpetuated disillusionment in national politics within the production of youth culture, which was not exclusively metropolitan, but tended to be more accessible in densely populated areas. "In cities, the young preferred to party their way through a time of newly intense self-awareness and absurd self-deception," Michael L. Lasser observes (154). Northeastern centers like New York and Atlantic City formed havens for youth culture's consumption, manic idleness, political inattention, and no less crucially, rootlessness.

Young artists, including the Fitzgeralds, took the figure of artistic youth as the hero of the new cultural order that was modernism, challenging the traditionalism of the Victorians; it was a revival of the earlier cultural revolution of youth that spurred the original Young American in Literature movement (coined by Emerson in the late 1840s to describe what became the American Literary Renaissance) based in New England, a period many literary critics were returning to after the popularization of Van Wyck Brooks's literary critical retrospective, *America's Coming of Age* (1915). Writing of how Joyce's *A Portrait of the Artist as a Young Man* evolved the Bildungsroman tradition, James T. Farrell noted how the vicissitudes of late nineteenth-century life encouraged a shift in the European Bildungsroman's previous emphasis on fame and success—for example, the writer character Lucien of Honoré de Balzac's *Lost Illusions*—to narratives about the "young man seeking freedom in the realm of feeling and culture." The

> character of public life changes and decreases the opportunities to be free. The idea of culture (as the realm of freedom) begins to grow. Thus, the logic of art for art's sake. The artist, crushed by the weight of contemporary

culture, adopts the attitude that art is its own end, becomes the rebel artist. (Farrell *The League*, 57)

One way in which the young artist rebelled was in their so-called "revolt from the village," according to Van Doren; but this rebellion left the young artist who felt cynicism toward the nation's aesthetic and political destiny to deliberate what might replace that stabilizing *place* in forms like the Bildungsroman, which had previously relied on that neat representability offered by regional characters, scenes, and plots. New York, even more so than Chicago, posed a wholly unrepresentable place. As discussed in Chapter 1, what "a man like Hurstwood could be in Chicago," *Sister Carrie*'s narrator informs us, "he would be but an inconspicuous drop in an ocean like New York" (Dreiser *Sister Carrie*, 245); unlike Carrie, whose incredible artistic successes on New York City's Great White Way unsettle the novel's verisimilitude by accelerating the timeline of her growth beyond what *vraisemblance* would allow.[1] Artists, too, were compelled to reconsider the relationship between character and social forms, by experimenting with new ways of representing development and mobility across both newer and more traditional social spaces.

Though the Künstlerroman can be traced back to the earliest developments of the Western novel, its narrative preconditions underwent a critical reorganization during the modernist period, when urbanism and the structures of mass production disrupted bourgeois concepts of creativity, genius, and aesthetic value. "The modernist *Kunstlerroman* works as a rarefied endgame for the novel of youth, with its artist protagonist committed to ceaseless change outside the normalizing routines of family, courtship, and vocation," writes Jed Esty (224n). That subgenre also self-referentially chronicled the processes driving modernist culture itself, in which narratives about developing artists—often not "native" to the metropolis that tests their artistic mettle—reflect differing regional

---

[1] Dreiser and Mencken were, in Fitzgerald's words, "the greatest men living in the country today." Dreiser's embarrassed millionaire Hurstwood inspired Fitzgerald's Anthony Patch of *The Beautiful and Damned*. He insisted to his editor Perkins in 1924 that Hurstwood and his own Tom Buchanan were two of the "best characters in American fiction" (qtd in Kruse *Fitzgerald at Work*, 96).

responses to the large-scale cultural mobilization that postwar patriotism brought to the forefront of public life, including widespread anxiety over the erasure of the local within the homogenization of mass culture. As the following two chapters investigate, the Künstlerroman's narrative delivers a "testing for artistic genius and, in parallel, the artist's fitness for life," according to Bakhtin (*Speech Genres*, 16). As the region was forming a new American literary integrative network combining heterogenous regional and transnational influences, as opposed to an assimilative nation center that combined all those influences into the one homogenous cultural mass, the Northeast formed an ideal setting for the test of the regional artist's "genius" and "fitness for life," in ways it had done since the nineteenth century. For, the untested artist who is shuttled away from their regional outposts brings fresh perspectives to a cultural revolution already underway. Their development thus allegorizes the "new" Northeast as an industrial vacuum absorbing the heterogeneities of "our decentralized literature" (Howells 177), as it shifted from provincial New England to metropolitan New York.

The regional imaginary of the Northeast in the Künstlerroman of the 1920s constructed long-range allegories of the region's shifting balance in the cultural order, as "provincial" New England's role as the nation's cultural hegemon shifted to "metropolitan" New York. Often, these allegories were managed through representations of a central young artist figure whose childhood is associated with regionalism and traditionalism, who negotiates their destiny among an immense forum of other artists who have likewise been lured to New York City, the pantheon of avant-garde modernist cultural production. These modernist developments were not defined by the erasure of local color and the rejection of literary regionalism as such, but rather emerged out of the collapsing of presumed differences between different regionalisms, and the heterogenous rural and metropolitan social formations they housed. The modernist Künstlerroman that narrativizes the cultural revolution emanating out of the Northeast, as a result, creates a peripatetic geography of mass production to make sense of the new position of the artist in a rapidly reorganizing national and global order. Scanning for innovative forms, characters, and narratives, the peripatetic artist comes to know themselves through regional difference, and their artistic development hinges on finding an aesthetics of "the new" that comprehensively represented the disorienting flux of modernity's uneven geographies.

The young artist hero often featured in topical debates of the 1920s over the future of American literature: the young aesthete, for example the Fitzgeralds; or the young New Negro, such as Jessie Redmon Fauset and Wallace Thurman. Unlike other subcategories of the Bildungsroman that are distinguished by plot and theme, the Künstlerroman is defined by a particular character type: the developing artist, who became one rebellious hero of the late nineteenth-century novel, as it contemplated the possibility of a post-nationalist modernity. That development is subject to the character of public life and the opportunities for artistic freedom. As opposed to naturalism's reliance on sociological types and deterministic plots, the artist novel ontologically relies on individualism and character development, and historically did "not feature average protagonists" (Mazzoni 267). The development formulation of the artist registers the artistic traditions the character will either conform to or reject, one reason why the Künstlerroman historically provided a useful testbed for tracking the changes modernity brought upon both art and the social role of the artist. "The developmental formulation itself is primarily a plot formulation rather than a character formulation," argue Phelan, Scholes, and Kellogg, as it regards "seeing the character at a long range, with limited detail, so that his change against a particular background may be readily apparent" (168). This is not necessarily the case in the modernist Künstlerroman, which often conveyed the artistic protagonist's unfolding development stylistically, rather than rely on the Bildungsroman's traditional narrative arc.

The following two chapters narrate the 1920s cultural revolution of the Northeast, from the perspective of young regional aesthetes at the center of four key Künstlerromane: Fitzgerald's *This Side of Paradise* (1920) and Zelda Fitzgerald's *Save Me the Waltz* (1932); and Jessie Redmon Fauset's *Plum Bun* (1928) and Wallace Thurman's *Infants of the Spring* (1932), two significant works of the New Negro Renaissance. These novels followed the same critical geography: a young character from a parochial regional outpost—either within the Northeast, or elsewhere—arrives in New York City looking to acquire a modern, cosmopolitan identity by joining the culture of rootlessness and newness flowering there, and instead finds themselves "tested" in Bakhtin's sense by the many unforeseen distractions. These novels simultaneously drew upon avant-garde technological innovations and forms made widely available during the 1920s, borrowing character models from film, theater, variety hall entertainment, modern dance, popular music, and visual art, interleaving these influences with regionalist tropes to stylistically test and suggest where the novel fit into the new media ecology and geocultural landscape. Although these Künstlerromane internalized and legitimized the Northeast region's cultural centralization, they self-reflexively insisted that these activities were peculiarly responsive to modernity's uneven geographies. The narrative determinants by which the Künstlerroman is defined—namely, the testing of the artist's "genius" and "fitness for life"—unfold in these novels through the artist's reflections on the tenuous dynamic between the local and universal impulses of modernism, as they attempt to reconcile their individual creative instincts and ambitions with the circuits of artistic production and exchange unique to mass culture.

Fitzgerald's *This Side of Paradise* (1920)

Although Fitzgerald was a Midwesterner by birth, and a nomad by nature (he was raised in St. Paul Minnesota; spent most winters outside of Washington D.C.; had relations in rural Maryland, where he often holidayed; trained in the armed forces adjoining Montgomery, Alabama, where he later lived with his wife, Zelda; and only lived in New York for a short period of his adulthood), his novels have long been construed as reinforcing the old-fashioned argument that modernism only thrived on the metropolitanism Manhattan fostered in the 1920s, which purportedly relied on the refusal of metropolitanism's antithesis: the regional imaginary. Few novels better "illustrate the moving tide of which the revolt from the village is a symptom than the presence of such unrest as this among these bright barbarians" in Fitzgerald's novel *This Side of Paradise* (1920), Van Doren noted, which he attributed to its depiction of youth who "play among the ruins of the old" and "reason randomly about the new, laughing" (173). No longer simply a precocious boy from St. Paul, Fitzgerald's first novel reputedly placed him among those "Western youth" who were instructed that "Art ... is something far away, and literary subjects must be something select and very civilized," as Hamlin Garland observed of regionalism and literary value in 1894 (14).

Fitzgerald's career as a serious writer, cosmopolite, and relatedly an 'ex-Midwesterner' thus seemingly confirmed the stereotypical allegory of American modernism as "liberated from provincialism and local allegiances, caught up in an ambivalent but creatively productive relationship with the fluctuating currents of modernity and modernization," a definition which critics such as Alexander and Moran argue neglects the regionalist tendencies within modernism (1). Like many modernist writers, Fitzgerald and his partner Zelda Sayre—from Montgomery, Alabama—have often been portrayed as icons of metropolitan modernism; yet their fiction appears preoccupied with the untidy local entanglements and regional affiliations that structured their own lives. After the success of *This Side of Paradise*, they soon became key figures in the establishment of the Northeast's new anti-provincialist cult of artistic celebrity and Flapper youth culture (Douglas *Terrible Honesty*, 58–9). As they commoditized their views on what it was to be a young American artist in the Jazz Age in stories and press clippings, Manhattan formed a useful muse for their portraits of the post-regional modernist artist after the fad of local color had supposedly played itself out, according to *The Nation*'s September 1919 editorial. Instead, the couple became associated with a transcontinental group of "lost" (read: geographically delocalized) modernists, as their social director of sorts Gertrude Stein famously dubbed them. That cosmopolitan collective convened in New York, London, and Paris, metropolises that were ostensibly disconnected from any definitive national heredities, and certainly not connected to any regional ones. In his art novels, Fitzgerald made a career out of the narrative possibilities of character and event that were offered to him by the cultural hegemony of New York, as it was imagined to be a cosmopolitan port to a rootless, global modernism. While it is tempting to assume that this self-mythologization of the author as an unfixed young aesthete might have erased local or regional aesthetics from his writing, in what follows I demonstrate that this was not the case—certainly not in terms of his first novel.

In the geographical imaginary of *This Side*, region plays a dynamic role—at times accelerating or decelerating the artist protagonist's growth, while stabilizing his development in an increasingly interconnected, yet fractured world. Such an interpretation places Fitzgerald's modernism in dialogue with recent regionalist approaches to studying emplacement in the new modernist studies, such as Andrew Thacker's argument that we ought not view location "simply as the place where modernism . . . ends up after its travels," but as facilitating "a dynamic role in the constitution of modernism in a way that does not seem that different from the model conceived . . . by certain proponents of transnationalism" (13). The debut novel of an unpublished Princeton drop-out, belonging to the "history of a young man" genre, *This Side* features a plot that appears to be entirely about a young Midwesterner's literary "revolt from the village," at least at first glance. A prodigious, white, bourgeois youth from Minnesota, Amory Blaine attends Princeton, romances beautiful debutantes, and attempts to gain entry into the Northeastern elite. However, in contemplation of his future career, Amory succumbs to blind disillusionment in the future of the nation's literature. Yet, upon closer inspection, the novel's geographic re-engineering of the Künstlerroman considerably exceeds this classic reading. Fitzgerald found new formal possibilities by charting the young, peripatetic protagonist's development across various regional lines, including the Midwest, South, and Northeast, contributing to an overall effect of stylistic unevenness in conveying the artist's troubled identity, at an age when he is most at risk of conforming to a quixotic cultural nationalism rooted in 100% Americanism. Throughout his social and artistic awakening, Amory shuttles between his provincial childhood home in the Midwest, the old culture of New Jersey and New York City's Upper East Side, and the decadent entertainment of Atlantic City, Greenwich Village, and Broadway, making various other detours along the way. Amory Blaine's mobility thus suggests how the seemingly stabilizing properties of regional identity interpenetrated rather than anchored the more fluid, yet uncertain, spatial dynamics of cosmopolitan modernism. *This Side* discloses a far more involved geographic imaginary than has previously been attributed to Fitzgerald's novels, while echoing wartime debates over nationalism and the future of the American novel.

By the early 1920s, Fitzgerald was conceiving of a solution to the exhaustion of the American history of the young man novel and the moribund aesthetics of local color that irked him. In a vitriolic letter in early 1921 to Thomas Boyd, literary editor of the local newspaper *St. Paul Daily News*, Fitzgerald lamented how the development of the artist novel had become the most "overworked art-form at present in America" (qtd in Thomas 68). He abjured Floyd Dell's *Moon-Calf* (1920), a semi-autobiographical Bildungsroman about an alienated young radical named Felix Fay from the economically impoverished Midwestern provinces, whose aesthetic horizons inevitably pull his "tramping steps" toward the "dark blotch in the corner" of his cultural map, "Chicago! Chicago!" (Dell 346).[2] Fitzgerald opined that clearly, the "writing of a young man's novel consists chiefly in dumping all your youthful adventures into the reader's lap with a profound air of importance, keeping carefully within the formulas of Wells and James Joyce," meaning that when the genre is attempted "without distinction of style it reaches the depths of banality" (Fitzgerald qtd in Thomas 68). If an author was to ascend to the heights of Joyce's *A Portrait of the Artist as a Young Man* (1916)—a novel that *This Side*'s itinerant artist protagonist Amory Blaine reads and finds bewildering—a stylistic intervention was required. The writer would need to emulate Joyce's formal innovativeness via his portrayal of a young character developing over time—and space—through stylistic changes, and not merely rework its plot by mapping the aesthetics of cynical localism onto the Bildungsroman's biographical time.

Inauthentic depictions of life in the regions, the main obstruction to the development of a serious national tradition in literature, were also resulting in the increasing banality of the Künstlerroman genre, in Fitzgerald's esteem. In one 1925 letter to his editor and

---

[2] Dell—remembered for editing the radical periodicals *The Masses* and *The Liberator* from Greenwich Village—began his career editing the Illinois-based little magazine *Friday Literary Review*, which published critical regionalists including Dreiser, Carl Sandburg, and Sherwood Anderson (Spears *Chicago Dreaming*, 213-19).

friend, Maxwell Perkins, Fitzgerald savagely ridiculed the hollowness of Tom Boyd's latest regionalist novel for having "discovered" the patriotic figure of the American peasant, "WHO IS, CLOSE, TO SOIL, AND . . . 'STRONG! VITAL! REAL!'"—only a decade after Robert Frost, Sherwood Anderson, Willa Cather, and Eugene O'Neill "exhausted" that local color "type" (Fitzgerald *A Life in Letters*, 119). Fitzgerald observed that this sociological type constituted "scarcely 10% of the population . . . and if possessing any sensitivity whatsoever," was "in the towns before he's twenty" (119). Such inauthentic representations of rural local color—unlike the authentic regionalism of Sherwood Anderson's *Winesberg, Ohio*, for instance—constituted a "stubborn seeking for the static in a world that for almost a hundred years has simply not been static" (119). Genuine literary geniuses, namely Edith Wharton, Henry James, and above all Gertrude Stein, realized that to "have a respect for people whose materials may not touch theirs at a single point" does not mean that they must, like "fourth rate + highly derivative people like Tom [Boyd]," reuse "the old, old bag" of the usable past that is "bound to the soil" through trite local color (119). Perkins had misread Boyd's "mere earnestness" in representing a static, immovable local America "for sincerity" (120).

After Joyce, Fitzgerald found that the artist character needed to serve as a sincere representation of the developmental processes of a character achieved through psychological realism; the artist character must also stylistically register the uneven development of an artist who becomes metaphysically dislocated once he absconds from the region of his childhood. In *This Side*, a *roman-à-clef* based on the author's own adolescence, the novel's formal experiments in high modernist narration clearly reinforce the novelist's incipient cognitive mapping of an undeveloped artist character whose artistic maturity transpires across an unstable geographical framework of contradictory regional codes. Many modernists were experimenting with new stylistic effects for conveying interiority, inner development, and the dialectical relationship between consciousness and the unconscious. Fitzgerald explored similar narrative techniques for conveying the protagonist's unconscious preoccupation with uneven development, his entire identity being shaped around his unfolding sense of the modernizing relationship between literature and the regional imaginary. In other words, *This Side* formalizes the protagonist's aesthetic maturation through its stylistic unevenness, thus insisting upon the unsettled dynamic between the protagonist's regional identity and his widening relationship to the world. The young egoist's movements across uneven and contradictory regional, national, and global heterotopias, as well as his unhappy realization that he has seen too much of the world and cannot return to his provincial youth, capture the warp and weft of modernity through stylistic inchoateness, structural fragmentation, and narratorial experimentalism. *This Side* speaks self-referentially to modernist formal experimentations that attempted in Pound's words to "Make it new!," thereby uncovering—as Theodor Adorno surmised—the unsettling possibility of "whether anything new had ever existed" (*Aesthetic Theory*, 19).

Fitzgerald portrays regional characteristics—e.g., accents, vernacular, or mannerisms—in contemptuous, unsentimental portraits of the middle-class Midwest in the opening chapters. Amory's characterization initially relies upon reproducing views of regionalism that his mother Beatrice Blaine impresses upon him, views that he will later attempt, and fail, to repress. Beatrice's diatribes to Amory reveal how "The Blaines were attached to no city. They were the Blaines of Lake Geneva; they had quite enough relatives to serve in place of friends, and an enviable standing from Pasadena to Cape Cod" (Fitzgerald *This Side*, 5). Cosmopolitan and yet provincial, Beatrice instills in her son a critical but disordered cultural compass. Her condescending view of regional character is exemplified in her description of the delocalized accents of "American women," "especially the floating population of ex-Westerners" who frequent Lake Geneva (6). However, what she appears to abhor most are these women's attempts to repress their own regionality:

> "They have accents, my dear . . . not Southern accents or Boston accents, not an accent attached to any locality, just an accent"—she became dreamy. "They pick up old, moth-eaten London accents . . . They talk as an English butler might after several years in a Chicago grand-opera company." She became almost incoherent—"Suppose—time in every Western woman's life—she feels her husband is prosperous enough for her to have—accent—they try to impress me, my dear—" (6)

Beatrice's satirical description in fact reveals the instability of localist aesthetics, challenging the nationalistic discourse of wartime America, which attempted to stabilize and solidify what had previously been only an abstract civic pride in the solidity of local culture. Beatrice's attempts to broaden her son's cultural education bring them to the port of New York, from which they intend to sail for Italy; however, fate traps him inside his narrow regional framework when his appendix bursts four hours into the trip and they are forced to return to shore, foreshadowing Amory's artistic struggles to come:

> Beatrice had a nervous breakdown that bore a suspicious resemblance to delirium tremens, and Amory was left in Minneapolis . . . There the crude, vulgar air of Western civilization first catches him—in his underwear, so to speak. (7)

The incident is a metaphor for the push-and-pull between localism and cosmopolitan worldliness that Amory will oscillate between for the entirety of the novel. Despite initially finding himself caught within a parochial social network in Minneapolis, this event makes Amory realize that culture and education are passports to other parts of the country and world, and thus determines to acquire more of these qualifications. As a precocious thirteen-year-old, Amory's geographical compass turns steadily northeast toward New York, as the financial and cultural capital of the United States, an essential theater for insisting upon the modernist artist's central role in narrativizing and contending with modernity's crisis of subjectivity, at a time when mass culture and morality laws were undermining the viability and autonomy of high art.

In establishing the artist character's Midwestern regional background as a constraining force inhibiting his artistic development, Fitzgerald was simultaneously locating the "testing" of his protagonist's "genius" and his "fitness for life" in the Northeast, leaving the Midwestern ingénue vulnerable to the unnarratable flux of newness converging within that region. Fitzgerald designed a character whose true artistic development occurs only at the level of style as opposed to plot; a technique Joyce pioneered in *Portrait*—a novel Amory reads in 1917, leaving him "puzzled and depressed" (192). *This Side* is structured into two books of four and five chapters respectively, with a short epistolary interlude containing Amory's letters to his friend Tom D'Invilliers and mentor Monsieur Darcy while deployed overseas with the U.S. infantry from 1917–1919. Although Fitzgerald interchanges the terms egoist and egotist throughout the novel, in titling the opening section as "The Romantic Egotist"[3] he clearly aligns himself with Ezra Pound's transformative vision for Dora Marsden's feminist literary publication, *The Egoist*.[4] Amory's artistic development emanates not in narrative, but in the style of the prose, responding to Joyce's technical invention in *Portrait*, which was serialized in *The Egoist*. But what Fitzgerald represents—especially in the scenes set in Princeton, which comprise roughly a third of the novel—is modernism's assault on the immovable, encrusted cultural chronotopes of Northeastern cultural supremacy, as the "new" filters in through New York City's cosmopolitan and regional cultural interfaces. Unlike the fixed New York setting of *The Beautiful and Damned* (1922), *This Side*'s events wander all over the Midwest, Northeast, and South. Fitzgerald represents the effects of modernism's transformations on the North's cultural hegemony, and the filtration of these vicissitudes into the regional cultures beyond the State of New York, observing the shift away from sentimental local color to the purportedly delocalized tenets of modernism.

Amory internalizes Beatrice's contradictory beliefs regarding place and culture value. He furthermore inherits his mother's method for dealing with her unshakable dissatisfaction with her region's cultural mediocrity, which is to repress it through liquor and impulsive spending. These matrilineal traits become starker in the wake of his father's death, during Amory's time at Princeton. Amory uncovers in the family ledger that she has not only burned through her own dowry but has also outspent what her husband earned on purchases including several expensive cars and transpor-

---

[3] Fitzgerald is also referencing George Meredith's influential novel *The Egoist* (1879), which critiqued women's role in Victorian society as the headstrong Clara Middle struggles to disengage from the egoistic Sir Willoughby Patterned.

[4] Amory seemingly espouses T. S. Eliot's landmark essay, "Tradition and the Individual Talent," published in *The Egoist* in 1919. He also references the institutional suspicion toward Pound's *Cathay* (138).

tation stocks: "'I am quite sure,' [Beatrice] wrote to Amory, 'that if there is one thing we can be positive of, it is that people will not stay in one place. This Ford person has certainly made the most out of that idea'" (93). Swept up in the desideratum of infinite mobility that the transportation revolution represents to her, she instructs the family's alarmed financial adviser, Mr. Barton, to "'specialize on such things [investments] as Northern Pacific and these Rapid Transit Companies, as they call the street-cars,'" and implores her son to go into finance (93). Amory's mobility appears driven by his mother's fear of emplacement: of becoming inert, trapped in a parochial regional framework.

In addition to his family estate in Lake Geneva, the campus of Princeton University in Mercer County, New Jersey forms a base from which Amory's many adventures spring as he avoids such inertia; there are scenes located in New York, Atlantic City in New Jersey, Philadelphia, Maryland, and various locations in Minnesota. Nevertheless, the most formative "non-events" in Amory's life take place in New York, in moments when he abandons his cultural and moral edification—the primary focus of the classic Künstlerroman—because he is "distracted" by the city's many intoxicating diversions. In these episodes, the novel's most ambitious formal experimentations with character take shape, and Fitzgerald's disjointed use of fragmentation and free indirect discourse enables him to show Amory internalizing the city's composite cultural networks, even if that egoist character is unconscious of his own unfolding artistic development. Amory's reluctant absorption of the Bohemianism that threatens to supplant the cultural hegemony of the old New England order is foiled by Tanaduke Wylie, a classmate who gradually disappears into the disreputable "futurist" Bohemianism of 42nd Street and Broadway, off Times Square. The "old Princeton," closed-off from the heightened mobility of modernity, "would never have discovered Tanaduke Wylie," the narrator indicates; but in Greenwich Village, "Tanaduke's genius absorbed the many colors of the age, and he took to the Bohemian life, to their great disappointment," in ways Amory finds difficult to comprehend while still creatively under the guise of a Princeton alumni (96). Tanaduke, alternatively, "talked of Greenwich Village now" instead of "noon-swirled moons," and "met winter muses, unacademic, and cloistered by Forty-second Street and Broadway, instead of the Shelleyan dream-children with whom he had regaled their expectant appreciation" (98), foreshadowing Amory's trip to Broadway in Manhattan shortly thereafter, where in a fit of Dionysian revelry he feels the fire of sin consume him and believes he encounters the devil (105–6).

In these ventures, Fitzgerald stages the unfolding process of Amory's artistic development in the Northeast through different styles that were the product of his own artistic interests in film and theater, deploying these styles as part of the wider map Fitzgerald is drawing of the contrasting cultural spaces through which the peripatetic Amory passes. Fitzgerald transposed the "dynamism" he "associated with the stage" into his fiction: with its "inflated dialogue," "emotional extremity," the "literal use of dramatic staging and presentation," the "abrupt [cutting] between scenes," a "relative disregard for the unities of time and place," and an "overarching variety-hall aesthetic," argues T. Austin Graham (22). Looking both to the dynamic potentiality of character in live theater and the logic of mechanical fragmentation in pre-montage film narrative as analogical maps for a characterological modernism, Fitzgerald engineers a style of novel that creates a critical geography of the "old" and "new" cultural orders, to calibrate its own place in the broadening media ecology.[5] Fitzgerald registers his ambivalence toward the rise of the "new media" in Amory's fears that he will find himself "lost in a clerkship, for the next and best ten years of my life"—a developmental possibility he derides as having "the intellectual content of an industrial movie" (Fitzgerald *This Side*, 198). Fitzgerald's splicing of literary approaches to character with those in film and theater was a necessary intervention to protect the novel form's dissolution into the warp and weft of mass culture—those same forces Fitzgerald would later capitalize upon as a magazine serialist and Hollywood screenwriter.

Fitzgerald's novel further narrates how federal politics increas-

---

[5] Like many modernists, in 1917 Fitzgerald read Henri Bergson, William James, and Arthur Schopenhauer; viewed D. W. Griffith's nationalist epics and Charlie Chaplin's comedies; listened to Irving Berlin; and explored New York's vaudeville, musical comedy, and theater scene (Raubicheck and Goldleaf 303).

ingly impacted on local life in the context of WWI, in ways that were having transformative effects on culture and identity. The year 1917 sees nativist patriotism—that is, ambient racism, anticommunism, and xenophobia—sweep across Amory's Princeton cohort, as the young scholars prepare to defer their studies and enlist in the armed forces. Only a few "Bohemian New York" rebels, pacifists like Amory's socialist classmate Burn Holiday, turn instead to the political line of "socialist magazines" and Tolstoy (135). Amory fails to convince Burn to resign from radical politics, which he suspects are being funded by pro-German spies (136–7). Before he meets Burn for the last time, Amory travels to Washington to enlist, taking the regional train, upon which the nativist "hysteria" catches up with him. He becomes overwhelmed by

> the spirit of crisis which changed to repulsion in the Pullman car coming back, for the berths across from him were occupied by stinking aliens—Greeks, he guessed, or Russians. He thought how much easier it would have been to fight as the Colonies fought, or as the Confederacy fought. And he did no sleeping that night, but listened to the aliens guffaw and snore while they filled the car with the heavy scent of latest America. (134–5)

Black Americans and Woodrow Wilson's "hyphenated Americans"—an abstract sociological type with no actual basis in geography—form easy strawmen onto which Amory can project his trepidations about the sudden interference of national destiny and world progress in his personal destiny, as both a young man conscripted into war and an aspiring artist without a community. Steadily, his hatred of the Germans brings him to shift the blame onto "the ancestors of his generation," who idolized Schiller and Goethe and "German science and efficiency" (137–8). Yet, his experiences as an aviator in the war effort—obliquely referenced in the four-page "Interlude" section—reflect Amory's broader disillusionment in the American patriotism for which the younger generation have fought and died.

Riding on the wave of that generational disillusionment, the narrative takes a formally radical turn, too; in *The Debutante*, the one-act play contained within *This Side*, the narrator becomes a stage director. The play narrates the drama of Amory's star-crossed courtship of the wealthy debutante living on the Upper East Side, Rosalind Connage, a character partially modeled on Fitzgerald's future wife, Zelda Sayre. The play presents how Rosalind, the primary love interest in the novel, comes to reject her lover Amory over his financial insecurity, prompting his sense of artistic impotence. Describing that character in the format of lengthy stage directions, Rosalind is introduced as no "model character" (156), meaning neither a stereotype nor a morally upright person. Her demeanor is "theatrical" (156), because she resides in a place where, like Princeton, nineteenth-century traditionalism still holds currency: East 68th Street, on the Upper East Side. If Manhattan formed a *"theatre of progress,"* the performance it stages cannot "progress in the conventional sense of dramatic plotting; it can only be the cyclic restatement of a single theme: creation and destruction irrevocably interlocked, endlessly re-enacted," Rem Koolhaas observes (13–15). Given how the novel's integration of a one-act play is set in this location, it explicitly contributes to Fitzgerald's overall prognostication that traditional character "no longer seems tenable," that "identity is performed and relatively unstable," a shift that "appears as a move from [*regional*] 'character' to [*metropolitan*] 'personality'" in this novel (James 3). Amory's attraction to the unobtainable Rosalind mirrors the nature of the environment in which their affair transpires: the Upper East Side's playground of the *nouveau riche*. "By the 1910s," writes Mike Wallace, "Fifth Avenue, from Rockefeller to Carnegie" and "the side streets of the 60s, 70s, and 80s that stretched east from Central Park" became the district of new millionaires, "piled into mansions," living virtually on top of their neighbors who were "stockbrokers, department store owners, commercial bankers, mine owners, real-estate moguls, railroad entrepreneurs, oil magnates, insurance executives—and the out-of-town monied" (294–5). The architects designing the new townhouses and converted brownstones were also social architects facilitating that class's "pretensions to cultural as well as economic hegemony;" in 1902, architectural critic Herbert Croly recognized that the new millionaire was attracted to buildings that suggested "time and stability," stemming from his desire to "emancipate his children and his fellow countrymen from the reproach of being raw and new" (Wallace 295). The rapid development of the city's affluent neighborhoods—which was more than partially financed by the industrial development of the regional hinterlands—was thus masked by illusive aesthetics of temporal depth, evoking a stable cultural past that never existed.

The mixed appearances and essences of that milieu force Amory to confront not only his cultural traditionalism, but furthermore, his aesthetic provincialism, as it grates against the city's modernizing features on the one hand, and, on the other, the architectural features of upper Manhattan that falsely suggest the historic depth and stability of the ruling class's claim there, as noted above. This situation forces Amory to choose between recycling the theme and remaining a *personality* or escalating the intensity of the performance to become a feted *character*. Amory chooses the latter, as he staggers into the world of Manhattan's elite. At this point, Fitzgerald chooses to dramatize Amory's experiences as he flirts with Rosalind in "No Man's Land" (her bedroom):

> HE: I'd like to have some stock in the corporation.
> SHE: Oh it's not a corporation—it's just "Rosalind, Unlimited." Fifty-one shares, name, good will and everything goes at $25,000 a year. (159)

Both the talk of dowries and the use of scripted dialogue implicate the immovable class operations at play in the structure of New York's elite. Throughout the novel, Fitzgerald characterizes Amory's different approaches to courtship with different women by creating conceptual links between the choice of experimental stylistic effects he uses, and the geographical connotations they conjure; for example, in his jejune romance in Maryland with Eleanor later in the novel, whom he woos by reading her romantic poetry, Amory contemplates why he "didn't at all feel like a character in a play, the appropriate feeling in an unconventional situation," as he had done in Rosalind's Upper East Side world (210). In the Upper East Side sections, then, the dramatic form serves on the one hand to ironize the most quotidian, bourgeois Bildungsroman plot device: the young hero's "Philistine" romance, the first of a series of trials on his regular path into adulthood, the destination of which Hegel described as "domestic affliction" and "the headaches of the rest of married folk" (Hegel 593). Yet, the use of dramatic staging further acts as a signature of formal atavism: a kind of metaphoric mimesis simulating the encrusted social forms of the Upper East Side environment, an elite world built on class pretension, cultural theatricality, and the architectural denial of its historical shallowness; a class the Midwestern ingénue wanders into only by "kismet." At the same time, Fitzgerald inadvertently presaged the hybrid artform Virginia Woolf would prophesize regarding the future of the novel: the "cannibal, the novel, which has devoured so many forms of art . . . will be dramatic, and yet not a play. It will be read, not acted" (Woolf 224).[6]

These tidings are also explicitly tied to the repression of regional affiliation as a core part of the developing artist's character and identity. In the following chilly exchange, for example, Amory's rival for Rosalind's affections, Gillespie, attempts to remind Rosalind of the Midwestern youth's provinciality, which, in this society, is equivalent to a character flaw:

> GILLESPIE: I've met Mr. Blaine. From Lake Geneva, aren't you? [. . .]
> (*Desperately*) I've been there. It's in the—the Middle West, isn't it?
> AMORY: (*Spicily*) Approximately. But I always felt that I'd rather be provincial hot-tamale than soup without seasoning. (168)

Gillespie's embarrassed stutter betrays the Northeastern elite's feelings toward the city's many newcomers from the Middle West, provoking Amory's sudden impassioned regionalism, which contradicts many of his earlier avowals of apathy toward the region. This exchange reveals the motivation for Amory's turn to Rosalind and New York's high society, which is driven by his desire to "overcome" his reprehensible regional roots, to broaden his opportunities through the acquisition of "global" culture that only the Northeast can facilitate, to engage in the broader cultural project of rootlessness often attributed to one canonical view of modernism.

---

[6] Theatrical intermediality became one defining feature of the modernist novel, reshaping the possibilities of the form. Fitzgerald's method antedates Joyce's *Ulysses* (1922), Jean Toomer's *Cane* (1923), Woolf's *Between the Acts* (1941), Faulkner's *Requiem for a Nun* (1951), and several Flann O'Brien novels.

It is the act of becoming a writer—not by writing, but by assuming the cultural capital that such a character plays in the nation's rapidly evolving culture industry—that will write him into the same social circle as Rosalind, despite his provincial roots:

> ROSALIND: What are you going to do?
> AMORY: Can't say—run for President, write—
> ROSALIND: Greenwich Village?
> AMORY: Good heavens, no—I said write—not drink. (169)

But unfortunately, Amory is not a successful author, not least because he is yet to discover any remarkable, fresh subject to write about: his own youth—as a young, ambitious Midwesterner who relocates to the East Coast in order to become a "personage" (read: an important public character), a narrative not unlike Floyd Dell's *Moon-Calf*, or countless regionalist novels. What Amory needs is a lesson in characterization achieved through style: to write about the only thing this egoist knows—himself—with bold formal inventiveness. Amory's subject's development—like Fitzgerald's—must come into view through the contrasting of the disorienting new places of modern(ist) youth and art with the novel's parochial regional settings.

After Rosalind leaves Amory for wealthier suitors, the Upper East Side farce is abandoned, in favor of anonymous escapades on Broadway, the Lower East Side, the Ritz, and Atlantic City. There, Amory embraces the stereotypical modernist lifestyle he decried in his flirtations with Rosalind—despite having distanced himself from Princeton's avant-garde, like Tanaduke. Fitzgerald negotiates the literary ideal with influences from the popular arts, such as silent film and Broadway productions, as evidenced in one intoxicated episode entitled "Experiments in Convalescence": "His head was whirring and picture after picture was forming and blurring and melting before his eyes . . . as the new alcohol tumbled into his stomach and . . . the isolated pictures began slowly to form a cinema reel of the day before" (184–5). The relationship between celluloid art and literary narratives cut both ways for Fitzgerald; if Hollywood required "'younger good writers' to improve the quality of their films," as Fitzgerald saw it (Seed 87), his novel also indicates that the Bildungsroman must perform "experiments in convalescence" by simulating the perplexing effects as newer and older forms and technologies coalesce, to properly convey the disorienting experiences of modernity.

Many of Amory's excursions reflect the Bildungsroman's "philistine" courtship plot, in Hegel's definition. In Philadelphia, Amory woos his third cousin, the "poverty-stricken" widow Clara Page (another nod to Meredith's novel), whose two girls are raised by "the little colored girl guarding the babies" while she entertains a "houseful of men of an evening" (126). While in Maryland, Amory seduces the intelligent, literary-minded Southerner Eleanor Savage. But the question not only of what it means to be inculcated into national-historical time, as well as a national-historical culture, but how to *represent* that abstraction arises in Amory's misadventure with a prostitute in an Atlantic City hotel—an event that nods to *Portrait of the Artist*. Amory and Alec Connage find themselves indicted under the White-Slave Traffic Act of 1910, legislation prohibiting the transportation of "any woman or girl for the purpose of prostitution or debauchery, or for any other immoral purpose" under federal law. Accompanied by a prostitute, Amory and Alec book into an Atlantic City hotel using New York numberplates, at which point the police swarm: "The burly man regarded Amory contemptuously. 'Didn't you ever hear of the Mann Act? Coming down here with her . . . with a New York license on your car—to a hotel like this'" (229–30). Under the Mann Act, the FBI could police a nationalist agenda based upon moral prohibition, by criminalizing sexual misdemeanors across state jurisdictions. This legislation has aesthetic implications for the Bildungsroman, too; for, while sexual experience is rendered as an implicit rite of passage in the narrative of young manhood, in which the protagonist "sows his wild oats" to seek out his destiny (Hegel), here it is subject to a federal injunction with its moral basis rooted firmly in regional politics; namely, Southern white supremacy and anti-miscegenation laws. While Fitzgerald is not redressing these xenophobic and racist aspects to the law, suddenly Amory's peripatetic pathways are directly constrained by national politics' intrusion upon everyday life, in a way that is suggestive of its increasing role in determining the possible pathways of development.

That event necessitates Rosalind's public announcement of her engagement—appearing in the same national newspaper issue that names and shames Amory for his inadvertent sex-trafficking misadventure in a New Jersey hotel—which triggers Fitzgerald's return to fragmentary, and typically free indirect narration. This stylistic choice assists the author in seizing the inchoate artistic subject let loose upon Manhattan, as he seeks to assert order in a disordered environment. This is where at the beginning of his authorial career, Fitzgerald—a future reluctant, mercenary Hollywood screenwriter (Murphet and Rainford 4)—looks to the character model not only of theater but film, to metaphorize Amory's modernizing perceptions of the cultural world he has inherited as a hero of the postwar younger generation. In 1919, the metropolis resembles "a movie set calling" resident artists like Fitzgerald "to live inside their 'own movie of New York'" (Douglas *Terrible Honesty*, 59). The intermittent use of the free indirect discourse, as well as a one-page experiment in stream of consciousness, serves to represent the action of Amory sinking into despair toward the end of the novel. Even as Amory repudiates the "industrial movie," Fitzgerald's experimentations with stream of consciousness and disjointed narrativization represent the unconscious as if it were shaped by the celluloid arts:

> Somewhere in his mind a conversation began . . . composed not of two voices, but of one, which acted alike as questioner and answerer:
> *Question.*—Well, what's the situation?
> *Answer.*—That I have about twenty-four dollars to my name.
> *Q.*—You have the Lake Geneva estate.
> *A.*—But I intend to keep it. . . . People make money in books and I've found that I can always do the things people do in books. (Fitzgerald *This Side*, 237)

Written like a script, this two-page internal dialogue formalizes the splitting of the character's actantial composition into two antagonistic semes: Q and A. But the theme of the interview is that even a Princeton graduate cannot "make money in books" from Lake Geneva or Minnesota; nor can he survive as a penniless writer in New York City, a geographical dilemma lifted straight off the pages of Fitzgerald's biography. The scene shifts to an establishing shot of a ferry ride along the Hudson River; in the narrator's words, the "dialogue merged into his mind's most familiar state—a grotesque blending of desires, worries, exterior impressions and physical reactions" (238). That disoriented psychic state is formalized through several subsequent paragraphs written in stream of consciousness, simulating the psychological processes of registering the differences between the metropolitan environment and his regional roots: "Apartments along here expensive—probably a hundred and fifty a month—maybe two hundred. Uncle only paid hundred a month for whole great big house in Minneapolis" (239). Not only the subject matter but the style of this episode reinforce the notion that Amory's blind, forward march into the future is also a geographical pathway away from the simple innocence of his childhood and the "paradise" of his years in the Midwest. Anxious at the prospect of the unknown future in a brutal economy, he nevertheless refuses to sell his family's estate, even when desperately impoverished, in a symbolic attempt to recover his lost innocence by retaining the option of returning to the place he associates with childhood, innocence, and the past. Princeton and provincial New Jersey offer backward-looking refuge from the unclear destiny of modernism that Tanaduke Wiley finds in Greenwich Village, while Atlantic City and New York seem to catapult him into a future-oriented metropolitan temporality, where personality and character become confused performances of subjectivity.

The geographical ambivalence Amory embodies mirrors contemporary disputes over the future direction of postwar American literary nationalism and the widely broadcasted "end" to local color. Tom D'Invilliers and Amory's debates regarding capitalism's globalizing effects upon the nation, literature, politics, and their futures, reveal the wandering writer's uncertainty over his geographic affiliation. Amory's most critical monologue emerges from these discussions:

> "Young students try to believe in older authors . . . countries try to believe in their statesmen, but they *can't*. Too many voices, too much scattered, illogical, ill-considered criticism . . . more confusion, more contradiction, a sudden inrush of new ideas, their tempering, their distillation, the reaction against them—" (197)

What Howells hopefully called "our decentralized literature" weighs heavily upon Amory's generation. Unlike his Princeton comrade Burn Holiday, Amory knows virtually nothing of local or national politics to write about; although late in the novel, he confesses in a condescending rant to a New Jersey taxi driver with more parochial, conservative political views that socialism may solve the difficulties his generation faces. But all Amory really knows well enough to narrativize is *himself*, as the final sentences of the novel affirm: "He stretched out his arms to the crystalline, radiant sky. 'I know myself,' he cried, 'but that is all—'" (260). This is as much an egoist's despondent cry as it is an artistic revelation: the unfixed youth, *Amory*, will become Amory's self-referential artistic subject, as much as it became Fitzgerald's. *This Side*'s miscellany form stylistically seizes the young artist's impressions of being an unfinished, unfixed character perambulating across uneven social spaces coded through differing regionalisms, in uncertain times. Amory, like Fitzgerald, will lay the foundational stones of a "new" school of novel imbedded in a cosmopolitan modernist network represented by New York's culture industry rather than in the elite scholarly institutions of the Old North; but his regional complex, the childhood "paradise" to which Amory can never really return even when physically there, haunts those prospects.

Matthew Bruccoli describes *This Side*'s "loose form" as resulting from the young author's "inexperience with structuring a novel" (139). Regardless, those stylistic effects register what the novel symptomizes and anticipates regarding the future of character in the modernist Künstlerroman, typified by narrative fragmentation, mimetic representation, and decentered subjectivity. Fitzgerald dramatizes the character's evolving regional imaginary to equip him with a set of conflicting aesthetic principles that update the traditional Bildungsroman by deploying a range of avant-garde experiments in style. The formal disorderliness itself gradually reflects the unevenness of Fitzgerald's literary modernism, as it transpires across divergent locales where the artist's "fitness for life" and "genius" are tested: Wisconsin, Minneapolis, or Princeton, but also Maryland, Washington, New York City, and Atlantic City. The repression of his regional roots brings Amory no sense of worldly belonging: only alienation and artistic failure. No edifying centralized core of modernist cosmopolitanism embraces him—even in the Northeast, Amory is conscious of always being on the periphery of an abstract center that never materializes. It is precisely this uncanny sense of emplacement and placelessness that simulates the young artist's experience of emerging in literature's national-historical time. *This Side*'s restless geographical imperative finds no stability or evenness in either local, national, or transnational aesthetics, and so, blends them into one stylistically uneven vision of a regionally displaced youth.

Zelda Sayre Fitzgerald's *Save Me the Waltz* (1932)

"I don't want to be famous and fêted—all I want is to be very young always and . . . to feel that my life is my own," a 22-year-old Zelda Sayre declared in 1919, writing from her home in Montgomery, Alabama to her future husband Scott Fitzgerald in St. Paul, Minnesota (Z. Fitzgerald *Dearest Scott,* 40). Her statement articulated the spirit of aesthetic egoism attributed to her generation, in which adult responsibilities are delayed and denied in favor of hedonistic pleasure, political disengagement, and all that jazz. Through their fiction, the Flapper icon and her husband Scott spearheaded a lost generation of rootless youths, drawing upon the increasingly homogenized representation of Flapperdom (youth culture) in popular magazines; films; Tin Pan Alley popular songs about the vicissitudes of young love; and variety shows and cabarets. To establish herself as not simply another ambitious regional outsider drawn to the Northeast's cultural capital, Sayre increasingly drew upon the cosmopolitanism of interwar popular culture in her novel writing; aspiring to the cosmopolitan *"culture"* that a young Henry James once declared lacking in the "vulgar" American national character (qtd in McCarthy 102).[7]

The protagonist of Sayre's semi-autobiographical 1932 novel *Save Me the Waltz*, Alabama Begg—a white Southern debutante—marries a Yankee painter named David Knight who has "revolted" from the parochial Midwest of his birth. Her struggles to develop artistically allegorically expose the nation's regional faultlines. Sayre's

---

[7] This theme recurred in several of James's female development novels, including *Portrait of a Lady, What Maisie Knew,* and *Daisy Miller.*

literary geography traces the protagonist's childhood in small-town Tennessee; her unstable marriage in New York State with David, with whom she has a child, Bonnie; the endless parties she attends on the French Riviera, with David's artist friends; her ballet career in Naples, after David commits infidelity; and her return to the South to bury her father, after a physical injury terminates her dance career. However, the novel's geographic imaginary is more complex than that stereotypical cosmopolitanism its modernist migration plot might initially suggest. Within the novel's widely roaming map, Sayre observes the radical cultural transformations that emanated out of Jazz Age Manhattan. Although the novel gradually disconnects Alabama from her cultural roots as a Southerner, the author does not necessarily reject that region as one crucial source of her young protagonist's creative destiny; rather, the novel engages actively, albeit ambivalently, with regionalist debates of the period. Though various Northern critics found Sayre's novel dense with "overwrought descriptive passages," her imagistic descriptiveness and tendency toward metaphysical reflection were arguably "a frequent mark of the southern novel in this period," Amber Vogel suggests (587). Sayre's regional imaginary also periodically aligned with ambivalent localist patriots like Dewey, but also approached the reactionary Southern Agrarians' regionalist manifesto *I'll Take My Stand*, published two years earlier in 1930. Like Fitzgerald's first novel, *Save Me* disclosed the regional complex looming within the cosmopolitan unmooring of Stein's Lost Generation.

The Fitzgeralds' strategy to conquer the Northeast's competitive culture industry fed into modernism's infrastructure of self-promotion and purportedly "rootless" literary aesthetics. Many modernists attempted "to create and expand a market for elite literary works" by reconfiguring "the textual signature itself into a means of promotion," as Aaron Jaffe argues (30). In the Fitzgeralds' case, that signature relied upon competitive acts of aesthetic self-promotion, as evidenced by Sayre's sharp-witted April review of *The Beautiful and Damned*.[8] From 1931–1932, while residing at

---

[8] "I recognized a portion of an old diary of mine ... [and] letters which, though considerably edited, sound to me vaguely familiar. In fact, Mr. Fitzgerald ... seems to believe that plagiarism begins at home" (Z. Fitzgerald "Mrs. F. Scott," 388).

919 Felder Avenue, Montgomery, Alabama, these tensions simmered: Fitzgerald furiously declared to Sayre's physician that "literally one whole section of" Sayre's manuscript was "an imitation of" his fifty-thousand-word draft of *Tender is the Night*. Consequently, Sayre's leading male character, the Irish American painter Amory Blaine, was renamed David Knight after Fitzgerald opined that she stole "the name of a character I invented to put intimate facts in the hands of the friends and enemies . . . my books made her a legend and her . . . thin portrait is to make me a non-entity" (qtd in Bruccoli 380). Another legend of their making concerned the New York-based modernist dancer Isadora Duncan, who publicly seduced Scott Fitzgerald at a celebrity-studded dinner party in 1925; Sayre then threw herself down the staircase in front of the guests (Cline 183). When Duncan died in a tragic accident in 1927, Sayre fixated upon becoming a professional dancer, even joining the Philadelphia Opera Ballet, leading Fitzgerald to confide in a friend that he suspected she was attempting to "replace Isadora Duncan now that she was dead, and outshine me at the same time" (qtd in Cline 213).

While salacious biographical imprimaturs have dictated the terms by which these two novelists' works have been interpreted, truth precedes the legend: Sayre's Künstlerroman self-reflexively drew upon the social formations of her regional upbringing and the cosmopolitan cultural circle of her young adulthood, to create an elaborate geographical matrix and cultural poetics of the radical feminist transformations of modernism. This was especially the case in terms of *Save Me the Waltz*'s depiction of the cultural impact of pioneering dancers including Duncan upon modernist conceptions of women's development and art. *Save Me the Waltz*—which Sayre called "the story of myself versus myself" (qtd in Švrljuga 125)—moreover engaged in an evolving consensus on female subjectivity and regionalism. Rather than simply evoke New York as a launchpad to transnational modernism, Sayre contrasted that venue against the South of her youth, including her uneasy transformation from a "Southern belle" into the cosmopolitan "flapper," as Linda Martin-Wagner observes (*Zelda*, 1–2). Written when the couple were living in Sayre's hometown, surrounded by the memories of youth it contained, *Save Me* tells the story of the protagonist's idealized cosmopolitan self (adulthood), versus the other self she must suppress, that is, her regional self: a metaphysical place of perpetual childhood and innocence.

The development of Sayre's ballerina protagonist, Alabama Begg-Knight, increasingly displays what Julia Foulkes has described as the anarchic "alienation and isolation of the artist from the larger society" that pioneering dancers including Isadora Duncan and Martha Graham "proudly exposed" (34). That development also suggests the transforming relationship between dance, literature, and gender in the modernist imaginary. In 1893, French symbolist poet Stéphane Mallarmé incited interest in the modern female dancing body with his prose-sketch of a solo performance given at the Folies Bergère in Paris by renowned American ballerina Loïe Fuller (Jones 13–14). That elegant figure danced her way into the imagery of the French Impressionists, and into English-language works by Oscar Wilde, W. B. Yeats, and T. S. Eliot, who in turn inspired the Ballets Russes (14). Eliot speculated over the "future for drama and particularly for poetic drama," and whether it might "not be in the direction indicated by ballet" (qtd in Taxidou 110); while Stein's modernist ekphrasis used poetic rhythm to create a conduit between language and dance within the reading act, as in "Orta or One Dancing," an homage to Duncan (Taxidou 110). While literary modernists imported dance into poetry, performance manifestos such as Isadora Duncan's 1915 *The Dance of the Future* staged the formal and thematic declaration of the body as a medium "just as a writer uses his words" (qtd in Taxidou 110–11). In turn, literary modernism's impact upon dance fused action and individualism in ways that "celebrated and explored definitions of womanhood" (Jones 6). Graham inverted this "emphasis on individualism" in her influential performance of *Heretic*, which choreographed a psychoanalytical lens onto female interiority and expressiveness, thereby disrupting the nineteenth-century "idea of the individual as rational public citizen" (Foulkes 33–4). Graham and Doris Humphrey's feminist models of modernist character staged new aesthetic possibilities for how race, sexuality, and gender might be staged; models that could be usefully applied to other forms and media, including the Bildungsroman. Indeed, Alabama's development mirrors their aesthetic disenchantment with conservative tropes of the dancing female body, by revealing an increasingly progressive feminist representation of the dancer's development, chapter by chapter.

Save Me the Waltz's regional juxtapositions, redolent of the migration narrative common to the city novel, are key to understanding that trajectory of the artist's development from a "decorative" Southern Belle into a disciplined, cosmopolitan dancer. Sayre's novel begins with the young adulthood of Alabama Begg, granddaughter of slave owners and born—as Sayre was—on a former plantation passed down from her grandfather, a Confederate general. Linda Martin-Wagner concludes that Alabama is "pigeon-holed from the beginning of her life into the proper female roles" ("An Assessment," 201), a pigeonholing that serves the text's regionalist revisionism regarding gender and artistry. The Southern setting complements the novel's initial traditional women's Bildungsroman themes of courtship, marriage, and maternity, which will strategically contrast Alabama's evolving artistic identity as she is drawn into New York City's cultural scene, which forms a port to Europe and the high culture of ballet. This becomes clear in the 1923 galley proofs with penciled corrections, in which Sayre's revisions to the original draft of Chapter 1 effectively sideline a young Alabama's naive and superficial desires for fame. The following dialogue between Alabama and her mother Millie suggests that the protagonist's quest hinges on obtaining personal autonomy outside of patriarchal conventions, something Sayre makes abundantly clear in her revised semantics:

> "I want to go to New York, Mama," said Alabama.
> "What on earth for?"
> "To be ~~famous.~~" [my own boss]
> Millie laughed. "Well, never mind," she said. "Being ~~famous~~ [boss] isn't a question of places. Why can't you be ~~famous~~ [bossie] at home?" (*Save Me the Waltz* Galley Proofs, 19-23)

This conversation insists upon a stereotypical North–versus–South spatial binary that reduces the geographical complexity of those regional identities in that period. The protagonist's development becomes contingent on her awakening, as it is brought on by a growing awareness of the gendered politics of aesthetics that underwrite modernism, including its purported revolt from the village. Sayre's revision displays uncertainty toward giving her protagonist the rather grubby motive of fame-seeking, leaning instead toward the nobler quest for autonomy. This early galley proof also stimulates geographical tension between the Beggs's Old Southern Kentucky values, emblematic of a cultural atavism in which a woman must find a domicile to "finish the story of her life," a phrase Sayre penciled onto the typewritten proofs (Galley Proofs, 23–6), and the modernizing North. The novel's early modal ambivalence teeters between Southern romance discourses and imagistic prose redolent of Northeastern modernism. She is soon after courted by the visiting Northern artist David Knight, whose connections to modernist cosmopolitanism beyond the Mason–Dixon line appear far more valuable to Alabama's aspirations than the immediate wealth of her other suitors: he is a gatekeeper to fashionable society, celebrity, but most importantly, Northern avant-garde culture.

Alabama's mother Millie errs in the sense that the ontological implications of being famous, and a boss, are to an extent determined by place. For Alabama, becoming an autonomous subject requires her to gather insights into the world by leaving her hometown and relocating to Manhattan, which in the 1920s was establishing itself as a locale where female dancers were transforming the political potentialities of radical female characterization. "One of the most radical aspects of the representations staged by New York City dancers is that, for the most part, women stood alone," writes Ellen Graff, "thus explicitly commenting on both the independence of the female body and its power" while enabling "the female body to be on stage as an abstraction rather than a representation of the dancer herself" (22). Inversely, the traditional nineteenth-century female Bildungsroman used the courtship plot as a means of curtailing genuine autonomy for women in ways that echoed the narrative choreography of both modern dance and ballet, in which female character development was "enmeshed" with marriage (Banes 5). The "coming-of-age" of the eponymous heroine of *Sleeping Beauty* was choreographed as an *"enforced passivity"* by Marius Petipa for the 1890 performance at St. Petersburg's Mariinsky Theatre; the prince's *"gaze, his kiss, brings* her to life," contra the standard 1895 choreography of *Swan Lake*'s Prince Siegfried, who "comes of age" and "goes hunting" (Goldberg 305-6). As a medium, dance "militates against depicting sedentary states (like domesticity)" by foregrounding "issues of sexuality and the social governance of mating through the marriage institution," Sally Banes observes (6).

    The regional dimension to Sayre's plot initially reads much like these romances, a mode which was historically significant to the development of Southern literature, as I shall elaborate in Part 3. Practically speaking, to get to New York, the Southern debutante Alabama—not a sleeping beauty, so much as a Southern Belle, lodged within a constrictive regional framework—must marry a Northern knight, i.e., David Knight, to increase her mobility. In the first third of Sayre's novel, the courtship plot reads as an unstable "waltz" between "Mr. and Mrs. David Knight," in which Alabama's role is to be "nothing but an aesthetic theory—a chemistry formula for the decorative," as David suggests, relegating her to a passive role (Z. Fitzgerald *Save Me*, 66). Twirling past celebrities including Charlie Chaplin and the celebrated bandleader Paul Whiteman, David and Alabama privately quarrel over their uneven rhythms, with David sighing: "I never could waltz anyway" (64). If modern dance was drawing upon nineteenth-century courtship plots to renovate in feminist dance pieces, Sayre here refurbishes the literary symbolism of dance—specifically, waltz—which thrived in women's Bildungsroman depictions of young womanhood. Edith Wharton's Lily Bart of *The House of Mirth*, a work Sayre and Fitzgerald both greatly admired, likened the emotional sensation of "youthful romance" to the "whirl of a waltz" (65). Lily's dance metaphor benchmarks Manhattan's ruling class's patriarchal hypocrisy: while her male counterpart Jack avoids a sexual scandal simply by remaining "'quiet" and marrying himself off, Lily must "calculate and contrive, and retreat and advance, as if I were going through an intricate dance, where one misstep would throw me hopelessly out of time'" (48). Lily inevitably does misstep, leading to the novel's tragic realization of the "central truth of existence"—signified through the simile of courtship as cosmic choreography—that men and women are "like atoms whirling away from each other in some wild centrifugal dance" (Wharton 311). When, mid-dance, Alabama similarly begins to feel her gendered alienation among her husband's artist friends, she does not interpret it romantically, but rather, understands it as "a hundred thousand things to be blue about exposed in all the choruses" (Z. Fitzgerald *Save Me*, 64), a jazz trope that reflects the gradual unanchoring of her self-perception from the conservative destiny laid out for her as a child in semi-rural Tennessee. By interchanging the steady waltz beat with the polyrhythmic sounds of New Amsterdam's popular music, Sayre renovates that clichéd social metaphor belonging to the female development novel. These cross-rhythms reinforce the notion that the Knight's rhythmic unevenness evidently stems from their regional differences: Alabama's expectations of marriage, molded by her atavistic small-town Southern upbringing, diverge from the looser marital values of the Northern metropolitan modernist David.

What aesthetic lessons Alabama absorbs in those early chapters hinges upon her regional difference, which is also problematically suggested through the racialized imagery of early 1920s Manhattan, focalized through a white Southerner who encounters for the first time the cultural revolution brought about by the exodus of African Americans out of the South. Alabama clearly retains a geographical imaginary over which the social relations of Jim Crow loom, detectable in the description of New Amsterdam music that "pumped in their eardrums" and in "unwieldy quickened rhythms invited them to be Negroes and saxophone players, to come back to Maryland and Louisiana, and addressed them as mammies and millionaires" (47). Alabama, we have already learnt, was "[i]ncubated in the mystic pungence of Negro mammies" (3). Sayre conveys the Great Migration through a kind of racist minstrelsy, a trope which recurs throughout Alabama's character development and never subsides; later in the novel, Sayre exploits racist tropes of the "primitive" Black dancing body to emphasize the protagonist's artistic awakening as she undergoes grueling ballerina training in Naples. Alabama measures her progress by "the strength of her Negroid hips, convex as boats in a wood carving," of which she feels "gladly, savagely proud" because such "complete control of her body freed her from all fetid consciousness of it" (174). The racial primitivism that shapes Alabama's artistic imaginary is more than partly linked to the Begg family history, which is revealed when Alabama returns to the South at the novel's denouement; her mother Millie Begg—whom Alabama believes exists not for herself but only as "part of a masculine tradition," i.e., the patriarchal Southern household (208)—cautions her not to dent an heirloom "'made by hand from silver dollars that the slaves saved to give your grandfather after they were freed'" (213). Simultaneously, Sayre's model of female characterization relies not only on the seriousness of the symbolic bodies of white dancers, but also their juxtaposition against the popularization of African American dancers—the most famous being Josephine Baker—who revolutionized modern dance in the 1920s in musicals, revues, and cabarets. Relocating from what Sayre depicts as the slower, homogenous regional chronotopes of the Jim Crow South to the fast-paced, polyrhythmic Northeast, Alabama's exposure to Bohemian Greenwich Village and her white touristic adventures uptown into Harlem's cabarets visibly reshape her regional imaginary.

The carefully choreographed "waltz," a metaphor of her marriage, becomes a visible impediment to Alabama's artistic development as a modern dancer who seeks to emulate Duncan, Graham, Humphrey, but no less crucially, Baker. To truly break with the gendered constraints of Alabama's unevenly regionalized identity, Sayre exploits the marital separation plot: a retiring of the waltz metaphor, and a shift into an aesthetic derived out of a richer, more complicated balletic tropology. Alabama's struggle to negotiate competing cultural influences in music, dance, and literature metonymizes the revolution occurring in the women's dance movement in New York during the 1920s. Dancers like Isadora Duncan emerged *"choreographically* as sexual revolutionaries" who danced "solos without male partners," thus "categorically [rejecting] the marriage plot entirely in their dances"; while others such as Martha Graham still utilized the marriage plot, but in a "troubled" fashion (Banes 6). Sayre's novel inhabits a middle ground between the novel of development as a template and those subversive expressions of female character that were embodied by modernist dance troupes. Sayre's thin yet muscular physique, contoured by ballet exercises, embodies the Southern artist's regionalized self-cultivation despite her brush with modernism in Manhattan. The narrator juxtaposes Alabama's muscular physicality with the sculpted "porcelain" body of a Hollywood actress they meet on the ship over to France, Gabrielle Gibbs, with whom David has a public affair (118–20). Not simply a rival for David's affections, Gibbs—a representative of the celluloid arts—poses an ontological threat to the ballerina's medium, which depends on live performance. When during the party given for a foreign princess, an event at which Gabrielle and David consummate their affair, Alabama finds that the princess used to be in the Ballets Russes, she begs her for a letter of reference (116). David's obnoxious, chauvinist friend Hastings, who attempts to seduce Alabama with his caustic wit, tells her she would be better off receiving "'the address of a Black-Bottom teacher,'" whom he notes is "of course colored, but nobody cares about that anymore" (116). More perceptively, he jokes that Alabama only wants to join the ballet for the same reasons she married David, a painter: to be "'almost as exotic,'" the implication being that she seeks classical training to overcompensate for her reputation as a parochial Southern girl (117).

As Foulkes notes, the "transience of one moment of dance speaks to the fragility of the artform as a whole" (6), an observation which Sayre insists upon. Whereas Fitzgerald cynically responded to the role film and screenplays were having upon the modern novelist throughout his career (Murphet and Rainford 4), Sayre insists upon the cultural incommensurability of dance and film; the latter might mechanically preserve, reproduce, or record dancing, but the power of dance as an artform is set into motion by tension between the presence of the body and the impermanence of live performance, which resists technological reproduction (Foulkes 6). Later, when Alabama's child Bonnie visits during rehearsals, she tells her mother that she will never wed, given how marriage is represented in "the movies" (184). David took Bonnie to see a film about "'dancing" and "a lady in the Russian Ballet" who has "'no children but a man and they both cried a lot,'" starring Gabrielle Gibbs, whom Alabama quips she has "'never seen her except in life'" (184). Gabrielle's role anticipates Greta Garbo's performance as Grusinskaya, the tragic Russian prima ballerina in *Grand Hotel* (1932), who delivers the immortal lines "I just want to be alone." Menaced by the presence of a film actress, Alabama's career is coupled with the dissolution of her marriage. As Sayre overlays two opposing modes of womanhood—Alabama the dancer, versus her celluloid simulacrum, Gabrielle—the novel's subterranean concerns over the film industry's effects upon literary character and live dance surface. Gabrielle's Garboesque character mediates Alabama's internal role as the tragic stereotype of the alienated ballerina. This subtext of cultural permanency and impermanency, the unsettling flux of tradition and progress, animates Alabama's decision to separate from her husband and child in Switzerland, and continue her training as a prima ballerina instead. However, her initial desire to become her own "boss" now shifts back to the lexicon on the original galley proofs of the novel, *"fame"*: "I am going to be as *famous* a dancer as there are blue veins over the white marble of Miss Gibbs" (Z. Fitzgerald *Save Me*, 122; italics mine).

The rivalry between women, and mediums, seems to tug at old insecurities Alabama feels as a regional outsider, which intensify as Madame informs her dance troupe that they will have to vacate their studio, for developers "are making a moving-picture studio of my place here" (193). As Alabama contemplates what the disestablishment of the studio will mean for her career, she stands, like Grusinskaya, "alone with her body in *impersonal regions*, alone with herself and her tangible thoughts, like a widow surrounded by many objects belonging to the past" (193–4, italics mine). The use of free indirect discourse here is crucial: Alabama, alone in her "impersonal regions" that are filled with objects of her past, begins to interpret the challenge that film poses to dance—and, more broadly, the challenge the popular arts will pose to those aspiring to high art—as an epochal shift. No less crucially, she interprets this crisis as a matter of geographical displacement, in which she has lost something significant as she has become unanchored from her regional specificity. Without the stabilizing solidity of region to anchor her growth, Alabama's self-determination wavers and her development process falters; the unfixed artist protagonist continues to wander, and by luck finds an opportunity to train with a prestigious ballet company in Naples. For the meantime, this opportunity offers Alabama a symbolic space of primitive creativity she feels she requires to resume her creative destiny.

If Paris is the epicenter of modernity for the New York expatriates, their "tumultuous friends drowning the Chopin in modern jazz and vintage wine" (221), Naples draws the female artist into a setting where the unacknowledged influence of Duncan and New York's feminist dance scene on her character returns. She initially fears the other dancers' "sagging breasts" and "pneumatic buttocks like lurid fruits in the pictures of Georgia O'Keefe" (178). The ballerinas in the stage wings are "mostly ugly" and "old," according to the narrator, with necks "twisted like dirty knots of mending thread," "flesh [that] hung over their bones like bulging pastry," and black hair "with no nuances to please the tired senses" (178). Despite Sayre's personal distaste for naturalism's "ugliness,"[9] she exfoliates away Alabama's previously glamorous façade: the ballerina's eyes "throb" with every "beat of her pulse," her hair clinging "like plasticine about her head," the rehearsal music trilling in her ears like "persistent gnats" (178). Her upper lip feels "cold and peppery with drying sweat;" she retires to bed with bloodied feet (208). Such characterization springs out of Sayre's "intense distaste for the melancholy aroused in the masculine mind by such characters as Jenny Gerhardt" or Gloria in *The Beautiful and Damned* (her own likeness) (qtd in Eby *Dreiser and Veblen*, 184). Alabama's outward performance of two contrasting regional stereotypes, firstly as a Southern belle, and subsequently as a metropolitan Flapper, both rely on the attractiveness of unextinguished youthfulness Alabama exudes to the male gaze.

Disgusted but captivated by the fleshy, sweaty, sagging, abject women hidden in the stage wings, Alabama perceives what the author herself seems to suggest: the gestural power of the artwork that transfigures decorative womanhood into a more radical femininity. If nothing remains "to please the tired senses" of the male, cosmopolitan gaze (178), Alabama's transformation signals how the authenticity of art is determined by a dialectic between beauty and suffering that never stands still. This is highlighted again when David and Bonnie send a telegraph, leaving an unsmiling Alabama disturbed by her daughter's enclosed drawing of "a clumsy militant figure with mops of yellow hair" (221)—an emulation of Duncan and Graham's radical characters. That hair symbolically foils her

---

[9] Sayre was repulsed by Frank Norris's *McTeague* (1899), advising Fitzgerald to "never be a realist . . . [who] thinks being ugly is being forceful" (qtd in Milford *Zelda*, 60).

father's "even Confederate gray" hair, which she later smooths on his deathbed (207).

Her travels bring Alabama only the illusion of personal autonomy. In her pursuit of the cosmopolitan ideal, she risks and loses all. Her Faustian debt to the cult of artistry is inevitably recalled along with the rest of Stein's Lost Generation of artists (Douglas *Terrible Honesty*, 471), her *coup de grâce* arriving at the apotheosis of her career as she stars as the prima ballerina in a production of *Faust* (Z. Fitzgerald *Save Me*, 223), before succumbing to a career-ending injury. When the family are set to return from Europe to the States, David offers to secure Alabama another dance residency, but she insists "she'd never dance in America" (210); that prophecy becomes true, in the novel's conclusion. The novel's elliptical narrative structure sees Alabama return to her small-town South to bury her father, where the metaphor of O'Keefe's vibrant flowers fades into the same shade of "Confederate gray" as her father's hair; a dusty, black-and-white image of an overfilled ashtray: "I just lump everything in a great heap which I have labeled 'the past,' and, having thus emptied this deep reservoir that was once myself, I am ready to continue" (272). The premise of unfixed youth in Sayre's novel recourses to a melancholy, but ultimately conservative, view of the cosmopolitan metropole as destructive to the stabilizing qualities of the regional, echoing the through-line of the Southern Fugitive Agrarians' *I'll Take My Stand* (1930). Sayre's imagery above echoes Donald Davidson's contribution:

> Our megalopolitan agglomerations . . . patronize art, they merchandize it, but they do not produce it. They despise the hinterland, which . . . somehow manages to beget the great majority of American artists . . . [who] often migrate to New York [and then Europe], at considerable risk to their growth. (Davidson 57)

Distanced from the urban melee, an injured Alabama stands alone once more in what she earlier called her "impersonal regions," contemplating her destiny; only, upon returning to Montgomery, it becomes clear that her experiences of the modernist art world have rendered her unfit to reinhabit either her former metropolitan or regional frameworks. Driving in her family's Ford past "Negroes, lethargic and immobile," to find her sister and mother across the "old town where her father had worked away so much of his life spread before her protectively," Alabama realizes that "to be a stranger in a land when you felt aggressive and acquisitive" was virtuous, "when you began to weave your horizons into some kind of shelter it was good to know that hands you loved had helped in the spinning—made you feel as if the threads would hold together better" (203-4). If the *roman-à-clef*, the elliptical "turning of the key," opens the music box and summons forth the ballerina to briefly dance her mechanical pirouette, Sayre's decisive final gesture is to snap the lid shut, leaving the estranged artist's development unfinalized in the region of her childhood. In that locale, *Save Me* visibly works through similar concerns to the Agrarians regarding regionalism and artistic development, at the novel's close. Yet, these contemplations do not necessarily nullify the novel's progressive outlook regarding what roles the New Woman might perform within those agglomerations, a perspective that such reactionary regionalisms as Davidson's effectively silenced and ultimately rejected (see Donaldson "Introduction," xv).

Save Me's position within the evolving history of the American Bildungsroman should not be defined by its late capitulation to the female antidevelopment narrative, nor its indulgence of an atavistic regionalism regulated by the seemingly incompatible logics of North and South. Sayre's novel ambitiously mapped new ways in which to formalize the young subject's internalization of gendered social relations, structured at local, national, and international scales. To simulate the disorienting effects of navigating differing levels of affiliation, Sayre infused aspects of character from the Southern romance with avant-garde models of aesthetic development; in this case, taking New York's women's dance scene as its muse. Alabama's development as an artist comes into view through the text's internal struggle to reconcile the protagonist's atavistic regional identity with the modernist cosmopolitanism she desires to embody through the symbolic form of ballet. Like *This Side of Paradise*, in theme and form, Sayre's *Save Me the Waltz* thus reflected upon where modernism happened, locating it not in New York, Europe, or the regions, but rather, in the dynamic cultural interfaces between these multiple localities.

CHAPTER 5

Thurman and Fauset's Portraits of Harlem's Regional Artist

This chapter resumes our tour of America's Northeastern region in the 1920s, led by its literary hero, the young artist character. Let us detour into uptown Manhattan, pausing above 110th Street. Harlem, a neighborhood comprising just 3.63 km² of the borough, is loaded with cultural mythologies, especially apropos its precipitation of the New Negro Renaissance c. 1919–1935, popularly referred to as the Harlem Renaissance: a cultural revolution that resulted from the Great Migration of Black Southerners to cities above the Mason–Dixon line. The Künstlerroman played a strategic role in contending with Harlem's geographical mythologies, as a self-reflexive subgenre that narrativized the Black nationalist hero who emerged out of the bloody Red Summer of race riots in 1919: the New Negro. With a nod to the cultural nationalism of the period popularized by literary critical publications including Van Wyck Brooks's *America's Coming of Age* (1915), the African American intellectual Alain Locke's exegesis on the Old and New Negro in his influential *New Negro* anthology (1925) indicated that

> if in our lifetime the Negro should not be able to celebrate his full initiation into American democracy, he can at least ... celebrate the attainment of a significant and satisfying new phase of group development, and with it a spiritual Coming of Age (Locke 16).

For Locke's collaborator W. E. B. Du Bois, the harbinger of the New Negro's getting-of-wisdom was the young artist, whom he felt was crucial to the development of a durable African American literary tradition. Du Bois and Locke's 1924 co-written essay for *The Crisis*, "The Younger Literary Movement," peddled Jean Toomer's *Cane* (1923) and Jessie Redmon Fauset's *There is Confusion* (1924) as leaders of a generation of literary works that were "[marking] an epoch" by creating feats in literature that unambiguously negated the lie of Black inferiority (Du Bois and Locke 288). Adjacent to the cultural federalism of the WWI context, which saw white literary critics including Brooks revive Ralph Waldo Emerson's Young American in Literature to consolidate a white nativist national tradition, the Young New Negro led Black nationalism's program of Du Boisian cultural uplift. As that figure was conceived by influential intellectuals such as Du Bois and Locke, its antagonist was the "immature" Old Negro, a tropological fixture of the peasant rural South often associated with provincialist, sentimental local color fiction. As an abstract collective united by the bonds of racial solidarity that was furnished by a shared sense of cultural unity, the New Negro movement was thus tethered by a regional imaginary that linked metropolitan Black modernity and cultural maturity with the future-oriented, cosmopolitan figure of youth.

Harlem was the spatial signifier of cosmopolitan, anti-regionalist Black modernity and the coming-of-age of African American art, a process that was predicated on the idea of a standardized nationwide culture (Locke "New Negro," 7). Locke looked to examine and redraw the lines of regional difference within Northern Black communities that the Great Migration had precipitated. He found that the "sectionalized" mentality facing the nation's "Negro population," caused by Southerners migrating en masse to the Midwest or Northeast, needed to be addressed. That population was no longer imagined to be primarily located in the premodern, "local and not peculiarly racial" mode of living of the rural South. Now, it was concentrated in great cosmopolitan cities and centers of industry where large Black communities comprised of individuals from diverse regional and national backgrounds were experiencing the full effects of the nation's modernization (5). The "flight" of the Negro out of the rural South was "not only from countryside to city, but from medieval America to modern," Locke observed (6). The mecca of Harlem was not "merely the largest Negro community in the world, but the first concentration in history of so many diverse elements of Negro life," having brought together "the African, the West Indian, the Negro American," as well as "the Negro of the North and the Negro of the South; the man from the city and the man from the town and village; the peasant, the student, the business man, the professional man, artist, poet, musician, adventurer and worker, preacher and criminal, exploiter and social outcast": each group with "its own separate motives" (6). Harlem, then, was no longer simply a place, but a cosmopolitan point of inquiry: how could these at times seemingly irreconcilable local differences and heterogeneities be reconciled?

Given its proximity to the nation's most prolific publishing firms, Harlem offered an advantageous political solidity to the movement. The concept of youth was the key metaphor of the cultural revolution that was concentrated there. As the genre that purportedly consolidates nationalism's many contradictions, the Bildungsroman proliferated in African American writing of the 1920s as a means of narrating and contending with such internal differences, becoming one of the defining genres of the Harlem Renaissance (Whalan "The Bildungsroman," 72). Harlem after 1919 signaled not only an imagined community of Black artists, but the imagined region of an unfolding generational shift, within which cultural nationalism was called upon to unite a heterogeneous collective of African Americans spread across the country in their uneven regionalisms, by bringing them into a centralized politico-aesthetic movement. The neighborhood drew scores of outsiders from beyond those four square kilometers in Manhattan, before and after "the five or six years generally allotted" to the renaissance, as the author Sterling Brown noted in his 1955 retrospective, *Southern Road*; nevertheless, most New Negro

> writers were not Harlemites; much of the best writing was not about Harlem, which was the show-window, . . . but no more Negro America than New York is America. The New Negro has temporal roots in the past and spatial roots elsewhere in America, and the term has validity . . . only when considered to be a continuing tradition. (Qtd in Singh 3)

Although numerous Bildungsromane of the period contemplated the effects of ethnic assimilation experienced by an individual who matures into that framework,[1] curiously, African American literature was often described in mainstream discourse as equivalent to a regional literature. Mimicking the essentialist commentary of the period, the novelist Wallace Thurman put it this way in his satirical Künstlerroman about the Harlem Renaissance, *Infants of the Spring*: just "[a]s the middle westerner and the southerner had found indigenous expression, so was the Negro developing his own literary spokesmen" (34). Raised in the Southwest and Midwest, educated on the West Coast, and spending only three years in Harlem at the height of the renaissance, Thurman was skeptical of this new cultural "region" of American literature. To declare Harlem the birthplace and center of the Young New Negro movement, and the ground zero of a consolidated, mature African American literary tradition, raised issues for many such as Thurman regarding individualism and assimilation, who found that the homogenized ethnic solidarity that was supposed to protect artists from cultural marginalization within an Americanist national framework might also alienate them from genuine creativity.

During the early 1920s, the novel genre became one of the most contentious literary arenas of New Negro culture for airing these debates. As James Weldon Johnson demonstrated in his monograph, *Black Manhattan* (1930), the 1920s political context had fashioned the defining "phase of the development of the Negro in the United States" in terms of "the recent literary and artistic emergence of the individual creative artist" (261). Johnson contended that "New York has been, almost exclusively, the place where that emergence has taken place" (261). The suddenness of Harlem's post-WWI cultural and social transformations did "not have the appearance of a development," but appeared "rather like a sudden awakening, like an instantaneous change" (261). While "for many generations the Negro has been a creative artist and a contributor to the nation's common cultural store" (261), until circa 1925, "'literary renaissance' Negro writers had been less successful in fiction than in any other field," Johnson notes, exempting Charles

---

[1] Works outside the African American literary tradition include *Bread Givers* (1925) by Jewish American novelist Anzia Yezierska; and Mourning Dove's (Hum-Ishu-Ma) *Cogewea: The Half-Blood* (1927).

Chesnutt and himself.[2] Because the Künstlerroman focuses specifically on a type of young character who registers their society's shifting artistic values, it became an important tool for narrating these developments in fiction, providing a self-reflexive window onto the Northeastern culture industry, while exposing the extent to which internal contradictory regionalisms informed the uneven geography of Harlem's development.

Complex regionalisms and cultural geographies were also at play within the New Negro movement's nationalizing framework, as exhibited in novels about the Harlem Renaissance. This current chapter explores how those geographies self-reflexively figured into novels that narrativized African American literature's Coming of Age, and in doing so, archived contemporary debates over ethnic identity and aesthetics, and regionalism's role in the national standardization of the New Negro movement. One prominent debate over the future direction of the New Negro novel arose between the Philadelphian Fauset and the Californian Thurman, a writer twenty years her junior. Despite those authors' contrasting ideological approaches to form, in both Fauset's respectable *Plum Bun* (1928) and Thurman's disrespectable *Infants of the Spring* (1932), the artist's unsettled development underlines the authors' ambivalent relationships to Harlem as a real location, and as a metaphor of cultural nationalism. The artist character's regional complex in *Plum Bun* and *Infants* conveyed the challenges of that developmental process of New Negro literature, and the pressures of the younger generation to fulfill their great potential.

In *Plum Bun* and *Infants*, the author's regional imaginary insinuates itself in the artists' attempts to integrate into the cultural renaissance already underway in Harlem. Representing youth on the verge of artistic maturity provided an important geographical metaphor for registering the cultural effects of the Great Migration, in which the geographical process of movement from the periphery to the center echoed the cultural process from immaturity to maturity. What resulted from that phenomenon, and the cultural national-

---

[2] These novelists included Du Bois, Toomer, Fauset, Thurman, Walter White, Nella Larsen, Eric Walrond, Rudolph Fisher, and Claude McKay (Johnson 275–6).

ism it encouraged, were narratives that equated artistic immaturity with regional difference. Artistic immaturity, as it was configured in *Plum Bun* and *Infants*, resulted not from their regional identity as such, but from the protagonist's geographical ambivalence. The protagonist, a regional migrant who is drawn to Harlem, discovers that beneath its mythic veneer, the social production of space there is dialectical, negotiating small-town customs they recognize, but also many other contradictory cosmopolitan social forms that operate across its street curbs and storefronts, rent parties, artist enclaves, and cabarets. The disoriented youth struggles to fulfill their potential for artistic genius in that locale, longs for simpler times, and their future remains unsettled. The failure of the Harlem Renaissance to fulfill its ambitions was thus allegorically configured in both Thurman's and Fauset's Künstlerromane through strategic geographic metaphors of regional difference which, in turn, illustrated the integrative difficulties facing the New Negro movement as a nationalist enterprise.

Jessie Redmon Fauset's *Plum Bun: A Novel Without a Moral* (1928)

When Du Bois and Locke upheld Jessie Redmon Fauset's novel *There is Confusion* as an exemplar of the younger generation of New Negroes, they glossed over the fact that Fauset, born in 1882, was in her forties, and was an established writer for *The Crisis* from 1913, before becoming its literary editor, 1919–1927. Cheryl A. Wall notes that Locke's "emphasis of youth" proved exclusionary for women, given many of the New Negro women "were not young" (*Women*, 12). In 1925, Fauset—then the literary editor of *The Crisis*, the leading African American periodical of the epoch—published an essay by the Radcliffe graduate Marita Bonner entitled "On Being Young—a Woman—and Colored." In that essay, Bonner articulated the frustrations impeding young, educated women's desires for cultural cosmopolitanism. "You hear" from elsewhere in the region "that up in New York this is to be seen" or "heard," and yet to be categorized as young, a woman, and colored means that the individual cannot "break away to see or hear anything in a city that is supposed to see and hear too much" (227). Bonner was describing how it felt to be young, a woman, and a New Negro: it was to loiter on the peripheries of Black cultural modernity. For Bonner, this metaphysical homelessness translated into the metaphor of a protagonist who is symbolically alienated from New York's cultural revolution, who resides in exile on its regional peripheries. Perhaps because most of her early essays and stories were similarly about young, intelligent, middle-class Black women from the respectable suburbs of Northeastern municipalities—who often fail to reconcile their cosmopolitan desires with the more conservative social customs of their regional framework—Fauset's fiction exemplified Du Bois and Locke's young New Negro ethos, while challenging its gendered imbalances, by using the same regionalist metaphor of alienation as Bonner. In *Plum Bun*, a novel of uneven development, a light-complexioned, Black young woman artist struggles to overcome her regional complex: not only determining which race she will live among under Jim Crow, but whether she will align her art with modernist New York or "regionalist" Philadelphia.

Fauset, like Du Bois, was disturbed by the approach of various "younger" writers whom Wallace Thurman represented; in kind, Thurman quipped to their mutual friend Langston Hughes that Fauset ought to be "taken out to Philadelphia to be cremated" (*Collected Writings*, 119). Such remarks, reflective of Thurman's incendiary style of literary criticism more broadly, indicate why Fauset's friend Du Bois labeled Thurman "the young upstart," as Thurman revealed to Claude McKay (*Collected Writings*, 166). Thurman was reacting against the successes of novels that reflected Harlem's "artificially constructed 'imagined community' of unified ideas and a common heritage," centered upon Du Bois's notion of the "Talented Tenth," which in practice projected an exclusionary "nationalistic, masculine, bourgeois, and heterosexist tone" (Keresztesi 18). This position formed the basis of his own Künstlerroman about the Harlem Renaissance's failures, *Infants of the Spring*. That novel purposively deviated from Fauset's style of Künstlerroman in *Plum Bun*, as one representative of a cluster of 1920s and 1930s novels that focused on the development of young, light-complexioned women from Black bourgeois centers such as Philadelphia, Boston, and New York, whose racial ambiguity left them in a state of ontological homelessness.[3] In the context of the "one-drop" legal principle—buoyed as it was by the recently resurrected Ku Klux Klan's "unceasing fight for 100% Americanism," as pointed out late in *Plum Bun* (666)—the dilemma of what it meant to be mixed-race, young, and a woman was mapped onto a protagonist's struggle to feel at home in either the white or Black worlds she traverses; either in the metropolitan scene, or the provincial clusters of the Northeast. Fauset conflates the artist's racial uncertainty with the "provincial" Philadelphian childhood she must leave behind to mature as a New York-based artist. But this is part of the novel's other dualisms, especially critical in terms of Fauset's engagement with what I have been calling the regional imaginary. As Cherene Sherrard-Johnson observes regarding *Plum Bun*'s relationship to visual culture, Angela's "visual mindedness" bears the influence of the Fourteenth Street School of painters who depicted Manhattan's urban scenes—observable in the detailed narrations of Angela's experiences in Greenwich Village and Harlem, which she later turns into an installation of local color portraits (Sherrard-Johnson 63–4). If Philadelphia instills in Angela a cultural provincialism that aligns her artistic practice with the school of American Regionalism in visual art in the 1920s, her time in New York exposes her to the Fourteenth Street School, a movement that shunned Regionalist aesthetics by focusing on the tension between traditional and progressive social customs as well as the effects of mass culture. This is the ambivalent territory through which Fauset's allegory of modernism treads in *Plum Bun*, thus becoming a novel—like Sayre's and Fitzgerald's—of uneven artistic development.

That aesthetic emerges not in the flight from regionalism to metropolitanism, but in the dialectical dynamic between those two seemingly oppositional aesthetics. The novel may be read as an allegory of the artistic social formations of the New Negro Renaissance to which Fauset, a Philadelphian, was not only party

---

[3] Other notable instances of this tendency include Fauset's *There is Confusion* (1924), and Larsen's *Quicksand* (1928) and *Passing* (1929). The categorical indeterminacy of the mixed-race characters informed nuanced characterological investments in these passing novels, especially those that attempted to disentangle the multiple jeopardies facing young, Black female artists.

but in which she was a tastemaker as the influential editor of *The Crisis*. *Plum Bun*'s protagonist, Angela Murray, arrives in New York City from Philadelphia, eager to leave behind the memories of her suburban childhood in Philadelphia, especially the untimely deaths of her parents, who were victims of medical negligence due to systemic white supremacism in the healthcare sector. She is free to migrate to Greenwich Village to launch her painting career, whereas her darker-complexioned younger sister Virginia relocates to Harlem as a musician. For the middle third of the novel, Angela chooses to remain downtown and pass as white, to her creative and social detriment.

Due to Philadelphia's rapid industrialization in the early twentieth century, which encouraged steady Black migration to the city,[4] it became a vibrant cultural enclave for Black artists and intellectuals, including Alain Locke, Fauset, and her half-brother Arthur Fauset, who was a prominent folklorist. Yet, in *Plum Bun*, Philadelphia is deliberately characterized as a "small-town" regional center, where the parochial, educated middle-class social formations were more resistant to the speeding up of industrial modernity and the cult of the "new" that affixed itself to New York City. As the Bildungsheld Angela attempts to shed those roots, but inevitably ends up clinging to them, *Plum Bun* deliberately sets her character development as temporally at odds with Harlem's cultural renaissance. Although throughout her entire middle-class childhood Angela comfortably identified as Black, upon her parents' premature deaths—caused by the medical negligence of racist nurses—she determines to move to a larger city where the anonymity that accompanies densely populated communities will enable her to pass as white. She initially resides in Union Square in New York, before securing a permanent residence in Greenwich Village on the West Side, where she continues to white-pass out of convenience. Though the formalization of her racial identity is a primary concern of the artist's character development, the overarching impediment to Angela's development as an artist—more specifically, a portraitist—is her outsider status as a regional migrant, which is sympatico in the novel's terms

---

[4] These transformations were abridged in Fauset's close friend Du Bois's influential sociological study, *The Philadelphia Negro* (1899).

with her outsider racial status. Metaphysically, she is never fully able to assimilate into white Manhattan.

This impediment was common in contemporaneous novels that narrativized female artistry in relation to a nationalist framework, which often explored the integrative difficulties of Americanism after the 1917 draft through the dilemma of ethnic passing, within which the individual artist character struggles to reconcile their individuality and cosmopolitan ambitions for their artistic destiny with the narrowing constraints of their ethnic identity and community. As Martin Japtok has argued of *Plum Bun* and Edna Ferber's pioneering Jewish Künstlerroman *Fanny Herself* (1917), although

> the artist's quest is more (stereotypically) connected to a flight from society and to an attempt to realize artistic vision untrammeled by societal restrictions, the function of art in the ethnic Bildungsroman . . . connects the protagonists to their ethnicity and ultimately to their ethnic group. (95)

Precisely *where* that ethnic group is to be located also determined whether that artist's integration would be successful, either personally or professionally, as is the case in *Plum Bun*. Beneath that novel's somewhat melodramatic plot, then, Fauset encodes how Angela's artistic and social dilemma—to identify as Black or white—hinges upon the resolution of her geographical restlessness. In terms of Bakhtin's definition of the Künstlerroman, both Angela's "fitness for life" and her potential for artistic "genius" are tested by whether her Philadelphian values of middle-class respectability, which at first seem to be more aligned with the customs of downtown "white" Manhattan where she passes, will carry her across the vibrant uncertainty of Harlem life and the cosmopolitanism of Greenwich Village. The novel works in that sense to secure her a middle ground between these two categories, which Tom Lutz has described as Fauset's regional cosmopolitanism (170). Angela's individual ontology of art is connected to her sense of the geographic emplacement of Black, white, and other racialized collectives: a nexus between space and cultural identity out of which the mythology of the Black nationalism of the Harlem Renaissance emerges.

For the geographical logic of a passing narrative to work, the author must erect spatial barriers around the region's racialized zones: those boundaries of Blackness and whiteness that separate ethnic groups into certain areas of the city, which only the mixed-race Black protagonist can freely navigate, while seemingly never belonging to either place. New York City's external spatial divisions catalyze the protagonist's interior struggles to integrate into either landscape, and thus coalesce with one of those two races. *Plum Bun* does not emulate the modernist techniques *du jour* for conveying the central character's interior thought processes as a fragmented patchwork, such as non-linear narration or stream of consciousness; rather, much of Angela's characterization as developing artist is registered through free indirect discourse that details her perambulations firstly in Philadelphia and, for much of the novel, in different racialized areas of Manhattan. This builds upon one idea outlined in a personal essay published in *The Crisis* in 1922 entitled "Sunday Afternoon," in which Fauset noted how to "the visual-minded all impressions come in a series of little pictures," as she could "remember only by opening and closing camera-fashion a little inward shutter—all my life stretches backward in a group of single detached visions" (Fauset "Sunday Afternoon," 162). Angela, it is noted five times throughout the novel, is "visual minded," often pausing to take mental images that she aggregates into a film-reel of memories. Angela also registers time spatially, as in one instance in which she imagines "the past years of her life falling into separate, uneven compartments whose ensemble made up her existence" (Fauset *Plum Bun*, 515). As revealed in her correspondences with the younger writer Jean Toomer, whom she mentored during her editorship at *The Crisis*, Fauset venerated Walter Pater and the French imagists, abjuring "the modern tendency . . . toward an involving of ideas . . . a sort of immeshing the kernel of thought in envelopes of words" (qtd in Foley *Jean Toomer*, 55). What Fauset "immeshes" in her own work are the variegated physical and cultural chronotopes of distinctive parts of the Northeastern region, mapping those onto the protagonist's visually oriented contemplations, which ultimately reflects those multiple jeopardies of—as Bonner's essay suggested—being young, a woman, and colored, and relegated to the fringe of the Northeast's culture industry.

The peripatetic Angela's ability to identify as both Black and white permits her to map the city beyond Harlem for the reader, including areas that darker-complexioned African American characters could not access due to racism. Angela finds herself overwhelmed by the "towering building" of Fifth Avenue, which in regionalist imagery appears to her like a "canyon" that "[dwarfs] the importance of the people hurrying through its narrow confines" (Fauset *Plum Bun*, 487). Within that geography, Angela creates an anthropological assessment of those people "living at a sharper pitch of intensity than those she had observed in Philadelphia," although none "of these people, black or white, were any happier" (487). As a "visual minded" painter, Angela interprets that metropolitan scene as a regionalist panorama: skyscrapers form a "canyon" towering above the "river" that is Fourteenth Street, "impersonally flowing;" in that terrain, Angela herself becomes an animal-like entity who "wandered, almost prowled, intent upon the jostling shops" but "above all intent upon the faces of those people" (487). For the first few months in New York, she can repress this feeling of self-imposed racial alienation, charmed as she is by the liberating effects of metropolitan mobility and anonymity: "She was seeing the world, she was getting acquainted with her life in her own way without restrictions or restraints; she was young, she was temporarily independent, she was intelligent, she was white . . . this was what it meant then, this sense of owning the world, this realization that other things being equal, all things were possible," though they are of course gendered, the narrator addends (487–8). At first, Manhattan and the whiteness and independence (adulthood) it facilitates for her seems boundless in its cosmopolitan possibilities, in contrast to the Philadelphia of her earlier Blackness and restricted circumstances (childhood), as a more provincial area in that it is yet organized by small-town customs and a lack of anonymity.

Inspired by this scene, Angela longs to paint the "'types'" she encounters on the sidewalk of Fourteenth Street, especially those white people standing in front of a pianola in a shop window wearing "one expression which [she] could only half interpret," which seems to appear on "those listening countenances usually at the playing of Irish and Scottish tunes" (489). It is a look of "utter remoteness" that dissipates as soon as a jazz song comes on. Where exactly those minds travel to hear those tunes, she does not know; but what emotion that countenance makes Angela feel is "'Homesick,' ... though she hardly knew for what,—certainly not for Philadelphia and that other life which now seemed so removed as to have been impossible" (489–90). Angela projects her inner inability to reconcile these questions onto the world around her, including in one instance while watching a film at the local cinema. The portraitist studies "the screen with a strained and ardent intensity, losing the slight patronizing skepticism which had once been hers with regard to the adventures of these shadowy heroes and heroines; so utterly unforeseen a turn had her own experiences taken" (490). It strikes her that she is on "the threshold of a career totally different from anything that a scenario writer could envisage" (490). As she peers "about her in the soft gloom of the beautiful theatre," she wonders if the other audience members would "begrudge her, if they knew, her cherished freedom and sense of unrestraint? If she were to say to this next woman for instance, 'I'm coloured,' would she show the occasional dog-in-the-manger attitude of certain white Americans and refuse to sit by her or make a complaint to the usher" (490)? As New York upholds and breaks down racial barriers in uneven ways, at a point when Jim Crow was legally hardening throughout much of the country, the cinema offers uniquely suggestive scenery for repurposing the mulatta character as a New Negro Woman through the paradigm of the development of the artist novel. The cinema provides a cosmopolitan space of temporal suspension, where Angela's racial/regional dislocation can rise to the surface of her thoughts. She finds that "Philadelphia and her trials"—meaning her childhood when she identified as Black—"were receding into the distance" as she assumes herself a future in which she will choose to be white (490). Nevertheless, Angela also uses cinema in the above instance to test a utopian possibility where genuine "social equality" might not only become available but normalized, socially and culturally.

To allay her homesickness for the lost innocence of childhood, feelings which intensify during these cultural excursions, the white-passing Angela makes frequent trips to the cinema and theater, urban interiors that allow her to project her internal aesthetic and racial development onto external screens and stages. The "happy, irresponsible, amused hours" she spends "in the marvellous houses on Broadway or in the dark commonplaceness of her beloved Fourteenth Street," as well as a local theater "on Seventh Avenue just at the edge of the Village," attract her not for the cultural entertainment but "for the sake of the audience, a curiously intimate sort of audience made of numerous still more intimate groups," as do the wistful white "men gazing in the music store" who dream of Scotland and Ireland (490). In these public venues, she realizes she has been "neglecting her Art," the reason she "'broke away from everything and came to New York.'" Angela determines to take painting classes; but what she finds there in Greenwich Village is a third option for the trajectory of her development among a cosmopolitan cohort of Jewish, Spanish, German, Scandinavian, white American, and African American artists including the man she will eventually marry, Anthony Cross, a commercial portraitist (492). Angela discovers that art's community-building function might potentially fill the void her provincial childhood in Philadelphia once occupied. Even when the vastness and busyness of metropolitan existence seems designed to alienate the individual from that network, art anchors her into the collective. Angela even begins to metaphorize her social relations through the mediums she works in; for instance, the narrator notes how Angela remembers her new art school friends like snapshots. The most vivid of her collection of mental photographs is Rachel Powell, the only dark-complexioned Black artist in their class, who acts aloof from the others, and who also serves as the racial double of the white-passing Angela, who renames herself Angèle Mory to ensure she remains unrecognized (492).

Harlem also becomes the implicit signifier of Angela's homesickness for the region of her fading youth—and it becomes attached both to her sister, Virginia, and her uncanny double Rachel Powell, who personifies all that Angela regrets about betraying her dark-complexioned sister by white-passing and leaving their idyllic childhood behind. Harlem she perceives as offering not an alienating cosmopolitanism but a regional cosmopolitanism: a blending of the provincial and the metropolitan, as elucidated in the following observation of the moiling groups on Lenox Avenue . . . [who] were gossiping, laughing, dickering, chaffing, combining the customs of the small town with the astonishing cosmopolitanism of their clothes and manners. Nowhere down town did she see life like this. (494)

Angela conceives of Harlem not only as a "city within a city" (494), but as a paradoxical aesthetic region radiating both the "customs of the small town" and "astonishing cosmopolitanism." For, "just as this city reproduced in microcosm all the important features of any metropolis, so undoubtedly life up here was just the same" as in any one of modernity's seemingly ubiquitous regions. Like Fauset herself, Angela converts anthropological observations about the different modes of local life, especially its racialized regionalisms, into her artistic subjects. In Harlem, this analytical tool makes sense to the "visual minded" artist: people seem to dress, walk, and behave in ways that are external reflections of their internal self-image; however, unlike the conspicuous consumption of Fifth Avenue's great spectacle, this "production" serves a community-building function and aesthetic, rather than the alienating, individualistic production she has observed downtown. Fauset's local color descriptions of Harlem's socially diverse and culturally dynamic avenues, where "black," "brown," "yellow," and "white" characters interact through the art of "strolling," transfigures these throngs into a troupe of actors within a great geographical "production" of social groups, united by their social marginalization in wider Manhattan (493).

In modernism's untidy geographies, the unfixed *flâneur* was often seen as the ideal representational vehicle for navigating the scale of modernity's cities, with their seemingly infinite possible events and character encounters. To register the incalculable spatial pathways and possible character networks through which Angela passes, Fauset relies upon New York's numeric sign system, a vast grid of parallel and perpendicular street numbers, elevated trains and streetcar networks, and the underground subway system. The vastness of that system is registered paratactically by Fauset, whose syntactic exploration of the city itself is configured as one elongated sentence:

> At One Hundred and Thirty-fifth Street she left the 'bus and walked through from Seventh Avenue to Lenox, then up to One Hundred and

Forty-seventh Street and back down Seventh Avenue to One Hundred and Thirty-ninth Street, through this to Eighth Avenue and then weaving back and forth between the two Avenues through Thirty-eighth, Thirty-seventh down to One Hundred and Thirty-fifth Street to Eighth Avenue where she took the Elevated and went back to the New York which she knew. (493)

As Fauset narrates Angela's perambulations through Harlem, the hypotaxis used to evoke meandering movement positions the artist protagonist as a *flâneuse*; her attentiveness to the visual functions similarly to James Weldon Johnson's anthropological lens onto the cultural art of "strolling": not "merely walking along Lenox or upper Seventh Avenue" so much as an appropriation of "these streets" as "places for socializing" in one's fanciest clothes "with friends," "acquaintances," and most importantly, "the strangers he is sure of meeting" (Johnson qtd in Robertson, White, and Garton 867). Street life was, by the mid-1920s, "central to the perception of Harlem as a black place," given how strolling through "Seventh Avenue in 1925 assured a visitor a rich picture of black life in Harlem, ... christened the 'Black Broadway' by writer Wallace Thurman" (Robertson, White, and Garton 867). "Strolling" accompanied the streets' public and commercial activities—from soapbox speakers, to prostitutes and "numbers runners" (gambling middlemen)— all conducted their business on the same sidewalks.

We can see Johnson's socializing impulse in Angela Murray's romanticized panorama of Lenox Avenue, when on "an exquisite afternoon," the painter goes strolling in Harlem for the first time (Fauset *Plum Bun*, 493). Like the many white tourists who traversed Harlem's streets via the subway, elevated lines, streetcars, and buses, or private cars, Angela attempts to interpret the meaning of adult society in this unfamiliar city through superficial surfaces and appearances: clothes, manners, and expressions all become the sum of these strangers' social function. One stranger's "sharp, high-bred face etched . . . on her memory" strikes her as possibly artistic, but Angela finds it "unlikely that he would be her kind of an artist, for how could he exist" (493)? He, a Harlemite, is the citizen of a different world than hers, as a white-passing woman who is caught in the ontological borderland between two similar yet separate "worlds" of social production. Though "in all practical things these two worlds were alike, but in the production, the fostering of those ultimate manifestations, this world was lacking, for its people were without the means or the leisure to support them and enjoy" (493). Unlike her sister, Virginia, who easily adapts to Harlem's regional cosmopolitanism and "seemed overwhelmed, almost swamped by friendships, pleasant intimacies" and "a thousand charming interests" (590), the white-passing Angela remains stubbornly alienated from it.

The "visual minded" Angela's "strolling" is ever accompanied by her personal dilemma as an artist: whether she will continue passing as white to further her career, or develop a racialized aesthetic like her sister Virginia, a musician who joins an artist enclave in Harlem. Angela here intuits one of the novel's key ideas regarding the politics of art and representation, determining who is considered the creator of art, and who is typically perceived as its subject within the limits of a white-supremacist marketplace of ideas and aesthetics. Such questions pose enormous implications for her artistic future: which part of her multiracial identity she will identify with on the canvas, and which will she emphasize within the competitive New York culture industry? Angela's objective detachment in Harlem is not that of the sociologist, but of the aesthete whose vision of life is structured upon her anthropological interest in the spatial formations of culture—yet, crucially, this is a position made available to her only on account of her regional difference, or, in Angela's words, her "natural remoteness" from Lenox Avenue. There, she feels vindicated in her decision to leave her childhood home, although "she could now realize that life viewed from the angle of Opal and Jefferson Streets in Philadelphia and that same life viewed from One Hundred and Thirty-Fifth Street and Seventh Avenue in New York might present bewildering facets" (493–4). This sense of dislocation becomes evident in the following observation, redolent of regionalist imagery:

> Unquestionably there was something very fascinating, even terrible, about this stream of life. . . . It was deeper, more mightily moving even

than the torrent of Fourteenth Street. . . . she already saw [these people] objectively, doubly so, once with her natural remoteness and once with the remoteness of her new estate[.] (494)

Unable to isolate any single focal point in this turbid cosmopolitan current, she finds herself "amazed and impressed at this bustling, frolicking, busy, laughing great city within a greater one. She had never seen coloured life so thick, so varied, so complete" (494). Angela's ethnic naivety, and her inability to understand her place in this racially zoned city, implicitly weighs upon her future as an artist. She, like every Harlem artist, begins to feel the pressure of "race-duty," and senses a resolution to this dilemma.

Despite the other cosmopolitan Greenwich Village community that Angela has entered among her art school friends, Rachel Powell serves as a frequent reminder of that unnamed region in Angela's mind where her dormant homesickness is located; a region that must be suppressed in assuming the role of mistress to her white-supremacist beau, Roger Fielding. Still psychologically traumatized by her Philadelphia classmates who abandoned her after finding out she was Black, Angela has internalized their racism, allowing herself to be seduced by Roger, a "young, rich and idle" (557) millionaire who made his fortune in managing his industrialist father's sawmill empire in Georgia (568) and believes she is white. He convinces her to live with him "in sin," which in the novel's lexicons constitutes a racial and sexual moral fall. Her white-passing identity, Angèle Mory, is not a character she respects, and the affair leaves her uninspired artistically:

> Gradually the triumphant vividness so characteristic of Angèle Mory left her, she was like any one of a thousand other pitiful, frightened girls thronging New York. Miss Powell glanced at her and thought: "she looks unhappy, but how can she be when she has a chance at everything in the world just because she's white?" (587)

Rachel Powell here operates as the ironic mouthpiece for what Angela, so long as she passes as white, cannot bring herself to articulate: namely, if Angela continues to pose as a white aesthete, she must remain locked out of the pantheon of genuine creative inspiration. After her relationship with Roger deteriorates, Angela commits to developing herself artistically:

> In her despair she turned more ardently than ever to her painting; already she was capable of doing outstanding work in portraiture, but she lacked cachet; she was absolutely unknown. (587)

If wooing does not inspire creative potential, inspiration must be sourced from *place*—one linked to her ethnic roots—in contradistinction to the modern spaces she inhabits.

Angela's regional bewilderment and sense of restlessness accentuates the sensation of double consciousness: of "ever feeling one's twoness," as Fauset's friend Du Bois wrote in *The Souls of Black Folk* (Du Bois *Souls*, 3); of feeling like a homeless signifier. During the social isolation of the art school summer holidays, when that feeling becomes most intense, she considers relocating to Europe, although "the urge to wander was no longer in the ascendant," and travel "did not seem as alluring now as the prospect of New York had appeared when she lived in Philadelphia," for it "would be nice to stay put, rooted; to have friends, experiences, memories" (590). Finding herself alone after her friends leave to return home, whether abroad or interstate, she finds herself envying her artist friend Martha for her "roots" in Long Island, which stirs in Angela a sudden desire for the "peace," "security," and "companionableness" of Philadelphia (590). Angela then projects her own sense of alienation—or what Angela feels as "homesickness"—onto the city's people, "particularly" its lonesome "young women" whom she observes during her daily commute (590).

That youthful restlessness central to the narrative logic of the Bildungsroman genre as the symbolic form of modernity—which results out of the abandonment of the country for the town (Moretti 4)—becomes concentrated in Angela's commute between her workplace and apartment across Manhattan's underground L-train network, the 14th Street-Eastern District line, a literal to-ing and fro-ing that mirrors her internal vacillations—and which will inevitably inspire the basis of her aesthetic as a portraitist. For Fauset, the enclosed venues of New York's trams, elevated train, and subway facilitate a character study of metropolitan life, to which the outsider Angela belongs, but from which she is ultimately distinguished as an artist:

> Her office was on Twenty-third Street and often at the noon-hour she walked down to the dingy Square and looked again in on the sprawling, half-recumbent, dejected figures. . . . She still carried her notebook, made sketches, sitting watching them and jotting down a line now and then when their vacant, staring eyes were not fixed upon her. (Fauset *Plum Bun*, 589)

Whereas the L-train routinely drops silent throngs of unremarkable, isolated characters at their destinations and their banal nocturnal distractions, "the evenings" find the artistically maturing Angela hard at "work" on "the idea of a picture which she intended for a masterpiece" (590).

The longer Angela remains a downtown resident ethnographically interpreting the cultural and social life of the uptown community, the more her geographical restlessness appears to externalize her unresolvable racial indeterminacy. Fauset's direction for Angela increasingly involves testing her artistic "genius" to resolve her racial and regional double consciousness, tensions that play out in the novel's courtship plot. Angela's gradual determination to identify once more as Black partly results from her growing awareness that she is in love with Anthony Cross, who in a melodramatic twist reveals he is the mixed-race son of a Black American sailor from Georgia who was lynched for protecting Anthony's mother, a Brazilian "with the blood of many races in her veins" (622–3). Fauset turns the screw: Angela discovers that her sister Virginia has fallen in love with Anthony. This revelation forces a distressed Angela to seriously commit to developing her artistic abilities; but still, she does not immediately think of engaging in any racialized aesthetic. When she wins a prize for her portrait collection entitled, "Fourteenth Street Types," a clear reference to her proximity to the Fourteenth Street School (Sherrard-Johnson 64), it receives an equal cash award to the prize bestowed upon Rachel Powell for "A Street in Harlem" (Fauset *Plum Bun*, 654). Her simultaneous competition with and desire to befriend Rachel Powell—whom Angela initially rejects to avoid being outed as Black—comes to a head when her rival is discriminated against by white organizers of a foreign art exchange to the Fountainebleau School of Fine Arts near Paris. One organizer demands to know if "'any other young coloured woman knowing conditions in America" has "the right to thrust her company on . . . people with whom she could have nothing in common except her art'" (661). The color-line within the artworld finally compels Angela to "out" herself as "young coloured woman," relegating herself to that same cordoned-off region of Blackness as Rachel Powell (663). What seems at first a sacrifice, in fact leads Angela into a more meaningful opportunity to expand her artistic range by returning to the "small-town" community of Philadelphia, and resultingly, her "authentic" Black identity. Yet her homesickness soon transfers onto her unresolved feelings for Anthony Cross. Angela, traveling through France on a scholarship, finds herself on her way to becoming a successful artist; and, at the last, Anthony crosses the seas to find her and propose.

Beyond the novel's sentimental conclusion, and despite its suggestive subtitle that defines *Plum Bun* as "a story without a moral," Angela's resolution reflects Fauset's overall standpoint: that African American literature must be morally sound to be politically constructive. It provocatively argued for a gendered literary geography that was mindful of how cosmopolitanism—the ability to freely traverse places, regions, nations—was part of the mobility afforded to whiteness and masculinity. Fauset's Künstlerroman thus bypassed hegemonic views of the Great Migration that dominated discourses of Black regionalism during the 1920s, while enacting a feminist intervention into narratives about the development of the New Negro literary renaissance. Beneath the veneer of a realist Künstlerroman which narrativizes the challenges of modern Black female subjectivity, Fauset mapped a more complex vision of the porous racial and cultural exchange routes that ebbed and flowed across the city and into the regions than many of her detractors recognized.

Wallace Thurman's *Infants of the Spring* (1932)

When, in 1932, Wallace Thurman—one of Fauset's staunchest critics—drafted what would remain an unpublished review of his second novel *Infants of the Spring*, he reflected on the shortcomings not only of that novel, but of the nationwide New Negro movement it chronicled:

> Had I waited five more years . . . it might have been more refined . . . [but] I might never have been able to produce anything else without these present unworthy characters willfully insinuating themselves, wreaking havoc. (Thurman "Review of *Infants*," 226)

He was neither the first nor last critic to describe *Infants* as an aesthetically "unsatisfactory novel" (226). His Künstlerroman nevertheless pursued a nobler desire to novelize the Harlem Renaissance from the perspective of those flawed, complicated artist characters who comprised Harlem's young literati. Many of those real-life characters had never appeared in literary realism; certainly not in a Fauset novel, whose body of "work was an ill-starred attempt to popularize the pleasing news that there were cultured Negroes, deserving of attention from artists, and of whose existence white folk should be apprised" (Thurman *Aunt Hagar's Children*, 245). Who would publish about characters like himself: a Black aesthete and queer decadent from the parochial backwaters of the Midwest, who even in Harlem cannot fulfill his potential to equal the greatness of Joyce, Flaubert, or Stendhal, because he labors under the pressure of representing what white America considered the culturally inferior race?

Thurman suggested that *Infants* "undoubtedly has contributed much to the author's individual growth, but which he fears will do little to impress a critical public," from which "no Negro novelist can expect intelligent critical guidance or encouraging appreciation" (Thurman "Review of *Infants*," 226). Nor did they receive it from him. Thurman singled out Walter White's propaganda protest fiction *Fire in the Flint* (1924) and *Flight* (1926), and Fauset's realist novel *There is Confusion* (1926), as two sorts "of literary works both Negroes and sentimental whites desired Negroes to write" (Thurman *Aunt Hagar's Children*, 244). Accordingly, "Negro literature and literary material" were being "exploited by fad finders and sentimentalists" so that a "'renaissance'" could be brought on by encouraging "indiscriminately anything which claimed a

Negroid ancestry or kinship" (245). Such had been the case in local color fiction about the South. Now, readers were "mollified because in addition to Claude McKay's primitive delineations" in *Home to Harlem* and *Banjo*, and Rudolph Fisher's *The Walls of Jericho*, "they have also had respectable volumes by Jessie Fauset and Nella Larsen" including "*Quicksand, Plum Bun*, and *Passing*" (245). In *Flight*, White glosses Mimi Daquin's "complex racial heritage," "heterogenous social milieu," and "duo-racial heritage," leaving her incomplete vis-à-vis truly great characters like "Emma Bovary, Nana, Candida," or "Clara Barron" (184). Mimi merely reflected "a general type," because propaganda does not require "an intense, vibrant personality," only "an alphabetic doll regaled in cliché phrases, too wordy sentences, and paragraphs pregnant with frustrated eloquence" (*Aunt Hagar's Children*, 184). Writing to Langston Hughes, Thurman used similar analogies to mock Nella Larsen's characters, which "always outrage the reader, not naturally as people have a way of doing in real life, but artificially like ill-managed puppets" (Thurman to Hughes in *Collected Writings*, 184).

Thurman's conviction was that forcing Black writers into a homogenous imagined "region" cordoned off from modernism's literary developments was conditioning an entire generation of young Black writers to produce sentimental mediocrity and faulty local color fiction. "Could it be that the *Zeitgeist* was not conducive to the fullest fructification of literary talent?" Thurman wondered (*Aunt Hagar's Children*, 236). That question informed his Künstlerroman's regional complex, as the author responded to that subgenre's quest not only to "[test] for genius" but also the "artist's fitness for life" (Bakhtin *Speech Genres*, 16). The immaturity of the Black writer, despite Locke and Du Bois's proclamation that literature's New Negro had splendidly come of age, is a point upon which the novel *Infants* insists, in its depiction of an aspiring, dark-complexioned writer from the Midwest, Raymond Taylor—modeled on Thurman himself—who fails to manifest his talent, despite his centrality within Harlem's young New Negro literati. The inability for the regional ingénue to mature in the context of Black society's internalized white supremacy had informed his breakout Bildungsroman, *The Blacker the Berry* (1929); but transforming his personal struggle to artistically mature into a metaphor for the failure of the young New Negro movement in Harlem to realize its potential was Thurman's intention for *Infants*. Kenneth Warren describes *Infants* as "one of the earlier works" in the establishment of an African American literary tradition "structured around the theme of black artistic immaturity and naïveté" (69), while Michael Nowlin corroborates that "Thurman entered the literary field ... believing he could write 'great literature'" even though "no African American had yet done so" (102). Fittingly, the only writing project that Raymond accomplishes in *Infants* is a review of a "silly," "sophomoric" novel by a writer who means to "apprise white humanity of the better classes among the Negro humanity" rather than further the development of New Negro modernism, the defining art novel of which was yet unwritten (Thurman *Infants*, 54). Fittingly, this is an acerbic reference to Thurman's review of Fauset's first Bildungsroman, *There is Confusion*.

Despite Thurman's protestations, Fauset's and Thurman's novels resembled each other in genre, setting, themes, and subject matter. No less critically, the idea of Harlem as staging multiple, potentially irreconcilable uneven regionalisms played a crucial role in their narratives about the struggles of the artist to develop in the Northeast's culture industry. Thurman was also an outsider to Harlem; he was born in Salt Lake City in the Southwest; raised in Boise, Idaho in the Rocky Mountains; and educated as a young adulthood in California, a location he returned to in the 1930s to work as a Hollywood screenwriter. While studying at the University of Southern California in 1922—then the editor of *The Pacific Defender* in Los Angeles, where he also produced *Outlet*, "the first western Negro literary magazine"—Thurman became the architect behind what he soon found was an unrealizable Black cultural renaissance of the Far West (Taylor 245). For this reason, Quintard Taylor situates Thurman among a collective of African American writers who "explored black life through the prism of their western experiences," even if "a regional literary aesthetic" failed to precipitate there in the first half of the twentieth century (245). Following his former postal clerk colleague, the novelist Arna Bontemps, over to the Black metropolis of the East Coast in 1925, Thurman set his compass upon Harlem. Thurman turned to novels after the failure of the literary "little magazine" *Fire!!*

A Quarterly Devoted to the Younger Negro Artists, and *Harlem,* which both folded due to untenable finances, despite boasting contributions from African American literature's brightest talents.[5] There was an autobiographical element, then, to Thurman's *The Blacker the Berry* (1929), as Emma Lou Morgan, who "fled to Los Angeles to escape Boise, then fled to Harlem to escape Los Angeles," suddenly realizes while staring at a Western Union sign that mobility has not improved her opportunities, that "these mere geographical flights had not solved her problems in the past, and a further flight back to where her life had begun, although facile of accomplishment, was too futile to merit consideration" (827). The struggle for the dark-complexioned Midwesterner to adapt to Harlem in *The Blacker the Berry* encapsulated the psychological effects of the racial politics surrounding regional migration: the uncanny cultural variances between West and East that Thurman not only experienced, but lucidly narrativized.

Though personal elements informed *The Blacker the Berry*, Thurman adopted a more explicitly real-life approach in *Infants*. It self-referentially processed Thurman's regional complex as a creative practitioner, at a moment when the pressure upon the African American artist to assimilate into a white marketplace of ideas was considerable, including the necessity to locate oneself in Harlem to be taken seriously as an artist. Like the Fitzgeralds, who both hailed from regions that were framed as geographically, socially, and ideologically distant from modernist Manhattan, Thurman's outsider perspective sharpened his objectivity in mapping the psychological and social contours of Harlem's cultural renaissance, the success of which he doubted could stand the test of time. His unflattering perceptions of youth culture in Black and white New York City, and the subsequent regional imaginary that underwrote it, were satirical, edgier, and more polarizing than Fauset's. Virtually none of the literature produced within the cultural spree that constituted the renaissance there even met, let alone surpassed, the feats of Western literature, his novel suggested. Thurman's friend McKay's *Home to Harlem* (1928), but above all Toomer's *Cane*, were the only

---

[5] Contributors included Langston Hughes, Zora Neale Hurston, Bruce Nugent, Countee Cullen, Gwendolyn Bennett, and the artist Aaron Douglas.

African American novels Thurman deemed worthy of beatification because, in his estimation, they dared to show Black life as it really was: filled with disarray, convolution, and contradiction, despite how white liberals neatly imagined it, fantasies to which Fauset's and Larsen's realism catered. McKay's charismatic ruffians emboldened Thurman to consider material closer to "home"; namely, the eccentric characters in the artist commune at 267 W. 136th Street, Harlem.[6] The "Niggerati Manor," named by Zora Neale Hurston in the novel as in life, formed Thurman's spatial referent of Black bohemia; but it was also an abstract architectural symbol of the New Negro Renaissance's unsteady foundations, as African American literature stood poised in a disorienting region of its own within the literary marketplace, staring down an uncertain future.

Repeatedly, Thurman's literary criticism had signaled the failure of a consensus on the politics of literary character to launch in African American aesthetics, in the hands of a group of young artists caught within the crosshairs of so many conflicting positions on what Black writers ought to convey; which members of an undeniably heterogeneous racial community ought to be depicted; and how certain racial types must be characterized to redress white supremacy. Ironically, then, Thurman's biographer Eleonore van Notten notes that "no single character is sufficiently developed to engage the reader's interest," and they "fail to come to life" (240). This was largely true of *Infants*. Instead of writing life-like characters with rich interior lives, Thurman formulated a *roman-à-clef* filled with superficial caricatures of people and works that defined the epoch. A satirical narrative mode meant his characters did not require interior character development, as they were intended to personify differing aesthetic positions in public debates circa 1926–1928 over the future of African American literature within modernism's melee. Thurman's skillful local color descriptions, coupled with his unparalleled sharpness in diagnosing the flaws in others' personalities and writing, transcended his quest for "life

---

[6] Like the Fitzgeralds, plagiarism also began at home in the "Niggerati Manor": Thurman's friend Bruce Nugent's unpublished novel *Gentleman Jigger* was concurrently written about the same events and characters, including the witty writer Raymond Pellman, i.e. Thurman (Worth 163).

like" characterization, which as the criticism above suggests, he evidently saw as central to literary greatness.[7]

The ironic, indeed, seditious, proposal that his generation had failed to produce anything more sophisticated than disposable sentimentalism animated *Infants*'s satirical complaint, which opens with an epitaph from Shakespeare's *Hamlet*, a play centered on a thirty-year-old character whom—according to Franco Moretti—modern Western "culture" elected as "its first symbolic hero" of youth's mobility and potential (3). "Youth to itself rebels, though none else near," Laertes counsels Ophelia, issuing a warning that even the young and beautiful are susceptible to death before their prime. Laertes' warning looms over Raymond's artistic circle, whose youthful potential and creativity will be asphyxiated by the pressures of a white capitalist economy that consumes the racial 'fad' with insatiable greed; whose discriminating tastes ignore any artistry that operates outside its narrow view of race, sexuality, and art. The difficulty Raymond faces as a competent but untested writer is the standardization of African American literature, which pours all Black writers into the one conventional mold, a mold which has not allowed young writers to develop and produce anything beyond the foibles of sentimental local color fiction. The omniscient narrator expresses these tidings early in the novel, focalized through the protagonist Raymond:

> There had been throughout the nation an announcement of a Negro renaissance. The American Negro ... was entering a new phase in his development. He was about to become an important factor in the artistic life of the United States. As the middle westerner and the southerner had found indigenous expression, so was the Negro developing his own literary spokesmen. (Thurman *Infants*, 34)

---

[7] George Schuyler's speculative satire *Black No More: Being an Account of the Strange and Wonderful Workings of Science in the Land of the Free, AD 1933–1940* had pioneered such inflammatory lampooning of the New Negro Renaissance in 1931. Schuyler and Thurman both extended aspects of Carl Van Vechten's incendiary *roman-à-clef Nigger Heaven* (1926), so convincingly "realistic" that it produced Harlem's newest "indoor sport, namely, the ascertaining which persons in real life the various characters were drawn from," as Thurman quipped in his review for *The Messenger* ("A Stranger," 192).

The narrator here implies that "the Negro writer," still in the throes of development, inhabits their own literary region, analogous to literatures of the Midwest or South, the literary value of which was often considered substandard to the universal pantheon of great art.

As we have seen already, a common motif within the Bildungsroman's geographical imaginary is to provide a lens onto modernity's transforming social environment through the unadulterated senses of a young regional outsider, whose mobility enables the author to create impressions of the modern scene that guide the reader through intensities of modernity's changing social, economic, and environmental landscape. This was a particularly salutary strategy for communicating the regional imaginary of the Künstlerroman, as a subgenre that narrativizes tectonic shifts in the cultural landscape and the way in which art is valued and consumed. In *Infants*, Thurman gives the role of "innocent foreigner" in Raymond's words to the newly arrived Stephen Jorgenson, a white Canadian tourist of Danish heritage, who becomes the protagonist's companion. Their homoerotic bond over mutual tastes in high culture forms a conceit that conveniently allows Thurman to introduce his personal views on decadence and modernism, and where his vision for African American authorship aligned with that tradition. Stephen, a foreigner who later calls himself a member of Stein's Lost Generation, feels drawn to Harlem's exotic underbelly. Yet, his reflections upon arriving in Harlem redress the primitivist mythologies of that place: when he alighted "the sub-way at 135th Street," Stephen "felt alien, creepy, conspicuous, ashamed" amid "strange dark faces, the suspicious eyes, the undercurrent of racial antagonism which I felt sweeping around me, the squalid streets, barricaded by grim tenement houses" (5–6). Where Angela feels a sense of wonderment in *Plum Bun* that almost compels her to out herself as Black, Stephen desires to "assume some protective coloration" and pass as Black to adapt to the uptown (Black) environment in which he is suddenly ensconced.

As Thurman's cynical mouthpiece in *Infants*, Raymond follows Hughes and McKay in their crusade against the polite tea-rooms of Fauset's and Larsen's Northeastern fictions, as he tells Stephen to trust those instincts, and desist in his crusade to romanticize the Black metropolis:

> "New York is a world within itself, and every new portion of it which gets discovered by the sophisticates . . . seems more unusual [. . . but] don't let the fact that it's black New York obscure your vision." (19–20)

Stephen's tourism allows Thurman to refuse the romanticization of Harlem as the frontier of Black modernity that had been mapped out by sensationalist white literary cartographers like Van Vechten. Instead, Raymond/Thurman explains to the reader Harlem's contradictory social production of space, filled with creative intensity yet mired by the inequality of resources one might expect of a redlined district, which Thurman chose to emphasize in his literary portraits of life in Harlem. "Harlem has been called the Mecca of the New Negro," Thurman wrote in 1927 in a guide to the suburb for the *Haldeman-Julius Quarterly* (Thurman "Negro Life," 39). Playing tour guide for a mixed-race socialist readership, Thurman describes the dialectical energy of Harlem's social production of space, at once full of abject poverty and vibrancy. Just as "the great south side black belt of Chicago spreads and smells with the same industrial clumsiness and stockyardish vigor of Chicago," New York's own Black Belt must "teem and rhyme with the cosmopolitan cross-currents of the world's greatest city" (39). Like Fauset's protagonist Angela noted in *Plum Bun*, that cosmopolitanism was intercut with the solidity of small-town culture. Thurman's topography of Harlem, home to over 200,000 Black residents by the mid-1920s, formed part of an interconnected interregional and international racial landscape that was simultaneously local, and yet teeming with many contradictory domestic and international cultural influences. Though Harlem is "a great city," and there are "no shanty-filled, mean streets," certain parts of "Little Africa" reveal the poverty of many of its inhabitants, who reside in "tenement houses" that "are darkened dungheaps, festering with poverty-stricken and crime-ridden stepchildren of nature" on "the edge of Harlem's slum district" (40), a perspective immediately impressed upon Raymond's friend Stephen. Harlem is only "part and parcel of greater New York. Its rhythms are the lackadaisical rhythms of a transplanted minority group caught up and rendered half mad by the more speedy rhythms of the subway, Fifth Avenue and the Great White Way [Broadway]," he observed (39), lines that clearly inform Raymond's own geographical assessment in *Infants*.

Among the many men and women, Black, white, or other who frequent the Manor, Raymond and Stephen are the only ones who are seen to be serious about aesthetic values and judgment. Much like Fitzgerald's Amory and Tom D'Invilliers, whose conversations on art and the future of the American novel confirm Amory's unfolding aesthetic sensibilities as a future writer, Thurman's pair devise a shortlist of genius novelists that includes Thomas Mann, Andre Gide, Sigrid Undset, Marcel Proust, Stendhal, Flaubert, Hardy, Tolstoy, Zola, Hemingway (the only American, who is only listed for capturing the zeitgeist of the twenties), and above all Joyce, about whose *Portrait of the Artist* they grow "incontinently rhapsodic" (Thurman *Infants*, 18). After devising their cosmopolitan canon, "their talk veered to Harlem," and on home soil they find themselves "sitting at opposite poles" (18). Raymond has explored "every nook and cranny of that phenomenal Negro settlement," which he admits "attained international fame, deservedly"; and yet he remains "disgusted with the way everyone sought to romanticize Harlem and Harlem Negroes" (18). What Raymond finds in Harlem cuts against the grain of its romantic mythologization that Stephen initially subscribes to:

> Word had been flashed through the nation about this new phenomenon. Novels, plays, and poems by and about Negroes were being deliriously acclaimed and patronized. . . . And yet . . . nothing . . . was being done to substantiate the current fad, to make it the foundation for something truly epochal. (34)

The development of African American literature, its coming to maturity, has been arrested. The narrator, speaking for Raymond, diagnoses a problem in American fiction caused by the popularization of literary "regionalism" as a mode, with its heightened interest in folk vernacular and rural panoramas, but also its sentimentalism and political sensationalism. Local colorism lacked both foresight and destabilized any genuine foundation upon which the New

Negro Renaissance could be anchored for it to reach a point of stable, lasting maturity. Modernism's drive to innovate by appropriating from what it regarded as the primitive and exotic may have involved introducing Black characters, voices, and material to avant-garde culture that flourished in cosmopolitan cities such as New York, but the effects of this vogue would not be long-lasting for African American literature, Thurman warns. Although "the Negro was more in evidence in the high places than ever before in his American career," for Raymond and his fellow Black artists "there would be little chance of their being permanently established" (34). Raymond is concerned with what he perceives as "the fact that most Negroes of talent were wont to make one splurge, then sink into oblivion," and wonders whether this is the result "of some deep-rooted complex," or "a lack of talent" (Thurman *Aunt Hagar's Children,* 34). Thurman's narrator echoes his critique of Fauset and Larsen; namely, "Negro writers who had nothing to say, and who only wrote because they were literate and felt they should apprise white humanity of the better classes among Negro humanity" (Thurman *Infants,* 54), another line lifted out of Thurman's literary criticism. The manor's "visionary" landlady, an artist and radical-turned-businesswoman named Euphoria Blake, assembled the renters on the basis that she "knew the difficulties experienced by Harlem artists and intellectuals in finding congenial living quarters," intending to profit "by turning this house over to Negros engaged in creative work" while benefiting "artistically from the resultant contacts" (19–20). As a landlady, Euphoria knows how to yield returns from Harlem's cultural revolution: not by engaging in abstract cosmopolitanism or nationalist fervor, but by offering a concrete, material *place* where creativity can converge—and pay dividends.

The rising action of the narrative follows Raymond's arrested artistic development and immobilization within that "Niggerati Manor." Having moved to Harlem from the West to assist his writing career three years prior to the novel's events, he must now climb what Thurman's friend Langston Hughes called the "racial mountain." In the landmark essay, "The Negro Artist and the Racial Mountain," the incipient poet upbraided the "high class" convention that was suffocating those "younger Negro artists who create," demanding they "pour racial individuality" into the national mold of "American standardization" (Hughes "The Negro Artist," 1267). Hughes's spatial poetics advocated for the politicized broadening of the racial aesthetics of space: a shifting away from subjects of the bourgeois parlor rooms; a wandering into the cabarets, sidewalks, subway trains, and other public spaces belonging to the masses; a co-mingling of extraordinary and ordinary characters who serve no didactic moral function. Harlem was not the exclusive spatial fix where this aesthetic principle of "realistic prose pictures" of Black life was rooted (Thurman "Negro Artists," 196–7),[8] so much as one provider of the "common element" (Hughes "The Negro Artist," 1268) that could be found on Seventh Street in Washington, or along State Street in Chicago, or in the West Indian tropics. Hughes, whose poetry is twice referenced in the novel, materializes as the "smiling and self-effacing" young poet Tony Crews, who attends Dr. Parkes's literary salon simply because he is "grateful . . . to slip away from the backwoods college he attended" in the Midwest (Thurman *Infants*, 142). But it is the racial mountain that Raymond holds in mind when he idles about Central Park one afternoon, a spatial environment that invites the processes of internal reflection. His writer's block registers in spatial terms: "He was going . . . he knew not where" (89). "Always he had protested that the average Negro intellectual and artist had no goal, no standards, no elasticity, no pregnant germ plasm," and

> now he was beginning to doubt even himself. He wanted to write, but he had made little progress. He wanted to become a Prometheus, to break the chains which held him to a racial rack and carry a blazing beacon to the top of Mount Olympus so that those possessed of Alpine stocks could follow in his wake. (89–90)

Thurman strategically positions his artist hero on the doorstep of an ostensibly transhistorical, transnational (and thus transregional) literary pantheon that he believed no other Black novelist had entered. Raymond's musings echo Eliot's modernist aesthetics of tradition,

---

[8] Reviewing *The Weary Blues* (1925), Thurman praised Hughes's exploration of Black society's "lower" provinces (*Collected Writings* 196–7).

individual talent, and "the historical sense," which "involves a perception, not only of the pastness of the past, but of its presence; the historical sense compels a man to write not merely with his own generation in his bones, but with a feeling that the whole of the literature of Europe from Homer and within it the whole of the literature of his own country has a simultaneous existence and composes a simultaneous order" (Eliot 55). Taking one step further, Raymond, simultaneously pressured by the world literary tradition on one level and the "literature of his own country" on another, as well as the literature of Black cultural nationalism beneath that, "wanted to do something memorable in literature, something that could stay afloat on the contemporary sea of weighted ballast, something which could transcend and survive the transitional age in which he was living. He wanted to accomplish these things, but he was becoming less and less confident that he was possessed of the necessary genius" (Thurman *Infants*, 90). His undeniable "modicum of talent" could not "guarantee his being catapulted into the literary halls of Valhalla," another Western idea of immortality. Raymond's "talent was not a sufficient prerequisite for immortality. He needed genius and there was no assurance that he had it" (90).

The scales over Stephen's eyes soon peel away after experiencing one too many corrupting instances of the Niggerati Manor's chaotic nightlife, including one infamous "Donation Party," which deteriorates into sexual debauchery and violent belligerence, driving a wedge between Raymond and the Canadian tourist. Stephen realizes he, too, was drawn to the Manor on account of what he thought would be the stabilizing force of its legendarily cosmopolitan community:

> "You see, I'm one of Gertrude Stein's lost generation . . . or rather post-lost generation. I'm too busy trying to find borderlines in this new universe of ours ever to strike out on my own. . . . The world has become too large. I can't see the skyline from the ground, and I'll probably become a Humanist just because they are interested in establishing boundary lines." (136)

Raymond wonders why he doesn't simply "revolt" (136), a word that echoes Van Doren's famous phrase regarding the New American literature. But as Stephen points out, Raymond's dilemma is unequal to his; Raymond's artistic blockage is not simply caused by him realizing he is caught adrift in the cosmopolitan uncertainty of his generation. Rather, he will always be relegated to the imagined region of Blackness, where there can be no development into genius, only immaturity, criticism, and failure.

Clearly, Raymond's regional complex derives from his outsider status as a Midwesterner. More crucially, however, it stems from his inability to radically break with the overly simplistic, "regional" framework imposed upon Black novelists in order to establish an individualist path for himself in the universal pantheon of art—a struggle that reiterated the broader concerns of Thurman's own literary criticism and nonfictional cultural geography. Raymond's diatribes against the zeitgeist parody the acerbic wit of the public jeremiads of Thurman, who attempted to define his own literary ambitions for the young New Negro by placing that figure in the center of an unflattering but realistic portrait of their locale, Harlem. The Black writer, but also their geographical symbol, Harlem, had become muddled in the racial imaginary of the "local color" fiction that attempted to depict it as exotic in all the ways that might appeal to the white touristic reader. Such realism, to Thurman, only further segregated the Black writer from the cultural and political avant-garde of modernism, thus in his mind preventing African American writers from reaching maturity. Such aesthetic concerns culminate in the event of the "first and last" Harlem literary salon, held by Dr. Parkes (Alain Locke), who brings together a motley crew of young literary artists from around the country. Cedric, the alias of West Indian-born author Eric Walrond, insists that

> "There is no necessity for this movement becoming standardized . . . Dr. Parkes wants us all to go back to Africa and resurrect our pagan heritage . . . Fenderson here wants us all to be propagandists . . . Madison wants us all to . . . fight the capitalistic bogey. Well . . . why not let each young hopeful choose his own path?" (148)

It is an individualist position with which the protagonist—and author—effusively agrees, joining his housemate and rival Paul Arabian (alias of Bruce Nugent) in his impish undermining of Dr.

Parkes's agenda. The meeting reinforces the flaw of all regionalisms, which risk either merging into a homogenous, standardized entity within the capitalist marketplace of ideas, or disintegrating altogether. Dr. Parkes implores Raymond to heed caution, and not succumb to decadence:

> "... remaining in this house, as notorious as it is bound to become ... is inimical to your development. You can't create to the best of your ability, being constantly surrounded by a group of parasites and drunken nonentities." (124)

The reluctance Raymond feels to accept what he knows to be true, that he must leave the Niggerati Manor to become a great artist, intensifies the issue of his unfixed standing within the young New Negro movement. The artists' tenement at least offers some physical semblance of cultural solidity, as disorderly as its frequenters may be. Without that stabilizing sense of place, the dilemma returns of where the Young New Negro artist can anchor his aesthetic: in the soils of Africa, which he has never known? In the fields of the South, which he has no interest in ever visiting? In the parochial Midwest, which bores the white reading public? Arising out of the miscegenated, avant-garde underworld of rent parties, bootlegging, orgies, cabarets, and fisticuffs—facilitated by those unrespectable postwar social spaces that the parochial Old Negro avoided, lest it confirm their white reading audience's preconceived views of Blackness as the primitive subregion of white culture—Raymond emerges as the driftingly aimless harbinger of African American literature's uncertain future. Those tidings of uncertainty register in the novel's final image of Paul Arabian's sketch of the Niggerati Manor etched onto his suicide note, drawn not as a tenement but a skyscraper crumbling under a sky of "dominating white lights" (175). Like the disintegrating building, Thurman suggests that Harlem, as a symbolic place entrenched partly in reality and partly in myth, could only temporarily stabilize the otherwise unsettled future of African American authorship.

Infants was not merely a Künstlerroman, then, but a richly conceived novel about Thurman's great unwritten art novel: the one that would surpass the "racial mountain," or rather, racial region inhibiting African American writing from reaching maturity in his perception; a novel which, crucially, never came into being. That unwritten novel haunts Raymond's musings on race, tradition, and individual talent, both publicly and privately, as he recursively emphasizes a point Thurman accentuated throughout his tragically short career:[9] the faddism of racial aesthetics within a white-supremacist marketplace of ideas would perennially disconnect the reality and realism of Black modernity, stunting the more radical formal interventions and developments he and others sought to pursue. He, like Raymond, may not have published a feted novel like Joyce's *Portrait* that could substantiate the maturity of the Black writer. The Künstlerroman form nevertheless enabled Thurman to fulfill his artistic ambition to demythologize overly simplistic accounts of the affiliative relationship between race and place that defined African American literature's uneven geographies for many of his contemporaries. In doing so, he joined Fauset in the quest to unsettle the narrowing discourses of regionalism, identity, and artistic development that constrained them as writers.

---

[9] A 32-year-old Thurman died of tuberculosis in December 1934 in virtual obscurity.

Part III

Southern Underdevelopment

CHAPTER 6

Imagining The Region of Underdevelopment

If the Bildungsroman is defined by its allegorical schema in which youth becomes the "symbolic form" of capitalist modernity, as Moretti argues (5), and if it is the geographical logic of nationhood that puts "the brakes" on youth's boundless development in the genre, as Esty has addended (5), then what shape does youth's development take when it is contoured by the geographical imaginary of a regionalism popularly distinguished by its stubborn antimodernization? Ever lurking at the peripheries of the imagined nation, the twentieth-century South has historically been imagined not only as a site of antidevelopment—as might align with Esty's hypothesis regarding the colonial imaginary of the Anglo-European modernists as issuing narratives of arrested development—but also one of economic underdevelopment. Those socioeconomic "characteristics" that distinguished region from nation were shared "with formerly colonial, underdeveloped peripheries around the globe" (Greeson 3). In both U.S. and world history, the South's story of underdevelopment has metonymized "broader narratives of the Western journey into modernity," Jennifer Rae Greeson observes (4). Literary accounts that projected "the South as premodern and undeveloped" also served a "forward-looking function," by delivering "a domestic site upon which the racialist, civilizing power of U.S. continental expansion and empire abroad may be rehearsed and projected" (4). In the early twentieth century, the South formed a geographic medium—part myth, part reality—onto which the uneven temporalities of national destiny and capitalist modernity could be projected, reinforcing the official narratives of nation-formation.

Many complex layers appear within that region's story of underdevelopment, which this present chapter shall briefly rehearse before proceeding in the following two chapters to the question of how these conditions influenced the regional transformations of the Bildungsroman. Between 1900 and 1960, unprecedented technological interconnectedness, on the one hand, meant media scrutiny documented the region's actual underdevelopment in terms of education, poverty, and civil rights relative to other parts of the nation. Yet on the other hand, the political trope of Southern regional underdevelopment also provided the liberal nation-state with the means to rationalize the racism, imperialism, and 100% Americanism that accompanied national expansion and development. As part of that narrative, the nation "required 'the South' to play a certain, immanently negative part within the *Realpolitick* struggles it was engaged in against the Soviet Union" during and after World War II, preserving "an anti-industrial, pro-agrarian matrix of mythemes in its accepted regional identity" in ways that "proved resistant to any overlay of socialist political semes" that might have destabilized the nation's "exceptionalism" and "anticommunism," Julian Murphet observes (26-7). That situation "provides a strong materialist explanation of the perseverance of romance within a national culture tending officially ... toward rational and modernist formal structures" (27). This all suggests why from the 1910s through to the 1930s, the progenitors of a Southern literary renaissance might have understood the relation between nationalism and regional difference as a matter of generic anxiety: a struggle between romance (the Old South)[1] and modernism (the Nation, including the capitalistically integrated New South), at a moment when the new media revolution "made the abstract 'nation' more of a material reality for more millions of people than at any moment in human history" (27). This also

---

[1] Richard King influentially wrote of the prevalence of the association between region, romance (genre), and family in the formation of a Southern literary tradition, mirroring how the plantation was "conceived of as structured like a family" (27).

indicates why the Bildungsroman that evolved there internalized the political struggle between romance and modernism, seemingly incoherent aesthetics that formally suggested uncertainty over the region's past, present, and future identity, but also what role the nation's region played in the ascent of the U.S. as a world hegemon.

The cultural trope of Southern underdevelopment was initially linked to debates over the region's sentimental depiction in local color fiction, as articulated in one essay entitled "The Local Novel," featured in Hamlin Garland's *Crumbling Idols* (1894). He predicted how an "unaffected, natural, emotional" caliber of colorism would "redeem American literature, as it has already redeemed the South from its conventional and highly wrought romanticism" (69), the implication being that Southern literature would graduate from that degraded mode of fiction—romance—to more mature modes of representation. In 1917, H. L. Mencken for New York's *Evening Mail* declared that the South was the region of anti-Bildung; it was "almost as sterile, artistically, intellectually, culturally, as the Sahara Desert," outside of developments in music and literature of the Black South (*Prejudices*, 229). Yet, according to Jean Toomer in 1923, the "maturation of sectional [i.e., regionalist] art" in New England and the Midwest had inspired interest in the South's "Factories, Main Streets, and survival of the old plantations," where a rich new plane of "physical environment" was complemented by its "stark theme of the white and black races" in "a land of the gret [sic] passions: hate, fear, cruelty, courage, love, and aspiration" (233). Toomer's Southern-focused "American scene" juxtaposed competing regional temporalities: "the restless mal-adjustments of the northern pioneer," beating against the "peasant-adjustment rhythm of the Southern Negro," as the "non-pioneer of the South" (233). Though the South was imagined as operating in a different rhythm to that of national modernity, Toomer insisted that it was no mere window into the nation's preindustrial, provincial past. Rather, its folk provided an integrative cultural component of a modern national identity that was rooted in the fact of land and human passions, rather than in the capitalist-industrial rhythms of development. These romantic observations formalized into Toomer's masterwork about the Jim Crow rural South, *Cane* (1923), a foundational text of the New Negro Renaissance.

That cultural revolution also precipitated counterattacks from white Southern nativists, who imagined their South as a young, heroic champion of a regionalism rooted in agrarian customs. Relative to the cosmopolitanizing industrial North, many areas within the Southern region appeared motionless, closed-off from the nation's drifts of people and capital, which later allowed Southern nativists like the Agrarians to loudly demand the preservation of the veneer of regional distinctiveness, at a moment when mass media was rendering the idea of nationalism virtually ubiquitous in everyday life. By 1910, 15% of U.S. residents were foreign-born, while in the South, that figure remained fixed at 2%, contributing to the persistent optical illusion that the South was immune from the sorts of changes other regions were undergoing in the early twentieth century (Bone 6). From Oxford, Mississippi in 1933, Faulkner regretted how "the New South" was not really "the South" at all, but "a land of immigrants" wrought into the image of "the towns and cities in Kansas and Iowa and Illinois" (qtd in Cobb 114). Echoing that sentiment, literary critics Allen Tate, Robert Penn Warren, Donald Davidson, and Andrew Lytle were among those scholars who contributed to *I'll Take My Stand: The South and the Agrarian Tradition* (1930), a collective manifesto revolting not against the village, but against what they felt was the cultural and political interference of domineering Northern modernism and its synecdoche, New York. "It is out of fashion in these days to look backward rather than forward," Ransom groused in his contribution; the Southerner, "the only American given to" looking backward in a forward-marching industrial society, "feels himself in the American scene as an anachronism" and a "quaint local character" (1). Writers like Dreiser—whom according to Ransom was the quintessential anti-regionalist, rootless communist, and metropolite—had pushed Southern writers to create their own market for "authentic" regional fiction and literary criticism, supported by a thriving local periodical culture.

By representing the region as an idyllic agrarian locale rather than an underdeveloped economy, thereby categorizing that authentic locale as endangered by the cultural homogeneity that accompanies capitalist development, the Southern Agrarians attempted to preserve, protect, and lament the loss of the local cultures, including their chauvinisms, creating a persuasive theory of regional affiliation symbolized through the white heroic figure of young manhood. That "anachronistic" Bildungsheld of *I'll Take My Stand* rebelled against the perceived tyrannical national industrial future and its protagonists: the New Negro, the New Woman, and immigrants (Donaldson xxxiv). The literary Agrarians' anti-modernism, especially Davidson's, led them to argue that regionalism only emerged into view as a cultural defensive against the unanchored cosmopolitans and their cynical satires of regional life that had erupted in the early 1920s, perversely coopting what Davidson perceived as "authentic" regionalisms: genuine, organic modes of living exclusively belonging to the rural and remote Southern region, with some exceptions in the Midwest. Davidson's historical logic only follows if one accepts his narrow definition of regionalism, which "as an 'ism' is only one phase of a general movement of revulsion and affirmation: the self-conscious phase, in which the artist discovers his own discontent and rebels against false guidance" (*Regionalism and Nationalism*, 80–1). Quoting Tate, he defined regionalism not as "quaintness and local color and folklore" that "are merely a titillation of the reader's sentimentality or snobbishness," but as "'the immediate, organic sense of life in which a fine artist works'" (83).

In such definitions, the Agrarians' regionalism "couldn't fully escape the romanticism they shunned, for" they petitioned a "nostalgic image of a vibrant and authentic regional culture" that rebuffed all "legal, economic, political, and social encroachments of what they saw as the bland and homogenous culture of the nation as a whole," Michael Bibler observes (50). The "hierarchical model of individual and regional differences" they espoused connected "explicitly to the legacies of the southern plantation" system, which Lytle went so far as to describe as not only a moral but a "natural" social system, meaning that the "destruction of it" could be "nothing less than catastrophic" (Bibler 51). The Agrarians' romance of Southern exceptionalism was ultimately unsettled by the New Deal, given the heightened scrutiny Roosevelt paid the region circa 1938, when he labeled it "the nation's No. 1 economic problem" (qtd in Bibler 12). Yet, the Agrarians' manifesto constituted a persistent theory of aesthetic regionalism that encouraged some curious transformations in the Bildungsroman about the rural South from the 1930s; though, in many instances, authors were reacting against it. The Agrarians championed the progenitors of a Southern Renaissance from the late 1920s, which included a proliferation of Bildungsromane by authors including Thomas Wolfe (*Look Homeward, Angel*), Ellen Glasgow (*Barren Ground*), William Faulkner (*The Unvanquished; Light in August*), and Eudora Welty (*Delta Wedding*), although many of those novelists reflected more ambivalent portraits of regional difference and did not engage in the exclusionary regionalism the Agrarians peddled.

How could the classical Bildungsroman's generic paradigms and teleology of development be modified to faithfully depict those processes, contradictions, and tensions? The trope of regional underdevelopment itself insists that a fundamental difference exists in the way we imagine regional and national time and represent those imagined differences through textual chronotopes. In the first half of the twentieth century, region was imagined as backward-facing, its primary mode of representation taking the form of romance, whereas the nation was imagined as fast-paced and forward-facing, its mode being modernism, in the most conventional sense of that term. As authors reflected on the instabilities of regional difference in modernist writing about the South, they responded to political models of regional difference from the 1930s that at times challenged but were at other times defined within discourses of U.S. nationalism. The overlapping of these seemingly incommensurate chronotopes was coded within the modernist text through "devolution, folkloric authenticity, romanticism, and Gothicism," as Leigh Anne Duck observes (4). In the case of the Bildungsroman, this meant that the usual biographical time of the genre's classical iterations underwent distortion in narratives that represented the South's underdevelopment, caught between two seemingly irreconcilable modes.

The following two chapters elaborate how the Southern Bildungsroman subsequently registered those uncanny cultural effects of the New South's abrupt entrance into modernity, and the challenges of integrating the region's heterogeneous but economically underdeveloped local cultures into America's nationalhistorical time, as those processes were filtered through the lens of an unfinished youth. In various novels, the genre's biographical time is disrupted and the process of *Bildung* left incomplete, as the narrative structure internalizes the struggle between national-historical time and regional temporality. In such works, regional difference is established in a number of ways: firstly, through the characters' use of local dialect and vernacular, which is distinguished from the omniscient narrator's uninflected language; secondly, in the juxtaposition of the banalities of everyday, small-town life against shocking, remarkable, and violent events; and thirdly, in extensive descriptions of the region's distinctive natural environment. These tendencies informed the blending of classical Bildungsroman conventions with the folkloric aesthetics in Zora Neale Hurston's *Their Eyes Were Watching God*; and the "gothic" aesthetics in Carson McCullers's *The Member of the Wedding* and Flannery O'Connor's *The Violent Bear It Away*. In both interrelated variations, the peasant South, caught between atavism and progress, found its ideal figuration in the unfixed figure of youth, whose uneven development came to register the region's coming into modernity as a fragmented, tormented, and furious growth spurt.

CHAPTER 7

The Way of the World: Hurston's Folkloric Bildungsroman

Zora Neale Hurston's *Their Eyes Were Watching God* (1937)

Zora Neale Hurston was among those authors who remodeled the Bildungsroman by appealing to Southern folkloric romanticism to narrativize how modernization would impact the region's peasant classes, as opposed to simply wondering how folk culture might serve modernists searching for the authenticity of ancestries and places. Although scholars have routinely described Hurston's 1937 Bildungsroman in more universalizing terms as an "individual quest for fulfilment" that "becomes any woman's tale" (Wall "Zora," 76), *Their Eyes Were Watching God* was suggestive of the author's commitment to correcting the perception of Southern regionalism as faulty and backward, blending elements of a regionally neutral biographical realism with appeals to folkloric authenticity rooted in idiosyncratic local cultures and the fact of land. The universalizing impulses in protagonist Janie Crawford's individual quest for fulfillment forms the narrative conceit by which Hurston, who was also an ethnographer, mapped the effects of capitalist development upon the preindustrial Black folk cultures of the early twentieth-century South. As a work that blends elements of the classical Bildungsroman's generic scaffolding—including its themes of labor, courtship, and domesticity—with oral dialect and folkloric storytelling conventions and appeals to Florida's sublime natural environment, Hurston's novel thematically and formally perpetuated an ideology of regional cosmopolitanism. The protagonist's ethnic identity expands, as does her appreciation for and affiliation with the many heterogeneous rural Black folk cultures she encounters as she traverses different communities and modes of living. In this way, Hurston's ethnographic window onto the region's labor and folk-cultural history in ways offered a corrective both to the official discourses of the Jim Crow South, and to Northern critics who misconstrued those communities as primitive and backward.

As Janie searches for personal fulfillment in a variety of settings—from household, to farmstead, to township, to "de muck" (the fertile Everglades, on Florida's southernmost tip)—her experiential geographical education widens in a southward direction. Her romantic view of the sheltered South of her childhood is habitually tested at these different locations by national and global forces that threaten the self-sustaining Black folk cultures of the region. Hurston's critical regionalist geography furthermore drew knowingly upon Florida's proximity to the extended Black South of the Bahamas and Haiti, where the novel was composed while its author conducted fieldwork for the ethnographical study, *Tell My Horse: Voodoo and Life in Haiti and Jamaica* (1938). As Janie's "little world" confronts the effects of the region's abrupt modernization, rural Florida becomes implicated in larger national and global forces of development, cutting against the perception of regional insularity, unworldliness, and primitivism that during the New Negro Renaissance were popularly attributed to the folk South.

Hurston's rural folk chronotopes were not synchronized with the modernist tendencies that united Thurman's and Fauset's Northeastern portraits of artistic development. In Thurman's *Infants of the Spring*, Hurston's likeness Sweetie May Carr is distinguished from the other New Negroes as a Southern "short story writer, more noted for her ribald wit and personal effervescence than for any actual literary work" (142). Like the character Thurman modeled on her, Hurston initially found a lucrative Northern market for Black Southern folklore and its "primitive" culture and dialect, as suited the tastes of her white patron, Charlotte Osgood Mason. "She was a great favorite among those whites who went in for Negro prodigies" for corroborating "their conception of what a typical Negro [i.e., a Black Southerner] should be," although "she did this with tongue in cheek," Thurman japed (*Infants*, 142). Although in jest, he raised a serious issue that Hurston's subsequent novels would redress: from the late 1890s, African American writers had struggled to find avenues of expression that counteracted the "inevitable co-optation of their self-representation within a system of capitalist exchange and racialized patronage" (Carr and Cooper 288). This weighed heavily on Hurston, who later suggested her weariness with the New Negro movement grew out of an innate dissatisfaction with the burden "to write about the Race Problem," rather than about "the human beings I met" who "reacted pretty much the same to the same stimuli" (*Dust Tracks*, 713).

This tendency toward racial, and relatedly, geographical untethering—in which the individual casts off the restrictive identities imposed upon them—became a defining element of Hurston's Black feminist individualism, which informed her regionalist readjustment of the novel of uneven development. Hurston was, at least according to Thurman's satiric portrait of her, "a master of southern dialect," a skill she deployed in her novels, "and an able raconteur, but she was too indifferent to literary creation to transfer to paper that which she told so well . . . and her written work was . . . turgid and unpolished" (Thurman *Infants*, 142). Alain Locke's review of *Their Eyes Were Watching God* extolled Hurston's provisional but "overdue replacement" for condescending "faulty local color fiction" about the Black South ("Review," 18); but he hoped she would come to "maturity" by exploring "motive fiction and social document fiction" and not resorting to "oversimplification" (18). Subsequent critics viewed Hurston's "folk material" as abandoning the "orderly duty" of "literary format," as Catherine Gunther Kodat summarizes; such conclusions overlook how "the southern black folk tradition *itself*" renders the "feminine quest for independence problematic" (Kodat 321). The regional imaginary of *Their Eyes*, then, suggests a South that is characterized by unevenness and filled with contradictory cultural and historical forces, as it formally reorganized the Bildungsroman genre through its extensive use of regional dialect and folkloric themes and imagery.

Though aspects of *Their Eyes* adhere to the biographical time of the realist novel of development, Hurston manufactures an aesthetic regionalism rooted in dark romanticism and the sublime.

The novel's setting produces a panoramic vision of the individual's confrontation of the racial sublime, which we might define as the oppressive forces of human civilization and nature that jeopardize both Black lives and the folk cultures that sustain rural and remote Black communities, which are more susceptible to ecological disasters and hardship due to economic instability. This perspective challenged the constructed parameters of race and regional difference. Her autobiography *Dust Tracks on a Road* later articulated her desires to expand her literary horizons beyond the demands imposed upon her novels by the literary institution:

> ... I know that goodness, ability, vice, and dumbness know nothing about race lines or geography. I do not wish to close the frontiers of life upon my own self [... or] deny myself the expansion of seeking into individual capabilities and depths by living in a space whose boundaries are race and nation. Lord, give my poor stammering tongue at least one taste of the whole round world[.] (796)

Within Hurston's critical regionalism, youthful characters—simultaneously bound and unbound by race or nation—formed an ideal receptacle for examining the contradictions and conflicts between modernization and industrial development on the one hand, and the stability and authenticity of folk culture and localist aesthetics on the other. Hurston's projection of her authorial identity as Southern writer did however recalibrate over time, during her anthropological field research.[1] *Their Eyes* depicted other injustices and injuries that comprise the racial sublime, through a hybrid mode—part folk romance, part realist—which allowed her to explore the contradictory effects of industrialism on folk cultures. This included documenting the exploitation of Black laborers that accompanied modernization driven by the profit motive of capitalist development, while highlighting the nodes of resistance that folk cultures and community organization offered.

---

[1] Working firstly with Franz Boas at Columbia University, her ethnographic research into Black folklore of the South and Southwest later expanded to include Jamaica and Haiti, before she commenced working for the Federal Writers' Project's Floridian chapter.

Hurston's novel thus simulated the effects of uneven development by appealing to what Bakhtin called the "realistic fantastic" of folklore, which he found not only commensurate with realism and the novel, but also "an inexhaustible source" for "all written literature" (*Dialogic* 151). For,

> the fantastic in folklore . . . relies on the real-life possibilities of human development—possibilities not in the sense of a program for immediate practical action, but in the sense of the needs and possibilities of men, those eternal demands of human nature that will not be denied. (150–1)

Put another way, Hurston's novel contrasted the hegemonic realist biographical time of the Bildungsroman with a regionally determined folk time, which blended elements of dark romanticism with folklore and dialect fiction conventions. In contrast to the metropolitan female development novel of Fauset and Larsen, Hurston's novel portrayed what Bakhtin argues are the key developmental characteristics of the Rabelaisian folk chronotope; namely, a regional aesthetic in which "Human life and nature are perceived in the same categories," and in which "seasons of the year, ages, night and days . . . ripening, old age and death" are "categorical images" that "serve equally well to plot the course of an individual life and the life of nature (in its agricultural aspect)" (*Dialogic* 208).

To achieve this parallel effect of a region ambivalently wedged between the modern and premodern, Hurston splits Janie's development into two narrative timelines: the first of these is the present-tense frame narrative, constituting a dialogue between Janie and her friend Phoeby Watson, to whom she narrates her story of development. That story forms the inner past-tense narrative. Each section of Janie's development transpires in a different mode of agrarian living, with each locale mirroring one historic aspect of the South's uneven development. Janie's mode of living shifts from the household; to the small-town; and finally, to the coastal sublime of the Floridian Everglades. The novel's first of these sections—the household—depicts Janie's initiation into West Floridian society, which occurs when she realizes the peculiarity of being raised by her Black grandmother, Nanny Crawford, a former slave, alongside the "quality white folks" for whom Nanny works

(Hurston *Their Eyes*, 21). Janie's childhood mirrors the situation of the prosperous twin towns of Hurston's youth, "White Maitland" and "Negro Eatonville," the first autonomous Black hamlet in the South (Hurston *Dust Tracks*, 566). Janie emphasizes how this relationship was cooperative, not coercive: Nanny works *with* the Washburns; Janie is raised *with* their children. Yet, Janie recalls to Phoeby Watson the moment that the reality of Jim Crow first dawned upon her through one key symbol of the modern, the photograph:

> "... Ah didn't know Ah wuzn't white ... but a man come long takin' pictures ... So when we looked at de picture and everybody got pointed out there wasn't nobody left except a real dark little girl with long hair." (21)

The photograph provoked Janie's first experience of double consciousness: spotting the difference between the unraced speaking "I" and the "real dark little girl" initiates her into how others internalize the irrational logic of segregation, which declares that appearances are essences. The Black "chillun" at Janie's school soon began "teasin' [her] 'bout living' in de white folks backyard" (Hurston *Their Eyes*, 22). Hurston uses this situation to establish the parameters of how regional customs and policies might determine the possibilities of literary form: if in the most conventional definition, a Bildungsroman represents a youth's apprenticeship into the adult world of courtship, education, labor, and culture, how might that form accommodate the effects of anti-miscegenation laws that dictate as much as determine who one might court; anti-integration laws, determining how and where one might be educated; and a racialized division of labor that relegates Black workers to menial domestic and agricultural positions, and situates women in inferior positions to men? Those questions had resulted in a pervasive cultural logic in response to this underdevelopment within the New Negro Renaissance: that rural, folk customs were backward, primitive, and urgently necessitated political and aesthetic modernization.

Though Janie's tone is ironical, in Chapter 2 she recalls to Phoeby the moment when the serious implications of that racial difference upon her future, which she did not understand in the incident above, were revealed to her by her grandmother, Nanny. In petitioning Janie to marry the propertied farmer, Logan Killicks, Nanny told the story of Janie's mother Leafy's conception during the Civil War. Nanny's former mistress became enraged to find that Leafy was born "'wid gray eyes and yaller' hair'" because it meant the planter raped his slave; enraged by jealousy, the mistress whipped both mother and child (33-4). As an adolescent, Leafy, a tragic mulatta, was raped by a white schoolteacher, and left town after delivering Janie. This *récit* braids Janie's fate into the region's history of slavery, including the history of sexual terrorism and miscegenation carried out to sustain the plantation system before and after chattel slavery. Though history repeats itself, Hurston breaks that continuum; Janie, an unfixed figure of youth charged with potential and mobility, is not to be a tragic heroine, but the embodiment of Hurston's oft-cited mantra: "I am not tragically colored" ("How It Feels," 827).[2]

The past is not the aspect of the South that Hurston wishes to dwell on; emphasizing the future-oriented present, Janie's unfolding development, which manifests as a peripatetic restlessness, gives the novelist the conceit through which to write the wider story of the region's development. The intergenerational history which has just registered the plantation as a site of oppressive violence takes a decisive turn: "Janie had had no chance to know things . . . Did marriage end the cosmic loneliness of the unmated" (Hurston *Their Eyes*, 38)? Janie's impressionability means she capitulates to Nanny's petition that Janie marry Logan, a preferable pathway to Janie's alternative future working within the region's gendered division of labor. Janie's first relationship with Logan, whose lessons in chopping wood, plowing, and peeling potatoes initiate her into the facts of land, further reveals to her the limited autonomy of women in this mode of production. In the rural South, employment opportunities remained subject to the logic of the traditional gender roles of the plantation hierarchy into the twentieth century. Already, Janie's indeterminacy over her prospects are formalized

---

[2] Hurston's heroine diverges from the tragic mulatta trope of earlier African American women's fiction and novels, including Frances Harper's *Iola Leroy* (1892) and Pauline Hopkins's *Contending Forces* (1900).

at the sentence level: there is a disjunction between Janie's use of oral dialect (the language of folk romanticism) in the previous scene, and the omniscient narrator's racially neutral third-person preterit tense in the above sentences (this was commonly used to convey the biographical time of the realist Bildungsroman). These folk dimensions underscored Richard Wright's notorious claim that Hurston's novel perpetuated the "facile sensuality" and even worse racist "minstrel technique" commonly used to apprise white readers' views of Black Southerners in local color fiction (Wright "Between Laughter and Tears," 25). Hurston's narratorial polyphony nevertheless was crucial to the author's strategic revision of the Bildungsroman's geographical logic: Janie's development bifurcates between her affiliation with regional folk culture, as insisted upon in that character's oral dialect and local vernacular, and the pressures of national progress, which the omniscient narrator's seemingly racially and regionally neutral use of standard English represents.

After Logan's death, Janie fortuitously meets the older, more socially ambitious Joe Starks, originally from Georgia, whose urban education in the North enables him to capitalize upon Black Florida's uneven development to his social and economic benefit. The contrast created by Janie's movement and her relationship with Joe Starks enables the ethnographic novelist to examine in more detail Florida's Black cultures, while testing the limits of regional customs and borders. After acquiring 200 acres from a white landowner and amassing a small fortune in property, Starks marshals Eatonville and Janie along with it into modernity, firstly by creating a housing market, then by financing the introduction of Sears and Roebuck streetlamps and other "modern" upgrades (71–3). In a procession of "every type of vehicle"—mule-drawn carriages, automobiles, bicycles—Starks's disciples congregate, united in a feverish modernism as the town is suddenly wired into the circuits of capital (72). At the ceremony in which the lights are turned on, Starks's sermon to the people of Eatonville is a study in such contrasts:

> "De Sun-maker bring [the Sun] up in de mornin,' and de Sun-maker sends it tuh bed at night.... All we can do, if we want any light after de settin' or befo' de risin,' is tuh make some light ourselves." (72–3)

This utterance elicits the locals' trust by infusing biblical discourse with homegrown vernacular to rationalize this technological revolution. Starks's speech spellbinds the villagers, the energy harnessed by his streetlamps transforming before their very eyes into magical circuits of hot, white light, delivering an unanticipated electric shock to the preindustrial Black South. Historically speaking, the events here are an abridged version of the socioeconomic and political transformations of Hurston's Eatonville that occurred during Southeast Florida's land boom, which were brought about "mostly" by "Northerners" (*Dust Tracks*), and subsequently by national corporations seeking to monopolize the region's resources and profit from its development, including Florida Power & Light (est. 1925), a conglomerate of several subregional corporations.

Joe Starks's plan implicates his entire community in a struggle between irreversible modernization and atavistic cultural traditions, a contradiction which causes the town's awkward growth spurt. As the hamlet's industrial potential expands, only one house seems to rise from the earth: the Starks's house looms with its "two stories with porches," its slick "bannisters and such things" casting the rest of the town into the aspect of "servant's quarters surrounding the 'big house'" painted in a "gloaty, sparkly white" (75). Its ostentatious veneer reflects Starks's changes in appearance and demeanor, as he transfigures into the uncanny double of both a Southern planter and a Northern mogul, his performances of power emanating from his "biting down on cigars" and spitting chewing tobacco into a "gold-looking" vase (75). As Leigh Anne Duck observes, Janie's more moderate "determination to prioritize folkloric pleasure over social status" facilitates a reconciliation between Starks's modernization and Eatonville's folkloric values (Duck 137–9), as symbolized by the instrumental role Janie plays in convincing Starks to host a funeral for the hamlet's famous "yelluh mule." Yet, even in this Black hamlet, the essence of a postracial utopia is washed out by the arrival of class. Janie, in acquiring fine "wine colored" dresses and a "little lady-size spitting pot" that outshines the other womenfolk's tincans, becomes implicated in this process. Putting on such Northern, metropolitan airs is "bad enough for white people, but when one of your own color could be so different it put you on a wonder," we are informed. The rapid assimilation of rural folk cultures into the accelerating rhythms of industrialization is likened through folk imagery to the shock one might experience in "seeing your sister turn into a 'gator. A familiar strangeness" (Hurston *Their Eyes*, 76).

It is a folk explanation for the serious risk that this modernization will pose to Janie's development, because it threatens to alienate her from the stability the folk cultures of the preindustrial world offer her. Although almost twenty years apparently pass during this marriage, her development is frozen; she withdraws from that community due to her proximity to Joe Starks. After his death, the parochial dimensions of small-town customs, and their views of how a young widow should behave, also inhibit her growth and autonomy, determining that she must leave to find a more authentic version of herself. To manage these competing sets of constraints upon Janie's development, Hurston reverts from the biographical time of the Bildungsroman to what Bakhtin distinguishes as the "adventure time" of the folk romance (*Dialogic* 105), which encourages a turn toward the aesthetics of dark romanticism whereby the racial sublime—in this case, signaled by the fallout after a naturalist disaster—anchors Janie back into the fact of land. When the town gossips focus on Janie after Starks dies from kidney failure, she elopes with her younger lover, known as Tea Cake, to join the seasonal workforce on "de muck": the Floridian Everglades, a tropical wetland system located on the southernmost tip of the United States. The swamp constitutes the novel's fourth "big," "strange" relocation, into an ecosphere with the "ground so rich that everything went wild" (191). The word choice "rich" is telling: $11 million dollars in crops were sold between the Everglades' major flood events of 1926 and 1928, one reason why Tea Cake informs Janie that "'Folks don't do nothin' down dere but make money and fun and foolishness'" (191). This adventure is not the retreat from the modern it first seems, as Janie and Tea Cake become initiated into a modernized agricultural industry, which churns astronomical profits out of Black migrant harvesters' labor. Yet, as Martyn Bone points out in his materialist account of Hurston's literary transnationalism, the novel's depiction of Florida's transnational agricultural industry reflected the deleterious effects of stringent immigration policies on the region between 1917 and

1924. Unlike in other regions, the Immigration Act of 1924 did not prevent the trafficking of Bahamian, Caribbean, and Central and South American workers brought into Southern plantations to prevent labor shortages through various loopholes, including the Department of Labor's Immigration Service's foreign guest-worker program; many were smuggled across the southern border (Bone 41). The covert nature of these operations meant those migrants were forced into precarious living situations.

Reflecting on the confluence of the forces of Jim Crow, 100% Americanism, and the Johnson–Reed Act upon the region's transnational peasant class, Hurston's ethnographic narrator probes as to how national foreign policies filtered down into regional labor practices and social relations, from the perspective of rural workers. Like her former collaborator Langston Hughes, Hurston centered these investigations on a single catastrophic event that disrupts the teleology of development perpetuated by the Bildungsroman genre: a hurricane. By the election year of 1928, when the narrative events Janie is recalling from the frame narrative are set, Florida had entered a deep recession, meaning that despite the devastating storm season of 1926, county and state governments, Congress, and industry continued to bicker over which body was liable to finance an estimated U.S.$20million in improvements to the levee and drainage canals girding the Kissimmee-Okeechobee-Everglades lake system (Grunwald 190–1). In 1928, a category five storm—one of the deadliest in U.S. history—ravaged Puerto Rico, the Bahamas, and Florida, before sweeping through South Carolina and Edisto Island, killing over 2,500 people and tens of thousands of livestock, and resulting in over U.S.$100 million in damages. The most catastrophic damage was caused when the dyke ruptured (Myers 107). Hundreds of the Black workers who had been brought in for the harvest season, many of whom were undocumented migrants, died in the flooding, though the precise figure remains an estimate (Bone 41).

Hurston's novelization of the hurricane accentuated the catastrophic effects of the racial sublime: the human cost of political inconsistencies between nation and region over migration and social policy, as well as the legislation and construction of public works. As the storm system swells over the Black seasonal workers' camp, Janie observes how "the drifting mists gathered in the west—that cloud field of the sky—to arm themselves with thunders and march forth against the world," an image that transfigures this moment from the context of local history into a world-historical event (Hurston *Their Eyes*, 234). The Seminole community, whose connectedness to the area enables them to anticipate the first signs of an approaching storm, advise the workers to evacuate. The Black workers' intuition, however, is disordered by their lack of local knowledge, as well as their precarious position within the muck's casualized seasonal labor system. Though they earn eight dollars a day in the height of the season, that work is temporary, disincentivizing them to abandon their work; they have no way to foresee that negligent public safety regulations and industrial laws will ultimately leave them at the mercy of nature's forces if they do not. Without appropriate shelter, and their white overseers having already abandoned them, Janie realizes that the "time was past for asking the white folks what to look for through that door" (235). In the aftermath, the focus shifts briefly to Tea Cake, who stumbles upon "the hand of horror on everything," a fractured scene of "Houses without roofs, and roofs without houses" (251). He is conscripted into

> a small army that had been pressed into service to clear the wreckage in public places and bury the dead. Bodies had to be searched out, carried to certain gathering places and buried. Corpses were . . . under houses, tangled in shrubbery, floating in water, hanging in trees, drifting under wreckage. (252)

While Janie hides inside the house, "sad and crying," Tea Cake and the "miserable, sullen men, black and white" dig graves and search for bodies (252). A shellshocked Tea Cake observes throngs of corpses wearing "fighting faces" with "eyes flung wide open in wonder," as white militia armed with rifles insist upon segregating the dead under "orders from headquarters" (252–33). They are heaved into Jim Crow unmarked mass graves by surviving Black laborers, as the national guardsmen and the police—who have been absent from the area throughout the agricultural season except to usher intoxicated whites away from the workers' camps to prevent race riots that would slow productivity—now reassert their authority with guns and orders.

Revolutionary violence haunted the classical Bildungsroman; world-historical events register only peripherally, given the form's originary symbolic function was to restore national cohesion in times of revolution and catastrophic social disorder through the harmony of the aesthetic. In *Their Eyes*, the hurricane's mythic violence is masked by the romantic veneer of folk mysticism common in the region's oral storytelling traditions. We see this in Hurston's reversion to what Bakhtin would call the folk chronotopes of the adventure romance in the closing chapters of the novel, rather than the biographical nation-historical time of the novel: "No matter how impoverished, how denuded a human identity may become in a Greek romance," writes Bakhtin, "there is always preserved in it some precious kernel of folk humanity . . . [and] the indestructible power of man in his struggle with nature and with all inhuman forces" (*Dialogic*, 105). Drawing upon folk-cultural responses to the catastrophe that she collected in her ethnographic fieldwork,[3] Hurston's representational strategy discursively deviated from traditional documentary methods, including the depersonalizing use of the indicative mood in the newspaper coverage (see "Waters Rise," 1). In listening to the interpretations those folk histories offered, *Their Eyes* became one of the few accounts that acknowledged the deaths of African American and undocumented migrant workers.

Ironically, such dimensions of her novel were curiously neglected in Locke's review mentioned earlier in this section, which pronounced that Hurston would never reach artistic maturity until she wrote social document fiction. Her Bildungsroman's portrait of the rural South's development broke with such anti-regionalist readings of dialect fiction on the one hand, and the belief that Black cultural modernization necessitated the author's removal from the "primitive" cultures of the Deep South, on the other. It

---

[3] In 1935, with Alan Lomax and Mary Elizabeth Barnicle, Hurston recorded folk singer Lily Mae Atkinson leading an unidentified choir singing the blues ballad referenced in the novel's title, "God Rode on a Mighty Storm," one of five recorded folk songs about the hurricane. Though not a firsthand witness to the hurricane, she spoke to witnesses in Florida, and obtained supplementary material during her research in Frederica, Georgia (Monge 132).

further unsettled the Agrarians' insular romanticization of the pastoral South, by connecting the individuals' precarity to the historic, large-scale problems of race and industrialization that structured their experiences of the world. It was difficult to situate generically as a Bildungsroman; *Their Eyes* brings the narrative to its cathartic conclusion via a courtroom scene in which Janie is astonishingly acquitted of killing Tea Cake by an all-white jury and cured of rabies by the medicine reserved for him. Janie's symbolic resurrection does not adhere to the expected narrative pathway of individual fulfillment through marriage and maternity. Her outlook is altered by the hurricane's aftermath, her sense of injustice toward what she witnessed in "the muck," symptomatic of the wider effects that regional and national development will impose upon Black Southern folk cultures, leaving her development unfinalized.

Although she is forty in the frame narrative, Janie has not physically aged, indicating that her folk heroism denies the realist verisimilitude associated with the Bildungsroman's novelization of development. Because Hurston did not feel "confined to the 'usual' *Bildung* model," as Geta LeSeur observes more generally of Black women's Bildungsromane (101–2), she shifted the genre's gendered emphasis from courtship, domesticity, and maternity to the "*[testing] of the heroes' integrity, their selfhood*" that Bakhtin saw as central to the folk paradigm (*Dialogic*, 105). If the biographical time of the Bildungsroman is unequipped to promote the teleology of Janie's, or by extension the rural Black South's, development, the author's late appeal to the folk adventure romance offsets these generic limitations. This blending of realist and folk-romantic modes is critical for the novel's geographical messaging, given how Janie's numinous status as a character seemingly marked by eternal youth mirrors the novel's geographic course southward, which consciously inverts the trajectory of the Great Migration.[4] Hurston's allegorical coordinates progress steadily into the southernmost tip of the nation, where its borders appear most visible and porous. Positioned at the sublime interface of the regional and the global, the novel culminates in an oceanic image of Janie dragging in her

---

[4] Hurston deliberately underemphasized those northward migration patterns in her autobiographical Eatonville records (Duck 133).

horizons "like a great fish-net" (Hurston *Their Eyes*, 286). A mystically youthful Janie lies in bed, imagining herself gazing at the southern horizon from the Everglades' coastline, contemplating the borders of the transnational Southern folk cultures she has encountered, the future of which flows outside the currents of national destiny. At the confluence of the past, present, and future, in a place within and without national time, the imperious, southward gaze of her mind's-eye forms a decidedly open-ended gesture of regional cosmopolitanism that defies the gendered, racialized teleology of the classical Bildungsroman.

CHAPTER 8

Caught and Loose: McCullers, O'Connor, and the Gothic Bildungsroman

The Gothic School

The underdevelopment of the rural South, caught between atavism and progress, that resulted from its uneven relationship to the industrial development that was more rapidly modernizing other parts of the nation, also informed a school of Southern fiction that was historically labeled the Gothic School. This mode predominantly represented the South's small rural communities, where provincial life appeared to operate at a visibly slower pace than that of the national-historical time (Bakhtin) with which a Bildungsheld must become synchronized. The Southern Gothic registered the South's sublime elements, including its rural vistas, but accentuated the liminal, uncanny, and grotesque social, economic, and political dimensions of geographical affiliation, creating the visage of a "peasant" region operating both within and without national-historical time. Often focusing on rural and remote places where the Depression had impoverished the local economy, where opportunities for education were limited, Southern women's writing accentuated the region's "contorted and fragmented bodies," as Sarah Gleeson-White explains, establishing the basis of what she calls the Southern grotesque as opposed to gothic ("Peculiarly Southern," 46). Eudora Welty, Flannery O'Connor, and Carson McCullers deferred to these textual strategies of estrangement to acknowledge "a tragic history in which they have partaken, even in silence," whether by perpetuating the South's "burdensome models of femininity" or by overlooking slavery's "tragic legacy and a literally fatal regional patriotism" (46). Southern women's "domestic" literature often welded "the 'trivial' and the 'historical'" through such depictions of "throwaway bodies in an economy based on white privilege, a national epistemology of racial unknowing," so as to "stir up new ways of thinking about labor and object relations" across different regional codes, Yaeger adds (*Dirt*, 254).

All Southern writers, according to McCullers, regardless of the authors' "politics, [or] the degree or non-degree of liberalism in a Southern writer," inherited a "peculiar regionalism of language and voices and foliage and memory" that bound authors to a "homeland within a homeland" ("Books I Remember," 515). Yet, McCullers's emphasis on the unsettling paradoxes of regionality through such juxtapositions as Yaeger and Gleeson-White observe, situated her novels in a "genre of writing" that was "sufficiently homogenous" by the 1940s for "critics to label it 'the Gothic School'" (McCullers "Russian Realists," 471). McCullers queried the use of the term "Gothic," which she believed was a mislabeling of the realist tendency in "modern Southern writing," which only appeared grotesque and alien to the Northern audience due to their unfamiliarity with the region (471). Although a Gothic tale resembled "a Faulkner story in its evocation of horror, beauty, and emotional ambivalence," that "effect evolves from opposite sources; in the former the means used are romantic or supernatural, in the latter a peculiar and intense realism," McCullers explained (471). Southern verisimilitude was only viewed as Gothic due to the South's estrangement from the nation, for it having historically constituted

> a section apart from the rest of the United States, having interests and a personality distinctly its own. Economically . . . it has been used as a sort of colony to test the rest of the nation. The poverty is unlike anything known in other parts of this country . . . the only part of the nation having a definite peasant class. But in spite of social divisions the people of the South are homogenous. (471)

The Bildungsroman—an idealist genre depicting an adolescent's development—was to form a metaphor of the uneven relationship of "literature in the South" to other national transformations, as "a young growth" that "cannot be blamed because of its youth," a period defined by speculation over "the possible course of its development or retrogression" (McCullers "Russian Realists," 474). The so-called Southern Gothic Bildungsroman, then—a term I use in this chapter in an historical rather than descriptive sense, to seize upon the antiquated, uncanny regional difference that label connoted—distinguished itself from other regional variations in its stark emphasis upon "freakish" bodies and events that disturb the idyllic projections of the region's social and environmental landscape. The individual's developmental process becomes visible in moments of estrangement, when modernization ruptures the stabilizing familiarities of regional identity through images of fragmentation, deterioration, and melancholia: juxtapositions which bring to light the unsettling effects of the logic of unevenness, whether social, political, geographical, or economic.

The novel that resulted from McCullers's reflections above, *The Member of the Wedding*, turned its compass inward to face the most "painful substance" of national life from the standpoint of a region that symbolized the divisiveness and violence of the modern world; as did O'Connor's *The Violent Bear It Away*. In these novels, an unfixed youth attempts to find their place in a world they know little about by mimicking the hypocritical behaviors of adults in their small-town South, thus discovering the region's internal incongruities in moments of uncanniness, grotesqueness, and violence without justice. Yet, both novelists looked expectantly to the prospect of a New South shaped by the younger generation.

Carson McCullers's *The Member of the Wedding* (1946)

We have arrived in a somnolent township a few miles outside of Columbus, Georgia. This town is not a real, physical location, but rather a memory projected over Brooklyn's suburbs and the "view of the Manhattan skyline" that surrounded the author Carson McCullers's Manhattan apartment (McCullers "Look Homeward," 431). The Georgia-born writer was drawn to New York as a promising young concert pianist in the 1920s, before turning seriously to writing, most notably stories and novels that were about poor people growing up in the South during the Depression. It was there she penned the essay I am describing, in which she observed in Manhattan's rooftops outside her window the symbolic landscape of Northern capitalism and national progress. She felt struck by a sudden curious "homesickness," which was not only her personal attribute as a Southerner adrift in Manhattan, but the "national trait" of all Americans, "as native to us as the rollercoaster or the jukebox" (431). To McCullers, homesickness was "no simple longing for the home town or the country of our birth," but the feeling of being "torn between a nostalgia for the familiar and an urge for the foreign and strange" and all "the places we have never known" (431). Americans must be the loneliest of all races in that sense, she mused, for their "hunger for foreign places and new ways has been with us almost like a national disease. Our literature is stamped with a quality of longing and unrest, and our writers have been great wanderers" (431). America's abrupt entrance into WWII forced the writer to turn "inward," into that "singular emotion, the nostalgia that has been so much a part of our national character" (434). For, like the protagonist of a Bildungsroman, "America is youthful, but it can not always be young. Like an adolescent who must part with his broken family, America feels now the shock of transition. But a new and serene maturity will come if it is worked for," McCullers advised. "We must make a new declaration of independence, a spiritual rather than a political one," to capture the heterogeneity of "our own familiar land . . . that is worthy of our nostalgia" (434), an image typical of many regionalist commentators who drew upon the organic metaphors of land and place to provide cultural nationalism with stable roots.

There is no clearer articulation of the American Bildungsroman's regional complex—the desire and apprehension to be caught and loose in the world, and the metaphysical unrest that encompasses—than in McCullers's explication of "homesickness." Tellingly, McCullers unpacks this concept through the analogy of a youthful protagonist who in every way resembles the protagonist of *The Member of the Wedding* (1946), a Bildungsroman set in small-town Georgia, in which McCullers explored this trope of a restless Southern youth who yearns for affiliative "membership" beyond what her underdeveloped regional framework offers. For McCullers, America was clearly a nation still in its youth. If America, as a nation, remained too "young" to play this stabilizing role for McCullers, then we must ask, what spatial force *could* give finished form to the subject of *The Member*? Would it be the region—the insular Old South, or perhaps some reconstructed version of it; the nation against which the region struggles; or the promise of a more nebulous global interface? The Bildungsroman as a genre always negotiates some dynamic combination of regional, national, and global scales, reconfiguring the relationships between them in ways that become visible through the dialectic of constriction and movement. For McCullers, this meant the Bildungsroman was the ideal form through which to narrativize how the imagined Southern identity was, in many ways, constrictive to a person like herself, whose identity neither conformed to nor abided the white-controlled South's ideological norms regarding race, sexuality, and gender; and yet, it remained an imagined regional affiliation to which she felt perennially drawn.

The Member presents a portrait of an adolescent who is increasingly aware that she is "living in a section apart from the United States," in McCullers's phrase above. The rural township where the novel is set encapsulates the South's insularity, but also accentuates its many interregional and international interfaces. The rapidly growing Frances "Frankie" Addams, the twelve-year-old protagonist of *The Member*, is one of McCullers's many young, liminal figures who hovers at the categorical borders between femininity and masculinity, and naivety and maturity, and queries the racial construction that governs the segregated adult society of her small-town, which, as signaled at key junctures by the motif of the ambient white noise of the Addams' wireless playing in the novel's background, is wearing the first effects of capitalist development and globalization. Frankie's mother has passed away; her father, a regionalist who refuses to shop at the town's new department store, is engrossed in his small business; and her older brother Jarvis, a soldier on the eve of marrying a "Southern belle" named Janis, has moved away. When she is not loitering around the adult spaces of her town, including the Blue Moon saloon, the visiting carnival's Freak Show, or the prison, Frankie endures the banal daily rhythms of the Addams' kitchen with their Black housekeeper, Berenice Sadie Brown, and Frankie's six-year-old cousin, John Henry West.

The Member's "dark and divisive" aesthetic tendencies draw upon the Southern Gothic to depict the South's rural proletariat—as observed from more domestic, feminized spaces like the kitchen; the masculine spaces of the café and saloon; and more indeterminate, liminal spaces of authority, such as the carnival Freak Show and the prison. For McCullers, these spaces exemplify how the South structures its uneven relations in contradictory and unequal racial, ideological, and sexual power dynamics, as the spaces and situations are entered and contemplated through the lens of an adolescent with a widely roaming imagination.

Resisting her bond with these "freaks" (the protagonist's term), preferring to imagine herself as akin to the heteronormative white American couple that her older brother and his fiancée represent, Frankie persistently attempts to reconstruct herself. Underwriting her uneven development are three personalities she performs: firstly, her everyday persona, Frankie, a child with cosmopolitan ambitions to explore the world; secondly, her regionalist persona, the histrionically feminine F. Jasmine, a Southern belle; and thirdly, her final transfiguration into the moderate persona, Frances, the adult (American) persona into which she develops. Yet it is the first of these, "Frankie," whose regional cosmopolitanism embodies the heterogeneous—in her terms, "freakish"—character of McCullers's ideal New South.

Set during WWII, Frankie's problematic romanticization of the war, and her intermittently racist and sexist mindsets in her attempts to imagine the world's unevenness, especially in terms of its underdeveloped regional and colonial locales, should not be conflated with McCullers's own views. Like the polysemic narration in Mark Twain's *Huckleberry Finn* and Henry James's *What Maisie Knew*,[1] the reader grasps more than what the unformed child Frankie herself registers regarding the social construction of her racial and gendered identity she grows into. To that end, McCullers sets her novel within a claustrophobic radius, constricting Frankie, John

---

[1] In these two novels about a child's initiation into the hypocritical adult world, epistemologies of racial difference form crucial lessons. This is obvious in Twain's novel, but one recalls James's subtler effects in Maisie's unexpected scandal over discovering her father's mulatta mistress from New Orleans.

Henry, and Berenice to a kitchen and the basic business district of a textile mill town based on Columbus, Georgia: McCullers's hometown on the Chattahoochee River. McCullers's constrictive, small-town landscape is stylized as an uncanny region of contraction and expansion; on the one hand, extremely narrow and parochial, but which facilitates various global encounters, including via the radio, or through the visitations of travelers and migrants. The setting's contradictory dimensions contribute to a regional aesthetic stylized by shocking uncertainty and incongruity, scars, wounds, disability, racial ambiguity, and queerness: the hallmarks of the Southern grotesque. This literary world is the beating heart of *The Member*, which ultimately denies "the significance of the event in its title," the wedding-event, which was central to the traditional women's Bildungsroman (Thurschwell 110). Pamela Thurschwell suggests that the "incoherent" child's body, as it subverts "narratives of development and growth" through Frankie's fear of "of literally growing too tall" (115-16), reflects Kathryn Bond Stockton's concept of "growing sideways": "a textual strategy coalescing around the figure of the child that works to subvert heteronormative development teleologies" (Stockton 13).[2] Frankie's concerns over growing too large—physically and emotionally responsive to what I have been describing as the central concept of uneven development in American Bildungsromane—underline the parochial sexual and racial norms that informed the hegemonic Southern identity, at precisely the moment she is expected to develop into its feminized ideal: the Southern belle. As Sarah Gleeson-White similarly observes, McCullers's grotesque foregrounds instances of unsettling paradoxes and contradictions to productively sublimate the literary region's constraints upon the individual's development, refusing the symbolic image of Southern femininity (*Strange Bodies* 125). Like Hurston, McCullers presents the younger generation as prepared for the transformative effects of a regional cosmopolitanism, brimming with the potential for revolutionary social reconstruction, which,

---

[2] Stockton's *Queer Child* theorizes the "sideways growth" of the queer child as "something that locates energy, pleasure, vitality, and (e)motion in the back-and-forth of connections and extensions that are not reproductive," as the child who "by reigning definitions can't 'grow up' [so] grows to the side of cultural ideals" (13).

in the novel's spatial terms, plays out in the characters' attempts to breach the borders of the South, whether physically or imaginatively. McCullers often destabilized such regional barriers in her fiction by foregrounding her adolescent protagonists' youthful cosmopolitan fantasies, which delay and deny the reality principle of their situation. Gleeson-White locates McCullers, along with Eudora Welty and Flannery O'Connor, among Southern women writers who disposed of the Old South's romanticized tropes of white womanhood, assuming "responsibility for" but ultimately discarding "this image" ("Peculiarly Southern," 49). Frankie's "warped and crooked" sense of her physical development creates a semiotics of the body in a "liminal," "unfinished" state of becoming that often recurred as the grotesque spectacle of "the freak" figure in Southern literature (*Strange Bodies*, 29). As Berenice notes, Frankie's most "'serious fault'" is that if "'Somebody just makes a loose remark . . . then you cozen it in your mind until nobody would recognize it . . . You cozen and change things too much in your own mind'" (McCullers *The Member*, 489). This is nevertheless Frankie's most powerful attribute as a narratorial focal point: her imaginative capacity "cozens" or manipulates the South's regional order in ways that undermine its isolationism, as well as its sexual, racial, and ideological power structures that conscript those bodies into the hegemonic discourse—or cuts them loose.

Frankie's unbridled geographical fantasies undermine the most conservative aspects of the Southern order. Consider, for instance, the motif of "the world," which recurs in several instances as a spatial signifier of Frankie's "homesickness." The novel begins with a vague reference to an unnamed event that has initiated her into that world:

> It happened the green and crazy summer when Frankie was twelve years old . . . when for a long time she had not been a member. She belonged to no club and was a member of nothing in the world. Frankie had become an unjoined person who hung around in doorways, and she was afraid.
> (McCullers *The Member*, 461)

The "it" that "happened" remains unspecified; although, the gradual implication in the novel is that the "it" presumably refers to her brother's wedding, but more crucially to an incident with a boy named Barney McLean who recently introduced her to an "unknown sin" (a sexual act). This uncertainty feeds into the recurring motif of the unnamable incompleteness haunting Frankie, as she loafs "around town, and the things she saw and heard seemed to be left somehow unfinished" (481). This incompleteness relates to her uncertainty toward the geography of unevenness; it is the effect of this being the first "year when Frankie thought about the world. And she did not see it as a round school globe, with the countries neat and different-coloured. She thought of the world as huge and cracked and loose and turning a thousand miles an hour" (479). Frankie's first foray into adulthood is to contend with the way—and shape—of the world. Unfortunately, her education on the matter is incomplete; the school's geography book "was out of date; the countries of the world had changed. Frankie read the war news in the paper, but there were so many foreign places, and the war was happening so fast, that sometimes she did not understand" (479). Where Frankie's real education begins is in the newspapers, magazines, and newsreels:

> She saw the battles, and the soldiers. But there were too many different battles, and she could not see in her mind the millions and millions of soldiers all at once. . . . Sometimes these pictures of the war, the world, whirled in her mind and she was dizzy. (479)

Like Studs Lonigan and Bigger Thomas—who learn about society, the world, and their place in it through prejudicial media representations—Frankie styles herself as a cosmopolitan "member" of a global collective that she consumes through film and the radio; that fantasy leaves her unsynchronized with the reality of the everyday, regional social spaces she inhabits. Frankie is too young to critically analyze these mental images: a pastiche of things about the world those popular mediums have taught her. Throughout the novel, understanding more about "the world"—huge, cracked, loose—preoccupies the protagonist. Frankie's gender prevents her from enlisting as a marine, which through her brother the soldier she understands to be the American way of encountering the world; she fantasizes about donating blood instead, so that "her blood would be in the veins of Australians and Fighting French and Chinese, all over the world, and it would be as though she were close kin to these people" (480).

These images merge into the psychological collage of an individual whose defining characteristic is her globalist preoccupation. The world, the symbol of adulthood, forms an antagonistic counterpoint to the local and regional coordinates that bind her to her hometown and to childhood. Yet visualizing "the world for very long made her afraid," for Frankie is overwhelmed by its scale (480), a fear that seems to signal not only her intense response to the size of the world but the implications of entering adulthood, which seems to be filled with violence and alienation. That scale is so vast that Frankie feels disconnected from it, though she "was not afraid of Germans or bombs or Japanese. She was afraid because in the war they would not include her, and because the world seemed somehow separate from herself" (480); hence, Frankie's intuition that "she ought to leave the town and go to some place far away" becomes the thematic driver of the narrative (480). In another instance, Frankie returns to the image of "the world" in a moment of insecurity as her brother's wedding that she has built up in her mind inches closer, finding that

> it was fast and loose and turning, faster and looser and bigger than ever it had been before. The pictures of the War sprang out and clashed together in her mind. . . . The world was cracked by the loud battles and turning a thousand miles a minute. The name of places spun in Frankie's mind: China, Peachville, New Zealand, Paris, Cincinnati, Rome. She thought of the huge and turning world until her legs began to tremble . . . But still she did not know where she should go. Finally she stopped looking around the kitchen walls [.] (492–3)

Frankie's romantic worldview projects a cinematic reel of composite panoramic and close-up images stitched together into a single visual stream, projected onto the walls of a Southern kitchen—just as "Frankie" becomes a pastiche of different phrases and idioms she has absorbed in her encounters with "the world," as she attempts to become the more ladylike cosmopolite "F. Jasmine." For the young individual who has never left her home-state, the "world" presents as a speeding up, a slowing down: a fluid chronotope which contrasts the unfluctuating "dog days" rhythm of regional timekeeping, blurring the lines of reality and myth. Above, McCullers transforms the Southern kitchen into Plato's allegorical cave, which illustrated "the effect of education—or the lack of it—on our nature," in which soldiers' shadows projected onto the cave's walls become the only reality for prisoners who have never experienced the world beyond their unenlightened darkness (Plato 220).

Frankie's older brother, along with the other undeployed soldiers from the nearby base, form a peripatetic counterpoint to Frankie's immobility, a reminder of the local scale of region to which she is confined and the collectivity she lacks:

> The soldiers in the army can say we, and even the criminals on chain-gangs. But the old Frankie had had no we to claim, unless it would be the terrible summer *we* of her and John Henry and Berenice—and that was the last *we* in the world she wanted (497).

It is nevertheless not that "good looking white couple"—Berenice's description of Jarvis and Janice—to whom Frankie most relates, but rather Berenice and John Henry, whom Frankie learns to regard as her true "we of me" (497). Her unacknowledged dependency upon Berenice is already palpable when the latter's beau T. T. and her foster brother Honey Williams visit the Addams' home, and Frankie, in her limited pre-adolescent vocabulary, finds that she cannot explain why Honey snubs her. Inverting the moment when Janie first realizes she is not white in *Their Eyes Were Watching God*, Frankie senses a disquieting degree of difference from Berenice. This realization is unsettling, because Frankie utterly depends on the surrogate mother's authority as the voice of her superego, to the extent that Frankie habitually has imaginary conversations with Berenice anticipating what she might say about things Frankie has done in her absence. Although Berenice later tries to explain in the simplest terms that they are not a *we*, that "'I am I, and you are you,'" and "'I can't ever be anything else but me, and you can't ever be anything else but you'" (567), Frankie's inability to comprehend cultural and racial difference persists, as she stubbornly refuses to entertain such distinctions. This lack of comprehension, for instance, occurs when she converses awkwardly with the Portuguese owner of the town's *Blue Moon*, motioning to doff her sombrero in a naive gesture of mutual cosmopolitanism, only to find she has forgotten it (512).

Frankie's deep concern over her alienation within her own family—a concern she cannot articulate—forms an ironic signifier of the Southern household as the social perpetuation of the historical "forced family" that originated with slavery. That system crammed "slaves, masters, indentured workers, and their offspring into the same house, creating tormented, yet creative, family models," as Valérie Loichot explains (15). This familial model relied on the reproduction of the "black mammy" trope, which as Jessica Adams suggests, demoted Black female caregivers from the "significant position of influence" they held over wealthy white families, and thereby prevented the "authority of black caregivers from becoming absolute" (70-1). Another outcome of the plantation family was that same-sex intimacy and queer ambivalence became central to the spatialized politics of the Southern household, as Michael Bibler notes apropos the plantation novel, in which domestic spaces including the kitchen and porch generated subversive sites for social relations that challenged the household's white patriarchal order (63-4). While Frankie's household is managed by her laconic, largely absent father, a widower and small-business owner with whom she has an emotionally estranged relationship, the "almost perfect" Berenice ensures the Addams household coheres—her one flaw being her glass eye, in Frankie's assessment, a token of the domestic violence Berenice endured in one of her four previous marriages (McCullers *The Member*, 463). The Addams household's cohesion requires Berenice's presence, even though she clearly has her own "we of me" outside of it: Honey, Big Mama, T. T., her lodge, and the Black church (497). Frankie's "homesickness," which is in Lukács's sense the transcendental "homelessness of a soul in the ideal order of a supra-personal system of values" (61), is thus a side-effect of the construction of whiteness that forms a crucial part of the Southern education: a need to claim her distant brother and sister-in-law as her "we of me," because everyone else "had a *we* to claim, all others except her," especially her proxy mother Berenice, whom she does not yet realize she loves more than anyone else in the world (497).

Berenice's foster brother, Honey, who is mixed-race but looks "as though he came from some foreign country, like Cuba or Mexico," becomes yet another central character in Frankie's imaginary global South. Like herself, Honey is penned inside the region's internal borders, namely, its policing of racial and sexual identity. Though he is "light skinned," "almost lavender in color," with "lavender lips" that "could talk like a white school-teacher" (493), Honey is immobilized by Jim Crow. Not fully understanding what that means, Frankie projects onto him her escapist obsession with cultural difference; she has been fantasizing about exotic "Esquimaux" and igloos (464); wearing a sombrero all summer and pretending to be Mexican (509, 513); and devouring magazine pictures of South America—one of her dream destinations, along with New York, Chicago, and Hollywood (482). Honey forms another, related canvas onto which Frankie can project her desires to transcend her own regional destiny. She later implores Honey to flee to Central America, lest trouble inevitably find him, cautioning him that he will never "'be happy in this town'" (578). When Frankie plots to run away after discovering she cannot accompany the wedding party on their honeymoon, she fantasizes about finding Honey and escaping to Cuba or Mexico. As her sense of regional confinement peaks in the novel's post-wedding anticlimax, Frankie's pendulous moods vacillate between an increasingly desperate desire to know and be known by everyone in the world, and a violent impulse to "'break something,'" or "'just tear down the whole town'" (481). Initially, she instinctively reroutes these feelings into what she considers "[getting] herself into trouble," such as petty theft and promiscuity, including the "secret unknown sin" committed with Barney McKean in his garage (482). Having internalized the desire to act like a "good" Southern girl, the only two things she fears are her "father," whose bed she has grown too big to share—which distresses her—"or the Law" (482). Because her budding sexuality also estranges her from the dominant ideology of her regional framework, Frankie feels a secret affinity with the isolated Honey that he cannot equally return.

Sitting in the Blue Moon café with an unnamed, red-haired soldier with bad intentions, as she tries to "play adult," Frankie believes she is finally connecting to the world around her: "Today she did not see the world as loose and cracked and turning a thousand miles an hour, so that the spinning views of war and distant lands made her mind dizzy. The world had never been so close to her" (523). She fantasizes about traveling with the soldier and the newlyweds through the glaciers of Alaska, moving through "a crowd of sheeted Arabs" in Africa, and visiting the Burmese jungle she has seen in *Life Magazine*. The prospect of her brother's wedding and the uncertainty of what will follow that event suddenly makes it seem as though "these distant lands, the world, seemed altogether possible and near: as close to Winter Hill as Winter Hill was to the town. It was the actual present, in fact, that seemed to F. Jasmine a little bit unreal" (523). Such is the case when she spies "two colored boys" in an alley during her downtown wanderings, a vision of "dark double shapes" presumably in a homosexual embrace, which her mind instantly associates with the pose of her brother and his bride on the picture of the Addams' mantelpiece (526). Frankie's "wedding mindset"—fueled by the Southern romanticism of white heterosexuality that her brother's wedding represents—again facilitates a cinematic, transferential screen in which real events morph into unreal events, collapsing the borders of time and space, as well as the physical borders between races and genders.

At another point, when Frankie, John Henry, and Berenice's conversation turns to "[criticizing] the Creator" over a game of bridge (547), McCullers demonstrates how useful the Southern kitchen—a traditionally feminized space—may be for a Bildungsroman that seeks to subvert the social order, by encouraging the unbridled imaginings of children who are yet to be indoctrinated into the social order. Having positively absorbed Berenice's earlier lesson about her male acquaintance who fell in love with another man and then "turned" into a woman, John Henry imagines utopia as a "mixture of delicious and freak," in which "people ought to be half boy and half girl" (547). John Henry does "not think in global terms;" rather, his childlike imagination breaks down geographical realism and natural imagery into the vision of a surreal world in which he might have "a long arm that could stretch from here to California, chocolate dirt and rains of lemonade, the extra eye seeing a thousand miles," and so forth (546). The "Holy Lord God Berenice Sadie Brown" does think in global terms; she preaches for a liberated world in which "[there] would be no colored people and no white people to make the colored people feel cheap and sorry," and "all human men and ladies and children" would belong to a more genuine family than the South's tormented family model; it would be "as one loving family on the earth" (546). There would be "'No war, and the young boys leaving home in Army suits, and no wild, cruel Germans and Japanese'" (546). Frankie cannot "completely agree with Berenice about the war," and would prefer a world with "one War Island in the world where those who wanted could go" (547). In Frankie's world, patriarchal constraints on women would vaporize as "people could instantly change back and forth from boys to girls, whichever way they felt like and wanted" (547). This fantasy stems from her fear that other members of the "war"—"war" being her synecdoche for the nation-state and wider world—"would not include her," whether because of her age, gender, general "freakishness," or indeed her outsider regional status as a Southerner, leaving her to feel "the world seemed somehow separate from herself" (480).

Frankie believes that by changing her name, she will develop into a different character type to the one she was assigned at birth, one that is licensed with a passport to traverse her constrictive regional framework. In more generic terms, changing her name will bring about instant *Bildung*, liberating her from a life stage defined by one's lack of free agency: childhood. Berenice shatters that fantasy by clarifying that individuals are all "caught" by their birthright: "'I born Berenice. You born Frankie. John Henry born John Henry. And maybe we wants to widen and bust free. But no matter what we do we still caught'" (567). Berenice tells the stunned children that she is "'caught worse than you is'" within their regional framework since "'I am black.'" The Law of Jim Crow "done drawn completely extra bounds around all colored people. They done squeezed us off in one corner by ourself" (567). When Frankie once more repeats to Berenice that she wants to "'tear down this whole town,'" her solidarity is with Honey and Berenice, the "most caught" members of her South, and her America (568). However, Frankie's response to Berenice, and her most perceptive insight in the novel, is to propose that people are both "caught" and "loose." The adult world is full of danger, she realizes, a moment of disbelief that is reinforced when the red-headed soldier—whom she discovers is not really the romantic, intrepid figure she imagined him to be, just another local from Arkansas—attempts to rape her in his hotel room. This lesson in the politics of divisiveness driving the social production of space, both in the region and in a nation rapidly becoming a military superpower, only hits home for Frankie after Honey's incarceration, after which the imaginative world beyond her post-wedding, small-town locality implodes.

As Frankie negotiates her own willful imagination against Berenice's mightier reality principle, her logic forms a testament to the chronotopic unevenness between the national foreign policy and the regional domestic policy regarding race: there is no way to feel at home in an imagined community that does not regard her "we of me"—Berenice, Frankie, and John Henry—on equal terms. Noah Mass describes Frankie's ideology as part of "the emerging, globally connected southern identity that McCullers had been working to articulate all along" (235). As a "cosmopolitan citizen," Frankie "doesn't replace her sense of self with some new vision of being part of a global entity, so much as she expands the boundaries of her regional self to include exchanges, engagements, and intersections with people and ideas that carry global resonance," he argues (235). In short, "Frankie needs to find a way to feel at home in the South but remain unencumbered by what she sees as its regional limitations" (235). McCullers, like Twain over half a century earlier, does not enunciate this point, but rather leaves the message unarticulated in the background of the youth's interpretations, allowing the "unfinished" individual whose education remains incomplete to symbolize the possibility of global encounters to positively transform the future of the New South. McCullers's contemporary, the white Floridian author Lillian Smith, described Southern children's understanding of segregation as "a vague thing weaving in and out of their play, like a ghost haunting an old graveyard or whispers after the household sleeps ... so big that people turn away from its size" (25). McCullers evokes this same trope of gothic haunting when Frankie, going by F. Jasmine, experiences an unnamable affect, a ghostly fear that wanders with her, recurring in frequent thoughts about the people she has known who have died, including her birth mother (542). Frankie wants to become a "'[member] of the whole world'" (566), as a solution to the small-town problem of passing "'alongside each other" without "conversation" or ever knowing each other (564); that is until Berenice, whose experience of childhood was limited (she was married by 13), and who has lived four decades in an adult world stylized by domestic violence, death, and apartheid, informs Frankie that there are people she would not like to know. Although Berenice names "the Japanese" and "the Germans" as examples (566), that implication also extends to the white supremacists who haunt their Southern framework. Guided by Berenice's insinuations if not her words, Frankie's proto-political rage ultimately wins out, feelings of injustice that McCullers displaces onto the protagonist's unexplainable violent outbursts; her morbid fixation with listening to the war updates on the wireless; and her ambiguous understandings of sexuality and race. Beyond having been interpellated by the hegemonic views of white regional nativism in her formal and social education, Frankie's instincts ultimately align with Berenice's. As in the classical Bildungsroman, which allegorically suppressed, deflected, and redirected the seeds of revolution, McCullers codifies her complaint against Jim Crow, which exists both as a set of banal "everyday" measures that structure the region's social relations, and in the brutality and deprivation that lurk in the primal scene of the narrated events.

If one's regional heritage is tattooed upon a writer's style, dialogue, and application of verisimilitude, as McCullers maintained throughout her career, the dual character of that heritage was captured in *The Member* through the jagged surfaces of the gothic mode: a blending of the familiar and the strange that speaks to the unsettling disquietude of what she called America's chronic "homesickness." The transfigurations that resulted enabled the novelist to integrate into the Bildungsroman form those characters who could not conform to national-historical time, due to the internal fragmentation that structured their everyday life. That fragmentation was most visible in moments when the child protagonist learns and unlearns the way of the world through the regional enforcement of such social disconnection, through the policing of race, ethnicity, and immigration, as well as the exclusion of those who challenged gendered, sexual, and ideological norms. The region's destiny—bound up with yet distinct from that of the nation—was symbolically configured through the development of a young individual, caught and loose within those competing temporalities, who struggles to realize their cosmopolitan desires within a narrowing regionalist framework. McCullers once observed that "[if] only traditional conventions are used an art will die, and the widening of an art form is bound to seem strange at first, and awkward" ("The Vision," 520). It is an apt description of how *The Member* widened the ideological horizons of the Bildungsroman genre through the strange, awkward effects of the gothic mode, to narrativize the South's underdevelopment.

Flannery O'Connor's *The Violent Bear It Away* (1960)

McCullers's *The Member of the Wedding* was one of many novels that presented the dilemma Southern writers faced regarding "how to represent regional time, which contained multiple and contradictory influences," as Duck explains of Southern literary modernism (210), by appealing to gothic traits beyond the generic borders of the Bildungsroman's biographical realism in their novels of uneven development. That tendency was shared with Flannery O'Connor. Marc Redfield leads the chorus of scholars who describe the Bildungsroman genre's transformations at large in terms of the undead: "The more this genre is cast into question, the more it flourishes," while "a more historically and philosophically precise understanding of *Bildung* does not appear either to keep the *Bildungsroman* healthy and alive, or to prevent its corpse from rising with renewed vigor each time it is slain" (42). This description aptly applies to both *Their Eyes Were Watching God* and *The Member of the Wedding*; but also, to the generic transformations apparent in O'Connor's *The Violent Bear It Away* (1960). That novel of uneven development tells the story of a fourteen-year-old, Francis Marion Tarwater, apparently possessed by the devil who convinces him to murder his disabled cousin to symbolically purify his bloodline and restore the Tarwater dynasty to its former glory. Francis has inherited an extreme religious pre-destiny, and a post-plantation property, Powderhead: a liminal, palimpsestic space that converges the dynasty's past and future.

Though like Hurston and McCullers,[3] O'Connor blended the Bildungsroman genre with gothic elements of Southern dark romanticism, the geographical logic of development in her novel was shaped by an ideology closer to the Agrarians' concerns over what they perceived as the increasing political and economic interference of the nation-state within the region. McCullers's younger rival, O'Connor, likewise described the Southern grotesque as the inheritance of Hawthorne's "dark and divisive romance-novel with the comic grotesque" and America's urban naturalism movement, which as we have seen in earlier chapters was emanating out of the Midwest (O'Connor "The Grotesque," 818). O'Connor suggested that historically, the most impressive "American fiction has always been regional," whether from New England, the Midwest, or the South. In her estimation, the South "has a degree of advantage" in regional writing: "a degree of kind as well as of intensity," which would "feed great literature if our people—whether they be newcomers or have roots here—are enough aware of it to foster its growth in themselves" (O'Connor "The Regional Writer," 847). Echoing the provincialist fervor of the Agrarians, O'Connor determined that many crude "southernisms" were thrust upon the Southerner by Northern critics, who demanded that writers produce works out of a recognizable mold rather than develop authentic regional aesthetics. What resulted out of those pressures were the "Gothic monstrosities" and "preoccupation with everything deformed and grotesque" that left the Southern writer wedged "between Poe and Erskine Caldwell" (O'Connor "The Fiction Writer," 803). While all fiction writers are in a sense regional, according to O'Connor— whom, it should be noted, directed such comments to a local white audience largely in support of regional isolationism—the Southern writer felt compelled to justify their regional literary affiliation to their cosmopolitan readership.

As evidenced in her short fiction, such as "Everything that Rises Must Converge" (1965), as well as her novels, *Wise Blood* (1952)

---

[3] Flannery O'Connor grudgingly acknowledged Faulkner's and Welty's influences, but snubbed McCullers. McCullers reportedly resented O'Connor's and Truman Capote's commercial successes as regionalist writers, believing they were "poaching on her territory" (Westling 137).

and *The Violent Bear It Away*, O'Connor's young male characters often embodied the hegemonic characteristics of an underdeveloped region; young, regional types who are caught in the interface between dynastic *noblesse oblige* and the incremental effects of modernization on agrarian districts. From her mid-1950s vantage in Milledgeville, Georgia, O'Connor characterized the modern condition as a "dark night of the soul": this worldview, she felt, "is what Nietzsche meant when he said God was dead" (qtd in Giannone "Dark Night," 12). The devout Catholic was overlooking the affirmation in Nietzsche's statement to meet her own political ends; that is, to read the South as the resting place of a benign God, whose earthly children have been asphyxiated by the fog of despiritualization that accompanied industrial capitalism. Though O'Connor reputedly avoided the Agrarians' manifesto, she was well-acquainted with several members; moreover, her letters, essays, and speeches often courted their regionalist fanaticism (Gordon 200). She promoted an aesthetic return to localism at a point when regional stability seemed threatened by the North's techno-industrial influence, which energetically unsealed the borders keeping the nation at bay. O'Connor was notoriously a writer of contradictions,[4] and the Agrarians' chauvinistic regionalism and anti-industrialism looms over her novels, which reflect anxiety toward the erasure of Southern culture, whether earnestly or ironically.

The Bildungsroman genre's typical dialectic between social indoctrination (education) and the formation of authentic selfhood (experience) plays out in the rural setting of *The Violent*, where the residual patriarchal racism of the plantational Old South, marked by death, terror, and poverty, haunts the romantic view of the region as an idyllic pastoral landscape. In Part One of *The Violent*, we ascertain through colloquialized free indirect discourse that after the violent death of Francis's parents, he was briefly fostered by his mother's highly educated brother, Rayber, an uncle he knows only as "the schoolteacher." As a seven-year-old, Francis was kidnapped

---

[4] O'Connor's 1959 snub of James Baldwin indicated how her "egalitarian treatment of race and gender" in her fiction contradicted "her well-known rigidities" in adhering to the Deep South's customs (Giannone "Displacing Gender," 76).

by "the old man" Mason Tarwater, his deranged septuagenarian great-uncle of the same maternal bloodline, whose precipitous death at the breakfast table marks the narrative's commencement (O'Connor *The Violent*, 331). The fiery sermons Mason preached to Francis Tarwater in life read as hyperboles of the Agrarians' position: he stands for "provincialism—which prefers religion to science, handcrafts to technology, the inertia of the fields to the acceleration of industry, and leisure to nervous prostration," and which above all is skeptical of capitalist development and the profit motive, as Andrew Lytle summarized in *I'll Take My Stand* (234). Mason owned Powderhead, an isolated property hidden in rural woodland that is predominantly populated and cultivated by poor Black people and equally poor whites. Tormented by fiery visions of destruction lifted out of the Book of Revelation, Mason believed himself to be a prophet, raising the kidnapped Francis in this mind frame by surgically removing the child from modernity itself:

> The old man, who said he was a prophet, had raised the boy to expect the Lord's call himself ... He had schooled him in the evils that befall prophets; in those that come from the world, which are trifling, and those that come from the Lord and burn the prophet clean[.] (O'Connor *The Violent*, 332)

Mason believed young Francis to be his prophet-heir, having failed to convince his schoolteacher nephew Rayber to become his male successor by baptizing his disabled son Bishop. By delaying his task to bury Mason's corpse, Francis Tarwater evokes an atavistic curse, in which an internal voice—either a hallucination of the devil posing as his guide, or the undead voice of his great-uncle—possesses him, telling him as he digs Mason's grave that the "dead are poor," and you "can't be any poorer than dead" (345).

Powderhead's dead owner Mason's dynastic mindset, inflected by the fire-and-brimstone discourse of the Book of Revelation, acts as a mouthpiece of the sociopolitical struggles that capitalism's uneven development posed to the rural South. Out of those struggles, a conservative regionalist rhetoric emerged from a perceived "minority group seeking to protect cultural traditions threatened by an advancing and adversarial modernization" (Duck 179), whom Mason represents. Reflecting those tensions stylistically, the narration unfolds in highly fragmented free indirect discourse, as Francis deliberates his new patriarchal responsibilities by contemplating whether to move the property's fencing in order to deter his uncle Rayber, whom he means to "'kill'" if he "'comes to claim the property'" (O'Connor *The Violent*, 337). Consider the description of Powderhead, the property he has inherited, which resembles a decaying monument to the plantation architecture of the Old South belonging to the region's unrecoverable past:

> Powderhead was not simply off the dirt road but off the wagon track and footpath, and the nearest neighbors, colored not white, still had to walk through the woods, pushing plum branches out of their way to get to it. Once there had been two houses; now there was only the one house with the dead owner inside and the living owner outside on the porch, waiting to bury him. (336)

Powderhead itself is a symbolic monument to the region's violent past, its volatile present, and its unclear future. Its residual social operations notably remain demarcated along the plantation South's racialized, patriarchal faultlines. In telling the story of the Tarwater dynasty's generational struggles over property ownership and moral values pronounced in the name of regional traditionalism, the novel allegorizes the refusal of the regionally conservative Deep South to accept the modernization that will accompany the region's assimilation into national destiny. At a formal level, this conservative regionalist anxiety is represented through the aesthetics of a dark romanticism stylized by the grotesque, which, in this case, juxtaposes idyllic visions of the South's landscape and community against unsettling gothic spaces like the Powderhead plantation, and liminal bodies in states of transition.

Francis Tarwater, one such transitional figure, struggles against the disembodied voice of the "stranger" (O'Connor *The Violent*, 345). His only other social relations are with the poor Black sharecroppers who reside nearby, including Buford Munson, and a "woman, tall and Indianlike" (356), a sage-like figure who has recently been visited by the restless soul of his great-uncle. The novel's rising action begins with Buford:

> Francis Marion Tarwater's uncle had been dead for only half a day when the boy got too drunk to finish digging his grave and a Negro named Buford Munson, who had come to get a jug filled, had to finish it and drag the body from the breakfast table where it was still sitting and bury it in a decent and Christian way [. . . for the boy] had never returned from the still. (331)

Unable to afford plumbing, the neighboring Black sharecroppers depend upon Powderhead's well. As a socially constructed space, Powderhead thus exemplifies Valérie Loichot's description of the Plantation not only as a physical locale, but as a chronotope that configures the "perpetuation and regeneration of the effects of a dead structure" as "a unit of space and time whose individual elements are fused by gaping holes between them: a community defined by its inherent discontinuity, pain, and violence" (117–18). In the Southern plantation ideology, the white male family heir of reproductive age (the quintessential Bildungsheld)—in this case, Francis Tarwater—is vital to the continuation of the plantation system, whose consanguinity assures the continuation of bloodline needed to reproduce the patriarchal dynasty. When O'Connor's isolated protagonist abandons his familial duty to bury his dead great-uncle, seeking out his last living blood relations and thereby cementing his position at the head of the Tarwater dynasty, he encounters modernity and civilization for the first time, setting him on a tormented path of re-education.

Mason's death leaves the Tarwater dynasty to drown in the thick Georgian Piedmont, symbolized in their own surname, unless Francis can fulfill his dead uncle's destiny to baptize Bishop. Francis, like Nietzsche's Zarathustra, has been absorbed into the solitude of the forest, the death of the great-uncle leaving the Bildungsheld with only the old man's lessons to guide him as he re-enters civilization. Part Two of the novel more overtly links the Tarwater dynastic turmoil to the widening crisis of regional underdevelopment, after Francis travels into town to find his last living "blood connection," a dynastic phrase that recurs throughout the novel (O'Connor *The Violent*, 339, 347, 364). That relation is Rayber, a college-educated schoolteacher—who shares the same "dark grey" eyes, "shadowed with knowledge" (365). He lives alone with his disabled infant, Bishop, whom Mason was never able to baptize; after Rayber's wife abandons them, a subtle wedge of resentment is driven between father and child. Francis Tarwater struggles against Mason's duty to baptize Bishop, while Rayber struggles against his own Oedipal battles that Francis Tarwater's dark grey eyes propagate. Though Rayber discards his uncle's views, his attempts to resolve the dilemma of the family's patrilineal madness through ratiocination lead him back to a mythological account of dynastic inheritance:

> The affliction was in the family. It lay hidden in the line of blood that touched them, flowing from some ancient source ... Those who it touched were condemned to fight it constantly or be ruled by it. The old man had been ruled by it. He, at the cost of a full life, staved it off. What the boy would do hung in the balance. (402)

The unconscious, atavistic "longing" (Rayber's word) to revert to the paternal-ancestral is "like an undertow in [Rayber's] blood dragging him backwards to what he knew to be madness" (402). In Francis Tarwater's eyes, shaped and colored by the old man's genealogical imprint, Rayber feels his own self-determined image is threatened, "subjected to a pressure that killed his energy before he had a chance to exert it" (402).

Rayber is a rational, atheistic scholar who understands the theoretical implications of indoctrination, but nevertheless cannot reason away the superstitious hold Mason's ideologies impose upon his bloodline. As the narrative shifts focus to Rayber, who heads to Powderhead to collect his uncultivated younger cousin, he realizes that "the place *was* his" now legally speaking (444), a fact Francis Tarwater later proves himself willing to kill to refute. Through Mason's lessons, Francis believes that there are two categories of men: the men of speech; and the men of action. As Rayber is clearly a theorist not an actor, according to Mason's family credo, Francis believes he must assume leadership by becoming a man of action, in fulfilling Mason's macabre destiny to baptize Bishop. The child's death by drowning symbolically preserves the bloodline, a sacrifice that would confirm who is Powderhead's true heir. In O'Connor's wider oeuvre, the omniscient narrator almost always remains ambiguously detached from moral commentary, meaning that the messages of her works are shrouded in indeterminacy. A moral reading might indicate that O'Connor uses "grotesque" aesthetics—such as the horrific drowning of a disabled child—not to shock the reader into political consciousness so much as stimulate Christian piety. However, disability as a literary "signifier of sacred or ritual processes" has often served a targeted social function, Ato Quayson observes, whereby "transgressions are considered as marking them with ritual danger, so that they have to be driven out to avoid the total destruction of the rest of the community" (46). In that sense, because Bishop's disability is construed by the fanatical Mason as resulting from Rayber's atheism and his ex-wife's insubordination in divorcing him, the Tarwater dynasty stands in for "the wider society" that, according to Quayson's theory, will seize the "boon that these disabled characters possess and which is seen as critical for the well-being of the society" (46). That society is the rural New South, still visibly haunted by the specters of the Old South that will not lay dead. To formally simulate this jagged effect, the grotesque, dark romanticism of the literary South, carried over from the nineteenth century, is recast through the disfiguring technical effects of modernist narrative, including nonlinearity, stream of consciousness written in regional dialect, and multiple shifting narrative focal points. As with Hurston and McCullers, these competing modes chafe against the Bildungsroman's biographical time in ways that strategically configure the aesthetic dilemma of an individual struggling to emerge in national-historical time, whose destiny mirrors the extensive growing pains of a region visibly but hesitantly coming into capitalist modernity.

O'Connor's Bildungsroman concludes with an ambiguous image of Francis Tarwater turning back toward the town intending to "educate" all God's "sleeping children," having murdered his cousin and set his birthright Powderhead alight, thus becoming the prophet of an unsettling future. O'Connor's novel conforms to the "masculinist model" in which "personal growth is possible" within "a particular social context;" yet, as Katherine Hemple Prown observes, Francis Tarwater's "journey from youthful ignorance and rebellion to a mature understanding of his relationship to the 'children of God'" does not conclude with "autonomous selfhood," but rather with his reintegration into "the social order" (137–8). Francis Tarwater's individual destiny seems less certain than he realizes as Buford reappears, riding a mule, "looking down on him with a scorn that could penetrate any surface" (O'Connor *The Violent*, 477). Regardless of whether it was O'Connor's intention, in Buford's figure the genuine torchbearer of regional reconstruction presents himself. He is the challenger to the Old Man's/Francis's attempts to suppress the South's internal Other: the Black indentured servants, sharecroppers, and rural underclass, as well as the women of the bloodline, whose notable absence from the narrative events is meaningful. As the master of the property where he believes he is "in charge," which Francis confirms to the "Indianlike woman," Francis's role only involves the fulfillment of symbolic rites. Given how Buford buries Mason and plows his cornfields while Tarwater is "laid out drunk" (477), the symbolic family estate of Powderhead is ultimately revealed to have been sustained by indentured Black labor but demolished by white poverty and pride.

Set in the gothic cradle of rural Georgia's dark night of the soul, *The Violent Bear It Away* substitutes the spiritual poverty of the novel's actual title for the economic impacts of the Southern rurality and economic poverty its working title conveyed. Originating out of a short story in *New World Writing* under the title, "You Can't Be Any Poorer Than Dead" (1955), the novel into which it developed conveyed the lived effects of global and national instabilities at the onset of the Cold War, from the vantage of an underdeveloped region in the backwaters of the world's richest democracy. As a novel of uneven development, the struggle its unfixed protagonist faces in integrating into his unevenly modernizing regional framework articulated the multiplying international, national, and local ideological crises of the 1950s, including the renegotiation of the role of region in the increasingly consolidated power of the nation-state apparatus. In stretching the formal attributes of the Bildungsroman genre, *The Violent* captured the uncanny effects of a region caught between the agrarian past and industrial capitalist modernity: an allegory that emulated the South's role within the national narrative, a developmental story to be perpetually reenacted in the metaphoric struggle between stubborn backwardness (region/youth) and progress (nation/adulthood). Although their outlooks were dissimilar, O'Connor thus joined McCullers, Hurston, and many other twentieth-century novelists whose regional complex led them to contend with the uncertainty of national destiny by depicting the symbolic unfixed figure of youth as being conditioned by the incommensurability of the past and present, regional and national, and local and universal forces that define them. Such forces directed that figure, and the Bildungsroman genre along with it, onto the precipice of an indefinite future.

Part IV

Southwest Frontiers

CHAPTER 9

Mathews at the Limits of the Bildungsroman's National Framework

One last excursion takes us west, across canyons and deserts to a location on the edge of the continent where "[there] is no there there," as the Oakland-born writer Gertrude Stein quipped; an approximation that spoke to the perception of the late nineteenth-century Southwest as central to the American nation-state's formation, but peripheral to its cultural developments. Saturated in the land's natural sublimity, and its social history of frontier skirmishes and invasion, the region's literature has nevertheless thrived, often contending with borders and interfaces of the transnational. The Southwest has often appeared in American literature in ways that envision the ideological borders of nationhood, if only to make geographical sense of the heterogeneous, multicultural histories, and subversive social spaces that region contains. From nineteenth-century Native American and Mexican writing about the frontier, to interwar Euro-American and Indigenous social realism that depicted the region as multiethnic and linguistically diverse, literature of the Southwest has often challenged as much as it officiated mythologies of exceptionalism that were perpetuated in settler-colonial local color realism—or their reified versions in the form of the official maps of the American nation-state. Themes of Emersonian self-reliance and youth percolated its early novels, as disparate in style and theme as John Rollin Ridge's counter-nationalist vigilante hero in *Joaquín Murieta* (1854); Bret Harte's Californian local color romances of a region (and nation) in the making; or Mark Twain's satiric visions of the chimeric gilded land to which his young picaro "lights out" at *Huckleberry Finn*'s conclusion. The early twentieth century saw the Bildungsroman become a prominent fixture of Southwestern literature. The novel of uneven development often presented the effects of land speculation and industrialized agribusiness, centered upon the unfixed figure of youth who struggles to integrate into the frontier mentality of perpetual growth that was mapped onto the region. Such was the case in Frank Norris's *The Octopus* (1901), Jack London's *Martin Eden* (1909), and Upton Sinclair's *Oil!* (1926); and later in the unsettling, documentary visions of rural poverty in Sanora Babb's *Whose Names Are Unknown* (1938) and John Steinbeck's *The Grapes of Wrath* (1939).

As Eric Gary Anderson crucially observes in tracing representations of migration and borders in Southwestern literature, as a region it "coheres geographically, demographically, ideologically, or argumentatively *as* the Southwest" only from "multiple, shifting points of view" that "have been set in motion toward, across, through, around, and away from each other for many centuries" (4).Though regionalism may imply parochial aesthetic reactionism in certain contexts, the desperado Southwest of Pat Floyd Garrett's *The Authentic Life of Billy, the Kid* (1882) being one example, Southwestern regionalism simultaneously operated a strategic referent through which the struggles against colonialism and cultural imperialism could be forcefully imagined, articulated, and in key instances, refused. The colonial arena and borderlands of the remote Southwest—mythologized not only through nineteenth-century local color fiction, but through the imperialist Western stereotype issued by popular media including Hollywood genre films—issued urgent questions about the relationship between the novel as a form and nation. I have selected this literary region to conclude this critical regionalist map precisely because it raises crucial ontological concerns apropos the Bildungsroman genre as a symbolic form, which allegorically managed the boundless mobility of capitalist modernity by imposing onto that logic of development the nationalist paradigms of borders and citizenship: the young hero's identity is shaped not only through the imposition of the nation's borders that are reified through statecraft, but also the metaphysical internalization of those borders. As I have suggested throughout this book, the reality of uneven development put significant blinders on that process, resulting not in any one generic tendency, but in multiple permutations that often constructed bounded, recognizable local environments to destabilize and unsettle them.

John Joseph Mathews' *Sundown* (1934)

Osage writer John Joseph Mathews did precisely that. To the novel of uneven development, he added the principles of an Indigenous regionalism always already at odds with the narrative of American national destiny, to express and dispute the effects of the ideology of westward colonial expansion that was driving the industrial development of the Middle West and Southwest. As a novelist who was born in Pawhuska in the Indian Territory in 1894, and died in Pawhuska, Oklahoma in the United States in 1979, Mathews' Indigenous regionalism emanated out of a set of political and aesthetic constraints relating to the homogenization of the American nation that came into effect in the early twentieth century as part of the ongoing colonialization of Indigenous lands and people. Like many Southwestern writers to follow, Mathews reacted against the cultural homogenization of 1920s urbanization, advertising and mass media, and general commodification (Snyder 63). Mathews' Bildungsroman *Sundown* (1934) narrativized the adverse situation facing Osage youth like himself, who were caught between their nostalgia for an idyllic tribal regionalism and the reality of bureaucratic colonial interference after the implementation of the Allotment Act in the Indian Territories. Although Mathews accepted many of the distinctive Southwestern environmental characteristics, vernacular, and conventions that render a regionalism recognizable, *Sundown* converged many competing perspectives that become visible through the unfixed protagonist's mobility. The cultural, political, and geopolitical unevenness that Mathews' novel communicated subsequently challenged the ideology of a nationalhistorical time that was furnished by capitalism's exploitative logic of uneven development.

Mathews' anthropological work *Wah'Kon-Tah: The Osage and the White Man's Road* became a Book-of-the-Month Club bestseller in 1932, cementing his position as a cultural mediator between white and Indigenous perspectives. Although he personally capitalized upon the commercial demand for local color portraits of a "decentralized" American literature, and the white liberal fascination with Indian culture of the 1920s and 30s, this was a part of a broader intellectual project to recover rather than exploit the cultural history of the Osage through literary representation. Refuting negative stereotypes of the Indian that were circulated to sustain American exceptionalism and white supremacism, Mathews told the Osage's history from the authority of his lived experiences. This strategy became an important politico-aesthetic signature of Mathews' oeuvre, including his two autobiographies, and crucially, his 1934 Bildungsroman *Sundown*, which depicted the coming-of-age of the Young Osages, whose destiny was to challenge the white man's claim to authority over them and their ancestral lands.

In his autobiography, unpublished in his lifetime, Mathews described the two separate sets of education he himself received. His own formal education, including his academic studies as a young man at Oxford University, "failed to disturb my feeling . . . because education was a matter of 'induction' and not, as was assumed, 'education'" (Mathews *Twenty Thousand Mornings*, 20). The tribal education he received had a far greater impact: throughout his young adulthood, "the pre-dawn prayer-chanter [that] had stirred my soul" remained within him. *Sundown* highlighted those implications of being inducted into the confluences of empire and its designs for regional development, from an Indigenous standpoint, told from the perspective of its mixed-race unfixed figure of youth, Challenge "Chal" Windzer, who is of French, Anglo-American, and Osage lineage. As a subject, Chal emerges in and outside national-historical time against the turbulent backdrop of the Southwest's oil boom, a time "when the god of the great Osages was still dominant over the wild prairie and the blackjack hills" (Mathews *Sundown*, 1). In the interstice between the traditional order and that of capitalist modernity, *Sundown* narrates the young protagonist's pressure to conform to settler-colonialist values of young manhood, which he describes as a process of entering "civilization," a word which recurs throughout. Chal's upbringing, amid the flood of wealth that petroleum capitalism brings to his community for renting oil-rich land on the reservations, leaves him socially underprepared for university. Ever in search of new thrills and experiences that might bring him closer to the settler ideal of the national citizen, and less like the "uncivilized" villager he worries white culture sees him as, he soon joins the Army Air Corps and war effort, self-fashioning himself into the epitome of American boosterism.

Sundown operates in a dynamic generic space: at once drawing upon naturalist aesthetics commonly used to depict the processes of Southwestern development in the first half of the twentieth century, and offering alternative Indigenous critical regionalist accounts of the impacts of that development on the land and its people. The novel's uneven development plot is set within the context of the Dawes Act, which promoted the idea that national citizenship was contingent on the legal recognition of whites as property-owning subjects, necessitating the removal of Indigenous communities from their sovereign lands. In 1907, President Theodore Roosevelt declared Oklahoma the forty-sixth state of the Union, after Native American and Oklahoma Territories officials certified a vote of statehood. Allotment operated "as a field of force working to reshape Native experiences of space and time," writes Mark Rifkin; but rather than interpret Native chronotopes as "instituting a fundamentally new and different kind of temporality (dividing Native time between tradition and modernity)," allotment might be understood as "something like gravitational influence on extant Indigenous trajectories" (Rifkin 96). Such a gravitational influence was visible in the nation's move to capitalize upon lucrative natural resources through the regional remapping of colonialist settlements in the early 1900s, including the formalization of the State of Oklahoma, even as it prompted an aesthetics of resistance rooted in Indigenous geographies. In the context of these struggles, region for Matthews appears as a more amorphous concept than nation, at times consecrating but often exceeding the boundaries created through the empirical mapping of territories. As a novel of uneven development, *Sundown* explores the new subject positions and "civilizing" individualism that national progress imposes upon the "uncivilized" young Osage, whose destiny is contingent on reconciling his ideals and values with the reality of the development that has befallen the region. With ironic awareness about the risks that assimilating into white civilization poses to Indigenous youth, Mathews casts his protagonist's individual maturation and his ambitions to develop into a dutiful American citizen against the national and corporate interventions in the formation of the State of Oklahoma, to imagine how Indigenous trajectories fit into and transcend those boundaries between tradition and progress.

Set from 1887 through to the early 1920s, the novel shows how the effects of the Dawes Act on the region's Indigenous population unfold through the eyes of Chal, the unfixed youth who appears to be positioned at the very center of American national destiny and progress, and yet stands apart and aloof from it. Mathews engineers Chal's unfixedness as a character within the categorical disjunction between the conditioning forces of legal and civic geography, and the messier, lived experiences of locality and space: complex geographical affiliations which Chal embodies as a mixed-race individual of Osage, French, and American heritage. His unfixed nature is the product of his internal disconnection between the Indigenous epistemologies and connection to land and community imparted to him through his Osage heritage (region); the way patriotic regionalism was instrumentalized to allow for the intrusion of "Washington" and the "guv'mint" (the nation-state) in his people's land and economic affairs; and the faceless corporations of petro-capital who invade the area not through military might, but through soft power interference. According to the omniscient narrator, it could be construed

> that Chal's early childhood was contemplative rather than one of action. Yet . . . it was both a life of contemplation and action. Contemplation, mostly in the form of dreams wherein he played the role of hero, whether in the form of man or animal. (Mathews *Sundown*, 9)

Chal's unevenness as a subject recalibrates the quintessential dynamic of the Bildungsheld: he is torn between contemplation and action. Only, contemplation here means the imaginative possibilities for heroism within the balanced order of nature, relating to the spiritual traditions of the Osage, while action is limited to what remains possible for a "contemplative" life, at the dawn of the Allotment Era. As previously noted, it is significant that the contemplation Chal indulges in reimagines the history of Indigenous heroic engagements in the first settler-colonial encounters with the British. Such is the case with his white relative Cousin Ellen, who attempts to impart severe Christian values by giving him pictures of Christ's crucifixion, with which he painfully identifies, but then scolds him when he hacks the images of the Romans to pieces (19-20). In these encounters, Chal finds himself returning to the image of the sunset, a spiritual symbol which, as the narrator noted in the novel's opening descriptions of the prairies, is the icon of the God of the Osage (1). In the context of Chal's white education, that imagery here accrues an ulterior meaning: it signals the desideratum of American exceptionalism, and the twilight of Chal's innocence, as the traditional mode of living he and his community have known is jeopardized by those imperialist designs (21). He resists such cultural assimilation in his encounters with the schoolteacher assigned to him by the Bureau of Indian Affairs, a chauvinistic Quaker named Miss Hoover, whose life's mission is to bring civilization to the "savage" children of the prairies (25). She inculcates him with romantic views of Indigenous–settler relations derived from James Fenimore Cooper's *Leather-Stocking Tales* and Henry Wadsworth Longfellow's *Hiawatha* (26-7), narratives that perpetuated the Vanishing Indian, a racist trope of ethnic decline used to rationalize Manifest Destiny, while imagining a social order in which the white, paternalist authority assumes a position of moral responsibility over their uncivilized Other. When Chal impishly refuses that image in his rebellious japes, Miss Hoover verbally abuses him: an important early lesson in how white authority figures will react to any challenge he poses to their influence.

These early childhood scenes, which narrate Chal's impressions of the confluences of the Osage's two contradictory cultural systems, establish the competing frameworks of contemplation and action. The markers of Chal's "mixed" ethnic identity resolve in favor of his identification with Osage customs, values, and traditions beyond the Agency, and his overall suspicion toward the designs and ambitions of white people. However, the community soon succumbs to the effects of modernization at the onset of capitalist development. In facing these changes and challenges, the Osage have subdivided into two ethnic political groups: the "mixedbloods" and the "fullbloods." Chal's father John Windzer belongs to the "mixedbloods," who form the council's Progressives: political moderates who are willing to negotiate with Congress and oil lobbyists, and adopt various aspects of white "civilization," i.e., basic changes including clothes and food, the use of automobiles, and the adoption of construction and engineering enterprises. The latter group are Indigenous radicals opposed to any white settler interference, headed by Bare Legs—an intimidating, legendary elder who carries a hatchet with which to gesticulate during council debates. Chal's father John becomes swept up in the fever of Osage national development, as one of the Progressives who negotiates with agents of the federal "guv'mint" and land developers for the Reservation Oil corporation, who covertly lobbied Washington to negotiate exclusive tenancy rights to the region's oil.

John does not intentionally sell Chal's generation's cultural inheritance down the river, for the inadequate price of a small fortune in U.S. dollars. To convey how Washington's annexation begins with soft power tactics, including the psychological manipulation John unknowingly succumbs to, Mathews momentarily shifts from the tight, ironic perspective of the child Chal to an omniscient view of John:

> John Windzer was almost continually thrilled these days in the atmosphere of growth and progress; that atmosphere which indicated that something momentous was about to happen, something cataclysmic and revolutionary, but which never quite happened; that something indefinite that would change the whole existence of people who lived at the Agency. (49)

Returning from Washington, however, John announces to his family that "'the guv'mint" have called the Osage Progressives traitors and expelled them from the council, for having given the leases to the wrong oil company, and not the Reservation Oil corporation that Congress supports. This resolution leads Chal to resent his father, leaving deep imprints upon his destiny.

Chal's young adult experiences are implicated in these negotiations between capital and government at state, regional, and federal levels, which interfere in the organization of the region's Indigenous communities, disrupting their local traditions and customs in the name of "modernization." Mobility forms an important narrative strategy in rendering these dialectical processes visible in the multiethnic literatures of the Southwest, which "propose and enact uneven, shifting migratory moves" to at times "define migration as a resistance or survival strategy rather than as an expansionist inevitability, and they often articulate in some way the problems as well as the possibilities of personal as well as cultural movement" (Eric Gary Anderson 3). Even as a collegian, Chal returns almost compulsively to the idyllic past before modernization reorganized his region, reminiscing about the Osage rituals and customs that informed his childhood. Displaced from that community and at a distance from the place of his past, he finds that he inhabits a middle stage between the enjoyment of nature and the wildness of his childhood, and the "civilized" shape into which he believes his university education is molding him, as he learns to repress those instincts to perform whiteness. His studies there are punctuated by a "vague but insistent yearning for something," which distracts him from his professors' "droning, soporific voices" and the "sticky," "uncomfortable" feeling of his citizen's clothes (152). He wanders aimlessly "out into the country by himself, but was ever careful to take the ... cow trails mostly, where he would not be seen," seeking out "pastures where the first green grass had begun to push up through the soil," and the cardinals "whistle cheerfully" in tune with the unintelligible voices of plowmen (152). He suppresses the urge to indulge in his childhood roleplaying memories, in which he would assume "the role of coyote." In the university context, these pastimes now inspire feelings of "shame," because he "was more civilized now and more knowing, and he was ashamed of his recent past" (152). Chal instead focuses on majoring "in economics, to prepare himself for business," while hiding "the fact that most of his blood was of an uncivilized race like the Osages" (153). He observes the effects of colonial displacement on other Osage youths who do not share his ambition: Sun-on-His-Wings returns "to wearing the blanket," the traditional garment of Osage men; while Running Elk wears "citizen's clothes but loafed around the Oil Exchange pool hall" (154), a facility funded by the very corporation that has co-opted their land. Running Elk descends into alcoholism, a fate Chal determines to avoid by becoming "a businessman" who "[amounts] to something" (154), if only by white American standards.

Feeling increasingly restless, Chal tries to fulfill his destiny as an Osage hero by enlisting in the Army Air Corps as a fighter pilot upon learning of the United States' entry into WWI. While deployed in France, he becomes a decorated serviceman due to his tactical prowess. Because the protagonist Chal is of Osage, Anglo-American, and French heritage, his development articulates into an unclear affiliative destiny that is further complicated by the legal criteria guiding how citizenship in the nation-state is either issue or denied; a key issue in the context of wartime critical discourses of 100% Americanism. Though, like his father, Chal's education and experiences abroad induce him to perceive his former village life as primitive relative to settler ideologies valuing modernization and capitalist development, Mathews carefully insinuates that Chal remains ambivalent. This ontological uncertainty translates into the theme of geographic restlessness, indicated by his refusal to settle in any one place. Though he views the Osage's mode of living in congruence with nature as dynamic, heterogenous, and filled with beauty and complexity, Chal's attainment of the genuine ideal of manhood is contingent on his negotiation of the two seemingly incommensurate value systems. He is torn between his internal, contemplative "Indian" identity—his true self, carried over from his childhood—and his external identity, the persona of action who is regarded as a "civilized" young man. Encouraged by the flattering glances of women at the local dances, Chal is "filled" with "self-assurance" that he is progressively "gilded by that desirable thing which he called civilization" and "becoming a man among civilized men" (230). Nevertheless, he retains "his Indian keenness," a secret trait which gives him the advantage of reading "many things in people's faces which they didn't know were showing" (230).

The novel's ending consolidates Mathews' critique of the ideology of development and civilization central to the Bildungsroman genre, revealing those concepts to be economically uneven and politically fraught. The ending sees Chal return to both the maternal and natural order. His concerned mother's perception of him forces him to recognize how complicit he has become in the imperialist destiny of white men. She suggests to him that his role as an aviator is not as remarkable as he thinks, for "'Many white men are flying across the sea now'" to engage in imperialism and total warfare (Mathews *Sundown*, 310). Chal, forced to confront what sort of "civilized" man he has become, momentarily retreats into a purer, childlike state; even as his mother transfigures before him into "an Indian woman . . . questioning a man's courage," he suddenly feels "warmed by a . . . primordial thing which thrilled him and made his stomach tingle, and he felt kindly toward his mother—toward this Indian woman who could see into a warrior's heart" (310–11). The primordial pull of the Indian maternal represents to him an alternative pathway to become a heroic agent of his people, a challenger to the white man he has been prophesized to become since his birth. Her unspoken call-to-arms brings him to resign from the future in which he remains a fighter pilot in the service of abstract patriotism he no longer supports; that profession no longer sublimates the courageous and heroic Osage warrior ideal he "contemplated" becoming as a child. Comparing *Sundown* with the individualism inherent in the "suspended transition from youth to maturity" that informs Ernest Hemingway's depiction of the Midwest in the *Nick Adams* stories, Christopher Schedler argues that Mathews offers an alternative subject position, and thus a view onto the character of the region that is devoid of Hemingway's nostalgic "modernist 'tribalism'" (82). This alternative positioning hinges upon reconstituting the crisis of gender that accompanies capitalist development, as the Indigenous protagonist attempts to find romantic fulfillment in a white patriarchal system that has disorganized the social relations of the tribal system he belongs to, including its gender roles, and has disrupted the continuity of the traditional ceremonies that sustained that organization.

Like Cather's protagonist Jim Burden, Chal resolves on the final pages to assume a reformist position: to study law at Harvard University, presumably to defend his community's regional interests against the tide of national progress, a possibility that fills him with "assurance and courage" (311). Though Alexander Steele has compellingly indicated that "*Sundown* places center stage the Anglo and Osage spatio-temporal disjuncture it negotiates, occupying alongside Chal a middle space that disrupts, like so many other modernist bildungsromans, any teleological sense of arrival" (230), the novel's final images of Chal falling into a serene reverie, listening to the sounds of animals moving in the vegetation, suggest that the hero's development is not necessarily arrested or fragmented beyond repair. He has worked through the core ideological assumptions of development itself, to pause in a powerfully subversive state of temporary suspension.

As Mathews reflected in *Sooner Magazine*, the notion that the "people of the hills, the blackjacks, the shortgrass, the desert, and the mountain creeks have not yet interpreted the soil through their own idioms, metaphors, dialects, and song" formed his literary and political muse (qtd in Snyder 141). On several fronts, the novelist's depiction of a generational shift occurring between the individualist capitalist America of the future and the community-based tribal mode of living of the past drew attention to the fraught geographical imperatives of white America's imperial national destiny, built upon capitalism's uneven developmental logic. According to Steele, Mathews disrupted "the genre in which he composes to enshrine a distinctly Osage sense and sensibility, distilling in the process an ineradicable remainder, namely the untranslatability of a sacred and pre-settler-colonial Osage world into a secular concept of time and space" (230). As a work guided by both Indigenous and settler-colonialist epistemologies of land and development—referring to both human growth, and industrial expansion—which determine the ideologies of space and time that govern the individual's experience in the world, the subversive aesthetic regionalism of *Sundown* contends with and deterritorializes the ethnic homogeneity of "local color" realism about the western regions.

Sundown adumbrated a provocative literary deterritorialization of the Southwest, rewriting the plot of uneven development from the standpoint of a mixed-race Osage youth whose connection to the land and region interferes with his acceptance of the ideologies of capitalist development that are forcefully recolonizing his community. Matthews thus redrew the ideological borders of the novel of development by engaging in a critical regionalism that challenged the romanticism of nature and the frontier that underwrote American exceptionalism. Mathews pioneered an unfixed figure of youth who represented a generation of Indigenous youth whose epistemologies of place and connection to the land were being eroded, appropriated, and replaced by the invested interests of white property rights. The limits of the national framework that his novel tested formed an important touchstone for novels that contributed to the Native American Renaissance, including its epoch-defining novel, Kiowa writer N. Scott Momaday's *House Made of Dawn* (1968). Another Bildungsroman centered upon an Indigenous youth in the pueblos of the Southwest who struggles to integrate into national-historical time, *House*'s protagonist becomes disconnected from his land, traditions, and community, losing himself within the center of the hegemonic culture industry of Los Angeles, a city built upon two things: racist zoning and development policies, and the pursuit of eternal youth. Leslie Marmon Silko's *Ceremony* (1977), set in the Indigenous Southwest, similarly depicted its mixed-race protagonist Tayo's troubled process to reconnect to his culture and land after serving in WWII. This suggests that Mathews' Bildungsroman anticipated new frontiers for the Southwestern novel of uneven development, as it traversed the concepts of migration and displacement to engage with and discard the myths of the settler-colonial West. As such, *Sundown* destabilized the immanent assumptions of the soul-nation allegory: the symbolic figuration of what it means to develop in national-historical time. As by the mid-century the perceived dilution of regional variety loomed with the growing concentration of power wielded by the region's culture industry, Hollywood, Mathews' representational strategy proved expedient for subsequent generations of writers, including Momaday, as well as Larry McMurtry and Cormac McCarthy (Snyder 63). Instead of fortifying the imperatives of nations and borders, as well as the identities they impose, the Southwestern Bildungsroman in the hands of Mathews and others formed a critical stage upon which the nation's ongoing disputes over literature, place, and land could be powerfully rehearsed.

AFTERWORD

Situating the Bildungsroman's Transnational Afterlives

This book's guiding theme has been the evolving role that the regional imaginary played in the American Bildungsroman—defined as the *novel of uneven development*—up until the mid-twentieth century, as the cultural expression and symbolic form of the asymmetrical, rapidly changing dimensions of the United States during that period. As the concluding discussions of the Southwestern Bildungsroman have already indicated, that region is an ideal launchpad for briefly contemplating what "happened" to the Bildungsroman at the turn toward the current post-nationalist stage in American culture—while simultaneously suggesting the limits, real and imagined, of the historical and geographical stakes this argument entailed. As the aesthetic hyperreality of late capitalism distorted the allegory of youth's transformation, region's function in the genre's geographical logic became unstable. The temporal limits of this map end at the onset of the 1960s, when the Bildungsroman was increasingly engaged in the representational dilemma of depicting development in post-industrial, post-nationalist, and postmodernist space—as the United States shifted into what Giles demarcates as the "transnational era," defined by "the necessarily reciprocal position of the U.S. within global networks of exchange" and deterritorialization (12). The dialectic between the search for authentic places in a world of simulacra and the uncertainty of postmodernity's boundless spaces correlated to the elongation of the passage from young adulthood to maturity in countless post-WWII antidevelopment narratives, which threatened simultaneously to immortalize and dissolve the coming-of-age paradigm in the satiric excesses of postmodern pastiche—literary or otherwise, in films, games, advertising, and television.

And yet, like the perennial unfixed figure of youth, the symbol of the dialectic between tradition and change, the local and the universal, or between situatedness and mobility, has nevertheless continued to form an important apparatus for earnest contemplations of how affective and local affiliations are intercut with other loyalties and identities. Numerous volumes about American identity politics and the Bildungsroman attest to that genre's continuing appeal,[1] its depiction of social development rendering it ideal for delivering on pluralist politics. Since the mid-twentieth century, many authors have utilized the Bildungsroman to foreground ethnic minority groups in America's literary canon, by adopting similar representational strategies to the political geography of that earlier period—a tendency still prevalent in contemporary literature, as scholarship investigating America's multiethnic literatures continues to insist. Indeed, regionally inflected interpretations of the Bildungsroman early in the twentieth century unsettled the dominant understanding of the genre as an expression of a stabilizing national culture, in ways that over time have proven useful for authors to widen the genre's ideological horizons beyond the narrowing borders of American exceptionalism's hegemonic discourses.

Despite its temporal parameters, this book has presented a case for what ground might be covered, and recovered anew, by historically rethinking the Bildungsroman through a critical regionalist framework, beyond the specific periods and places that have occupied these pages. A more detailed map would have included discussion of the literatures of the Pacific Northwest; expanded discussion of the literature of the West Coast and Californian fiction; and given a more extensive consideration of the literatures of the Southern and Southwest borderlands. Another scholar's map might have selected different novels or traced another path across the map; nevertheless, they would have certainly encountered the imperative role that the regional imaginary played in the genre's development at

---

[1] For a comprehensive list of key studies of the Bildungsroman and multiethnic American literature, please refer to the Introduction (5–6n).

that point in American literary history. Individually, these chapters present materialist accounts of generic innovations that emerged in response to the nation's regional complex c. 1900–1960. I have showcased some of the most profound transfigurations of the Bildungsroman in American literature, and underlined how those transformations were implicitly informed by the geographic unevenness of the nation-state as it was guided by the temporal rhythms of capitalist modernity. Given the heterogeneous generic shapes into which the novel of uneven development evolved, the case studies discussed indicate more broadly how writers' investment in regional difference across the U.S.'s variegated places and locations—the substance of regions and nations—produced new variations that traced a wide spectrum of frontiers. From remote rurality to polyglot urban centers, these regionalisms ultimately revealed the untidiness of the nation-building project at the center of the Bildungsroman genre.

In the first half of the twentieth century, the inadequacies of national-historical time to counteract modernity's disorderly global geographies left writers with a difficult task: to find the means of representing an increasingly composite civic body and unevenly developing nation with no consensus on a centralized cultural identity. What resulted were the many diverse formal innovations on the Bildungsroman genre this book has discussed. Although it seemed that one could "know myself—but that is all!" as Amory Blaine cries at the end of *This Side of Paradise*, the American Bildungsroman's variegated model of modern development discovered that perhaps to "know oneself is" really only "to know one's region," as Flannery O'Connor speculated ("The Fiction Writer," 806). The ideal figure for navigating modernity's entangled geographic complexities from a literary standpoint was the unfixed figure of youth: a perennial figure both caught and loose in the world; the subject of not only imminent but immanent change, uncertainty, and uneven development.

WORKS CITED

Abel, Elizabeth, Marianne Hirsch, and Elizabeth Langland, editors. "Introduction." *The Voyage In: Fictions in Female Development*. U of New England P, 1983, pp. 3–19.
Adams, Jessica. *Wounds of Returning: Race, Memory, and Property on the Postslavery Plantation*. U of North Carolina P, 2007.
Adorno, Theodor. *Aesthetic Theory*, edited by Gretel Adorno and Rolf Tiedemann. Translated by Robert Hullot-Kentor, Continuum, 1997.
—. *Current of Music: Elements of a Radio Theory*, edited by Robert Hullot-Kentor, Polity Press, 2008.
Agyeman, Julian, and Rachel Spooner. "Ethnicity and the Rural Environment." *Contested Countryside Cultures: Otherness, Marginalisation, and Rurality*, edited by Paul J. Cloke and Jo Little, Routledge, 1997, pp. 197–217.
Alexander, Neal, and James Moran, editors. "Introduction: Regional Modernisms." *Regional Modernisms*. Edinburgh UP, 2013, pp. 1–21.
Anderson, David D. "Chicago as Metaphor." *The Great Lakes Review*, vol. 1, no. 1, Summer 1974, pp. 3–15.
Anderson, Eric Gary. *American Indian Literature and the Southwest: Contexts and Dispositions*. U of Texas P, 1999.
Aronoff, Eric. "Anthropologists, Indians, and New Critics: Culture and/as Poetic Form in Regional Modernism." *Modern Fiction Studies*, 55, no. 1, 2009, pp. 92–118.
Arthur, Jason. *Violet America: Regional Cosmopolitanism in U.S. Fiction*. U of Iowa P, 2003.
Ashbaugh, Carolyn. *Lucy Parsons: An American Revolutionary*. Haymarket Books, 2012.
Atherton, Gertrude. "Why is American Literature Bourgeois?" *The North American Review*, vol. 178, no. 570, May 1904, pp. 771–8.
Bakhtin, Mikhail M. *The Dialogic Imagination: Four Essays*, edited by Michael Holquist. Translated by Caryl Emerson and Michael Holquist, U of Texas P, 1981.
—. *Speech Genres and Other Late Essays*, edited by Michael Holquist and Caryl Emerson. Translated by Vern W. McGee, U of Texas P, 1986.
Baldwin, Davarian L. "Chicago's New Negroes: Consumer Culture and Intellectual

Life Reconsidered." *American Studies*, vol. 44, no. 1/2, Spring/Summer 2003, pp. 121–52.

Baldwin, James. *The Fire Next Time*. 291–348. *Collected Essays*, edited by Toni Morrison, Library of America, 1998.

—. *Notes of a Native Son*. 1–129. *Collected Essays*, edited by Toni Morrison, Library of America, 1998.

Banes, Sally. *Dancing Women: Females Bodies on Stage*. Routledge, 1998.

Barnes, Deborah. "'I'd Rather Be a Lamppost in Chicago': Richard Wright and the Chicago Renaissance of African American Literature." *The Langston Hughes Review*, vol. 14, no. 1/2, 1996, pp. 52–61.

Berman, Jessica. "Toward A Regional Cosmopolitanism: The Case of Mulk Raj Anand." *Modern Fiction Studies*, vol. 55, no. 1, 2009, pp. 142–62.

Berman, Marshall. *All That Is Solid Melts Into Air: The Experience of Modernity*. Penguin, 1988.

Bibler, Michael P. *Cotton's Queer Relations: Same-Sex Intimacy and the Literature of the Southern Plantation, 1936–1968*. U of Virginia P, 2009.

Blair, Sara. "Local Modernity, Global Modernism: Bloomsbury and the Places of the Literary." *ELH*, vol. 71, 2004, pp. 813–38.

Boes, Tobias. *Formative Fictions: Nationalism, Cosmopolitanism, and the Bildungsroman*. Cornell UP, 2012.

Bone, Martyn. *Where the New World Is: Literature About the U.S. South at Global Scales*. U of Georgia P, 2018.

Bone, Robert, and Richard A. Courage. *The Muse in Bronzeville: African American Creative Expression in Chicago, 1932–1950*. Rutgers UP, 2011.

Bonner, Marita O. "On Being Young—A Woman—And Colored." 1925. Reprinted in *The Crisis Reader: Stories, Poetry, and Essays from the N.A.A.C.P.'s Crisis Magazine*, edited by Sondra Kathryn Wilson, The Modern Library, 1999, pp. 227–31.

Braeman, John. "The Extension of Federal Power." 1964. Reprinted in Upton Sinclair, *The Jungle*, edited by Clare Virginia Eby, Norton, 2003, pp. 459–65.

Bremer, Sidney H. *Urban Intersections: Meetings of Life and Literature in United States Cities*. U of Illinois P, 1992.

Bruccoli, Matthew J. *Some Sort of Epic Grandeur: The Life of F. Scott Fitzgerald*. Cardinal, 1991.

Cappetti, Carla. *Writing Chicago: Modernism, Ethnography, and the Novel*. Columbia UP, 1993.

Carr, Brian, and Tova Cooper. "Zora Neale Hurston and Modernism at the Critical Limit." *Modern Fiction Studies*, vol. 48, no. 2, Summer 2002, pp. 285–313.

Cather, Willa. "Nebraska: The End of the First Cycle." *The Nation*, vol. 117, September 1923, pp. 236–8.

—. *My Ántonia*. Penguin, [1918] 2018.

—. "Walt Whitman" [1896]. 902–90. In *Stories, Poems, and Other Writing*, edited by Sharon O'Brien, Library of America, 1992.

Cline, Sally. *Zelda Fitzgerald: Her Voice in Paradise*. Arcade Publishing, 2002.

Cobb, James C. *Away Down South: A History of Southern Identity*. Oxford UP, 2007.

Corkin, Stanley. "*Sister Carrie* and Industrial Life: Objects and the New American Self." *Modern Fiction Studies*, vol. 33, no. 4, 1987, pp. 605–19.

Davidson, David. *Regionalism and Nationalism in the United States: The Attack on Leviathan*. 1938. Routledge, 1991.

—. "A Mirror for Artists." 1930. *I'll Take My Stand: The South and the Agrarian Tradition*, by Twelve Southerners, edited by Susan V. Donaldson, Louisiana State UP, 2006, pp. 28–60.

Dell, Floyd. *Moon-Calf*. 1920. Sagamore Inc., 1957.

Denning, Michael. *The Cultural Front: The Laboring of American Culture in the Twentieth Century*. Verso, 1998.

Dennis, Richard. *Cities in Modernity: Representations and Productions of Metropolitan Space, 1840–1930*. Cambridge UP, 2008.

Dewey, John. "Americanism and Localism." *The Dial*, vol. LXVIII, no. 6, June 1920, pp. 684–8.

—. *The Public and Its Problems*. Henry Holt and Co., 1927.

Donaldson, Susan V., editor. "Introduction: The Southern Agrarians and Their Culture Wars." In *I'll Take My Stand: The South and the Agrarian Tradition*, by Twelve Southerners, Louisiana UP, 2006, ix–xi.

Douglas, Ann. "*Studs Lonigan* and the Failure of History in Mass Society: A Study in Claustrophobia." *American Quarterly*, vol. 29, no. 5, Winter 1977, pp. 487–505.

—. *Terrible Honesty: Mongrel Manhattan in the 1920s*. The Noonday Press, 1996.

Dowd, Christopher. *The Construction of Irish Identity in American Literature*. Routledge, 2011.

Dreiser, Theodore. *Interviews*, edited by Frederic E. Rush and Donald Pizer, U of Illinois P, 2004.

—. *Sister Carrie*. 1900. The Riverside Press, 1959.

Du Bois, W. E. B., and Alain Locke. *The Souls of Black Folk*. 2nd Ed. A. C. McClurg & Co., 1903.

—. "The Younger Literary Movement." 1924. Reprinted in *The Crisis Reader: Stories, Poetry, and Essay's from the N.A.A.C.P.'s Crisis Magazine*. Edited by Sondra Kathryn Wilson. The Modern Library, 1999, pp. 288–92.

Duck, Leigh Anne. *The Nation's Region: Southern Modernism and U.S. Nationalism*. U of Georgia P, 2006.

Eby, Clare Virginia. *Dreiser and Veblen: Saboteurs of the Status Quo*. U of Missouri P, 1999. —. "The Psychology of Desire: Veblen's 'Pecuniary Emulation' and 'Invidious Comparison' in *Sister Carrie* and *An American Tragedy*." *Studies in American Fiction*, vol. 21, no. 2, Autumn, 1993, pp. 192–3.

Eliot, Thomas Stearns. "Tradition and the Individual Talent, Part I." *The Egoist*, no. 4, vol. vi, September 1919, pp. 54–5.

Ellison, Ralph. *Going to the Territory*. Random House, 1986.

Emerson, Ralph Waldo. *Nature*. 1836. *Essays and Lectures*, edited by Joel Porte, Library of America, 1983, pp. 1–230.

Esty, Jed. *Unseasonable Youth: Modernism, Colonialism, and the Fiction of Development*. Oxford UP, 2011.

Evans, Brad. "Howellsian Chic: The Local Color of Cosmopolitanism." *ELH*, vol. 71, no. 3, Fall 2004, pp. 775–812.

Farrell, James T. *The League of Frightened Philistines: And Other Papers*. The Vanguard Press, 1945.

—. "Social Themes in American Realism." *The English Journal*, vol. 35, no. 6, June 1946, pp. 309-15.

—. *Studs Lonigan: A Trilogy Containing Young Lonigan, The Young Manhood of Studs Lonigan, and Judgment Day*. The Modern Library, 1938.

Fauset, Jessie Redmond. *Plum Bun: A Novel Without a Moral*. 1928. *Harlem Renaissance: Five Novels of the 1920s*, edited by Rafia Zafar, Library of America, 2011, pp. 433-685.

—. "Sunday Afternoon." *The Crisis*, vol. 23, no. 4, February 1922, pp. 162-4.

Fetterley, Judith, and Marjorie Pryse. *Writing out of Place: Regionalism, Women, and American Literary Culture*. U of Illinois P, 2003.

Fitzgerald, Francis Scott. *F. Scott Fitzgerald: A Life in Letters*, edited by Matthew J. Bruccoli, Penguin, 1998.

—. *This Side of Paradise*. 1920. Penguin, 1996.

—. and Fitzgerald, Zelda Sayre. *Dearest Scott, Dearest Zelda: The Love Letters of F. Scott and Zelda Fitzgerald*, edited by Jackson Bryer and Cathy W. Barks, Scribner, 2002.

Fitzgerald, Zelda Sayre. "Mrs. F. Scott Fitzgerald Reviews *The Beautiful and Damned*, Friend Husband's Latest." 1922. Reprinted in *Zelda Fitzgerald: The Collected Writings*, edited by Matthew J. Bruccoli, Macmillan, 1991.

—. *Save Me the Waltz*. Galley proof with author's corrections; dates not examined. Zelda Fitzgerald Papers Box 1, Folder 8-10. Manuscripts Division: Department of Rare Books and Special Collections, Princeton University Library.

—. and F. Scott Fitzgerald, *Dearest Scott, Dearest Zelda: The Love Letters of F. Scott and Zelda Fitzgerald*, edited by Jackson Bryer and Cathy W. Barks, Scribner, 2002.

Fleissner, Jennifer L. *Women, Compulsion, Modernity: The Moment of American Naturalism*. U of Chicago P, 2004.

Flynn, Dennis. "Farrell and Dostoevsky." *MELUS*, vol. 18, no. 1 (1993), pp. 113-25.

Foley, Barbara. *Jean Toomer: Race, Repression, and Revolution*. U of Illinois P, 2014.

—. "The Politics of Poetics: Ideology and Narrative Form in *An American Tragedy* and *Native Son*." *Richard Wright: Critical Perspectives Past and Present*, edited by Henry Louis Gates, Jr. and K. A. Appiah, Amistad, 1993, pp. 188-99.

—. *Radical Representations: Politics and Form in U.S. Proletarian Fiction, 1929-1941*. Duke UP, 1993.

Foote, Stephanie. *Regional Fictions: Culture and Identity in Nineteenth-Century American Literature*. U of Wisconsin P, 2001.

Foulkes, Julia L. *Modern Bodies: Dance and American Modernism from Martha Graham to Alvin Ailey*. U of North Carolina P, 2002.

Garland, Hamlin. *Crumbling Idols: Twelve Essays on Art Dealing Chiefly with Literature, Painting and the Drama*. Penguin, 1894.

Giannone, Richard. "Dark Night, Dark Faith: Hazel Motes, the Misfit, and Francis Marion Tarwater." *Dark Faith: New Essays on Flannery O'Connor's* The Violent Bear It Away, edited by Susan Srigley, U of Notre Dame P, 2012, pp. 7-34.

—. "Displacing Gender: Flannery O'Connor's View From The Woods." *Flannery O'Connor: New Perspectives*, edited by Sura Prasad Rath and Mary Neff Shaw, U of Georgia P, 1996, pp. 73-95.

Giles, Paul. *The Global Remapping of American Literature*. Princeton UP, 2011.

Gilman, Susan. "Regionalism and Nationalism in Jewett's *Country of the Pointed*

Firs." *New Essays on* The Country of the Pointed Firs, edited by June Howard, Cambridge UP, 1994, pp. 101–16.

Gilroy, Paul. *The Black Atlantic: Modernity and Double Consciousness.* Verso, 1993.

Gleeson-White, Sarah. "A Peculiarly Southern Form of Ugliness: Eudora Welty, Carson McCullers, and Flannery O'Connor." *The Southern Literary Journal,* vol. 36, no. 1, Fall 2003, pp. 46–57.

—. *Strange Bodies: Gender and Identity in the Novels of Carson McCullers.* U of Alabama P, 2003.

Goldberg, Marianne. "Homogenized Ballerinas." *Meaning in Motion: New Cultural Studies of Dance,* edited by Jane C. Desmond, Duke UP, 1997, pp. 305–20.

Gordon, Sarah. *Flannery O'Connor: The Obedient Imagination.* U of Georgia P, 2000.

Graff, Ellen. *Stepping Left: Dance and Politics in New York City, 1928–1942.* Duke UP, 1997.

Graham, Sarah, editor. "The American Bildungsroman." *A History of the Bildungsroman.* Cambridge UP, 2019, pp. 117–42.

Graham, T. Austin. "Fitzgerald's 'Riotous Mystery': *This Side of Paradise* as Musical Theatre." *The F. Scott Fitzgerald Review,* vol. 6, 2007–8, pp. 21–53.

Greeson, Jennifer Rae. *Our South: Geographic Fantasy and the Rise of National Literature.* Harvard UP, 2010.

Grunwald, Michael. *The Swamp: The Everglades, Florida, and the Politics of Paradise.* Simon and Schuster, 2006.

Hakutani, Yoshinobu, editor. "Introduction." *Theodore Dreiser's Uncollected Magazine Articles, 1897–1902.* U of Delaware P, 2003, pp. 15–35.

Hapke, Laura. *Labor's Text: The Worker in American Fiction.* Rutgers UP, 2001.

Hardin, James, editor. "Introduction." *Reflection and Action: Essays on the Bildungsroman.* U of South Carolina P, 1991, pp. ix–xxvii.

Harvey, David. *Cosmopolitanism and the Geographies of Freedom.* Columbia UP, 2009

—. *The Limits to Capital.* Verso, 2018.

Hathaway, Rosemary. "Native Geography: Richard Wright's Work for the Federal Writers' Project in Chicago." *African American Review,* vol. 42, no. 1, 2008, pp. 91–108.

Hawthorne, Nathanial. *The Dolliver Romance, and Kindred Tales.* Houghton Mifflin Company, [1864] 1904.

Hegel, G. W. F. *Aesthetics: Lectures on Fine Art, Volume One.* Translated by T. M. Knox, Clarendon Press, 1988.

Herring, Scott. "Regional Modernism: A Reintroduction." *Modern Fiction Studies,* vol. 5, no. 1, Spring 2009, pp. 1–10.

Hicks, Granville. "The Case Against Willa Cather." *The English Journal,* vol. 22, no. 9, 1933, pp. 703–10.

Howells, William Dean. *Literature and Life.* Harper & Brothers Publishers, 1902.

Hricko, Mary. *The Genesis of the Chicago Renaissance: Theodore Dreiser, Langston Hughes, Richard Wright, and James T. Farrell.* Routledge, 2009.

Hughes, Langston. "The Negro Artist and the Racial Mountain." 1926. Reprinted in *The Norton Anthology of African American Literature,* edited by Henry Louis Gates Jr. and Nellie Y. McKay, Norton, 1997, pp. 1267–71.

—. *Not Without Laughter.* 1930. Penguin, 2018.

Hurston, Zora Neale. *Dust Tracks on a Road*. 1942. *Folklore, Memoirs, & Other Writing*, edited by Cheryl A. Wall, Library of America, 1995, pp. 557–808.

—. *Their Eyes Were Watching God*. 1937. *Novels & Stories*, edited by Cheryl A. Wall. Library of America, 1995, pp. 173–333.

—. "How It Feels to Be Colored Me." 1928. *Folklore, Memoirs, & Other Writing*, edited by Cheryl A. Wall, Library of America, 1995, pp. 826–9.

Jaffe, Aaron. *Modernism and the Culture of Celebrity*. Cambridge UP, 2005.

James, Pearl. "History and Masculinity in F. Scott Fitzgerald's *This Side of Paradise*." *Modern Fiction Studies*, vol. 51, no. 1, 2005, pp. 1–33.

Jameson, Fredric. *The Antinomies of Realism*. Verso, 2013.

Japtok, Martin. *Growing Up Ethnic: Nationalism and the Bildungsroman in African-American and Jewish American Fiction*. U of Iowa P, 2005.

Jeffers, Thomas L. *Apprenticeships: The Bildungsroman from Goethe to Santayana*. Palgrave Macmillan, 2005.

Johnson, James Weldon. *Black Manhattan*. Alfred A. Knopf, 1930.

Jones, Susan. *Literature, Modernism, and Dance*. Oxford UP, 2013.

Katz, Wendy J., and Timothy R. Mahoney, editors. "Introduction: Regionalism and the Humanities: Decline or Revival?" *Regionalism and the Humanities*. U of Nebraska P, 2009, pp. ix–xxviii.

Keresztesi, Rita. *Strangers at Home: American Ethnic Modernism Between the World Wars*. U of Nebraska P, 2005.

King, Richard H. *A Southern Renaissance: The Cultural Awakening of the American South, 1930–1955*. Oxford UP, 1980.

Kodat, Catherine Gunther. "Biting the Hand That Writes You: Southern African-American Folk Narrative and the Place of Women in *Their Eyes Were Watching God*." *Haunted Bodies: Gender and Southern Texts*, edited by Anne Goodwyn Jones and Susan V. Donaldson, U of Virginia P, 1997, pp. 319–42.

Koolhaas, Rem. *Delirious New York: A Retroactive Manifesto for Manhattan*. The Monacelli Press Inc., 1994.

Kruse, Horst H. *F. Scott Fitzgerald at Work: The Making of* The Great Gatsby. U of Alabama P, 2014.

Lasser, Michael L. *City Songs and American Life, 1900–1950*. U of Rochester P, 2019.

Lefebvre, Henri. *The Production of Space*. Translated by Donald Nicholson-Smith, Blackwell, 1994.

Lehan, Richard Daniel. *Realism and Naturalism: The Novel in an Age of Transition*. U of Wisconsin P, 2005.

LeSeur, Geta. *Ten Is the Age of Darkness: The Black Bildungsroman*. U of Missouri P, 1995.

Lewis, R. W. B. *The American Adam: Innocence, Tragedy and Tradition in the Nineteenth Century*. U of Chicago P, 1955.

"Local Color and After." *The Nation*, vol. 109, no. 2830, September 1919, pp. 426–7.

Locke, Alain, editor. "The New Negro." 1925. *The New Negro*, edited by Arnold Rampersad, Atheneum, 1992, pp. 3–16.

—. "Review of *Their Eyes Were Watching God*." Reprinted in *Zora Neale Hurston: Critical Perspectives Past and Present*, edited by Henry Louis Gates, Jr. and K. A. Appiah, Amistad, 1993, p. 18.

Loichot, Valérie. *Orphan Narratives: The Postplantation Literature of Faulkner, Glissant, Morrison, and Saint-John Perse*. U of Virginia P, 2007.

Lukács, Georg. *The Theory of the Novel: A Historico-philosophical Essay on the Forms of Great Epic Literature*. 1920. MIT Press, 1971.

Lutz, Tom. *Cosmopolitan Vistas: American Regionalism and Literary Value*. Cornell UP, 2004.

Lytle, Andrew Nelson. "The Hind Tit." 1930. In *I'll Take My Stand: The South and the Agrarian Tradition*, by Twelve Southerners, edited by Susan V. Donaldson, Louisiana UP, 2006, pp. 201–45.

McCarthy, Harold T. *The Expatriate Perspective: Americans Novelists and the Ideas of America*. Farleigh Dickinson UP, 1974.

McCullers, Carson. *The Member of the Wedding*. 1936. *Complete Novels*, edited by Carlos L. Dews, Library of America, 2001, pp. 459–605.

—. "Look Homeward, Americans," pp. 431–4; "Books I Remember," pp. 464–468; "The Russian Realists and Southern Literature," pp. 469–75; "The Vision Shared," pp. 518–21. *Essays and Other Writing*, edited by Carlos L. Dews, Library of America.

Martin-Wagner, Linda. "*Save Me the Waltz*: An Assessment in Craft." *The Journal of Narrative Technique* vol. 12, no. 3, Fall 1982, pp. 201–9.

—. *Zelda Sayre Fitzgerald: An American Women's Life*. Palgrave Macmillan, 2004.

Mass, Noah. "'Caught and Loose': Southern Cosmopolitanism in Carson McCullers's *The Ballad of the Sad Café* and *The Member of the Wedding*." *Studies in American Fiction*, vol. 37, no. 2, Fall 2010, pp. 225–46.

Mathews, John Joseph. *Sundown*. 1934. U of Oklahoma P, 1988.

—. *Twenty Thousand Mornings: An Autobiography*, edited by Susan Kalte. U of Oklahoma P, 2012.

Mazzoni, Guido. *Theory of the Novel*. Harvard UP, 2017.

Mencken, H. L. *Prejudices: First, Second, and Third Series*, edited by Marion Elizabeth Rodgers, Library of America, 2010.

Meyerowitz, Joanne J. *Women Adrift: Independent Wage Earners in Chicago, 1880–1930*. U of Chicago P, 1988.

Milford, Nancy. *Zelda: A Biography*. Harper & Row Publishers, 1970.

Monge, Luigi. "Their Eyes Were Watching God: African-American Topical Songs on the 1928 Florida Hurricanes and Floods." *Popular Music*, vol. 26, no. 1, 2007, pp. 129–40.

Moore, David Chioni. "Local Color, Global 'Color': Langston Hughes, the Black Atlantic, and Soviet Central Asia, 1932." *Research in African Literatures*, vol. 27, no. 4, Winter 1996, pp. 49–70.

Moretti, Franco. *The Way of the World: The Bildungsroman in European Culture*. Verso, 1987.

Murphet, Julian. *Faulkner's Media Romance*. Oxford UP, 2017.

—. Lydia Rainford, editors. "Introduction." *Literature and Visual Technologies: Writing After Cinema*. Palgrave, 2003, pp. 1–11.

Myers, Robert M. *Reconciling Nature: Literary Representation of the Natural, 1876–1945*. State U of New York P, 2019.

Norris, Frank. "A Plea for Romantic Fiction." 1901. Reprinted in *The Literary Criticism of Frank Norris*, edited by Donald Pizer, U of Texas P, 1964, pp. 75–8.

Nowlin, Michael. *Literary Ambition and the African American Novel*. Cambridge UP, 2019.

O'Connor, Flannery. *The Violent Bear It Away*. 1960. *Collected Works*, edited by Sally Fitzgerald. Library of America, 1988, pp. 329–79.

—. "The Fiction Writer and His Country," pp. 801–6; "The Grotesque in Southern Fiction," pp. 813–821; "The Regional Writer," pp. 843–8. *Collected Works*, edited by Sally Fitzgerald, Library of America, 1988.

Oppenheim, James. "Poetry: Our First National Art." *The Dial*, vol. LXVIII, no. 1, January 1920, pp. 238–42.

Pizer, Donald. "Late Nineteenth-Century American Literary Naturalism: A Re-Introduction." *American Literary Realism*, vol. 38, no. 3, Spring 2006, pp. 189–202.

Plato. *The Republic*, edited by G. R. F. Ferrari. Translated by Tom Griffith, Cambridge UP, 2003.

Pratt, Annis, and Barbara White, "The Novel of Development." *Archetypal Patterns in Women's Fiction*, edited by Annis Pratt, Barbara White, Andrea Loewenstein, and Mary Wyer, Indiana UP, 1981, pp. 13–38.

Prown, Katherine Hemple. *Revising Flannery O'Connor: Southern Literary Culture and the Problem of Female Authorship*. U of Virginia P, 2001.

Quayson, Ato. *Aesthetic Nervousness: Disability and the Crisis of Representation*. Columbia UP, 2007.

Rampersad, Arnold. *The Life of Langston Hughes: Volume I: 1902–1941, I, Too, Sing America*. Oxford UP, 2002.

Redfield, Marc. *Phantom Formations: Aesthetic Ideology and the Bildungsroman*. Cornell UP, 1996.

Robertson, Stephen, Shane White, and Stephen Garton. "Harlem in Black and White: Mapping Place and Race in the 1920s." *Journal of Urban History*, vol. 39, no. 5, 2013, pp. 864–80.

Robinson, Cedric J. *Black Marxism: The Making of the Black Radical Tradition*. University of North Carolina P, 1983.

Roediger, David R., and Philip S. Foner. *Our Own Time: A History of American Labor and the Working Day*. Verso, 1989.

Rowley, Hazel. *Richard Wright: The Life and Times*. Henry Holt and Company, 2001.

Ransom, John Crowe. "Reconstructed but Unregenerate." 1930. In *I'll Take My Stand: The South and the Agrarian Tradition*, by Twelve Southerners, edited by Susan V. Donaldson, Louisiana UP, 2006, pp. 1–27.

Raubicheck, Walter, and Steven Goldleaf. "Stage and Screen Entertainment." *F. Scott Fitzgerald in Context*. Edited by Bryant Magnum. Cambridge UP, 2013, pp. 302–10.

Rifkin, Mark. *Beyond Settler Time: Temporal Sovereignty and Indigenous Self-Determination*. Duke UP, 2017.

Schedler, Christopher. *Border Modernism: Intercultural Readings in American Literary Modernism*. Routledge, 2002.

Scholes, Robert, James Phelan, and Robert Kellogg. *The Nature of Narrative: Fortieth Anniversary Edition*. Oxford UP, 2006.

Seed, David. *Cinematic Fictions: The Impact of the Cinema on the American Novel Up to World War II*. Liverpool UP, 2009.

Seltzer, Mark. *Serial Killers: Death and Life in America's Wound Culture*. Routledge, 1998.

Sherrard-Johnson, Cherene. *Portraits of the New Negro Woman: Visual and Literary Culture in the Harlem Renaissance*. Rutgers UP, 2007.

Shields, John P. "'Never Cross the Divide': Reconstructing Langston Hughes's *Not Without Laughter*." *African American Review*, vol. 28, no. 4, 1994, pp. 601–13.

Sinclair, Upton. *The Autobiography of Upton Sinclair*. Harcourt, Brace, & World, Inc., 1962.

—. *The Jungle*. 1906, edited by Clare Virginia Eby, Norton, 2003.

—. *Mammonart*. Published by the Author, 1925.

—. *Manassas: A Novel of War*. The Macmillan Company, 1904.

—. "Our Bourgeois Literature—The Reason and the Remedy." *Collier's*, vol. 34, October 8 1904, pp. 22–5.

Singh, Amritjit. *Novels of the Harlem Renaissance: Twelve Black Writers, 1923–1933*. Pennsylvania State UP, 1976.

Smith, Lillian. *Killers of the Dream*. 1949. Norton, 1994.

Smith, Neil. *Uneven Development: Nature, Capital, and the Production of Space*, 3rd ed. U of Georgia P, 2008.

Snyder, Michael. *John Joseph Mathews: Life of an Osage Writer*. U of Oklahoma P, 2017.

Spears, Timothy B. *Chicago Dreaming: Midwesterners and the City, 1871–1919*. U of Chicago P, 2005.

Spivak, Gayatri Chakravorty. "Nationalism and the Imagination." *Lectora*, 15, 2009, pp. 75–98.

Stecopoulos, Harilaos. "Regionalism in the American Modernist Novel." *The Cambridge Companion to the American Modernist Novel*, edited by Joshua Miller, Cambridge UP, 2015, pp. 21–34.

Steele, Alexander. "Sacred Space, Secular Time: *Sundown* and the Indigenous Modernism of John Joseph Mathews." *Modernism/Modernity*, vol. 28, no. 2, 2021, pp. 229–50.

Stockton, Kathryn Bond. *The Queer Child, Or Growing Sideways in the Twentieth Century*. Duke UP, 2009.

Švrljuga, Željka. *Hysteria and Melancholy as Literary Style in the Works of Charlotte Perkins Gilman, Kate Chopin, Zelda Fitzgerald, and Djuna Barnes*. The Edwin Mellen Press, 2011.

Taxidou, Olga. "'Do Not Call Me a Dancer' (Isadora Duncan, 1929): Dance and Modernist Experimentation." *Moving Modernisms: Motion, Technology, and Modernity*, edited by David Bradshaw, Laura Marcus, and Rebecca Roach, Oxford UP, 2016, pp. 110–26.

Taylor, Quintard. *In Search of the Racial Frontier: African Americans in the American West, 1528–1990*. Norton, 1998.

Thacker, Andrew. *Moving Through Modernity: Geography and Space in Modernism*. Manchester UP, 2003.

—. "Placing Modernism." *Moving Modernisms: Motion, Technology, and Modernity*, edited by David Bradshaw, Laura Marcus, and Rebecca Roach, Oxford UP, 2016, pp. 11–26.

Thomas, J. D. "F. Scott Fitzgerald: James Joyce's 'Most Devoted' Admirer." *The F. Scott Fitzgerald Review*, vol. 5, 2006, pp. 65–85.

Thurman, Wallace. *The Blacker the Berry.* 687–831. *Harlem Renaissance: Five Novels of the 1920s.* Edited by Rafia Zafar. Library of America, 2011.

—. *Infants of the Spring.* Dover Publications, 2013.

—. "Negro Life in New York's Harlem: A Lively Picture of a Popular and Interesting Section [1927]," pp. 39–62; "A Stranger at the Gates: A Review of *Nigger Heaven*, by Carl Van Vechten [1926]," pp. 191–2; "Negro Artists and the Negro [1927]," pp. 195–200; "Review of *Infants of the Spring* [1936]," pp. 226–7; "Aunt Hagar's Children" pp. 234–88. *The Collected Writings of Wallace Thurman*, edited by Amritjit Singh and Daniel M. Scott III, Rutgers UP, 2003.

Thurschwell, Pamela. "Dead Boys and Adolescent Girls: Unjoining the Bildungsroman in Carson McCullers' *The Member of the Wedding* and Toni Morrison's *Sula.*" *English Studies Canada*, vol. 38, no. 3–4, September–December 2012, pp. 105–28.

Toomer, Jean. *A Jean Toomer Reader: Selected Unpublished Writings*, edited by Frederik L. Rusch, Oxford UP, 1993.

Tracy, Steven C. (ed.). *Writers of the Black Chicago Renaissance.* U of Illinois P, 2011.

United States Congress House Committee on Immigration and Naturalization. "Immigration from Countries of the Western Hemisphere: Hearings Before the Committee on Immigration and Naturalization." House of Representatives, Seventieth Congress, First Session on H. R. 6465, H. R. 7358, H. R. 10955, H.R. 11687. February 21 to April 5, 1928, Hearing No. 70.1.5. U.S. Government Printing Office, 1928.

Van Doren, Carl. *Contemporary American Novelists: 1900–1920.* The MacMillan Company, 1922.

Van Notten, Eleonore. *Thurman's Harlem Renaissance.* Rodopi, 1994.

Vogel, Amber. "Novel, 1900 to World War II." *The Companion to Southern Literature: Themes, Genres, Places, People, Movements, and Motifs*, edited by Joseph M. Flora, Lucinda H. MacKethan, and Todd Taylor, Louisiana State UP, 2002, pp. 582–92.

Wald, Alan. "Farrell and Trotskyism." *Twentieth Century Literature*, vol. 22, no. 1, February 1976, pp. 92–3.

—. *Writing From the Left: New Essays on Radical Culture and Politics.* London: Verso, 1994.

Wall, Cheryl A. *Women of the Harlem Renaissance.* Indiana UP, 1995.

—. "Zora Neale Hurston: Changing Her Own Words." Reprinted in *Zora Neale Hurston: Critical Perspectives Past and Present*, edited by Henry Louis Gates, Jr. and K. A. Appiah. Amistad, 1993, pp. 76–97.

Wallace, Mike. *Greater Gotham: A History of New York City from 1898 to 1919.* Oxford UP, 2017.

Warren, Kenneth W. *What Was African American Literature?* Harvard UP, 2011.

"Waters Rise Again in Okeechobee Area; Florida Aid Pressed." *New York Times*, September 23 1928, p. 1.

Welty, Eudora. "Place in Fiction." 1957. *Stories, Essays, and Memoir*, edited by Richard Ford, Library of America, 1998, pp. 781–96.

Westling, Louise. *Sacred Groves and Ravaged Gardens: The Fiction of Eudora Welty, Carson McCullers, and Flannery O'Connor.* U of Georgia P, 1985.

Whalan, Mark. "The Bildungsroman in the Harlem Renaissance." *A History of the Harlem Renaissance*, edited by Rachel Farebrother and Miriam Thaggert, Cambridge UP, 2021, pp. 72–88.

—. *World War One, American Literature, and the Federal State*. Cambridge UP, 2018.

Wharton, Edith. *The House of Mirth*, 1905, edited by Martha Banta, Oxford UP, 1994.

Williams, Raymond. *The Country and the City*. Oxford UP, 1973.

Woolf, Virginia. *Collected Essays, Vol. 2*. Hogarth Press, 1966.

Woolley, Lisa. *American Voices of the Chicago Renaissance*. Northern Illinois UP, 2000.

Worth, Thomas H., editor. "Editor's Commentary on *Gentleman Jigger*." *Gay Rebel of the Harlem Renaissance: Selections from the Work of Richard Bruce Nugent*, by Bruce Nugent, Duke UP, 2002.

Wright, Richard. *12 Million Black Voices*. 1941. Basic Books, 2008.

—. "Between Laughter and Tears." *New Masses*, October 1937, pp. 22–5.

—. *Black Boy: A Record of Childhood and Youth*. Harper and Brother Publishers, 1945.

—. "Blueprint for Negro Writing." 1937. Reprinted in *The Norton Anthology of African American Literature*, edited by Henry Louis Gates Jr. and Nellie Y. McKay, et al., Norton, 1997, pp. 1380–8.

—. "How 'Bigger' Was Born." 1940. *Early Works*, edited by Arnold Rampersad, Library of America, 1991, pp. 853–81.

—. Introduction. *Black Metropolis: A Study of Negro Life in a Northern City*, by St. Clair Drake and Horace R. Cayton. 1945. U of Chicago P, 2015, lix–lxxvi.

—. *Native Son*. 1940. *Early Works*, edited by Arnold Rampersad, Library of America, 1991, pp. 443–850.

—. *White Man, Listen! Lectures in Europe, 1950–1956*. 1957. HarperCollins, 1995.

Yaeger, Patricia, editor. *Dirt and Desire: Reconstructing Southern Women's Writing, 1930–1990*. U of Chicago P, 2000.

—. "Introduction: Narrating Space." *The Geography of Identity*. U of Michigan P, 1996, pp. 1–38.

INDEX

100% Americanism, 11, 18,
  47–8, 67, 71, 73, 79–80, 83,
  85, 103, 109, 147, 149, 180,
  196, 240

Adorno, Theodor, 78–9, 112
Allotment, 22, 233, 235, 236; see
  also Dawes Act
antidevelopment, 8, 20, 75, 86,
  139, 179, 244
Appeal to Reason, 37, 38
Atlantic City, 103, 109, 115,
  121–2, 124, 125

Bakhtin, Mikhail, 2, 6, 21, 105,
  107, 149, 162, 190, 195,
  198, 199, 201
Baldwin, James, 97, 220n
ballet, 127–38
Bildung, 33, 34, 75, 89, 96, 181,
  185, 199, 215, 218
Bildungsheld, 77, 201, 223, 236
Black Belt, 64, 70, 85, 86, 88–9,
  91–2, 96, 168
Bronzeville, 61, 69, 89, 91
Brooks, Van Wyck, 1, 103, 140–1

Cather, Willa, 20, 37n, 49–60,
  64, 111, 241
Chicago, 25–44, 64, 65, 67,
  69–97, 101, 104, 110, 112,
  168, 171, 213
  School of Sociology, 28,
  69–70, 72, 82, 88–9, 94
Chopin, Kate, 33n
Civil War, 1, 36
Communist Party USA (CPUSA),
  88, 94–5
cosmopolitan *-ism* suffix, 9, 13,
  16–17, 49, 61, 64, 101–2,
  107–8, 109, 112–14,
  125–31, 137–9, 141–2,
  145–6, 149, 151–7, 160,
  168–70, 173, 182–3, 186,
  200, 206–7, 209, 212, 216,
  218–19; see also regional
  cosmopolitanism
Crisis, The, 141, 145, 148, 150
critical regionalism, 12–20, 69,
  110n, 187, 189, 232, 235,
  242, 245; see also regionalism

Davidson, Donald, 138–9,
  182–3; see also Fugitive
  Agrarians
Dawes Act, 235–6; see also
  Allotment
Dell, Floyd, 110, 121
Dewey, John, 4–5, 10, 127
Dixon, Thomas, 36

Dreiser, Theodore, 20, 26–34, 43–4, 45, 47, 52, 53, 63, 69, 72, 104, 110n, 137, 182; *see also Sister Carrie*
Du Bois, W. E. B., 140–1, 144, 145–6, 148n, 158, 162
Duncan, Isadora, 128–9, 134, 137

Eliot, Thomas Stearns, 114n, 129, 171–2
Ellison, Ralph, 84
Emerson, Ralph Waldo, 1, 6, 103, 141, 231
Entwicklungsroman, 33
Esty, Jed, 8–9, 104, 179

Farrell, James T., 20, 61n, 69–84, 85, 86, 87, 92, 93, 94n, 96–7, 103–4
Faulkner, William, 120n, 182, 184, 219n
Fauset, Jessie Redmon, 21, 106, 141, 144–68, 170, 175, 187, 190; *see also Plum Bun*
Federal Writers' Project (FWP), 70, 91, 189n
Fitzgerald, F. Scott, 21, 37, 94n, 101–28, 132, 135, 137n, 147, 164, 165n, 169; *see also This Side of Paradise*
Fitzgerald, Zelda Sayre, 21, 103, 106–7, 109, 111, 108, 118, 126–39, 147, 164, 165n; *see also Save Me the Waltz*
Foley, Barbara, 5n, 29, 35–6, 41, 62, 80, 83, 87–8, 150
Fugitive Agrarians, 13, 21, 138–9, 182–4, 199, 219–21

Garland, Hamlin, 47, 108, 181
global –*ization* suffix, 2, 4–5, 8–10, 17–20, 36, 48, 73, 84, 90, 97, 105, 108, 112, 120, 124, 187, 199, 205, 207, 209–10, 213–14, 216, 226, 246; *see also* transnational
Goethe, Johann Wolfgang von, 45, 53, 117; *see also Wilhelm Meister's Apprenticeship*
Graham, Martha, 129, 134, 137
Great Depression, 63, 72–5, 83, 92, 201, 203
Great Migration, 61, 63, 68, 78, 85, 133, 140–1, 144, 160, 199
Great War, 48, 102, *see also* World War I (WWI)
Greenwich Village, 109, 110n, 115, 121, 124, 134, 144, 148–9, 153, 157

Harlem, 133–4, 140–75
  Renaissance, 140–75
  see also New Negro
Harvey, David, 10, 15–16, 18
Hawthorne, Nathanial, 1, 219
Hegel, Georg Wilhelm Friedrich, 93, 119–20, 122
Howells, William Dean, 4, 29, 37–8, 47, 101, 105, 125
Hughes, Langston, 20, 49, 60–8, 73, 85, 146, 162, 164n, 167, 170–1, 196; *see also Not Without Laughter*
Hurston, Zora Neale, 21, 164n, 165, 185–200, 207, 219, 225, 227; *see also Their Eyes Were Watching God*

Infants of the Spring, 21, 106, 143–5, 160–75, 187–8; *see also* Thurman, Wallace

James, Henry, 29, 37n, 72, 111, 126
Jameson, Fredric, 7, 29
Jazz Age, 108, 127

Jim Crow, 12, 64, 65, 67, 84, 87, 96, 102, 133–4, 146, 152, 181, 187, 191, 196, 197, 213, 215, 217; see also segregation
Johnson, James Weldon, 143–4, 155
Johnson–Reed Immigration Act, 71, 75, 78, 92, 196
Joyce, James, 73, 74, 94n, 103, 110, 111, 113, 114, 120n, 161, 169, 175; see also *Portrait of the Artist as a Young Man, A*
Jungle, The, 26, 28, 34–44; see also Sinclair, Upton

Künstlerroman *–e* suffix, 21, 73, 102–75

Larsen, Nella, 144n, 147n, 162, 165, 167, 170, 190; see also *Passing*
Lefebvre, Henri, 7, 14; see also social spaces
local color, 2, 4, 13, 15, 26–7, 37–8, 43–5, 47, 53, 62–4, 67, 69, 101, 105, 108, 110–11, 114, 124, 141, 162, 166, 169–70, 173, 181, 183, 188, 192n, 193, 231–2, 234, 242
Locke, Alain, 140–1, 145–6, 148, 162, 173, 188, 198
Lukács, Georg, 7, 29, 212

McCullers, Carson, 22, 185, 201–19, 225, 227; see also *Member of the Wedding, The*
McKay, Claude, 144n, 146, 162, 164–5, 167
Manifest Destiny, 45, 56, 59, 237
Mann Act, 122
Mason–Dixon line, 21, 55, 131, 140

Mathews, John Joseph, 22, 231–43; see also *Sundown*
Member of the Wedding, The, 22, 184, 203–18; see also McCullers, Carson
Mencken, H. L., 82, 96, 104n, 181
Midwest, the *–ern* suffix, 3, 20, 25–97, 107–8, 109, 110, 112, 113–14, 120–1, 126, 141, 143, 161, 162, 164, 167, 171, 173–4, 181, 183, 219, 241,
modernism, 9, 13, 18, 20, 21, 101–75, 180–4, 187, 194, 218, 225, 241–2
Momaday, N. Scott, 243
Moretti, Franco, 6–8, 27, 28, 45–6, 52–3, 158, 166, 179
My Ántonia, 20, 49–60, 64, 68; see also Cather, Willa

national–historical time, 2–4, 10–11, 22, 29, 38, 48, 50, 56, 59, 68, 97, 122, 126, 184–5, 201, 217, 225, 243, 246
national destiny, 4, 8, 41, 44, 49, 51, 55, 86, 90, 117, 179, 222, 227, 233, 236, 242
Native American Renaissance, 243; see also Mathews, John Joseph
Native Son, 20, 69, 71, 84–97; see also Wright, Richard
naturalism, 3, 25–97, 106, 137, 219,
New Negro, 61, 63, 66–7, 106, 140–8, 152, 160175, 181, 183, 187–8, 191; see also Harlem Renaissance
New York, 21, 33, 51, 52, 55, 59, 63, 101–75, 181, 182, 203, 213

Norris, Frank, 28, 39, 47, 63, 69, 81, 137n, 232
North, the *-ern* suffix, 21, 67, 85, 87–8, 96, 101–75, 181, 182, 187, 193, 194, 202, 204, 219, 220
Northeast, the *-ern* suffix, 3, 21, 33n, 35, 43, 47, 62, 101–75, 187

O'Connor, Flannery, 12, 22, 185, 201–3, 208, 218–27, 246; *see also Violent Bear It Away, The*
Osage, 233–42
overdevelop *-ment* suffix, 3, 27, 32, 69, 81, 94, 96

passing (racial), 149, 150, 152–3, 155–8
Passing, 147n, 162; *see also* Larsen, Nella
plantation, 1, 91, 130, 180n, 181, 183, 192, 196, 212, 218–20, 222–3
Plum Bun, 21, 106, 144–60, 162, 167, 168; *see also* Fauset, Jessie Redmon
Portrait of the Artist as a Young Man, A, 73, 75, 95n, 103, 110, 113–14, 169, 175, 122; *see also* Joyce, James
Pound, Ezra, 112, 114, 114n
Progressive Era, 25, 34
proletarian
  Bildungsroman, 41, 62, 80, 87–8
  regionalism, 20, 62–4, 85
  see also regionalism

regional
  complex, 2–3, 18–19, 21, 44, 73, 84, 86, 97, 125–7, 144, 146, 162, 164, 173, 204, 227, 246

cosmopolitanism, 16, 66, 149, 153, 156, 186, 200, 206, 207
regionalism, 2–22, 25, 27, 37–8, 41, 46–53, 56, 60, 62–3, 64, 67, 68, 69–70, 73, 80, 82, 84–5, 86, 90–1, 93, 101–2, 104, 105, 107, 108–9, 111–12, 120–1, 125, 127, 128, 130, 139, 141–2, 144, 146, 147, 151, 154, 156, 160, 163, 169, 174, 175, 179–85, 186–9, 198, 202, 205–6, 218, 219n, 220, 221–2, 232, 233, 235–6, 242, 245–6; *see also* critical regionalism; proletarian regionalism
roman-à-clef, 111, 139, 165, 166n
rural *-ity* suffix, 3, 8–9, 17, 20, 21–2, 28, 37, 43–4, 45–68, 69, 71, 85–6, 105, 107, 111, 133, 141, 169, 181–5, 187–227, 232, 246

Save Me the Waltz, 21, 106, 126–39; *see also* Fitzgerald, Zelda Sayre
segregation, 14, 61, 66, 68, 86, 191, 216–17; *see also* Jim Crow
Silko, Leslie Marmon, 243
Sinclair, Upton, 20, 26–9, 34–45, 47, 52, 63, 69, 72, 232; *see also Jungle, The*
Sister Carrie, 26, 28–34, 104; *see also* Dreiser, Theodore
slavery, 36, 38–9, 85, 192, 202
Smith, Neil, 9–10, 14, 54
social spaces, 1, 10, 14, 43, 46, 52, 69, 104, 125, 174, 209, 231; *see also* Lefebvre, Henri
soul-nation allegory, 8, 21, 71, 243
South, the *-ern* suffix, 3, 21, 36, 48, 58, 63, 64, 67, 71, 74,

85, 86, 87, 90, 91, 94, 95, 96, 102, 127, 128, 130, 132, 133, 134, 138–9, 142, 143, 162, 166, 174, 179–227, 245
South Side, Chicago, 69–97, 168
Southwest, the -*ern* suffix, 3, 22, 80, 84, 143, 163, 189n, 231–43, 244, 245
Stein, Gertrude, 108, 111, 127, 129, 138, 167, 172, 231
Studs Lonigan trilogy, 20, 69–84, 92, 94n, 209; see also Farrell, James T.
Sundown, 22, 233–43; see also Mathews, John Joseph

Their Eyes Were Watching God, 21, 185, 186–200, 211, 218; see also Hurston, Zora Neale
This Side of Paradise, 21, 94n, 106–26, 128, 139, 246; see also Fitzgerald, F. Scott
Thurman, Wallace, 21, 106, 140–6, 155, 160–75, 187–8; see also *Infants of the Spring*
Toomer, Jean, 120n, 141, 144n, 150, 164, 181
transnational -*ism* suffix, 2, 9, 14, 16–17, 32, 84, 102, 105, 109, 126, 128, 171, 195–6, 200, 231, 244; see also global
Twain, Mark, 206, 216, 231

underdevelop -*ment* suffix, 3, 21–2, 87, 92, 179–85, 191, 201, 204, 206, 218, 220, 223, 226
uneven development, 2–4, 8–10, 12, 14–15, 17, 19, 22, 29, 33, 34, 36, 38, 44, 46, 49, 61, 65, 69, 71, 72, 85, 90, 97, 111, 146, 185, 188, 190, 193, 206, 207, 218, 219, 221, 226, 232–3, 235, 242, 243, 244, 246
unfixed figure of youth, 3–4, 17–18, 29, 43, 46, 48, 50, 57, 60, 63, 66, 68, 86–7, 89–90, 108–9, 125, 136, 138, 185, 192, 203, 226, 227, 232, 233, 234, 236, 244–5, 246
Upper East Side, Manhattan, 109, 118–21

Van Doren, Carl, 13, 53, 56, 101, 104, 107–8, 172
Van Vechten, Carl, 166n, 168
Violent Bear It Away, The, 22, 185, 203, 218–27; see also O'Connor, Flannery

Welty, Eudora, 12, 184, 201, 208
Wharton, Edith, 33n, 111, 132
Wilhelm Meister's Apprenticeship, 52; see also Goethe, Johann Wolfgang von
Woolf, Virginia, 120
World War I, 11, 56, 79, 117, 141, 143, 240; see also Great War
World War II, 180, 204, 206, 243, 244
Wright, Richard, 20, 60n, 69–71, 72, 73, 84–97, 193; see also *Native Son*

Young American in Literature, 1–2, 103, 141; see also Ralph Waldo Emerson
youth culture, 65, 103, 108, 126, 164

Zola, Émile, 28, 30, 34–5, 89, 169